Praise for

The Velveteen Daughter

"*The Velveteen Daughter* seamlessly weaves fiction into reality, and reality into fiction, quickly merging to become one truth that vividly reveals Bianco's secret heart. This book is not only mesmerizing to read but of great importance, bringing Pamela Bianco as an artist to find her rightful place in the history of art."

—GLORIA VANDERBILT

"". . . the novel fascinates. . . . Huber's reliance on primary sources, coupled with her luminous prose, creates an unforgettable sojourn into the lives of early 20th-century artists. . . . fast-paced and difficult to put down."

—KIRKUS REVIEWS

"Huber's richly textured language is a wonder to behold, her prose every bit as luminous, inspired, and wise as either Bianco's or Williams's own work."

—FOREWORD REVIEWS

"Huber excels in depicting . . . complex family dynamics, and her subject is strikingly original. Combining the elegance of literary fiction with realistic period atmosphere and an emotional openness reminiscent of personal memoirs, the prose is entirely immersive. A compelling read. . . ."

—BOOKLIST

the velveteen daughter

the

velveteen

daughter

‡‡‡

A NOVEL

Laurel Davis Huber

SHE WRITES PRESS

Published 2017
Printed in the United States of America
ISBN: 978-1-63152-192-8 pbk
ISBN: 978-1-63152-193-5 ebk
Library of Congress Control Number: 2016961869

For information, address:
She Writes Press
1563 Solano Ave #546
Berkeley, CA 94707

She Writes Press is a division of SparkPoint Studio, LLC.

Cover design by Julie Metz, Ltd./metzdesign.com
Interior design by Tabitha Lahr
Cover: Pamela in her studio, age 17, photograph © The Vassar College Archives and
Special Collections Library, Louise Seaman Bechtel Papers, Folder 5.63

Rabbit drawing by William Nicholson (for the original cover of *The Velveteen Rabbit*)
© Desmond Banks

To the memory of my parents,
Marcia Cady Davis and
Gordon Delano Davis

‡‡‡

And to the memory of my first-grade teacher at Lincoln School,
Florence Chaplin, who gave me *Beginning with A*

Margery and Pamela, c. 1917

contents

"What is REAL?" asked the Rabbit one day. . . . "Does it mean having things that buzz inside you and a stick-out handle?"

"Real isn't how you are made," said the Skin Horse. "It's a thing that happens to you. When a child loves you for a long, long time, not just to play with, but REALLY loves you, then you become Real."

"Does it hurt?" asked the Rabbit.

"Sometimes," said the Skin Horse, for he was always truthful. "When you are Real you don't mind being hurt."

"Does it happen all at once, like being wound up," he asked, "or bit by bit?"

"It doesn't happen all at once," said the Skin Horse. "You become. It takes a long time. That's why it doesn't happen often to people who break easily, or have sharp edges, or who have to be carefully kept. . . ."

‡‡‡

From *The Velveteen Rabbit* by Margery Williams Bianco

part one

‡‡‡

‡‡‡

September 1, 1944

9 Livingston Place, Stuyvesant Square
New York City

(Late Morning)

margery

*I*t's a lost day, I'm afraid. Pamela's here. I hadn't counted on that. Just one look at her this morning and despair flew into my heart. She had the look I dread, her eyes overbright, shining with that queer mix of euphoria and terror. And she talked incessantly, a very bad sign. She was going to start painting again, she said, and went on and on about the large canvasses she seems to have had in her head for so long. I encouraged her, naturally, but I knew by the way she was acting that it was only talk, that she wasn't near ready. If she really meant it, we wouldn't see her at all, she'd disappear. She'd be too busy *painting*.

When she stopped talking it was midsentence, her thoughts trailing off into a dramatic yawn. She was awfully tired, she said. Did I mind if she just lay down for a while? I didn't need to answer, though of course I said, "Certainly, darling!"

She gave my shoulder a squeeze as she passed by. But I didn't look up. I find every way to avoid it, but the truth will look me right in the face: there is madness in my daughter's eyes.

This heat's unbearable.

The fan blowing back and forth across the ice hypnotizes me with its jerky rhythm—the faint *scriiitch* as it hesitates at every rotation, the cool breath of air across my face. My manuscript sits in front of me on the kitchen table, but I know I won't touch it. The desire to work has fled, it ran off down the hallway along with

Pamela. Worry occupies me now, and the same questions roil in my brain: Will it be a bad one? Will it go away of its own accord? Or—God forbid—will we have to bring her to the hospital again?

When Francesco left for the printer's studio at dawn, saying he'd be back by suppertime, I was quite glad to have the day to myself, all the time in the world, I thought, to do a final reading of *Forward, Commandos!* A nice, long stretch of solitude. . . .

I suppose you could say I'm alone now, here in the kitchen, but somehow it's not the same, not with Pamela just a few feet away, asleep in her old room. We heaved a sigh of relief when she moved into an apartment of her own a few years ago, but her "independence" has been tenuous at best. Little has changed. Her place is only a stone's throw away. Inevitably, she shows up on our doorstep when she is feeling not quite herself.

She'll sleep the day away, I can count on that. Another bad sign. There's trouble ahead when the little genius takes to bed.

The little genius. Why on earth did that pop into my head? We haven't called her that in years. . . . I suppose it was Pamela's attempt to discuss the past, her childhood. I had to cut her off.

Thank God there aren't any of those minefields to navigate with Lorenzo. Still, I should have realized that my hopes for a day alone would be futile when he appeared first thing this morning— I should have known that it was only a matter of time before his mother showed up.

Lorenzo burst into the apartment, vibrating with that match- less energy of youth, and planted himself in my kitchen. A bright pinwheel, spinning even when sitting still. His mother didn't feel like cooking, he said, she'd told him he could help himself to some Wheaties. He looked at me sheepishly then, not wanting to ask. "Scrambled eggs and cinnamon toast sound okay?" I said, and he grinned. While I fixed his breakfast, he chattered about his great plans. It's the start of Labor Day weekend today—naturally, he's determined to cram in all the last-minute adventure he can before school begins.

It's a miracle that Pamela produced such a solid, uncomplicated child. He shows none of the fragile jumpiness of his parents. Not that I ever knew Robert very well, but he was a type. And Lorenzo is not at all that type. He's blessedly normal. He likes the sorts of things most boys his age like, sports and model airplanes and listening to *Boston Blackie* on the radio. And roller-skating. "It's swell, Grams, you should try it!" he tells me. Well, I'm tempted. With the gas rationing going on, the streets aren't nearly so busy these days as they used to be. Lorenzo goes down to the financial district on weekends, when it's all but abandoned. He and his friends can skate right in the middle of the road all the way from Wall Street and Broadway, past the New York Stock Exchange and Broad Street, and never have to dodge an automobile!

Lorenzo finished his breakfast and ran off to meet his friends for a swimming party at McCarren Park. He seems to have a great many friends. They all call him Larry, or sometimes "Red," which irritates Pamela no end. But what twelve-year-old boy—what boy at all—wants to be called Lorenzo?

When Pamela showed up a few hours later, I sighed inwardly as I told her, all cheerful, that I'd make us some tea, thinking, *How does this happen?* She's seemed so much better in the last year or so. I was sure it had to do with the fact she was out in the world for a change—doing her bit in the war effort, volunteering at the Department of Censorship. It's the perfect job for her, translating letters in the Italian Division. Francesco and I've often talked about how good it's been for her, for her confidence, to see that she's needed, that she has skills to offer that have nothing to do with art.

Well, I suppose I've done the talking. Francesco has been mostly silent on the subject. He's glad, of course, that Pamela's stronger. At least she seemed to be. But—he won't say this to me, I know—he's dying to get her painting again. Would strong-arm her if he could.

I put the tea things down, talking all the while about Lorenzo's visit, his plans for the weekend. The only response from Pamela was a slight nod. She stared at her teacup with that serious thinking expression of hers, her eyebrows drawn together in a way that, since she was a child, has always made us exclaim, "There, Pamela's at it again!" Only now it's a bit harder to read. She always had strong, dark eyebrows that almost met over her nose and now they are gone. Completely erased. I do wish she hadn't shaved them off. It gives her such a fixed look, a false sophistication.

I will say this, though, the penciled lines are beautifully done. If anyone can draw in a perfect eyebrow, it's Pamela.

She started up again about painting. *I must try . . . I want to . . . I can see the images so clearly . . . my childhood.* And somewhere amongst all the talk she wondered aloud, as if it were something she'd just thought of, something that had never occurred to her before, that she supposed her childhood had ended that day in Turin. Yet another bad sign, that ancient story. I had no energy for it. We had both, in our own ways, returned to it too many times.

And so I smiled and went over to hug her, and said something like, "Well, here we are now, and I suppose we must concentrate on what's in front of us." Some such platitude, meant to be comforting. And meant to change the subject. After all, she's a grown woman now, and I did not want to revisit the past. Not that particular past, at any rate, a time when I may have let her down—I will never know, not really—and a time when Francesco and I turned a corner and could not look back.

How easily, in the end, I gave in to him. I try not to think of it. But there it is, it's inevitable. I feel the quick clenching of my stomach, the twinge of guilt running through me even now. It's simply wearying.

The fact is that when Pamela started in on that subject, my first thought was not a comforting platitude at all. The mind goes where it will. I've learned to forgive myself its quirky meanderings. We are all the same, aren't we? The most angelic among us must sometimes have thoughts that are mean or vengeful or idiotic or perverse. Just yesterday I was shopping at Balducci's and came across an elderly couple huddled in the aisle. They were examining the pudding boxes. And what should spring into my mind but a picture of them naked in bed. I even heard the man groaning. Wretched, horrid thought. I went back to hunting down the Colman's.

I do wonder, though, about these thoughts that fly into our minds from God knows where, shocking our decent and amiable selves. I suppose it must be a filtering mechanism of sorts, sanity's system of checks and balances.

At any rate, I confess that my immediate thought when Pamela talked of her childhood ending was, "I'm afraid, my dear, it never really has."

Now here she is, and not a thing I can do.

I hear nothing. The door to her room is shut, there is no sound of movement. She's utterly quiet, as if she's not here at all—yet somehow she fills the apartment so that I feel there is no room for me in this place.

pamela

I had to come over to Mam's, I just had to, I couldn't stay at home another minute. All that pacing, it's no good. I know what it means. Up and down the hallway, over and over. Picking things up, putting them down, not thinking what I was doing. Lorenzo's room . . . his desk. . . I stood there forever, moving his things about. His beloved Socony pen with the flying red horse floating in oil, the pack of Black Jack gum, the tin dish full of Cracker Jack prizes. I held the pen a long while, tilting it this way and that, the winged horse gliding back and forth, back and forth. I lined up Lorenzo's treasures. The pen, the tiny tin battleship, the pack of gum, the plastic green soldier, the skull charm. Lined them up in a neat row. Picked up the pen, went back to pacing.

Up and down the hallway, I couldn't seem to stop. My shoes on the wood floor. *Tap. Tap. Tap.* I kept thinking it was rain on the roof though I knew perfectly well that it was sunny outside. *Tap. Tap. Tap.* Faster. It was rain, I was sure of it.

I flipped the Socony pen. The little red horse slid downwards ever so slowly.

Flipped it again. Upwards. Downwards. I don't know how long I stood there. I had to put it back. Lined it up with the other things on Lorenzo's desk. Walked out the door, headed to Mam's.

They followed me, though. I looked up and there they were, a flock of horses in the sky, red wings beating, beating. There were so many of them, racing sunward. Hundreds. Then out from behind a cloud another horse emerged, a different sort of beast altogether, huge and white. . . .

He flew earthward, toward me, so that I could feel the wind, his great wings beating the air. When I looked up past him I saw that all the red horses had disappeared. It was just the white one now. He hovered above me, looked at me with ancient black eyes. Eyes both sad and deeply kind. I reached up, but he shook his head, tossing his mane, and off he flew, into the high white clouds over the city.

I know that horse and his black eyes.

My mother's horse. I *drew* him.

An illustration for Mam's book. *The Skin Horse.* The story of a boy who lies dying in the hospital and the toy horse he loves—a worn-out leather horse with a wobbly leg and just five bare nails on his back where his mane used to be.

And later, that other horse, the huge one with wings that flies to the boy's bedside. . . .

I drew the child and the white winged horse, but I didn't draw the empty bed.

Some people didn't like the book, they didn't understand. They said that the story was too sad for children. But Mam knew better. *Children can deal with sadness,* she would say. *Death is natural to them.*

But, of course, I didn't really understand, either. At the time I never thought a thing about it, never thought that my mother was talking of herself.

I had to come over here. I didn't know what else to do. It's safe here in my old room, the door shut, Mam just down the hall.

I run my hands over the ridges of the old chenille bedspread, the soft tufts outlining white daisies. One by one, I touch the little buds that make up the oval pattern, over and over. Like a rosary.

I want to talk to Mam, but I can't seem to formulate what I want to talk about because, really, it's just everything. *What's wrong?* I want to ask her. Something is wrong with me, everything is wrong with me, and I want my mother to tell me what it is, but how do you have a conversation when I don't want to talk about this or that. I just want to say to Mam, *I'm tired of everything.*

How can I tell my mother such a thing?

I can't explain it to myself, not in words. If I tried to talk to Mam, I know the way she would look at me and it would be too much for me to see in her eyes the love and the worry and, worst, the knowledge that she can't help me, not really, not ever.

There is nothing and no one else in the world when my mother fixes her gaze on you that way. I've never seen such eyes on any other person. You could say they were large and blue and it would be true but also meaningless because so are Doris Day's and so are my downstairs neighbor's, yet their eyes might as well be from another species entirely. Mam's eyes are vast almond-shaped seas, liquid navy, flowing with an endless depth of understanding and compassion. When she listens to you, she takes you in and you can't help it, you simply give yourself over to her. Everyone does, I've seen it time and time again.

You have to turn away or you will tell her everything.

margery

Well, here we are now, and I suppose we must concentrate on what's in front of us.

What is in front of me? This very minute?

There is this bit of sunlight, and I am grateful for it. I always gravitate to the kitchen, settle in like a cat. In the other rooms I feel the weight of darkness. I've done what I can in the parlor, but I'm no magician. There's only one window and it faces south, so the room never quite brightens up properly. Just last week, I pulled down the velvet maroon curtains—heavy, ugly things—and put up those new cloth blinds they've been advertising at Gimbels. It made me feel better for a bit, but it didn't really help very much. At night, though, the parlor's transformed. Then it's a fine place, with the lamps and wall sconces illuminating Pamela's paintings. Her *Guggenheim Madonna* blazes in beauty, all reds and golds.

I shouldn't complain about this place, I know we're lucky to have a roof over our heads. The Great Depression didn't spare us, and why should it? Even before Francesco had to close his bookstore, I knew a move would be inevitable. But the truth is, I miss our home on Waverly Place more than I could ever have imagined.

Funny . . . it's the Kelvinator I miss most of all. All that shiny white porcelain, the door shutting with a satisfying, luxurious thud, the food magically cold. But now it's back to a peeling old icebox with bad hinges, back to chasing the iceman down the street. And there's no end in sight, not with another war on. . . . The papers say that the war has bolstered our economy, but its benefits seem to be dispersed elsewhere.

So pretty, how the sun lights up the china cabinet, piercing the little green glasses from Turin, casting emerald halos over the white dinner plates.

Sunshine dances over the glass and china like the flickering of a silent film, calling up fragments from the old days. The family dinners in Turin with Nonna and Uncle Angelo. And all those nights in London and in Harlech. . . . A velvet skirt pulled flirtatiously over a crossed knee, a spilled drink, a game of charades gone a bit risqué, bursts of laughter. How we would go on and on, talking of poetry and sea voyages, of the strengths and weaknesses of PM Lloyd George. Of bookbinding and opera and Welsh history, and who was doing what in the Royal Academy.

The green light hovers and shimmers. Another old film unreels.

Paris.

Our flat on the Rue Mayet. A fire blazing in the hearth. The mantelpiece crowded with photographs. And wafting throughout, the enticing fragrance of *blanquette de veau* simmering on the stove.

A little wooden goat.

Pablo Picasso has come to dinner.

Francesco and I had had a little disagreement that morning. A minor affair, yet. . . .

In those days Francesco was head of the rare books department at Brentano's. It was a coveted post. Signore Brentano himself had interviewed him. *All starched and bespectacled,* was how Francesco described him. There was no question that Francesco was thoroughly qualified for the position. Signore Brentano had sent a long and formal letter ahead of the interview emphasizing that erudition was vital, but just as critical were good manners and impeccable grooming. Well, Francesco surely fit the bill. In his finely tailored Italian suits—he has always been choosy about these—he has the manners and bearing of a Medici. As for erudition, it sounds ridiculous I know, but . . . well, he does seem to know just about everything. He can translate from Latin and Greek; he's fluent in five languages. He knows scads and scads about poetry, opera, and architecture.

Oh—and this: he is *the* expert in Papal Bulls.

At the conclusion of the interview, Signore Brentano asked Francesco if he had any further questions. Francesco's response was typical. "Yes," he said, I have one question: "Are you going to hire me? Because if you do not hire me, you will not sell so many books!"

Francesco laughed, and then Signore Brentano laughed, too, his starch suddenly gone all limp. My husband could charm anyone, it seems.

Even Pablo Picasso.

The young Spanish painter came in to the store one day to browse, and ended up talking to Francesco for hours in a mixture of French, English, and Spanish. It would have been quite natural for Francesco to extend an invitation to his new friend.

"Come to dinner, Pablo! And bring your Fernande. You must meet Margery."

And of course the painter said yes. Who can say no to Francesco?

Pamela and I spent the morning of Pablo's visit in the kitchen. She dragged in great long pieces of brown paper and made herself at home at my feet, drawing ducks and rabbits. I was preparing the *blanquette de veau*, cutting pieces of meat, dredging them in flour, and dropping them into a fluted dish. Sometimes a sprinkling of flour would fly from the table, dusting Pamela's pictures, and she would laugh.

A tiny skylight let in some rare Parisian sun that splashed over the red-tiled floor, the cobalt-blue table, and the white porcelain sink.

Francesco came in, holding a sheaf of Pamela's drawings, and the atmosphere shifted. You always know when something is on his mind. He doesn't exactly *charge* into a room, but it seems as if he does. He stood just under the skylight and a shaft of sunlight lightened his red hair to copper.

He's a bit vain about his hair—or was, I should say. I'm afraid it's rather deserted him these days. Soon after we met, I made the mistake of calling his hair red. "Not red, *Titian*," he corrected me, then laughed at his own absurdity.

The first time I saw Francesco it was at Heinemann's, the publisher. I was twenty, a string bean of a girl in a long tweed skirt and loose sweater, clutching my mother's moth-eaten carpetbag. Moth-eaten, but distinguished just the same, for Mother had glued a large enamel swan to the clasp—an old brooch with the back pin gone missing. *Why waste such a pretty thing?* she'd said. The bag held my manuscript for *The Price of Youth,* and I had an appointment with Mr. Heinemann himself. Just as I started down the main corridor, a young man emerged from a dark hallway off to the side. When he stepped round the corner and saw me, he stopped.

A few years earlier, in America, I had crossed paths with a moose in the woods of Maine. It was winter. A few inches of snow brightened the ground. I heard a crashing through the trees, and before I had time to think what it was the moose had leapt right in front of me, across the path into a clearing. He stopped and just stood there, dark and huge, looking at me, his warm breath rising from his nostrils. He simply stood, solid and calm. But I could feel it like waves washing over me, how he was throbbing with life.

There was nothing of the animal in Francesco's looks, it wasn't that. He was well-dressed and polished. Elegant, even. But the vision of the moose came to me straight off. A feeling of something . . . feral. I felt even then his pulsing energy, his intelligence. This was someone out of the ordinary, I knew it at once.

He asked if he could help me. A deep voice, Italian. He fixed his blue eyes on me, and something ran straight through me, I can't describe it. But all I did was tell him thank you, I knew my way.

"Well, then . . . may I help you with . . . anything else?" And he grinned that grin that will disarm you no matter what has come before. He nodded in the direction of my carpetbag. "Allow me to guess, you have a first novel in there."

When I told him, unable to disguise my pride, that it was my second, I saw his surprise. "Ah," he said, and I saw that I had risen a notch or two in his estimation. He said he was the poetry editor, and added, very formally, that he would be delighted if I would stop by for a visit when I was done with my appointment. He pointed in the direction he'd come from. Second door on the left, he said.

"Francesco Bianco," he said, and offered me his hand. When I gave him mine, he kissed my fingertips. It sounds rather silly and old-fashioned now, I suppose, but there's no pretending that it didn't thrill me utterly.

Poetry Editor. Well, that was a bit of wishful thinking. More like poetry editor in training. The first door on the left had a little plaque—Hingham, or Higby, it said. And, underneath, *Poetry Editor.* The second door was quite blank.

At any rate, there he stood, sunlit, holding out Pamela's pictures as an offering.

"Pablo would be interested in these, don't you think?"

It took me a moment to answer.

"Oh, Francesco . . . no . . . I don't think so . . . I mean, yes, I'm sure he'd like to see them, one day. But perhaps not tonight . . . not the first time he comes over here. . . ."

Francesco was quiet, staring at the pictures. Then he shrugged.

"You may be right, not tonight . . . but . . . I don't know . . . it does seem someone ought to see these besides us, Margery."

pamela

I came over here, really, just to hear my mother's voice. To reassure myself that she exists. And to stop doing what I was doing. I really don't want to talk at all, but I can't stop my thoughts from boiling up, and when I got here, of course, I couldn't stop talking, but it was about nothing.

I'll study the wallpaper, that always calms me.

A spray of lavender flowers, bunches of two or three or four. I focus on the pattern, how it slants upward and I can go right or left, up to the molding, then down again. Zig. Zag. I count them though I've counted them hundreds of times before. Eight up, nine down. If I keep counting, keep running my hands over the daisies, I'll be fine.

The flowers on the wall are not lilacs. They are some sort of wildflower, I don't know the name.

Still, I smell them, just as I did that morning. *Lilacs.*

Turin.

The bedroom on the second floor. The wallpaper that's rich and red like dark wine and soft as chenille. I can't help touching it.

I am eleven years old. It is early in the morning and I lie in bed waiting for the sounds of Signora Campanaro emerging from her kitchen. My daily ritual. I can count on her—the old landlady is as predictable in her movements and as unchanging in her appearance as a painted clock figurine. Idly, I trace the velvety flocking of the deep-claret-colored wallpaper with my finger. The gorgeous geometries of the pomegranates, the whorled leaves. I love the repeating patterns and often copy the designs into my sketchbook. Sometimes I work them as a border to my pages.

A door groans, and I jump up from the bed to stand by the casement window. A cool breeze, the scent of first lilacs. Below, in the courtyard, Signora Campanaro appears in her heavy black dress, a faded striped dishtowel in her hand, and pads across the ancient flagstones to the henhouse. As she heads back, the warm eggs wrapped in the towel, she looks up and gives an almost imperceptible nod. The signal. I smile and wave, and just at that moment, a jolt of memory strikes and I remember that today will not be like every other day. My hand drops. I close the window.

I never thought to show my art to the public, to anyone at all. Why should I? But my father thought of it.

When one of the galleries in town advertised for entries for a children's art show, my father took it upon himself to enter my work. He never said a word to anyone.

I was with Mam when she found out. We were in the kitchen, assembling the ingredients for *grissini torinese*, the breadsticks seasoned with rosemary that Daddy loves so much. We heard knocking. Someone was at the front door, banging the old boar's head knocker in an official sort of way.

A messenger stood on the doorstep, a young boy wearing a blue wool cap. His bicycle lay against the curb.

"Bianco?" he said, and when Mam nodded, he gave her the large portfolio he had under his arm. A letter was attached to the portfolio, secured with string. It was addressed to me.

The imprint on the back flap of the envelope said *Circolo degli Artisti*. I recognized the name of the gallery, we passed by it often. The black portfolio was new. I'd never seen it before.

"Well, let's get it to where we can look at it properly," my mother said in an unnaturally subdued voice, and we made our way back to the kitchen. I untied the black ribbons. Mam and I stood there, looking at my drawings. She was quiet for ages. Something was very wrong, but I wasn't sure just what it was. I reached for the letter, looking at my mother for approval.

She nodded. "Yes . . . you'd better read it, I suppose."

I read it to myself. It was a polite letter of rejection explaining that the gallery was looking not for mature artists who drew children, but for child artists. They were quite sorry, they said, these were beautiful pictures, but there had been a misunderstanding.

"I don't understand . . . ," I said, though somehow the image of Daddy was already forming in my mind. I gave the letter to my mother.

She held it for a long time without looking at me.

"I should have known when I saw all the posters and your father never mentioned them once. I should have known," my mother said softly, mostly to herself, still looking at the letter.

margery

As soon as Pablo came through the front door that night with his girlfriend, Fernande, he handed me a little wooden goat. It fit in the palm of my hand. It was a real-looking goat, but rough-hewn—the nose a bit too fat, the ears a bit too long.

"For the children. I did it with this," he said, pulling from his pocket a simple one-bladed jackknife.

"It's a lovely little goat! It was quite thoughtful of you, Pablo."

Pablo nodded at Fernande, a smoldering young beauty, taller than Pablo, with a roll of dark hair crowning her head.

"I take no credit. It was her idea."

Fernande smiled at me and shrugged. "Pablo forgets that some people actually do have children."

Pablo looked around the apartment approvingly. He said he felt right at home, and I believed him. Some, though, might have thought our apartment was a bit of a mess. Books were everywhere, piled precariously—heaped up on tables, pushed against the sofa, spilling out from under the stairs. Charlemagne, the canary, was flitting from room to room, and Narcissus, our pet white rat, roamed free.

We settled in the front parlor with vermouth in the little green glasses, and after a while I left to check on the dinner. According to Francesco, they were talking about Apollinaire and Chagall, who had just arrived in town, when Pablo went over to the fireplace and tossed in his cigarette. That's when he picked up Pamela's drawing on the mantelpiece—a small piece of paper, postcard-size, resting among the photographs.

"Who did the *cobayo* . . . what is the French, Fernande?"

"*La même chose—cobaye.*"

"In my language it's *cavia*," Francesco said, and looked up with amused triumph in his eyes as I returned to the room. "Guinea pig to you, Margery. Pablo was just asking who drew the picture."

"Oh! The little guinea pig. Pamela did that this morning."

"Pamela? Your daughter? But no . . . she is only . . . I'm sorry, I can't remember these things. How old did you say she was?"

"Four."

"*Quatre!* It cannot be so . . . do you have anything else to show me that this four-year-old has done?"

Pablo studied the drawings that Francesco proudly handed to him.

"*Incroyable!* Such command for one so young . . . impossible, I think." He went through the drawings again, then looked up at me with an intensity that I felt was almost hostile. "I think I would like to have a visit with your little daughter."

"Oh, I don't . . . she's just getting ready for bed . . . now, do you mean?"

"Yes, I wish to see her now."

I called to Pamela as I headed up the stairwell.

"Come downstairs for a bit, Pamela . . . our friend Pablo is asking for you . . . bring your drawing board. . . ."

Pamela looked as though she couldn't believe her luck. A summons downstairs! To where the fire was blazing, where grownups were talking and laughing and drinking. Where everything was happening. I held her hand and led her down the narrow, unlit stairway. She was in her nightgown, barefoot.

When we entered the parlor, she leaned into me, suddenly shy.

Pablo was seated cross-legged on the floor.

"Come! Sit here next to me, Pamela."

She obeyed. As she sat close to him, I wondered what she thought of the rather odorous dark-haired man at her side. He smelled of many things—tobacco and sweet smoke and something sharper, like old soup, or Narcissus's cage.

"I've heard you like to draw animals . . . well, so do I! I am an artist, did you know that?"

Pamela nodded. She had heard us talking about Pablo and his paintings.

"I thought you and I might draw one picture together before you go to bed, would that be all right with you? How about a picture of this little goat that I made?"

She nodded again. Pablo set the goat down on the rug.

Pamela knelt over her drawing board. She worked fast, the way she always did, rarely picking the pencil up off the paper. But Pablo finished first, and watched as Pamela drew.

She stopped a moment and looked up at him.

"Is it a girl goat or a boy goat?"

Pablo laughed.

"Hmm, a girl goat, I believe."

Quickly, Pamela drew a collar of flowers around the goat's neck, and put down her pencil.

Pablo said, "You must sign it now."

She printed in neatly rounded letters on the bottom right: *Pamela*.

"And now I'll sign mine."

Pablo scrawled his name in capitals: *PABLO*.

"Shall we trade?" he asked.

Pamela nodded and handed her picture to the man with the wild black hair falling over his forehead.

Before he left that night, long after Pamela was asleep, Pablo asked to see her again. Francesco always says that I looked terribly startled then, and Pablo had roared. "No, no, don't worry . . . I won't wake her. I won't make her draw again!"

In monkish silence all four of us tiptoed up the narrow stairs. We stood around Pamela's small bed like shepherds watching over the Christ child. A rectangle of pale moonlight fell across her face.

"*Incroyable*," Pablo muttered again.

pamela

*W*hen Daddy came home, we were still standing in the kitchen with my drawings spread across the table. He immediately grasped the situation.

He flung himself down before my mother, wrapped his arms around her legs, pressed his face to her belly.

"Margery . . . Margery . . . Margery." He always put the emphasis on the second syllable, as in *frittata* or *bongiorno*. He looked up at her, pleading.

"It will be good, very good, you will see. Forgive me, please, Margery. . . ."

The words somehow came out as a poem from his lips. Mam looked into his dancing, begging eyes and shook her head. But she didn't seem as angry as I had thought she would be.

"Get up, Francesco," she said, and glanced at me, even managing a smile, as if to say, *He's right, you know, it will be all right.* But her attention turned to Daddy and I was quite forgotten. That was fine with me. I cared only that there was peace between my parents.

I realize now that what they had that day was not a true peace. That would have to come later. Mam's gesture of forgiveness was put on for my sake. Still, I think now that something *shifted* in my mother that day. She saw the way it was, the way it would be. She decided simply to free herself up. Mam's always been magnificent that way, she can simply go forward, not holding grudges or anything. I'm afraid I've never gotten the hang of that.

When Daddy had recovered, he read the letter carefully. He laughed.

He turned to me.

"So," he said, "they think you are a 'mature' artist? We will show them."

He promptly returned to the gallery with the drawings— and me—and let the gallery owner know that *this young girl, my daughter, is the artist. She made several of the drawings, in fact—see this one? And this?—when she was only seven or eight years old.* I nodded agreement, and smiled at the astonished owner. He murmured apologies and assurances that most certainly the committee would agree to show my work.

At the time, I thought I understood what had happened. I thought that it was simply the one thing, that Daddy hadn't talked to Mam about it, that he'd just gone off on his own. I couldn't see the truth, that everything had changed in that instant. Daddy's crime was not a simple one. It would set our world on edge, spinning off out of control. And Mam had seen it from the beginning.

The consequences for me . . . well, I never considered them at all. Years later—the hospital . . . the kind doctor, Henry—I saw the truth.

margery

I suppose it was all set in motion as long ago as that, the night Picasso came to dinner. Pamela's future. Our future. I had tried to hold Francesco back, and he had acquiesced, but what difference did it make? Pablo saw the drawing. He asked questions, studied the way Pamela drew.

Francesco and I had discussed our daughter often enough, it's not that we didn't know that our child was unusual. That a little girl who slept with her drawing board, who panicked if she couldn't find it, was not an average child. Yet—who was to say, things change, and I thought it was possible that in a year or two she'd move on to something else. Perhaps become obsessed with dancing or writing poetry or playing the flute.

How many times did I say to Francesco, *We must wait, she must decide for herself when she is ready*?

But he did not see it that way at all, he was all for striking while the iron was hot. He did not want to miss a chance. I couldn't stop him.

Or did not. When Francesco wanted to send Pamela away to San Remo after the exhibition in Turin, I said no. I said she was too young to be without her family.

After a while, though, I came round, said it was fine, that I'd been wrong to stand in her way.

And there was Pamela, running headlong into fame, on the heels of her father.

‡ ‡ ‡

Francesco came to me the night before Pamela left to stay with his artist friend in San Remo, all pleased.

"I told her to take Picasso's goat, Margery."

He put his hands on either side of my face, made me look at him.

"Margery, *cara*, I put the little goat in her case and told her it would bring her good luck. She gave me her big smile—she's *fine* now. I could see it—she's happy to be going. You don't have to worry about her any more."

He wrapped his arms around me and pressed me to him, and I decided to believe him.

I woke in the night, remembering his words.

I put the little goat in her case and told her it would bring her good luck. . . .

Perhaps he's right, I thought. Perhaps he's been right all along. Pamela will be fine.

Well. All that was a hundred years ago. I must stop this. Focus on what's happening now.

Pamela is thirty-seven and in her old room, and I wonder, is there anything I can do? I cannot think what. Urge her to paint again, tell her she really must try? If the large paintings seem daunting, could she not at least begin the process, sketch her ideas? Start on a small scale? But it's ridiculous of me to suggest such a thing. She is the artist, she'll begin when she's ready. Or when Francesco convinces her. It's not my affair. There's nothing I can do. I can't fix a thing.

Well, I can fix some tea.

Perhaps it will help, ease this headache I seem to have developed.

Strange, I never get headaches.

pamela

*W*hy do I keep it up? All this *if* business.

My thoughts get me nowhere, just a circle over and over, like a toy train.

The same story repeats itself. But I've changed it. Daddy, in Turin. He's on his way to the bookstore. He sees the posters advertising for young artists. He makes up his mind. He buys a new portfolio, puts a dozen of my pictures inside. Confidently, he heads to the Circolo degli Artisti. And this is where it changes, near the beginning. Daddy slows as he nears the gallery. He is hearing my mother's voice. *Wait, Francesco. Let her decide for herself.* He comes to a stop, holds the portfolio out as if asking it a question. He looks pained. He sighs, but then makes a brisk turn, a neat about-face as if he were still in the military, and marches home. He returns my drawings to the closet. The boy, the messenger from the gallery, never knocks at the door. Mam and I make *grissini torinese,* and when Daddy comes home from the bookshop he laughs and hugs us both and stuffs himself with warm bread. I draw, play with the cat, run out to meet Cecco when he comes home from school.

But after that—how would the story go then?

Would I find fame on my own? In my own time, as Mam predicted? Would it have worked that way?

Is that what I would have wanted?

I don't know. I cannot *know.* I only know what actually happens: Daddy brings my pictures to the gallery, and a few weeks later when I wave to Signora Campanaro in the courtyard my heart feels leaden.

It is the day of the exhibition.

We breakfast on boiled eggs and raisin toast. I study my brother as he butters his third piece of toast and feel a tug, a sadness. He is twelve—we are little more than a year apart—and we have perhaps been unusually close. I have known for long time that at the end of summer he'll be off to England, to boarding school. But I cannot imagine this. I do not believe he will really go away.

I think for the millionth time how like Mam he is. Steady, cheerful. He resembles her, too, with his dark hair and slender build. And his eyes—the kindness in his eyes. It is not just an impression given.

Once, when we were very small and living in Paris, Uncle Angelo sent Cecco some money for his birthday. Everyone had an idea of what he might buy. A puzzle. A wooden train. A packet of the almond torrone that he loved. A few days later he handed me a small package. Colored pencils! He said he'd heard me wishing aloud about how I wanted to draw with color, not just charcoal and pencil.

And later, in Turin, it was his idea to write the letters to the soldiers. The war was on, and Daddy was away, a captain in the Italian army. It was a hard winter for us. We were never warm enough. We shut all the doors and lived in one room of the apartment. There was little to eat. Mam made us calico bags to keep our bread rations in. She gave English lessons to earn a bit of extra money.

In the springtime, it was better. We hiked up San Vito to pick flowers and filled baskets with violets and primroses. We tied up handfuls with string to give to the wounded men at the British Military Hospital. I see my brother's face, alight as he thought of his plan. "Can we write notes to them, too, Mam?"

And so we cut little squares of paper and wrote a few words on each. *I do hope you will be quite strong soon. We hope you will be home before long. I know you are a brave soldier and will soon be well.* We hid the notes inside the bunches of flowers.

‡ ‡ ‡

Cecco jumps up, grabs the canvas book bag off the back of his chair. He calls out his good-byes over his shoulder as he rushes out the door. I sit, still and gloomy, feeling just as if that's it, he's gone, he's gone off to England and left me here.

Daddy pushes his chair back and announces that he is going to the gallery to "check on things."

Mam turns to me, ignoring the panic on my face, and smiles. "Shall we go to the park in a bit?"

At Valentino Park, Mam and I speak in French as we wander among the gardens. She points out weeping willows (*saules pleureurs*) and, by the riverbank, tulips (*tulipes)* and mallards (*colverts*). I hardly think of it that way, but I am having a lesson. A few years before, I'd trotted off with Cecco to the Istituto Bracco, but I'd had a bad time. I was horribly shy, and never made any friends. I might have survived that, but I couldn't survive Suora Ignatia. She rapped my knuckles when I drew rabbits at the end of my addition columns! I can still see her fat forefinger tapping my paper as she warned me to *never again* draw on my school papers. Her words made me feel empty. *Not draw?* The rabbits caused no harm, they didn't interfere with my rows of sums. Why did she tell me I couldn't draw? Even though a classmate came up to me in the playground later and told me she really liked my rabbits and she hated Suora Ignatia, I didn't feel better. I didn't answer. I was simply too paralyzed.

After one year at the Istituto, I declared that I'd never go back. There was no argument over it, my parents readily agreed—they could teach me all I needed to know. It would be better that way, they said, my mind could develop more naturally, and there would be time for art whenever I wished. At eight, my formal education had ended.

My parents taught me English and Italian and French, math and history. They took me to the Pinacoteca where I'd race to the Botticelli room to admire the angels and slender nymphs in diaphanous dresses. They took me to the ancient churches whose shadowy walls were lit by votive candles and hung with small oil paintings of Madonna and Child. I loved all the fat, naked babies, the serene faces of Mary, and the gilt halos—some like dark copper, some flashing pale gold in the candlelight. I drew and drew and drew.

Mam and I wander by the beautiful squares of gardens and find a bench near the river. I tear pages from my drawing notebook so that we can make paper boats. My mother is a wizard at paper folding. When Cecco and I were too small to make the folds ourselves, we'd watch fascinated as she took pages from her own hand-sewn manuscript book of shiny yellow paper and made perfect swans, two-seated boats, and tea kettles. When we were old enough to learn, she taught us to make the same object over and over, ensuring that our folds were precise, that we pressed ever so carefully with our fingertips, until we could do it perfectly all by ourselves.

We set our boats loose upon the Po. They bob and separate, abandoned orphans bravely heading out to sea. Soon they are no longer boats at all but only glints of white in the water. I watch them disappear, and suddenly I am overcome with a feeling I have never had before, and I have no name for it.

Today I can put a name to that feeling, with no trouble at all. *Melancholy.*

Mam, of course, can read my face. She leans in close to me and speaks gently.

"You know, Pamela, I suspect you'll have great fun at the gallery tonight. It will be your special time with Daddy, he'll be at your side every minute, and you know how he is—he'll have everyone quite entranced in no time!"

margery

Some nice English tea. And a biscuit.

There. That's better.

I'll just make myself as comfortable as I can, put my feet up on the chair Pamela abandoned.

I see her face across from me still.

It's not her real face, not the face of my Pamela. Good lord, those eyebrows. . . . Such a shock when she first shaved them off. And before long, another shock. When she dyed her hair blonde, it had rather terrified me, the way it changed her. But—well, it was 1932, and half the young women in America were walking around trying to look like Jean Harlow. Garish, to my eyes anyway. Still, it was an odd thing for Pamela, who'd never followed fashion. She's a Williams bohemian through and through. One thing, she didn't cut off her hair. I think at that time she was the only female in the city under forty whose hair wasn't short and sleek and waved. Pamela stuck to the style she's worn since she was fifteen, long braids wound in spirals round her ears.

What did any of that mean? I'm not sure. The transformation came right after Robert left, and perhaps that explains it all. Robert . . . he was so . . . so *what*? He was a flash in the pan. A charmer. Not a *dependable* sort, that much was obvious. It was hardly a great surprise when he left. Well, at least not to Francesco or me.

It all happened so very fast. If only I'd had time to talk to Pamela a bit, perhaps she would have been less impetuous. But there was no time—what was it, a few months? We only saw the boy two or three times. I liked him well enough. I do have a special affection for poets. And he was quite a good-looking poet. Easygoing, friendly. Not the brooding sort. But I never had a proper conversation with the boy. He always traveled about with an entourage, his literary friends from Harlem.

But there was something . . . I never could put my finger on it. Something about the look I saw that passed between his friends one time. Robert was talking to me, and he put his arm around Pamela, and I happened to see one of the boys look at the friend next to him with . . . how can I put it . . . a sort of arch amusement. It seemed to say, *There he goes again, what's he thinking?* I don't know how it is I read it that way, but sometimes you catch the barest glimpse of someone's expression and immediately a feeling registers and somehow you are sure that you know just what that person is thinking. You have no doubt at all.

Even so, what on earth could I have said to Pamela?

When Robert's letter came, she was silent. Catatonic, more like. She can get like that, she simply shuts down. You just have to wait it out. All she told us was this: *Robert's gone back to Oregon.*

At any rate, when she changed herself so drastically I tried to think it meant that she was hopeful again, that she wanted to start anew. After all, she'd just emerged from one of her black times. A particularly bad one. Things had truly begun to unravel right after Lorenzo was born. Even in the beginning, it was all Pamela could do to care for the child. Soon she wasn't capable at all.

In the end we'd all agreed it was best if I took them both to Merryall, my sister Cecil's house in Connecticut. The quiet of the countryside would calm her, was the thought. But her recovery, if it could be called that, was slow beyond imagining.

pamela

$\mathcal{N}$ot long after my father knelt on the kitchen floor in Turin, begging my mother's forgiveness, Daddy and I walked together out into the spring air and headed to the exhibition at the Circolo degli Artisti.

We were in a hurry.

Daddy strode over the cobbled piazza and I danced at his side, the ribbons on my braids bouncing and fluttering like butterflies. I tried to make a game of it, skipping to the staccato of my father's boots as they struck the stones. We were on our way to the gallery where my drawings were hung for the world to see.

I wasn't eager to go to the exhibition. I had no idea what to expect. Would it be crowded and noisy? Would people ask me a lot of questions? What if they didn't like my drawings?

As Daddy and I neared the gallery, it was not just nervousness about me, about my art, that I was feeling. There was something else, something that worried me most of all—*would Gabriele d'Annunzio be there?* I hoped more than anything that he would, though it wasn't for myself that I hoped, it was just that Daddy cared so very much. Mam had tried to warn him. *Oh, Francesco, don't get your hopes up, you really mustn't count on it,* she had said more than once.

Daddy slowed down and stopped at a storefront to check his reflection. Turning slightly sideways, he gave a little tug on his cream-colored suit jacket, and rearranged his fedora a centimeter or two. He needn't have bothered, he was always impeccable.

The shop we stood in front of sold candy and gelato, and the window was full of gay decorations. The centerpiece of the display was a doll, perched atop a silver box and loosely dressed in a long white tunic with huge buttons. Pierrot, the clown. Daddy pulled me in front of him, his hands on my shoulders. We stared at ourselves; Pierrot stared at us.

"So, Pamela," Daddy said to my image in the glass, "very soon now the people of Turin will discover the treasure we have kept buried in our house. They will be very surprised, don't you think?"

I nodded. I didn't know what to think. I knew Daddy wasn't really talking to me at all. He cocked his head, contemplating the doll.

"What do *you* think, *Pedrolino*?" Daddy laughed.

We turned away. We'd moved along just a step or two when Daddy twirled around as if something had caught his eye.

"Ah, did you see that, Pamela? He saluted us—it is the best of luck!"

We laughed together, then. It was good to believe that it might be true.

margery

*A*nd so we were off to New Preston, Connecticut. I packed up Pamela and Lorenzo, and we took a train to Waterbury. Jerry, a local farmer who looked after Merryall when it was deserted, met us at the station in his old black Ford pickup truck. I told Pamela to ride up front with Jerry, and I settled down with Lorenzo into the back on a pile of horse blankets. I knew he'd think it a lark to bounce around the back of the truck and watch the world go by—automobiles, birds, trees. We rode along miles and miles of dirt road. It was a glorious day. The hills glowed yellow-green in the sunlight. Puffs of clouds moved across an aqua sky, casting their fleeting shadows across the countryside.

Merryall. How fond I am of the place, an old farmhouse stretching itself out in the middle of a stone-strewn field like a contented cat. It isn't derelict, exactly, just a bit . . . neglected. That sort of thing doesn't bother Cecil and Teddy. No one seems to notice if the white clapboard is in need of paint, or that most of the shutters have come loose and hang drunkenly off the windows. Once when Francesco offered to nail up the shutters, Teddy looked at him quizzically. *Oh . . . the shutters? There's something wrong with the shutters?*

Inside, things are much the same. There's all the charm of creaking floorboards and low-beamed ceilings, but no time or money's been wasted on furnishing the house. A bed and dresser for the bedrooms. Cupboards with no doors in the kitchen. And in the living room, one of Aunt Agnes's old horsehair settees, a low painted table, all chipped and gouged, and several plain wood chairs that look like rejects from the town meeting hall. And so it was the perfect retreat for us. I didn't have to worry about Lorenzo ruining anything. Any spilling or banging he did simply added another bit of character to the place.

Most of the time—and we were almost a year at Merryall— Lorenzo and I were on our own. Pamela seemed to be eternally napping. Or eternally distracted.

One afternoon I was outdoors reading in the shade while Lorenzo played in the field. I heard his voice calling me, high and shrill, and when I went to him he pointed to a small, dead animal lying in the meadow. The creature was not very much bigger than a mouse, soft and rounded and silver-gray. His tiny paws were almost translucent, his face just a ball of fur with a pinkish, pointed nose. I picked him up and sat down on the grass with Lorenzo and I told him the story of the time his mother and her brother—Uncle Cecco—had found a mole in Hampstead Heath.

We were living in Golder's Green, then, such a peaceful place in those days, with only the occasional horse-drawn carriage rumbling by. I let the children roam free. Of course, most of the time they headed for the heath. Cecco came home one day, cradling something in his cap, Pamela at his heels. Cecco held out his cap for me to see. *He has no eyes, Mam! What is he?* I explained that he did have eyes of a sort, tiny slits, really. *Still, all moles are blind, you know,* I told them. They were quite impressed with themselves for having found such an exotic creature. They buried the poor thing in the backyard, and wrote a poem for his gravestone. I could still remember the poem, and recited it for Lorenzo.

In this dark hole
Lies Mr. Mole
He died of fright
Because he had no sight.

In the kitchen I folded over an old cloth napkin to make a bed for the little animal, and let Lorenzo carry him as we went to find his mother. The boy was bright as a Christmas ornament in his excitement. I thought surely this was something that would awaken Pamela, penetrate through the fog, encourage her to share more of her childhood with her boy. But she just nodded as we talked. I was frustrated.

"You do remember, darling, that time you and Cecco brought home the mole?" She said, "Oh, yes, I remember. . . ." But she very much looked as though she didn't.

In those days Pamela fulfilled her motherly duties mainly by worrying. Not the usual things, like is Lorenzo eating enough or should he be wearing a sunhat. She worried obsessively, and I could not reassure her, no matter what I said, about intruders, about Lorenzo being kidnapped. It was absurd, yet there was a grain of reason behind it. The Lindbergh baby was kidnapped just months before Lorenzo was born. It had stunned us all, naturally, everyone was horrified, and terribly, terribly sad. But Pamela was beyond all that, she was deeply traumatized. Her fears, far from subsiding, were acute now that Lorenzo was the same age as the Lindbergh boy, almost two. I have to admit he did look a bit like him, too, chubby and red-cheeked, with thick curling hair.

The idea that an evil person might enter our house at night tormented Pamela, and at bedtime she'd always ask, "Did you lock the doors, Mam?" I assured her I had, but still she'd go round checking. She set rows of pebbles on all the windowsills thinking we would hear them falling when the prowler tried to get through, and she insisted that not one window should be left open at night.

But I cannot bear to sleep without fresh air. I would pile the pebbles on my dresser, careful to rearrange them on the sill first thing when I woke.

margery

$\mathcal{A}$t last Pamela emerged from the darkness. We stayed on at Merryall for a while, and she felt well enough to take on a commission—illustrations for a new edition of *The Little Mermaid*.

When I was a child I was entranced by Hans Christian Andersen's fairy tales. I must have read *The Little Mermaid* a thousand times. Though I knew it almost by heart, one day, while Pamela and Lorenzo were shopping in town, I thought I'd read the story again.

When I came to a certain passage, I stopped reading. Or, I should say, I read the same lines over and over.

> *As the days passed, she loved the prince more fondly, and he loved her as he would love a little child, but it never came into his head to make her his wife. . . .*

These lines struck me as they never had before. Would Pamela dwell on these words? It seems such a trivial thing, but I was terrified. It was just the sort of thing that could set her back, this tale of a girl who does everything for love, sacrifices everything. But she never wins the one she loves. She is of a different world. She is made quite differently.

But it wasn't Robert I worried about when I read the story. I prayed that, after all this time, Pamela was not still thinking of Diccon.

She does hold on to things so.

What really worries me, and I cannot say it aloud, is . . . well, I fear that Pamela will never find love. It plagues me, this fear. What if she never does find a man to adore her, respect her? To balance her?

So, there it is. We can't talk about it, of course. But I feel she just . . . cannot judge people. She is too fragile for this world. Perhaps I am being unfair, too dramatic. But Pamela does seem to me awfully like a flesh-and-blood version of Hans Christian Andersen's little mermaid—both such tender and sensitive creatures, pinning their hopes on the impossible.

I try to be optimistic, yet I can't dispel the image of Pamela as an old woman, alone, puttering about in a daze. To imagine that my daughter could live all her life and never, ever know what it is to truly love a man, to have him love her back. . . .

My heart splinters to think it could be so.

Pamela fears it, too, she has said as much. And I have denied it utterly. I have lied to her. *Oh, darling, of course it will happen! You just never know when . . . you must be patient. You're still a young woman, for heaven's sake.*

pamela

*W*e were almost there.

I felt Daddy's excitement as we walked up to the gallery, felt his apprehension as he raised his hand to the door. All my worries about the exhibition were now telescoped into one: *Would Gabriele d'Annunzio show up? Would he?*

Tinkling bells announced us as Daddy pushed on the gallery door, but, over the low buzz in the interior, our entrance went unnoticed. People were milling about, some holding glasses of wine. Once in a while, the sharp voices of very small children flew up over the hum of the crowd.

I looked around, anxious, praying that Gabriele d'Annunzio might magically appear. But in my heart I was sure he wouldn't. It didn't seem possible. My father had written him about the exhibition, but there had been no response. I thought that was not very much of a surprise—d'Annunzio was the most famous, the most revered man in Italy. Why should he want to come to see my drawings?

In his youth, Gabriele had been an acclaimed poet. Later, he wrote plays, stories, and novels in a style so beautiful the critics fought each other to find the most ecstatic praise. All Italians were obsessed by Gabriele d'Annunzio. Often I'd overhear snippets at the butcher's or on the street corner. My parents discussed him over dinner. Women fought each other over him—if you wanted to follow his love life, you had only to pick up a newspaper.

Now the Great War had just come to an end, and Gabriele had returned from the front a hero, a fearless poet warrior. He'd fought heroically on land and on sea, but it was his exploits as a daredevil pilot that riveted the country. Once, to avoid enemy fire, he flew to the unthinkable altitude of 14,000 feet—it was seventeen degrees below zero! From his plane he dropped tricolor flags and thousands of messages, messages he had written himself to lift the spirits of the Italian soldiers. Daddy had kept one in the breast pocket of his uniform and showed it to us proudly when he came home from the war. It was tattered and dirty, but you could still read the words.

> *Courage, brothers! Courage and fortitude! I tell you,*
> *I swear to you, my brothers, our victory is certain!*
> *Courage! Constancy! The dawn of your joy is imminent.*
> *From the heights of heaven, on the wings of Italy, I*
> *throw you this pledge, this message from my heart. . . .*

Cecco was enthralled. He idolized the hero. For weeks he worked on making a model of d'Annunzio's biplane. He worried over the painting, getting the lettering right. I offered to help, but he wanted to do it himself. In the end, it was perfect. Cecco had managed to fit d'Annunzio's motto—*The Lion Roars Again*—in small print on the side of the plane. Blue tongues of fire shot through the words, surrounded by seven gold stars.

This famous man came into my father's bookstore on occasion, and Daddy had been helpful in finding some rare books of poetry for him. Most likely, Daddy regarded Gabriele d'Annunzio as a friend. After all, they both loved art and language and poetry and beautiful books. They had both served Italy in the war. And Daddy was always quick to become intimate with people.

In any event, my father had written to Gabriele, an invitation to see my work, and enclosed a picture I had made when I was seven—a pen-and-ink drawing of two girls sitting back-to-back on a large stone, naked, flowers strung round their waists. Gabriele had not written back.

‡ ‡ ‡

In the gallery, my drawings filled the back wall. When I first saw them, I was mesmerized. It was as if I had never seen them before. In a sense, that was true. I drew hundreds of pictures, shoved piles of them under my bed. Sometimes Mam would pull out the lot. *No use having them collect dust,* she'd say. I thought for a long time that she threw them out. It didn't matter to me. Each day I drew new things, and it was only the newest picture that held my interest. As soon as it was finished, I'd toss it aside, eager to begin the next.

Now I saw the world I had created.

Such a busy, happy, intricate world! The drawings were stylized and primitive at the same time. The landscapes were crowded, the flora unreal. Stalks of flowers ran tree-high. A cactus sat among roses. Vines ran rampant among ferns and climbed the slender trees topped with leafy heads. Children, starry-eyed, tumbled through the sylvan scenes. Some were naked, others wore airy dresses trellised with spade-like leaves and floating cherries, and idealized blossoms. Rabbits and ducks and kittens frolicked with butterflies. Chubby cherubs, sporting patterned wings, flew overhead.

I sat on a stool by my father. People came up to me, shaking their heads, smiling, their faces bemused. They offered many compliments. I responded politely, but really Daddy did most of the talking. He would always talk to anyone who would listen. *She started at four—we knew right away! She has never had a lesson, no—no, we feel she should find her own way, we don't want to meddle with her talent, it is a gift!*

Late in the evening, a change in atmosphere swept through the gallery. People whispered and turned to the entrance.

Gabriele d'Annunzio!

The gallery owner threw open his arms, hailing the hero. He beat his fists upon his heart. Someone rushed to get the great man some wine. When Daddy saw who was taking the attention away from us, his joy increased, and he gave a beckoning wave from across the room. Gabriele nodded at Daddy, but he took his time, holding amiable court as he ambled through the gallery, gazing at the paintings and drawings on the walls.

When he came to my drawings he stopped still. It seemed then that the whole gallery grew silent.

At last he turned to me.

"So it is you who have created these beautiful pictures? Truly? I would not have believed any child could draw in this way."

He introduced himself, and with a gloved hand reached for mine. He bent over and kissed my fingertips. I studied the famous man: the narrow bald head, the stiff waxed mustache, the gleaming boots. His strong cologne enveloped me, and I wanted to move away, but I couldn't.

Daddy happily regaled Gabriele about the evolution of my talent, the way my very first lines were so sure, so delicate yet so strong, the way I held a pencil, then a pen, and how I was beginning to work in oils. Gabriele listened politely, then gestured towards a large drawing just behind me—a pen and ink of a girl with a lyre washed with yellows and reds.

"This one . . . I will take this one," he said.

Gaslight danced in bright puddles across the piazza as we walked home.

"D'Annunzio . . . just imagine, Pamela. *D'Annunzio!*" Daddy's voice was excited, but low. Full of wonder.

I didn't understand—how could I?—that on that night my life had changed, that everything was tumbling into place, that the perfect and pure days of my childhood were over. That night we might as well have walked directly out the gallery door onto the gangplank of the *RMS Carmania*, the ship that would take us to America. There was no stopping the tide of fame that would sweep me up and carry me—and all my family—along to a distant shore. And there was no stopping Daddy.

....

Gabriele d'Annunzio Writes to Pamela
Turin, 1918

Commandant Gabriele d'Annunzio stares at the delicate drawing. A girl in a forest glade. She wears a flowing tunic, tied with a wide sash. She holds an ornate lyre, the stems curving into perfect coils.

What is it that draws him so? The otherworldliness? The mastery, the confidence to create such utter beauty? He examines the picture closely. A pen, in the hand of a small girl—yet, no mark of hesitancy, no small mistake, no sign of redrawing. The bit of color washed here and there, yellows and reds, just enough to bring the whole to life. It is perfection.

Gabriele sighs dramatically, shakes his head. He is truly moved. A *child* has made this picture! He remembers her eyes upon him, large and compelling. What color were they? Blue? Gray? In general, though, he has to admit, Pamela Bianco was a rather un-extraordinary-looking child. A quiet little girl with braids. Somber, even.

Eleven, her father says. She looked barely nine.

Gabriele has fallen in love with Pamela's drawings, and for him it is no different than when he falls in love with a woman. He cannot keep it to himself, but has to run shouting it from every rooftop, every street corner. He needs to honor this new love.

He will write a poem for the girl.

He takes some paper from his desk drawer.

Yes, he will write a poem and then he will send it to the newspapers. The editors will be ecstatic. Who in Italy will not want to buy a paper with this combination: the story of an extraordinary child artist *and* a poem about her by the great Gabriele d'Annunzio? It will be irresistible.

Gabriele is happy to do his part, to ensure the future of the little artist. Soon she will soar. Before long, he is sure, the whole world will know of her.

And to think, he almost did not go to the exhibition. Francesco's letter had irritated him—the man had assumed an intimacy that did not exist. But when he saw the drawing Francesco had enclosed, he had been unable to tear his eyes away.

A girl . . . whose name is like a flower. . . .

The poem is finished. But now he must write a letter to the child.

He holds his pen high in the air—even with no one to see him, he cannot not help the drama—then brings it down, writing in great flourishes.

Cara Pamela. . . .

He signs the letter and sits quietly a while, looking absent-mindedly at the objects on his desk. A pair of porcelain cats, a rhinoceros of lapis blue, a tortoiseshell crab. The war photos: d'Annunzio standing by the Ansaldo SVA, his reconnaissance biplane; d'Annunzio aboard his beloved MAS 96—the *Motoscafo Armato Silurante,* the famed torpedo-armed motorboat that he had commanded in so many victorious sea battles; and d'Annunzio with his flying partner, Rinaldo, whose death he still mourns.

And then his eye falls on the box.

The old box is beautiful, made of teak, and decorated with finely carved fighting stags. It has been in his family for generations. He hesitates only a moment.

He folds the letter, places it in the box, and rings for his adjutant.

pamela

I see Mam so clearly, the way she sits at her desk, her long legs swung off to one side of the chair. With infinite care, she wraps layers of old newspaper around a vibrantly colored vase. For weeks, whenever she'd walked by the shop on Via Battisti she had stopped to gaze at the beautiful glass from Murano, drawn to the brilliant azure and ruby and honey-gold. She could scarcely afford such things, but she'd recently received a letter from her sister Cecil in America announcing that Cecil's daughter Agnes had run off and married a playwright, a man she had known only a few months. *Good for her—a literary man,* she'd said to Daddy. Then—*Well, if I can't have that vase, Agnes can have it.*

I sit cross-legged on the floor, sketching my mother—the strong nose, the small chin, the concentrated brow, the dark hair rolled up loosely at the nape of her neck. I draw her long, slender fingers tying a great bow on the wedding present. The ends of the ribbon fly upwards from the bow, cascading around the edges of the page.

Mam sets the vase, now a swollen mummy, into a box cushioned with paper. She picks up Cecil's letter again.

Dearest Sister,
I write with rather astounding news. I cannot say
whether it is good news or not! It seems that our
Agnes has gotten married. Teddy and I were not at
the wedding—no one was there, in fact—a minister in

Provincetown seems to have married the happy couple in his parlor.

The young man's name is Eugene O'Neill—we know little about him, only that he writes plays. Agnes—who never to our knowledge has had any interest in the theatre—tells us that two of his plays were produced last fall and were well received. She is convinced that she has married a great playwright! That may be true, of course, but I can't help wondering if Agnes will be supporting him with her stories. . . .

Cecil writes on, philosophizing in her hazy way about marriage, child-rearing, choices one makes. Had she and Teddy been too bohemian themselves? Perhaps in some ways. Then again no, she didn't really think that was possible. They had wanted their girls to be "free spirits"—and they had succeeded—this was a good thing, wasn't it?

Dear, dear Margery—do keep your Pamela close by you!

That is how Cecil ends her letter.

Do keep your Pamela close by you. I've often wondered about that. What did she mean, exactly? Did she regret her permissive parenting? Was it a real warning, or just a random thought—a bit of Cecil's ironic humor? Did Mam take it to heart? I think she did worry about me, awfully. And she did keep me close, always. Or . . . perhaps it was the other way around.

My portrait is almost finished: Mam's head bent over her work, her ankles crossed, her Indian peasant skirt just hitting the tops of her laced shoes. At her feet I sketch in a cat, one paw on a wedding bell. On the bottom of the page I write, in my very precise handwriting, *Mam and the Wedding Bell, Turin.*

I fling my board aside and jump up. Where *is* Miss Betts, anyway? I run upstairs to find the cat.

‡ ‡ ‡

It's Cecco who spies the soldier approaching our apartment.

"Mam! A soldier!"

Cecco gets to the door first, with Mam and me close behind. Outside, an officer stands holding a box of dark wood.

"For Miss Pamela Bianco, with the compliments of *Commandante* Gabriele d'Annunzio."

Cecco looks as though he's just seen Napoleon on our doorstep. He stands rigid, staring, until the officer disappears from sight.

The heavy teak box is ancient, and decorated with finely carved fighting stags. Inside, there is a letter for me.

You are Italy's treasure . . . I am a poet, I worship beauty
. . . you are beauty, you must always remember this.

He asks me to keep all future correspondence from him in this box, a box that had been in his family for hundreds of years.

Later when I watch Daddy read that letter, I almost turn away, afraid he may weep from joy. Even Mam is awestruck.

The letter means little to me. But the box—I do love the box. I run my finger over the smooth wood, over the majestic stags with their great curling horns.

I have done nothing, but overnight, I am famous.

Photographs of my drawings are reproduced in Italian newspapers and all over Europe. Art critics fall in love with my pictures. The public adores me, their ardor enflamed to great heights by d'Annunzio, whose poem declares that I am "this wonderful child whose name is like the name of a new flower."

Pamela: honey, sweetness. *Bianco*: white. *White honey blossom.*

I love it, the idea of being a flower, and I dance about the house, bending and blowing about in imaginary winds.

Daddy is thrilled by all the attention. In his euphoria he takes me in his arms and swings me up, crowing. *Now you are famous . . . now all Italians are happy to claim you as one of their children!*

As he holds me aloft, I see myself reflected in his eyes. A prize. A child of gold.

I laugh with pleasure. I don't really give two figs about d'Annunzio or being famous. I certainly don't care about the critics or even all the people of Italy. But I have pleased my father greatly. For me, there is no greater joy.

margery

$\mathcal{P}$erhaps I should have let her talk this morning.

Turin, the beginning of it all. That's what she meant this morning when she started on about her childhood ending, and I cut her off.

I've rationalized it all a thousand times. Could it have made any difference if Francesco had listened to me? Who is to say that things would have gone any better for Pamela—for any of us—if I had succeeded? It's quite possible that all it would have accomplished is a terrible rift in our marriage. An irreparable one.

I'm glad that I let it go.

Of course it stays in her mind. I understand. What child forgets the sight of her father falling to his knees in front of her mother? She understood some of what had happened, in the way children do. That her parents had disagreed, that they had somehow reconciled. She was blind to the consequences, of course, but now that she's an adult . . . surely she sees the whole picture? Does she want me to say it should have gone differently, that it would have been better for her?

Well, if she wants to return to that time, I will listen.

In the long run, though, did it matter at all?

I think what's true is that I could have done all the insisting in the world, but there's every chance that Pamela would have done what her father wanted anyway, thinking to please him. Perhaps I failed my daughter, giving in the way I did. But I tell myself this: that if Pamela had to choose to follow her mother down one path or her father down another . . . well, I may have been her sun and her moon and her stars, but her father was God, and off she would have trotted.

pamela

It wasn't long after the exhibition at the Circolo degli Artisti that Daddy gathered us together. He had an announcement to make, he said. He'd made some plans.

Daddy often made "announcements." We were all used to his sudden enthusiasms, ideas that were really commands, and most of the time we were quite happy to go along. *Come! Angelo has lent us his boat—we shall have a picnic! Margery—I've found some fabric you will like, you need a new skirt—it's beautiful, so many different colored threads running through it—come see!*

But this . . . well, this was quite different.

Daddy said that he was going to London, to arrange another exhibition of my work. But, he said, he'd made other plans for me.

He told me that I would be going to San Remo to live by the sea. He was very clear, very emphatic. He'd made all the arrangements. I was to stay with one of his artist friends, Vittorio Petrella da Bologna, to whom he'd given strict instructions: Vittorio should make no attempt to coach me, but simply to see to it that I was provided with all the right materials. In San Remo, I'd be exposed to new landscapes, new people. It was a magnificent opportunity for me, Daddy said. And I would be well cared for—Vittorio's wife, Sophia, would watch over me. His friends would treat me as their own child. They had no children of their own, he said, as if it was obvious they'd love to borrow one of his.

Daddy's speech was greeted with silence. He looked at me, beaming.

"It will be wonderful, Pamela . . . the flowers, the sea, the people! You are happy to go to such a beautiful place...?"

I couldn't speak. I couldn't think what to say.

My mother was distraught. This had hit her too fast. It wasn't like the time Daddy had sent off my drawings to the art gallery, when she'd had time to process what had happened. Now she seemed, for the first time I could remember, truly angry.

"Francesco, I know what we agreed, that you'd be in charge, but this . . . this is too much. It's—"

"Can you not see this for what it is, Margery? Such a great chance for her. . . ."

"I see that it would be a wonderful opportunity, perhaps in a year or two . . . but Pamela's simply too young!"

"It's a few hours from here, not China. You won't be far away. If Pamela needs you, you can go to her."

"Let her stay here with me, Francesco . . . for heaven's sake, you know she'll draw all day on her own, she doesn't need Vittorio to watch over her."

"If she stays here, yes . . . as you say, she will draw as she always has. But that is not what she should be doing. Now she must see new things, try new things."

There was silence.

Tell him I don't need to try new things, Mam.

When she did speak her voice was quiet.

"You seem to forget, Francesco, she's only *eleven*. She really should be with her mother. . . ."

Daddy's voice went quieter still, signaling the end of the discussion.

"It's only for a little while. A month or so. It's the best thing for her, Margery. You will see."

Mam was quiet for days.

Cecco and I whispered to each other our hope that our father would give in just to see Mam happy again. But the mood in our home stayed somber.

Each day it was worse. I hated everything about the situation—the idea of leaving my family to stay with strangers, the palpable tension between my parents—but most of all I hated the thought that would not leave me alone, that pounded like a heavy drumbeat in my brain: *all this trouble is because of me.*

I was miserable. But I said nothing.

Daddy had made plans, and I knew that that was that.

In the end, Mam capitulated. She brightened, became her old self. She told me that she realized, now, that it was probably the best thing after all, that she'd been selfish to want to keep me for herself. She would write me lots and lots of letters, and she expected lots and lots in return. I was a lucky girl, she said. She wished *she* were the one going off to the seashore.

The night before I left, Daddy came to my room and sat by my bedside. He assured me over and over that it would be a great adventure, that I would have such lovely times and draw such beautiful things.

"And—oh! You must take this!" Daddy sprang up and lifted the little sketch off the wall above my bed. Picasso's goat.

He tucked the picture among the clothes in my trunk. "It will go to San Remo with you, it will bring you luck. And inspiration!"

He kissed my forehead.

margery

*I*f I went in to her now, tried to talk, would it be too late? Would she turn her face to the wall? Is it all beginning again, the cycle? Sometimes she can slide down so fast there's no hope of catching her. That nonstop talking today, that feverish look of hers—if it's the beginning, then. . . .

I'm being silly. Exaggerating. I mustn't jump to conclusions.

Yet a terrible fear runs through me. It doesn't surface often, but when it does it's always the same. The sharp tingling running up my back, as if a million pincered insects were attacking my spine all at once.

Pamela was what—twenty-two? Twenty-three?

Not so very long ago, really.

It was Sara, Pamela's sculptress friend from the Whitney Club, who put the idea into my head. Not that I blame her. She meant well when she came to see me that wintry day years ago. She was quite apologetic. And quite distressed. She said she wasn't at all sure if she should mention it, but she knew that Pamela was . . . *fragile* was the word she used, and she thought somehow I ought to know. She'd seen something disturbing, she said. Pamela standing on a curb near Gramercy Park, the northeast corner of 20th and Park, she thought it was. Perhaps it was 19th Street, it didn't really matter. Snow was falling. Sara was across the avenue, heading south. She thought Pamela seemed to be waiting for something or someone. And then a taxi came hurtling down the street and Pamela didn't flag it but stepped in front of it—*she sort of seemed to march in front of it*, was how Sara put it—and there was the squeal of brakes and the cab swerved away just in time. Some people helped Pamela back to the curb.

I never mentioned it, not even to Francesco.

I *am* sure Sara meant well, but there's every chance she misconstrued what she saw. Still, a thing like that, the image it forms . . . it will not leave you.

pamela

The white-washed house in San Remo was nestled high on
a hillside far from the sea but close enough that, when the
wind was right, I could breathe the salt air that freshened the citrus
and rose scents. It was a pretty, three-sided villa with a roof of red
tiles. The inner walls formed a square horseshoe edging a garden
courtyard lush with fruit trees and overflowing flowerbeds. Inside,
the house was cool and dark.

The da Bolognas were kind enough, but we talked little.
At home, with my family, I chattered endlessly, but in the outside world I was withdrawn, never comfortable conversing with
strangers. And most likely Vittorio and Sophia had no idea about
what to say to an eleven-year-old girl.

They made it clear, though, that they would be sleeping late,
that I was to have breakfast on my own. Sophia, plump and sleepy-
eyed, showed me how to shave off just the right amount of chocolate from the slab, how to melt it with a bit of water and a good
dose of sugar before slowly pouring in the milk. In the mornings
I rose early and took my steaming chocolate and some of Sophia's
homemade crusty bread to the banquette by the kitchen window
where I could look out over the garden awash with pink and white
anemones. It was so beautiful, but it hurt to sit there alone. In those
earliest hours, I thought only of my family, and I felt the tightness
in my chest would stop me from breathing entirely.

After breakfast, I'd run straight to the art shed to get my supplies. I was happiest working outdoors, surrounded by the palms

and orange trees and bushes thick with wild beach roses. Almost as soon as I set up my easel and began to draw, the lump of homesickness broke apart, dancing away and disappearing as quickly as dropped mercury.

Just as Daddy had predicted, I was drawing new things. But my inspiration was probably not of the sort that my father had envisioned.

Vittorio and Sophia had taken me along with some of their friends one night to the Casino, a local theater, to see a tall, raven-haired singer named Garden Rose. Garden Rose flashed over the stage in swirling silk skirts with embroidered sashes, shining layers of necklaces cascading over her breasts. And her headdresses! Dazzling networks of marcasite and colored beads and sequins splayed out around her head in a geometric sunburst. I was mesmerized by Garden Rose. I began to draw women and girls with fantastic intricacies of dress and hair decoration. And I began to dream of dancing. When I was alone in my bedroom I'd leap and kick, and pirouette until I was dizzy. I dreamed of being a famous ballerina.

Those dancing dreams never left me. Later, when I was so ill in the hospital, they were sad dreams. Visions of a dark and joyless Garden Rose filled my head. And I knew I'd have to paint her like that. The sad dancer, poised to step off into the abyss.

I would have been desperately lonely in San Remo if it had not been for Mimmi, the little girl who lived down the street. With her ruddy cheeks, coal-black eyes, and mop of twisted curls, she looked to me exactly like the Raggedy Ann doll Aunt Cecil had sent me from America. Even her checked gingham dresses seemed doll-like. Her hair was black, though, not Raggedy-Ann red. I was happy when Mimmi was around. It was as if I had a little sister, and I felt almost like myself again.

Mimmi was only five years old, but the fact that I was so much bigger didn't intimidate her in the least. She was very bossy, which made me laugh. She'd arrive with an armload of dolls and together we'd make clothing for them out of the bits of fabric from Sophie's "rag bag."

No, she doesn't need a hat!

No, Pamela—the bow should go in the back, not the front!

Not the pink one, the yellow *one!*

None of my suggestions were ever any good. I always did whatever Mimmi wanted.

I couldn't get her to sit still, but I drew her once, just her face. *The Strong Child,* I called the picture.

It was Mimmi who rescued me the day the letters came.

pamela

I was outside, painting the riot of anemones. Seeking shade, I had set up my easel under a grape arbor. Vittorio came out the kitchen door and headed towards me with a more purposeful step than usual. He had two envelopes, and I could see he was excited.

"You will be happy with this news from your father, very happy!" he said. "He wrote to me, too—the English, they love you—you are a grand success!"

One envelope was quite large and bulky, the other one letter-size. I took them, thanked Vittorio, and ran straight to my room. In the dim bedroom I sat on the cool stone floor and opened the big envelope first, the one with the London postmark.

This wasn't the first time I'd heard from Daddy. He had written me often, telling me all about the plans for the exhibition, how my reputation had reached London long before he had, and the great success he'd had when he called on many old friends of his and Mam's to help. Jimmie Manson—Royal Academy artist and respected art critic, had secured the prestigious Leicester Galleries for my show and had agreed to write an essay for the catalog. William Nicholson said he'd be delighted to print two of my studies in *The Owl*, his journal of art and literature. A third friend was the novelist and children's poet Walter de la Mare. My parents called him "Jack." Jack had befriended my mother years earlier when, at the age of nineteen, she had published her first novel. Mam was exceedingly fond of him. *He truly understands children*, she would say. Jack had, in a way, lived with us for most of my life. How many times had Cecco and I heard our mother's voice softly chanting: *"There is a wind where the rose was;/Cold rain where sweet grass was;/And clouds like sheep/Stream o'er the steep/Grey skies where the lark was."*

Daddy said that Jack responded with a childlike glee when he asked him to write the introduction to my catalog. The introduction turned out to be a poem. A lovely poem, ending with these lines:

> This happier child at peace in that first home,
> As yet untravelled, need no further roam;
> But over her paper and her colours bent
> Can paint the bliss 'tis to be innocent.
> Life add thy wisdom, and at length bring us
> Where springs the fountain of her genius.

Genius. The word was so often attached to my name in my childhood that I never thought it extraordinary. *Pamela, the little genius . . .* well, it was the same to me as *Caroline, the girl with the red hair,* or *Edward, the boy who plays the violin.*

The envelope from my father was stuffed with newspaper clippings. I shook them out impatiently. I didn't have to read them very carefully to know that my show—Daddy had titled it "Babes and Fairies"—had caused a sensation.

"Child Prodigy Shows Rare Gift." "Pamela Bianco, Child Miracle, Dazzles Art World." "'Miracle' Artist Draws Crowds at Leicester Galleries."

In the *Weekly Dispatch*, beneath a photograph of one of my drawings, was a quote from Langton Douglas, director of the National Gallery of Ireland.

> *I have very little sympathy with rhapsodies over infant prodigies . . . but the earliest drawings of this girl can be judged without consideration of her age. She has an extraordinary quality of line and a natural gift for composition.*

The heaps of praises fell around me like confetti. It was wearying to read all these strange things about myself—they seemed to be about some other child, a child in London, far away in a world that Daddy had created all on his own.

I wanted my old world back. I longed only for the sound, the touch of my family.

I pushed the articles aside and drew out what I was really looking for. Daddy's letter. His elegant handwriting covering the thick stationery seemed larger than usual. Perhaps it was a sign of his enthusiasm.

> *Everyone—great artists and writers—are praising your*
> *work. And, Pamela, the crowd! I wish that I could*
> *name everyone who attended—they were fighting*
> *over the pictures—Lady Sackville! John Galsworthy!*
> *And almost every piece has sold—perhaps soon you*
> *shall buy a grand house for us all! Remember to draw*
> *new things—forget your Madonnas and rabbits and*
> *fairies—draw from life! Our good friend Mr. Manson*
> *has written a wonderful article about you and says he*
> *will be writing to you soon—be sure you write him a*
> *nice letter in return.*

Daddy's delirium vibrated through the letter in my hands. I should have been thrilled, too. I didn't understand why I wasn't. Was it that Daddy wasn't here with me, that I couldn't see his face? Surely he would be beaming at me. I tried to feel the warm bolt of happiness that would have surged straight through me. But I felt nothing. The stone floor ran cold on my legs.

The sea air gently nudged the lace curtains.

Child miracle.

Was that what I was, really? I didn't feel like one at all. I thought again of home—teasing Cecco about his cap with the red tassel, darning socks with my mother, the little morning ritual with Signora Campanaro. Watching my guinea pig, Tiddles, scrabbling about the floor as I drew. But I wasn't at home. I was in San Remo, sitting on a chilly floor in the house of strangers.

Why was I here?

Because it was important to Daddy.

Why was it important to Daddy?

Because . . . I was a child prodigy. Italy's little flower. England's miracle.

It was true. I was not like other children.

I opened Mam's letter.

> *Tiddles has been eating ever so much lettuce and*
> *cabbage, and now he has learned a new trick—he sits*
> *on my lap and drinks tea out of a teaspoon! And guess*
> *who has been asking about you? The silent Signora*
> *Campanaro! She caught me as I was heading out to*
> *market, and I had the impression she had been waiting*
> *for me. There was no hello for me, just "Dov'è tua*
> *figlia dai capelli d'oro?" ("Where is your golden-haired*
> *daughter?") I think you have charmed her, Pamela. . . .*

My mother's letter, I knew, was meant to cheer me. But it knocked me right down. I was consumed by a fierce homesickness, suddenly grown tenfold.

Our family was all broken apart. It wasn't right.

I read my mother's letter over and over, and each time her words became less real, as if I were reading an echo and it kept fading and I strained to hear her voice, but in the end I lost her. She disappeared into a void.

I followed her. I drew my legs up against my chest, pulling my dress down to my feet. I rested my head on my knees and inhaled the unfamiliar but pleasant scent of the linen. Sophia used starch in the laundry and hung the clothes outdoors to dry. I smelled the sea.

Through the window I could see the sunlit fruit trees. Vittorio stood on his rickety ladder, pulling down oranges with a rake. I couldn't face the sun. I closed my eyes.

I was a weight, drawn down to the stone floor. A thick pain spread all inside. I couldn't seem to move. This time, no tears would form.

In my rigid silence I was keening.

Mam!

"Pamela! Pamela!"

It was Mimmi's voice, out in the garden.

I heard Vittorio.

"I think she's in her room. . . ."

I heard the quick, soft footsteps in the hallway, and I roused myself.

The door opened.

"Pamela!"

Mimmi's determined little face lit up when she saw me.

"There you are! Why are you sitting on the floor? Come on . . . I've brought Doria and Lisabetta, and they need us to make *hats* for them . . . ! Get *up*, Pamela!"

Because of Mimmi, I shook loose and jumped to my feet. I outran the darkness.

margery

*P*amela never complained when Francesco made plans for her, never made a peep. Even when he sent her off to San Remo.

I knew, of course, that she was terrified to leave home. But as the days passed in Turin, I began to see that a quiet villa by the sea was, in fact, the very best place for her. Francesco, though I was loath to admit it, had been right. Turin was not a good place for a child in those days. Everything was in turmoil at home, everything was topsy-turvy.

I was quite alone. Francesco had taken Cecco to Oxfordshire, got him settled at boarding school. Now he was managing things in London, and Pamela was off with the da Bolognas.

But being alone turned out not to be the worst of it. Soon I lost more than my family—I lost my home.

It was such a terrible, volatile time in Turin! Everyone was on strike—the factory workers, the postal workers, the railroad workers. So many had gone off to fight in the war and returned to find their jobs gone or their pay cut. There was bloody fighting in the streets. There were no supplies coming in. I was forced out of town by the chaos. Still, I was lucky enough. Friends who owned a villa in the hilly region north of the city offered me safe harbor.

One morning I sat on the hillside terrace. Just beyond the stone wall that surrounded the villa was a little orchard of delicate cherry trees, their white blossoms shivering in the breeze. And in the distance I could just make out the tiny chapel perched on the summit of Tre Denti. Such a lovely place, I thought. Yet I was fighting off a sadness, a strange, desperate sort of sadness such as I had never felt before. I'd just received a letter from Francesco. Quite a cheerful letter. Exuberant, in fact. Yet. . . .

Francesco said that things were going swimmingly in London. He'd arranged an exhibition for Pamela at the prestigious Leicester Galleries. Jack de la Mare had agreed to write the introduction to the catalog. And—this is what had Francesco so happily agitated—he'd enclosed an advance copy of the article that our friend Jimmie Manson was going to publish in *International Studio*. I could understand Francesco's excitement. It was a gorgeous piece of writing, a beautiful paean to our little girl. I was well aware that Jimmie was among the most esteemed art critics in Great Britain, that I should be ecstatic, but as I read—and reread—his worshipful words, I felt quite uneasy.

> *Here is a case, remarkable and beautiful, of a child*
> *. . . being moved to produce art as fine, in essence, as*
> *that of Botticelli, Piero della Francesca, Giotto. . . . I*
> *fancy that some old Chinese poet like Tu Fu, or Li Po,*
> *dreaming in the garden of the king . . . would have*
> *understood the beautifully serene art of Pamela Bianco,*
> *the new star in the artistic firmament, whose radiance*
> *lightens the murky light of our present*
> *day consciousness.*

I pushed the pages aside.
Pamela Bianco, the new star in the artistic firmament.
My Pamela?
I sat for a long while gazing towards the cherry orchard, the mountains.

I picked up my pen.
My letter was quite candid. I felt that I could unburden myself to Jimmie.

Dearest Jimmie,

There is a general strike in Turin, and I got away just in time. Our communication is cut off, but letters arrive by military service for the time being. Heaven knows how long I shall be here!

I'm staying with some Italian friends up here in the beginning of the mountains—and although I am fairly miserable, I am calmed by the beauty here—all chestnut trees & vineyards and ivy-covered balconies.

You would love to paint here. I wish you could.

I wish I didn't worry so. Pamela's success has been extraordinary—bewildering, really—I worry that when I see her again I shall find her somehow altered by it all, though I know she isn't. It is terrifying to see one's children make giant leaps—to places that one has dreamed of but somehow never reached. I feel that while Pamela and Cecco are growing up, I remain steadfastly stuck as I am.

And Francesco—I hardly know what to tell you except that he is so wildly excited over Pamela—it's as if he himself were the artist. It's all fine at the moment, but of course I can't help worrying about the other end of things—you know what I mean, Jimmie. I have never forgotten your real help and friendship in those days of his illness many years ago—I feel in a way you are the one real friend that we have, either of us.

I don't know whether we are to move back to London someday, or what we are going to do— Francesco maintains a lofty silence on all such trivial matters. But I hope so.

pamela

When I left San Remo it was to go to a new home, in London. Daddy had rented a place for us in Chelsea—a comfortable home, larger and airier than what we were used to. A host of pets padded about our flat and in the little patch of garden out back. Besides Caxton (the dog Daddy had bought for my mother when he sold a rare Caxton edition) and Narcissus and Charlemagne, there were cats, guinea pigs, rabbits, and hedgehogs. Once again I painted and drew in the quiet company of my mother. Cecco ran in and out with neighborhood boys. In the evenings, when Daddy came home from his bookstore, he was whistling. When I asked him, all serious, if he thought he might send me away again soon, he laughed and drew me to him. "No, *cara* Pamela, I order you to stay at home!"

My family was intact. Golden circles of happiness wound round and round me until I was all one bright piece again.

part two

‡‡‡

The Letter: January 11, 1977

428 Lafayette Street
New York City

....

It's raining. I must get out.

From her third-story window, Pamela can see that the rain has caught many by surprise. A man scurries past, holding a newspaper over his head. Others, with nothing to protect them, clutch their coat collars, hunch down into themselves.

She puts on coat, hat, boots, then goes to the window to check again—is it still raining?—and sees the postman. He's just turned right off Astor Place. He lowers his head, tugs ineffectually at his cap. The rain has not let up. She is glad.

He'll be here shortly, she thinks, but the fact holds no interest for her. She doesn't care about the mail. It's never anything, just bills.

There's just enough money in her pocket for some canned soup—chicken noodle, or perhaps split pea—and those soda crackers she likes. Her errand is a brief one, a few blocks to the grocer on East Third Street. But, once outside, she decides to take a walk first. To the old neighborhood. Macdougal Alley. Washington Square. These days the park is always so crowded, so full of noisy, scruffy-looking young people. But today, in this weather, it will be quiet. More the way it used to be.

She'll pick up the mail when she gets back.

As the postman approaches No. 428, he sees a small, bright figure leaving the building. An old woman, a tiny woman, in yellow rain boots and a huge floppy yellow rain hat. He cannot help smiling at the sight, a dandelion bobbing about in the gray rain of the city.

He reaches the last entrance on Colonnade Row, enters the lobby, stamps his feet on the rubber mat that says Welcome. He knows the history of this building, once one of the grandest addresses in Manhattan, home to Astors and Vanderbilts. But thoughts of the past register only in ghostly fashion, in the way a commuter's thoughts waft by at certain signposts along the way, too insubstantial and too repetitive to ponder.

His rubber-soled shoes squeak as he crosses the marble floor. The lobby is wide. Shadowed. Bare. Four mailboxes on the right wall. Against the left wall, a black enamel table holds a Chinese vase with a few tall silk flowers. White lilies, now pale gray with dust. The mirror behind—a towering piece of glass etched with art deco lines—doubles the arrangement.

Under the mailbox for Apartment 4, *Bianco* is typed on a little rectangle of paper framed in brass. Into this box the postman puts a meager handful of mail—the flyer he's put in all the boxes that day (Macy's is having a furniture sale), a bill from Con Edison, and a letter, addressed by hand. At the top left of the envelope: "R. Schlick," written with a bold artistic flourish, the last downstroke of the R swooping down, underlining almost the whole of Schlick. Inside the faint-blue circle at the top right: *Portland, Oregon, Jan. 8, 1977.*

He has no idea that the Pamela Bianco whose name is on

those few pieces of mail is the old woman in the yellow hat and boots. He has no idea that once she was an artist famous on both sides of the Atlantic. A young girl hailed as a "child miracle." A child of gold.

The postman has done his job. He has protected the mail from the elements, transported it safely. But what has he really done, what has he orchestrated? He moves on, oblivious. He will never know the import of a letter shoved through a slot. Words pushed into the tunnel of a dark box.

The envelope is thin. Just two brief pages, but they contain secret folds that open like an invisible fan. Pamela will see them immediately, the encrypted images: the jazz and glitter of old Harlem, the gilt of a seaborne Madonna, the filigree ring sinking into the Hudson River, and all the rains of Oregon.

‡‡‡

September 1, 1944

9 Livingston Place, Stuyvesant Square
New York City

(Midday)

margery

*T*his morning sun is lovely, yet now I find myself wishing for rain. A good, hard rain to clear away this stifling air.

I'd turn on the radio, get the weather report, but I don't want to wake Pamela.

Rain. That's what we need.

We—all of us—are rain people. You won't find us running inside when the skies open, to sit all safe and dry in our parlor.

Pamela, especially, has always loved the rain.

When she was little, she'd toss off her hat to let her hair get soaked. She'd yank off her Wellies and run barefoot through the wet fields, twirling about, her head lifted high, as if she were celebrating some wonderful news. You could hardly get her to come inside. Sometimes she'd stand for ages in the street, watching raindrops hit the puddles. "*I hear music!*" she'd tell me. It was like the plinking of the notes in her ballerina music box, she said.

Today, though, when Pamela seems so precarious, I suppose I should be happy the sun is shining. Rain draws her like a siren call. Most of the time, the call is innocent. But not always. Sometimes it's . . . well, I don't understand it. I think she *hears* things. It does sound mad, but I think—I think *she* thinks—the rain talks to her. Somehow it beckoned her out that terrible night.

We were still living in Macdougal Alley then. Pamela was working furiously in those days, and she often spent the night in her studio, just across the alley. She was already twenty or so, too old for me to monitor, but still I would look to see if she was there, if the light was on or not. On nights she knew she'd be up late working, she'd come over or ring us up to say good night. But that night we didn't hear from her.

How it rained! A relentless rain. Drenching. No light was on in Pamela's studio. When I couldn't bear it anymore, I went over to check. She wasn't there, of course. Francesco said not to worry. *She's grown up, you can't keep doing this.* But I couldn't help it, all night I kept getting out of bed, looking for a light across the way. Sometime towards dawn I threw on my robe and ran barefoot across the courtyard. It was so dim in the studio I could barely see. But I could feel that she was there.

I found her all curled up on the sofa, lying in the dark, soaking wet. Water stains blackened the velvet cushions. When I touched her, she felt hard, tense. Her fingers were clenched into tight fists. I worked them open, and smelled a meadow, a wet field. In her fists were the smashed stems of flowers. *Where on earth had she been?*

She wouldn't talk to me. I calmed her as best I could, rubbing her back, but it was a long time before she'd let me help her out of her wet clothes. I loosened her hair, toweled it, brushed it out as I hadn't done since she was a child. I stayed with her until she slept.

In the afternoon I went back to the studio, determined to get through to her. I thought if her misery had anything to do with Diccon, and I was sure it did, it was time to face things. Things were quite different now. We needed to talk about Nancy.

I came armed with the latest B. Altman catalog, a distraction tactic. Something easy and amusing, I thought, before I broached the subject of Diccon. It was one of our favorite diversions, poring over the fashions together, laughing at the hats and dresses we'd never own.

Pamela was just as I had left her, lying on the sofa in her nightdress.

I sat by her and thumbed through the pages until I found "Evening Wear." That autumn—it was the autumn of 1928—someone highly placed in the world of haute couture had decided it should be the season of metal. Perhaps, I thought, these improbable, gorgeous dresses would draw Pamela away from her gloomy thoughts.

"Listen to this dress, Pamela! 'French blue silk crepe blooming with a copper and gold floral design, a tracery of metal lace.' Lovely, don't you think?"

Pamela was silent. I tried again.

"Or this evening wrap—how can we live another moment without 'a glimmer of metal tissue against velvet?' Really, we must run out and get one for each of us."

Still there was no response. I closed the catalog.

"Pamela . . . perhaps we should talk about Diccon . . . ?" She cringed slightly but made no sound. I went ahead anyway.

"Diccon is . . . well, of course you know how fond he is of all of us, and you especially, but Nancy has been . . ."

She edged away from me then, huddling close to the wall.

"Please, Mam. I don't want to talk."

It was just a whisper. She turned her face to the wall.

pamela

I have to close my eyes, they're so awfully tired. All that counting, all the going up and down the wallpaper, it makes me dizzy.

Just the daisies now.

I lie in a meadow of daisies.

You must pluck all the petals, you must. You must find out
the answer.

He loves me, he loves me not. *Pluck.* He loves me. *Pluck.* He
loves me not. *Pluck. Pluck. Pluck, pluck, pluck.* It always comes out
wrong, it's always *loves me not.*

No, it's not true, it's not right. . . . Just one more flower and it
will come out all right. He loves me, I'm sure of it.

The scent of lilacs fades, disappears.

The air is cooler, wilder, behind my eyelids.

Apples. I can smell apples.

Diccon.

Once, just to say the name *Diccon* to myself could open a
hole in my heart. For so long Diccon meant—simply—almost
everything to me. Though at the time it was anything but simple. I
thought I would die of it.

margery

Well, it was no use. Pamela turned her face to the wall, and I had to leave her. I would get nothing out of her.

What had drawn her from her studio out into that stormy night? Whatever it was, the rain had fooled her, turned against her. I had no idea where she'd been or what she'd done, but I was sure we were in for a bad time.

And I knew she could not—would not—let go of Diccon.

It wasn't just Pamela. I suppose we all fell a bit in love with Diccon that summer in Wales.

Diccon, the Pied Piper of Harlech. That summer, none of us would have dreamed of planning a picnic or a hike to the top of Snowdon without racing over to find Diccon, to dig him out of his stone cottage where you'd find him writing a new poem or painting dragons on the walls.

He looked a bit like that actor they're all swooning over now, Errol Flynn. No, that's wrong, Diccon wasn't handsome in a movie-star way. He was too irregular, too professorial with his high, pale forehead and longish nose. He looked like what he was—a poet. Still, it just takes a little squinting of the mind to imagine him in the role of Robin Hood, or Captain Blood, his dark hair blowing wild in the wind. I see him now, tall and purposeful, striding over the windswept hills, waving his walking stick in the air as he belts out one of those old Welsh fighting songs he loved. He's wearing his lumberman's shirt, red-and-black-checked wool, and rough pants tucked into greased boots.

Diccon was twenty, about to enter his final year at Oxford. Pamela was thirteen.

We were staying with William Nicholson and his family in their summer home, an ancient stone cottage. William was a well-known figure, a brilliant artist and the publisher of a literary journal in London, *The Owl,* but to us he was simply an old friend. Over dinner one night in London, he'd asked if he could do a portrait of Pamela. And then he'd made a suggestion.

"Why not do it over holiday at my cottage in Wales?" he said.

"Yes, why not?" we agreed. We were happy to leave the city.

It was on our very first night in Harlech that William announced that there was someone he wanted us to meet, a poet who was staying nearby.

"Richard Hughes. Diccon, he calls himself. You'll quite enjoy him, we'll have him to dinner."

We were a large group crammed around the table—six of the Nicholson clan, the four of us, and Diccon. We feasted on roast lamb and creamed potatoes, and blackberry compote. We drank quite a lot of wine. The talk turned to poetry and literature. Francesco could quote anyone—Donne, Dante, Paine, Petrarch. . . . But Diccon was nearly as good at that game, and William and I were not so bad, either, so there was a good deal of touché-ing going on, and lots of glasses clinking. Pamela and Cecco were quite merry, too, raising their small tumblers of wine diluted with water.

Diccon was a natural storyteller, and he gestured wildly in his enthusiasm. When he got excited, color crept into his face and he seemed a small boy. But he was changeable. Sometimes when he grinned he looked all innocence, sometimes he looked wicked. Pamela could not pull her eyes away from him.

Ah, first love, I thought, smiling to myself. It seemed a very natural thing to me, a young girl's first crush. Soon, naturally, to be replaced by the next boy who took her fancy.

I didn't know it yet, but nothing was "naturally," when it came to Pamela. Who would have thought that there would be no next boy at all?

Still, it was a magical, merry evening, in the way you wish all dinner parties would be but rarely are—lovely food and drink, and the conversation unpredictable, and a feeling of warmth running like cognac through your veins all night long. It had to end, of course, but before it did, Francesco declared that we must all recite "The Fiddler of Dooney." We stood with glasses held high, and shouted out the lines.

For the good are always the merry,
Save by an evil chance,
And the merry love the fiddle,
And the merry love to dance:

And when the folk there spy me,
They will all come up to me,
With "Here is the fiddler of Dooney!"
And dance like a wave of the sea.

"Once more!" Diccon insisted.

And we all shouted even louder and tapped our feet on the floor, and Diccon grabbed Pamela and danced with her round the table. She only came up to the middle of his chest, and she was laughing, her head tilted back so that she could look at his face. I see them flashing by in the candlelight, Diccon hopping about like a great crow and Pamela with her braids flying every which way.

pamela

*I*t's always the same, the first memory that rushes back. I hold it a while, cupped in my hands. It pours out like liquid. But it always comes back.

We are standing on the windswept hillside of Harlech. It's summer. I'm thirteen, and I'm wearing a muslin dress Mam made for me and it's whipping against my legs. We stand gazing over the hillside, past the zigzag of slate-roofed cottages, all the way to the sea.

"This is *it*, Pammy, the very breath of Wales! And I shall breathe her in and make her mine! Watch me!"

Diccon's waving his cap over his head, and his dark hair blows every which way in the wind. His voice is a man's voice, but he's so excited he sounds like a child. Again and again he takes huge gulps of Welsh air, then blows it out. And grins at me. I am familiar with this Diccon by now—his fierce exuberance, his playfulness. Always saying whatever enters his mind.

And always coming up with ideas that you couldn't resist. Like the hotcakes.

I *was* hungry, though I would have followed him anyway.

I woke early that day, the day of the apple tree and the hotcakes. I was determined to draw the apple tree at dawn, if only the weather was right.

I threw on my dress and tied up my shoes and stood by the window, watching as the sky slowly lightened. Soon I knew the weather was cooperating—it was neither clear nor threatening rain. I grabbed my pencils and charcoals and sketchpad and ran up to my "sitting rock" high on the hill behind our cottage. Mists still clung to the earth, shrouding the low fruit-laden tree. I'd drawn the tree in midday, the sun dappling the ground through the gnarled branches. And at sunset, the yellow-red apples reachable against the orange-streaked sky. But never in the mystery of dawn.

There was a familiar music in the air. An intermittent, tinkling tune, as if perhaps angels, or fairies, hidden in the mists, were singing as the sun rose. But I knew what it was. Someone—it could have been a tramp, it could have been William—had fashioned a sort of wind chime made of bits of glass and shells—scallops and razor clams—and nailed it to the branch of one of the trees in the copse behind me. Soft breezes blew the music across the hillside.

I drew quickly, and the tilting tree hovered on the page, fantastical, like a troll's gnarled umbrella. Or an ancient ballerina, ghostly on the hillside.

The music changed. Much louder, faster.

I was perplexed; the wind had not picked up. I turned round. Diccon!

"Sorry, Pamela!" He waved his walking stick. "I was announcing my presence, didn't want to frighten you!"

I was almost finished with my tree, and Diccon sat down next to me to watch.

Diccon admired my drawing—*superb, Pamela, lovely*—then, impulsively, he invited me to Ysgol Fach. His cottage.

"I'll make you hotcakes, I'm quite good at it, you know."

Diccon poured me a glass of buttermilk and set the pitcher on the table. While he made the batter he told me more tales of his long journey by foot from London to Harlech. He said he'd just finished a poem about one of the scenes he had witnessed along the way: gypsy girls dancing in the moonlight. And he told me about the cottage. He was allowed to live there in exchange for three days' work, two pots of honey, and four pennies per year. The rent was fair, he said, as the 150-year-old cottage had been neglected for years. When he'd first taken over, great mounds of dirt, mud, and leaves had accumulated throughout, the roof was leaky, and there were giant holes in the floor—spring water gurgled up from beneath the fireplace, traveling unchecked over the stones. He'd spent all of the previous spring fixing up the place. Diccon's little home was still crude, but the fireplace was working and the roof was patched. Now, when it rained, the water that seeped up through the stone floor was just a trickle.

My eye went to what was clearly a letter on the makeshift desk by the window.

"Who are you writing to, Diccon?" I asked with the utter impertinence of youth.

"Nosey little brat, aren't you?"

He picked up the letter, though, and said, "It's to my mother, since you show such interest, and I'll even read you what I've written, you'll be pleased—

'The Biancos leave on Tuesday, for Chelsea, and I am very sorry to lose them: I have seldom met people I liked so much, or folk so informal and sensible in their ways. Mrs. B especially is wonderfully nice. . . .' Now what do you make of that?"

He looked at me with that mischievous look I'd seen so often.

"It's terribly nice, Diccon, and if you're trying to get me to take offense you've missed your mark—I've always known you liked Mam best. Everybody does, you know!"

It was true. Everyone wanted to be near her, to trust her with secrets.

The hotcakes were thin and buttery and sugary. "Mmmm," I said.

Diccon plunked down his tin plate, sitting so close to me that his woolen shirt grazed my arm when he reached for the buttermilk. He devoured his hotcakes.

"Mmmm," he said, widening his eyes, teasing me. "Told you I was good at it."

"More?" he asked.

"Yes, please," I said. He reached for my plate, then stopped. He looked at me with great concern. Before I could react his face was on top of my face and his tongue ran around my upper lip. It was over before I could even think.

"Don't want to waste even the littlest bit of that lovely buttermilk, do we?"

Diccon looked at me, his eyes widened—he was terribly amused, I could see—and let out a great laugh.

I didn't know what to think. I sat there frozen, feeling my face burn.

Diccon was at the stove, humming.

Had he just *kissed* me? Could that have been a *kiss*?

Diccon was letting out little whoops of glee as he tossed the hotcakes in the pan, and by the time he sat down again he was back on the subject of gypsy girls, and it seemed as though nothing had happened at all.

"I think you'll quite like this one, Pammy—I shall give it to you."

He bounded across the room to his little desk. He came back with a handwritten copy of his new poem, "Gipsy-Night."

I walked home slowly, all warm inside, light as a milkweed seed floating in sunlight. I stopped again at the rock by the apple tree and sat down to read Diccon's poem. He wrote of a dark night, rain dancing on roofs, wind sliding through the trees. Of Dobbin, the horse, stabled with bracken up to his knees. And wanting to dance with gypsy girls. . . .

My heart—foolish, innocent, tender, untrammeled—beat with newfound happiness.

Apple trees.

Hotcakes.

Poetry.

Gypsies.

Buttermilk kisses.

And Diccon—tall and strong, clever and kind—was *mine*.

We would be together forever, just as soon as I was grown up.

margery

William told us, in confidence, of Diccon's tragic past. So many deaths in the family, and now he was an only child with an overly protective mother. That summer in Wales was, I think, the first time Diccon experienced the warmth and comfort of family life, and the personal freedom he was never able to feel under his mother's roof. He was like a frisky colt, nosing among the herd. We all felt his eagerness, his curiosity, and his pleasure, and were glad of it.

Diccon may have been happy in our company, but, truly, he was ecstatic just to be in Wales. He could trace his ancestry to ancient Welsh kings and felt a strong connection to the land, though he'd only just visited it for the first time the year before. But that was all it took. Diccon had so fallen in love with Wales—every bog, hill, and rock, he said—that it had inspired him to change his name. When he returned to Oxford, he announced that he'd no longer answer to that inelegant English name, "Dick." In future, he declared, he would be known by his Welsh name, "Diccon."

It's true that Diccon did seem to spend an inordinate amount of time with Pamela that summer. He took her on day-long hikes, cooked hotcakes for her in his tumble-down cottage, and rode around with her on that motorbike of his, Pamela holding on to him, screaming deliriously into the wind as they bounced off over the moors and the old Roman roads.

And he could do no wrong in her eyes.

One day he said something extraordinary about her. Right in front of her. It was terrible, really. Diccon had made some sort of joke, and Pamela laughed, and then Diccon looked at her and cocked his head and said, "I've got it, Pammy . . . I've been trying to think, and now I've got it, what you look like sometimes . . . half pig and half cat!" I was aghast. How could he say such a thing? But Pamela just laughed.

And then *I* saw it. It was when she grinned. He had it precisely. My beautiful little Pamela, *half pig and half cat!*

It's easy to think now, should I have said something to her? Something like, "He is *twenty*, Pamela, not someone for such a young girl like you to be hanging her dreams on. . . ." But I never thought to, I simply didn't think beans of it at the time, and anyway she wouldn't have listened. She would have made her "Oh, don't be silly, Mam" face.

Nothing I did or didn't do would have mattered. Even in the beginning I couldn't have dislodged Diccon from Pamela's heart.

No, that summer in Harlech I never worried at all. Pamela may have been spellbound, consumed by first love, but I could see that to Diccon, she was just a little girl. He was oblivious to the yearnings of a thirteen-year-old, especially one who looked so very childlike still. I thought I understood why he wanted to spend so much time with her. He was fascinated by her. She was, after all, a girl with preternatural talent. He admired that terribly. And she was a very *famous* little girl. After Turin, there'd been her first solo exhibition, in London. The Leicester Galleries. It was a wild success. At the end of the show, there was only one drawing left on the wall—a cauliflower and some onions done in pencil and gouache. William and a friend tossed a coin for it. William won.

After that exhibition, everyone in Europe knew the name Pamela Bianco, the famous child prodigy, the little flaxen-haired girl who drew with the confidence of an Old Master. A genius, all the critics said. They called her a "child miracle." The things they wrote in those days!

Perhaps Diccon even had some vague hope that her great success would rub off on him. He never hid his ambition, always talking of books he hoped to publish, plays he thought he'd write one day. He longed for recognition. And here was this golden child. . . .

pamela

*G*od, what am I doing?
This rocking, rocking. It's worse than the pacing.
But he is back now, and I cannot send him away.
Swaying, rocking.
A hammock, in Wales, blown by breezes.
Dawn. Diccon lies asleep.

Our time in Wales is running out. We have to be back in the city soon. One last long hike, we decide. We'd all go.

Diccon leads the way, tall and sure-footed—swashbuckling, I think—striding like the lord of the land in his greased boots and red-and-black-checked lumberman's shirt. He sings an ancient Welsh battle song in a loud, exaggerated baritone, striking his walking stick on the ground for emphasis.

> Men of Harlech! In the hollow
> Do ye hear like rushing billow
> Wave on wave that surging follow
> Battle's distant sound?
> Tis the tramp of Saxon foemen
> Saxon spearmen, Saxon bowmen
> Be they knights or hinds or yeomen
> They shall bite the ground!

Dark clouds appear, and it seems only an instant before the storm rushes at us—such a wild, fierce thunderstorm! A drenching rain quickly turns to a tumble of hail, pelting us mercilessly. Daddy yells, pointing. *Over there—coal mine!* We scramble in, huddle together in the black, dank space.

I shiver from cold. I am not afraid, though; the storm excites me.

A long, low rumble breaks into a loud crack above our heads, and Diccon reaches over to put his long arm around me, to reassure me. He speaks in his now familiar, teasing way. *Don't ye be worrying yourself, lassie, it'll blow by soon.* I want him to know how I love the rain, the storm, the great adventure of it all. But I am quiet. His warm hand on my arm makes me mute. I feel a sort of thrumming, an exquisite happiness. I most definitely do not want Diccon to remove his hand. The feeling is so new, so strange. Daddy and Cecco often put their arms around me and of course that's wonderfully pleasant and comforting, but this . . . this is altogether different.

When Diccon releases me, he edges away just a bit, and a chilly draft flies up in the space between us. Where his hand has held my arm there is an imprint of ice. I try to recapture the thrum, but of course it's no use.

Diccon has forgotten me. He fills his pipe. It takes all his attention.

It seems to me a loving act—the cradling of the pipe, his graceful fingers holding the match over the bowl; his lips around the stem, making little sucking noises as he draws in air. I imagine him kissing me then and a pure, galvanizing desire shoots all through me. That is what it is, though I cannot name it. I have no idea.

Diccon sits so close, he seems an extension of myself. But I can't touch him. I can't say anything. I sit there, dumb and tingling, as the aromatic smoke wraps itself around me. It is almost unbearable.

margery

*T*he last time we saw Diccon that summer was when we hiked to Cwm Mawr, an abandoned farm high in the hills. I shall never forget it, but not for the shadowed hills or the stone relics or the surprise of the storm, though all those things were enchanting. It's an image of Francesco that stays etched in my mind.

It happened so fast, that storm. The blackness simply barreled down over us, bringing wind and rain and hail. We ran, laughing, hopping like rabbits, until we found shelter in an abandoned mine where we sat together huddled, listening to the cracks of thunder and the wind whistling by. It all passed quickly. Still, by the time we reached the farm, it was close to midnight. The skies had cleared, and the moon was high and brilliant. We traipsed into the ancient barn, exhausted, and collapsed on piles of hay. In the morning we woke all in a heap, Pamela curled up against Diccon's back, Cecco at his head.

Francesco was the first one to crawl out. He stood in his drawers and chemise, picking off bits of straw. Then he lifted off the clothes that he'd draped over a stall. The expression on his face was just like a baby who's got a spoonful of mushed peas being jabbed at him over and over. He slumped his shoulders in an exaggerated fashion, and spoke with a mock peevishness.

"Oh, God! Oh, God!" he said, "I can't bear it—the thought of putting on these cold, wet things. It makes my soul turn somersaults inside of me!"

It was pure Francesco. We all laughed, and it was just then

that the emotion struck, catching me entirely off guard. I watched Francesco standing there, rumpled and bowlegged, and solidly male, and as everyone laughed and stomped about and complained of the wet, my insides swelled in an intense celebration. A sudden thankfulness: all was well with us, no great rift had ruined what we had.

I knew that I could never change Francesco, that I could never subdue him. Nor would I want to. What I wanted was to run over and grab him and let him know what I was thinking, how happy I was, but of course one never does those things.

I've seen how other women look at him sometimes. It's not surprising. He's handsome and terribly charming and all that. He's also Italian—you do not want to debate with the man. Women like his forcefulness. *Now there is a man I could count on,* they think, *a man who is in control, sure of himself.* Strange, though, for all that he does seem oblivious. There are many things Francesco loves about himself, but I don't think he's ever appreciated his sexual attractiveness. His goal is not to seduce women. He simply wants to charm the entire world.

pamela

"But now I see another image—another man sprawled. Not a hammock, this time. A bed. Taking up too much room. This man is in Italy. A beautiful man, naked, unconscious. I don't know him.

He is my husband.

Robert.

I am too tired to dwell on those days.

Still . . . *Lorenzo.*

I should talk to Lorenzo about his father.

I really must try to do better for my son. I haven't provided much of a family for the boy, not that I could help it. It can't be easy for him, always being the only one with just a mother. Knowing so little about his father. I wouldn't talk of him. When Lorenzo was small he asked me lots of questions. I was always quite vague. *Your father went out west, that's all I know. He didn't really do anything, he fancied himself a poet. He was good-looking, I suppose, but you get your looks from your grandfather.*

There's not much I can tell him. And the one thing I know with certainty about Robert is not a thing to tell his son. Lorenzo knows only this: that his father left when he was a baby, went back to Portland.

It's been years since Lorenzo asked anything at all. He gave up long ago. Still, I know he'd treasure any little scrap of information. Perhaps, now, I could tell him a few things. Tonight, over dinner. I could tell him about how I met his father, about those gay times when we were running all over the Village and Harlem. He'd like to hear those stories. Why not? What harm could it do?

Tonight. Lorenzo and I will have a fine supper. We'll talk.

I've been wrong to be so silent.

margery

*A*fter the idyll in Wales, Diccon was a regular visitor in our home in Chelsea. He showed up on our doorstep almost daily. It seemed that we'd adopted each other, and we were all quite pleased with the arrangement. Often, of an afternoon, it would be just the two of us. Francesco was at his bookshop, Cecco was off at boarding school, and Pamela was working day and night, preparing for her second solo exhibition at Leicester Galleries.

Sometimes Diccon would read his poems to me. He said I had a good ear. There would always be tea—he was mad for my ginger scones, he said—and of course, we would get to talking on every subject imaginable.

It was on one of those quiet afternoons that he talked to me about his lonely upbringing, the shadow of death that hovered over his early childhood. His older brother, Arthur, had died at thirteen months, just eight days after Diccon's birth, and his sister Grace had died at four, when Diccon was just two. When he was five, his father died. He had only the vaguest memories of his father and of course none at all of the infant brother who had died before he was born, so it wasn't that he mourned terribly, he said, but that he lived every day with the cruel repercussions of so much death. He'd never been able to escape the atmosphere of sadness, the feeling of having got a bad lot in life. You could just see how it all weighed on him. He told me that even still, he felt in his house a load of grief.

"Like a heavy fall of snow," he said.

I nodded. I understood.

His mother hovered over him, he said. Even now. It was quite suffocating.

"Not that I blame her, she's lost so much, and I know she can't stop worrying that she'll lose me, too. I do love her, of course. Still, it's difficult. I feel I must be watching out for her always. And she seems to be ill so often—she needs me to be with her all the time, and I feel like a caged lion, but she doesn't seem to notice, just smiles at me sadly and tells me what a good son I am."

I thought of my own mother. Her sorrow had been no easier to bear, no less heartbreaking, but in her grief she was altogether different. She had never clung to Cecil and me as life rafts, quite the opposite. More than ever, she encouraged us in our freedom. This would have been natural to her. She would find her way out of the wreckage, and she would expect us to find ours. I remember my father saying that that's why he'd married her. *Your mother has the spirit of Diana, she could live on a mountain, talk to the animals. Your mother is a wild woman, Margery!* And he would laugh.

If it was what he loved most about her, it was also the reason his parents had been against the marriage. Florence Harper was not at all what they'd dreamed of for their son, an up-and-coming barrister. Not the right class, that was bad enough, but worse, a bohemian, a girl who insisted on wearing unacceptable clothing— crazy gypsy dresses, sometimes even turbans. With feathers! Who could take her to Claridge's for tea dressed like that? And Mother worked. That, too, was unacceptable. A *piano teacher*.

But my father had his own wild streak. He was both sides of a coin—on the one side, a barrister and a classical scholar of some renown, and on the other a devil-may-care liberal and fun-loving adventurer. When he died, the obituary in the barristers' journal referred to him as "that crazy Bob Williams." Together, my parents reveled in all the absurdities of life.

What I remember most about that time, before it was all taken away, was that the house was filled with laughter.

‡ ‡ ‡

When Mother lost her husband and daughter, she suffered through the funeral services and the burials. And the official visits of the rector. Apparently, it was this messenger of the Lord who unnerved her. She found his assurances about God's plan for all of us curiously cold. She could not find a crumb of comfort in any of it. The Church had not eased her burden, it had hardened her heart.

Mother was a woman of action. She would not look to others, she would not sit back and wait to see what happened next, she would orchestrate it herself. She quickly made two decisions.

The first was to leave the Anglican Church.

She told the story to Cecil and me often enough. It was Ellen, the housemaid, who'd made the impression on her. After my sister Agnes died, Ellen came to Mother, holding a little card. *Don't mean to be disturbing, Mum, but I wanted to give this to you, I've been praying for you. To Saint Anne especial, she's always been of help to me in my troubles. She'll look out for you, help you find comfort.*

Ellen handed the card to my mother, who'd never seen such a thing. *It's a prayer card, Mum. I've been praying for your family, and I've been lighting the candles at St. Mary's, too.*

I still have that prayer card. On the front is a drawing of a beautiful woman standing in a field, her hands clasped in prayer. She wears a flowing, pale-blue dress. A gilt-edged scarf is draped over her head, and falls to her knees. She smiles down at three peasant children, who kneel at her feet.

A prayer is printed on the back of the card. *O good St. Anne, filled with compassion for those who invoke you, I cast myself at your feet. . . .* That much I can remember still.

Mother always said that right away she felt peace creeping into her heart. This Anne, mother of Mary, the saint with the sweet smile and open arms, was welcoming her. Was welcoming her *especial.* It was then that my mother decided that she—and naturally, Cecil and I—would convert to Catholicism.

As if converting were not enough, my mother made another sweeping decision. We would all move to America, she said. She had a cousin who had a farm in Sharon, Pennsylvania. There was a Catholic girls' school nearby.

I never return to those saddest days. There is no need, I carry them with me always. But for Diccon, I made an exception. He would understand, he would know how the past gets stitched inside you and though the threads may come loose you can never rip it out entirely.

I told him only the barest of facts. Even so, as I told my story, a sea of sorrow flooded in, washed over my heart. And Diccon nodded sadly, his usually piercing eyes gone soft with pain. *Like a heavy fall of snow.*

I am seven years old. A carriage is coming to take my father away, and I listen for the clomping of horses and pray that the carriage never comes.

The house in London is dark, the curtains drawn. I sit cross-legged on the floor in a dress that yesterday was yellow but today is black. The dress smells funny. I know how it got that way. I stood on tiptoe to watch as Ellen poked a broomstick about in the tub full of black dye, pushing the clumps of sunny dresses every which way, turning them to thunderclouds. *Daddy is dead.*

My father lies in the parlor. It's all wrong, that's all I know. Surely in the afternoon, just before suppertime, he'll burst through the doorway as he always does, and swoop down to lift me up, kiss my forehead. *Ah, my little mistress Margery! How did you fare today? Tell me, what did you read?* My father's mantra: read, read, read. *No school till you are ten . . . read anything you wish . . . expand the brain!* He teaches me the names of flowers and insects and trees, and how to draw the Greek letters. He demonstrates Latin roots at every opportunity. Each Christmas, he points at the cornucopia, spilling over with fragrant pine and silver balls. *From the Latin* cornu, *Margery—it means 'horn'—see how it's shaped like a horn?*

I sit on my bedroom floor in my awful dress, filled with fear and unknowing. My stomach feels funny. A book lies open on my lap. *Illustrated Natural History*, a gift from Daddy. The book has been my steadiest companion. For hours and hours I have painstakingly traced the animals and cut them out to make a paper zoo. My favorite toys are by my side: the skin horse, the jointed wooden dog, and the soft velveteen rabbit that St. Nicholas left in my stocking.

My twelve-year-old sister, Agnes, lies sick in the next room. I've not been allowed to see her. In a few days, Agnes is dead.

My world now contains only my mother and my oldest sister, Cecil, who is sixteen. I wonder if they will die, too.

I find my greatest solace in the horse, the dog, the bunny. I confide in them, cry with them, hold them tight at night. They whisper promises. *It's all right, we're here. We love you very much. We're not going away. We won't die.*

margery

Perhaps I should go check on her.
   I'll admit I'm reluctant, afraid of what I might find. What if she's talking to herself again? What should I do then?
   But she's not. I'm sure of it. I could hear her from here.
   I mustn't worry so much.

I wish Francesco were here. Perhaps he'll surprise me, come home early.
   It seems forever ago that I said good-bye to him, quite joyful, knowing he was happy to be off to work on the book of poems. A local poet, he says, an unknown. He's doing just the one edition. A favor, really. Still, the book will be beautiful. Francesco is a perfectionist. The handset letters will be crisp, the sewing that no one will see will be flawless, the binding simply tooled but elegant. He says it will be ready soon. He seems eager to show it to me. Not that I'm in any hurry to have him finish his project. Hours that Francesco spends at the print shop are hours I have to myself, for my own work. And this morning I was so grateful to have a day to myself to get through my manuscript.
   But now that's all changed, I don't feel the same.
   I'd rather not be alone with Pamela.

‡ ‡ ‡

Sometimes it's hard to remember that she was such a jolly little girl. Running around in her linen dress and sturdy brown shoes. Dragging lengths of brown paper under the kitchen table where she'd lie on her stomach, legs bent up in the air, and draw for hours. Perched on a chair with a fistful of custard creams, face all serious, nibbling away ever so carefully around the diamond pattern. Laughing and laughing at the funny balloons in Paris, pressing her hands to her face, over and over like a little wind-up doll.

Even now she can be frivolous and gay, when she is flying high. Just last month, we were out at Merryall with Cecil's girls, Agnes and Budgie, and all the children and Pamela put on quite a show. Somehow, she got on the subject of her new underpants—of all things!—and how they had roses on them. Well, the children, naturally, were very intrigued. Suddenly Pamela started dancing about the room, singing something about, *Rosies, rosies, pocketsful of posies*, or some such pretty nonsense, and she hitched up her skirts, flashing her underwear. The children laughed themselves silly. They were quite delighted with their crazy Aunt Pamela!

But times like that are rare, I'm afraid. She can still fly high, but it's the landings I worry about.

I do hope Francesco gets home early. Pamela tends to be on her best behavior when her father's around. With me, she lets down her guard.

pamela

I see them now, the large canvasses.
 I've always seen them.

> *A chandelier. A girl who has grown too tall, like Alice.*
> *The many-tiered chandelier hangs from a ceiling*
> *impossibly high. The girl's head grazes the crystal*
> *pendants. She's stuck in place, imprisoned by beautiful*
> *patterns.*

> *A pomegranate. Prismatic, precise. Jewel colors.*
> *Dizzying, a stilled kaleidoscope of glass shards. The*
> *pomegranate is fragmented, yet whole. A perfect*
> *geometry.*

> *A maze. It travels out to the horizon. There is no end. A*
> *platform cuts through the middle, flanked by busts on*
> *pedestals, a boy and a girl. Behind them, a tiny girl in*
> *a white dress holds a silver hoop. A wrong step and she*
> *will fall into the sunken maze. Into the abyss.*

I have to paint them.
There are so many in my head. . . .
I *must* paint them.
I'll get my easel from the basement.
Tomorrow I'll begin.

I'll begin to sort things out at last, fix things. Put them in their proper place.

And I *will* talk to Lorenzo. Absolutely I will. Tonight!

I won't put it off a moment longer.

margery

I'll just wait a bit longer. It's almost noon. She'll come out when she's hungry.

Though she's perfectly capable of forgetting to eat. Whether it's because she's in one of her funks or because she's painting, it's all the same. Those days in London, when Diccon was visiting so often, she was as a shadow in the house—she worked constantly, appearing for meals only when she remembered to. Often I'd slip into the studio to leave her a sandwich and a thermos of tea.

As the date of her opening at Leicester Galleries neared, there was a tension in our home. Just an undercurrent, nothing like the earliest days. And, thank God, it had nothing to do with me. Francesco was nervous. It seems absurd now, but at the time I understood.

Pamela's art had changed dramatically. Her early work, the pictures that had stunned the critics and entranced the public, were intricate and fantastic, filled with imagined flora and starry-eyed children tumbling through sylvan scenes. But now her work was quite different. The fairies and butterflies were a thing of the past. Her landscapes of Wales and of our Chelsea neighborhood were quite somber. Her still lifes were dark. There was a moodiness, a melancholy in her art. It came from within, and I suppose it was a natural thing. Pamela herself was evolving rapidly, her own moodiness was growing.

Francesco worried over everything. What would the critics say? Would the pictures sell? Would the crowds come or had they had their fill of the prodigy? I was quiet. He'd heard me tell Pamela often enough that her art should be judged only by herself, that she wasn't to listen to critics or anyone else.

I worried only that Pamela might get hurt. I was certain that this worship of my daughter could not endure. She could hardly remain the child genius forever. Not for much longer at all. If the furor died down, if the critics were less than ecstatic, it might not be such a bad thing, I thought.

In the end, Francesco needn't have worried at all. The crowds came, and they bought. The critics swooned. Pamela's show was another triumph. She was still a star, burning ever brighter.

Pamela paid little attention to reviews, that was Francesco's lookout. But there was one she read over and over. The November issue of the 1920 *Oxford Review* ran an article on the Leicester show. The author was Richard Hughes.

Diccon reminded the art world that they had in their midst not a prodigy, but something far, far more rare—an artist. And he chastised those whose earlier enthusiasm for her jolly fairies and bunnies clouded the real issue.

Many famous people came to that exhibition, I can't remember them all. John Galsworthy, Lady Sackville. . . . Francesco could tick them all off today if you asked. One, though, I can never forget. She stepped into our world and, just like that, twisted the arc of our lives.

margery

Gertrude Vanderbilt Whitney, the American heiress, appeared at the gallery all draped in fur, and purchased two of Pamela's drawings. She took us aside—rather overeager and terribly sure of herself, I thought—and asked if we'd all join her in her rooms at the Ritz for tea. The following afternoon would be convenient, she said.

What does she want? I wondered. I was sure that she didn't just want to have a cozy little chat with the Bianco family.

The next day the sky gods unfurled a pewter blanket over London. It's their favorite trick, they never seem to tire of it. Before long the rain came. It wasn't a hard rain, and we easily could have walked to Piccadilly, but Francesco said we mustn't arrive looking like retrievers just out of the lake, so we took a cab.

Gertrude's suite at the Ritz was more like the wing of a palace. A ceiling that seemed a hundred feet high. Giant windows, framed by heavy blue velvet, overlooked Green Park. A formal French rug filled most of the room. A golden chandelier floated down from the ceiling, and its light reflected off the polished serving table and the silver tea tray loaded with delicate cakes and scones and jam pockets.

We sat, rather timidly I'm afraid, in formal high-backed chairs upholstered in an embroidered fabric that featured repeated domestic scenes of a royal Chinese family. Gertrude sat erect, enthroned in the middle of the facing sofa, and presided over tea. Behind her was a massive painting of some biblical scene—three angels peering down over clouds to robed men and women reaching skyward, beseeching. Surely, I thought, the angels would rather be looking at our hostess.

Gertrude was impressive. She was not beautiful. Her thick, dark eyebrows were untamed, framing wide-set, heavy-lidded eyes. Eyes that could smile kindly, but more often projected supreme self-confidence, even arrogance. She wore a navy-blue silk dress with a low neckline anchored by a diamond brooch. She sparkled—a band wound round her dark wavy hair was set off by a large jewel-encrusted beetle. Stones of red and green and blue glinted at us as she bent to pour the tea.

Gertrude wasted little time over small talk.

"Pamela must come to America," she said.

She was gracious but quite adamant. "The American public must see the work of this child!"

There was nothing to discuss, she really would not hear any argument on the subject. She would find a home for us—and a beautiful studio for Pamela, of course—near her own in Greenwich Village. Many, many artists had studios nearby. We would love it there. We could stay as long as we liked.

For just a moment, my heart rose. I thought of my mother and Cecil and Teddy and all their girls. They were still in Pennsylvania. I could see them all the time.

But in the next moment I felt quite anxious. What about Pamela? What would this mean for her? William, who was connected to the American art world, had told us how Gertrude loved to collect artists. That she'd set up studios for many painters and sculptors, people like Jo Davidson and Daniel Chester French. The whole idea made me feel uneasy. It wasn't just Pamela who would be uprooted. What about the family? And . . . we would be beholden to this woman. I flinched at the thought. It was all too much. I couldn't take it in.

I looked at Francesco, tried to give him a signal. *Caution, Francesco, caution.* . . . But I would lose this battle as well, and I suppose I knew it even at that moment. The juggernaut was already unstoppable, and, truly, by that time, I had no idea if it would be right to stop it even if I could. At any rate, my worried looks had no effect on Francesco. He was looking at Pamela, and I knew what he saw: his daughter cast in a Madonna glow, gilding that dull London afternoon, outshining the tea tray, the polished wood, the chandelier. Outshining even Gertrude's jewels.

His radiant child. His child of gold.

pamela

I came over here to tell my mother secrets. Unburden myself. *Everyone wants to be near her, to trust her with secrets.*

But I told her nothing this morning.

These paintings, these memories . . . these *feelings*. Caught in mazes. Trapped. Frozen. Stepping into a black void.

The panic, even as we sailed to America.

And it was all my doing. All of it. All of it was because of me. If not for me, we'd never even be in New York. We'd still be in London.

Does Mam think of that? Ever? Often?

I see my mother that first night on the *RMS Carmania*. She is lovely. Happy. And she is surrounded by men.

Soon after we boarded Mam discovered that the *Carmania* had bowed to the times—ladies were now allowed in the Smoking Room. We went there after dinner. It was a grand, vaulted room, full of jeweled lamps, dark paneling, and red velvet sofas and chairs. There were many conversations going on, lots of laughter.

Some young people sat at a table against the back wall, playing rummy, and Mam and Daddy somehow made it clear that I should join them. The grownups gathered in the front, near a large bar. There were only perhaps a half dozen women sprinkled among the men, but my mother would have stood out even if there had been hundreds. She had a kind of lovely quirkiness. From across the room, I studied her. She wore a simple ivory dress with an emerald sash she'd wrapped several times round her hips. Out of the same fabric—an old silk curtain from Chelsea—she'd fashioned a hair ornament that knotted at the nape of her neck. The ends fell like streamers down her back. She looked like a royal gypsy.

Though soft-spoken, Mam has a lively way of expressing herself, cocking her head and gesturing gracefully with her hands. A group of men quickly gathered around my parents. I could see how they were attracted to my mother.

My father's voice traveled to where I sat with my new friends, ". . . what *I* thought when I was courting her!"

The men all laughed. Mam laughed, too, and put her hand to Daddy's cheek. I watched the men watching my mother. The other women were quite lovely, chic and glittery in their low-slung dresses, and matching pumps, and eye-catching ropes of beads. But Mam shone in an altogether different way. She was softly lustrous—a pearl, perhaps, that each man felt he had discovered on his own.

Somehow as I watched my parents, I felt a sudden panic. There were Mam and Daddy, in the belly of a huge ship, laughing and talking as they were carried across the ocean. To America! And it was all because of me. *What were we doing?*

Panic overwhelmed me.

I excused myself, said I'd forgotten something. I tried not to run as I left the card table. But as soon as I found the stairwell I raced up and up, up to the sea air.

The fog had traveled with us. Even the sea was invisible from the high decks. The only sights to be seen were the hazy yellow circles of the ship's lights. I found the darkest place I could and stood against the railing, staring into the void. I thought of my parents. Watching them across the room I had seen a part of them that had nothing to do with Cecco or me or writing or old books.

I thought of Diccon. Would a child of ours ever watch us across a room and think, *Ah, there's that, too . . . ?*

Why were we leaving England, leaving Diccon? What were we doing here, on this ship, rushing to New York across this sea of fog, hurtling blindly into the unknown, leaving behind everything and everybody that was familiar?

I wanted to turn the ship around, go straight back to Chelsea.

It's all because of me.

The thought sickened me.

And what if . . . what if the Americans didn't like my art, what if no one bought my paintings?

New York City—what was New York City? A vast nothingness. I squinted into the blackness, trying to conjure up a gay life in a golden city. My efforts backfired.

A nightmare galloped through my mind, horrible and absurd. Like a decrepit mansion, a towering gallery loomed in the dark. Inside, my pictures were hung in warren-like rooms, too high to be seen properly. I stood alone at the end of a bleak corridor. Giant Americans—men, women, children—were pointing up at the walls, scoffing at my drawings, jeering at me. They turned towards me and crowded around me and lifted me up, crying, *Who does she think she is? She's no good, no good at all—take her away!* They carried me up stairs and more stairs and locked me in the attic just like that madwoman in *Jane Eyre*. I called out for Mam and Daddy and Cecco, but I knew they couldn't hear and I knew it was the end, that I would never see them, that I would live in darkness and never paint or draw again.

I gripped the ship's rail, telling myself how silly it was, just a string of bad thoughts. But it was no good. I panicked.

I spun away and ran from the ghostly night back to the gay rooms I'd been so desperate to leave. As I flew down the stairs, my shoes clanging wildly on the metal, a single thought repeated itself over and over.

Everything, everything—everything is because of me!

margery

When Diccon found out about Gertrude's offer, that we were planning to sail to New York, he tried to talk us out of it.

"Perhaps for a few weeks or so, for Pamela's exhibition, but to stay? You'll despise it. Bloody Americans. They can't produce any decent art or literature on their own—who's there been since Hawthorne? They have to import it, like Pamela. What will you *do* there?"

It wouldn't be bad, I said, I had my mother and Cecil and her family. And it would be a great adventure, wouldn't it?

As the time for leaving came near, Diccon brought flowers. Every day. There were so many arrangements in the house it began to feel as if we'd had a death in the family. One day he brought an armful of bachelor's buttons. He sat by me in the kitchen as I arranged the blue flowers in a milk-glass vase.

"They're beautiful, Diccon, but you really must stop! We aren't having a funeral here, you know, we're only going to New York. . . ."

"It *is* a funeral, then," he said.

Pamela made Diccon promise to come see us in the summer. "You absolutely will come, won't you, cross your heart?" Diccon groaned, but he promised.

At the end of February, he came to Liverpool to see us off. We'd told him he needn't bother, but he'd held up his hand and shaken his head as if to say, *I won't hear of it.* We were like family, he said, "And doesn't one always see one's family off on an ocean voyage?"

At the pier he shook hands with Francesco and Cecco, and kissed Pamela and me on the cheek.

"I fear I shall be quite lost without you."

This was not the usual wry, arch Diccon speaking. He actually did look quite lost.

"Oh, it's not for very long!" Pamela cried. "We'll see you this summer!"

We all waved to him from the deck of the *Carmania*. Pamela blew him kisses. In the city he'd traded his Welsh country cap for a fedora, and he was waving it back and forth like mad. I looked at his lone figure and saw the little boy who'd lost his father and brother and sister. We were his family now, and we were deserting him. It did seem rather cruel.

The seamen flung the massive hawsers to the deck, and the ship eased away from the pilings. Unseasonably warm air had spawned a fog that erased the land almost before we left the dock. There was no watching Diccon get smaller and smaller until he was a speck and then only a mirage. In the blink of an eye, he simply vanished.

Pamela looked up at me, her changeable eyes turned gray.

"But—we'll be coming back to England soon, won't we, Mam?"

"I don't know," I said, "But I should think so."

We drifted down the Mersey, out to sea.

part three

‡‡‡

The Letter: January 11, 1977

428 Lafayette Street
New York City

....

Before she enters the lobby, Pamela stamps her feet, shakes the rain from the yellow sou'wester, and searches in her pocket for the keys. She is halfway up the first flight of stairs when she stops and turns around, remembering the mail.

Why do I bother? she thinks as she draws out the thin pile. Still, she stands a moment to see, exactly, what she has retrieved. It never seems to matter how many days go by with only the most mundane, the most impersonal communications filling the mailbox—with every delivery there is just that bit of hope raised, the promise of *something*.

And now, here is something.

Pamela reads the Oregon postmark, but she has already recognized the handwriting.

She stands still a while, just looks at the envelope. This is what she sees: the gray of the East River, the gold ring, that last letter of Robert's in her hand. But it no longer resembles a letter at all. It is transformed, ready to carry out its final mission.

Why?

It's all she can think. Why on earth is he writing to her now? What possible reason could he have, after all these years?

Perhaps I simply won't open it at all, she thinks as she heads back up the stairs, though even as she has the thought, curiosity shoves it aside. She will open the letter of course, see what Robert has to say.

The cat, Byzantine, hears the apartment door opening. He stretches himself across the couch, his usual greeting.

"Hello, you old thing," Pamela says. And Byzantine *is* old. Sixteen in the spring. She fingers Byzantine gently behind the ears, strokes him.

She hangs her coat and hat on the doorknob to let them dry before putting them back in the closet, then walks over to the table heaped with haphazard piles of bills and coupons and flyers she's never bothered to throw away. She throws her handful of mail on top.

"Hungry?"

She opens the cabinet under the sink, takes out a box of *Tender Vittles.* She picks up the heavy green bowl from the floor, opens the pouch of cat food. *New! Seafood Flavor!* It smells like sweetened manure to her, but Byzantine seems to think it's all right.

Pamela watches the cat as he tentatively approaches the bowl. He will not finish his serving, she knows. Age has diminished his appetite.

She sighs. Is it a sigh for Byzantine? Or for the weariness that descended on her when she saw the letter from Robert? Or is it just an old woman's sigh, for nothing in particular?

She may be tired, but underneath, she feels it. The bit of adrenalin stirring.

Why does he write? What can he possibly say?

She returns to the table full of papers, retrieves the envelope.

It's awfully thin. He doesn't have very much to say, it seems.

‡‡‡

September 1, 1944

9 Livingston Place, Stuyvesant Square
New York City

(Early Afternoon)

margery

I'll go check on her. In just a bit.

Look at me. What am I doing? Wrapping my hands around my arms, hugging myself as if it were freezing in here. God.

And this awful headache. I suppose it's all these memories pushing and clamoring their way to the surface of my brain. They rush in like schoolchildren, breathless, tumbling, unstoppable. All that excitement over Pamela when we arrived . . . !

When I think of that icy wind when we sailed into New York Harbor—well, I almost *can* believe that it's cold in here. The snow may have been half-hearted, just bits blowing about, but the wind was quite serious. Low whitecaps rolled across the steely gray water as the *RMS Carmania* nudged up to the dock.

It seemed ages before we were allowed to disembark, but at last we got the signal. Edging our way down the gangplank, we jostled for position among the crowd of passengers. We were perhaps halfway down when we caught sight of the men on the dock. They were holding up huge dark boxes. Bulbs began to explode.

People looked around, craned their necks. Who was the celebrity, everyone was wondering. Was there someone we had we missed on board—Mary Pickford? Charlie Chaplin?

Then, the shouting. Reporters' voices rising into the air.

"Miss Bianco, over here! Miss Bianco!"

"Good God, Pamela," Francesco said, "They're after you!"

pamela

$\mathcal{M}$y fears about New York quickly vanished. So many glorious things were happening in those early months, one
after another. My exhibition, the glowing articles in all the papers,
my photograph in *Harper's Bazaar, Vanity Fair.* And meeting all
the artists in Macdougal Alley and around the Village.

Now I try to string the days together, try to make a whole of
it. A geometry of jewels, as ornate as a queen's coronation necklace. But just like such a necklace it is too much, really. As soon as
it is put away, you are no longer sure of its design.

Yet the centerpiece is solid. It shines just as brightly in my
mind now as it did then.

The studio. *My* studio.

At first, all I could do was follow the feather.

Gertrude moved about the rooms with a rapid efficiency,
pointing out features—closets, hidden storage areas, the light. Her
hat, a soft gray turban with an ornate pewtery clasp, sprouted a
long, thin, curling feather that whipped about as she moved. It left
trails in the air, like wisps of smoke.

I couldn't focus on what she was saying. My mind buzzed
with incomprehension. *This is not all mine, surely . . . ?*

In all those days crossing the sea, I had tried to envision the
new studio Gertrude had promised. I'd dreamt of a well-lit room,
big enough to comfortably hold a drawing table, easel, and all my

supplies. Room to paint and draw, but also room to breathe in, that was what I'd hoped for. But this! I could have a tea party—no, a *ball*—in this place. The space was truly luxurious: thirty-foot ceilings, a huge latticed skylight, a workroom three times the size of the parlor in our Chelsea flat.

There was even a tiny kitchen, a dining room, and an upstairs loft.

Gertrude handed me the key.

Just come see me if you need anything, Pamela, dear . . . don't hesitate. . . .

Through the skylight I watched a bank of steely winter clouds slowly steepening. Absentmindedly, I ran my hand over the great oaken worktable, covered with the fine dust of old clay and mottled by the gouges and nicks of previous artists. A cool, earthy odor still hung in the air. The walls were bare except for an abandoned charcoal sketch of a nude and an old Provincetown Players schedule someone had tacked by the front door.

I envisioned canvasses filling the studio, paintings like the one I'd imagined in Gertrude's suite at the Ritz in London.

A frisson of purest joy ran through me.

This space, this gorgeous studio, was *all mine*.

I raced up the stairs to the narrow loft—already thinking, what treasures would I store up here?—and down again to the little strip of kitchen where a dented black tea kettle sat atop a two-burner stove. It was, far and away, the dearest tea kettle I had ever seen.

But there was no time to luxuriate. The exhibition at Anderson Galleries was only a few weeks away.

margery

Gertrude had installed a telephone in our new home in Macdougal Alley. It rang all the time. The reporters could not get enough of Pamela. Someone was always calling up to ask for an interview. They all wanted Pamela to talk about her earliest drawings, the bunnies and children. They wanted to know what she thought and did when she was six years old. What could she say? She was like any little girl, she'd tell them. But she never had to say very much. Francesco was always with her. I was happy to have him take over. I had enough to tend to, just trying to take stock of this new world we inhabited.

New York. Greenwich Village. I had no idea.

Before our arrival, my idea of the city was a collage of postcards. A park, not so very far from our neighborhood I'd figured, that had pagodas and dome-topped structures all lit with thousands of electric lights: Luna Park, in a place called Coney Island. Fashionable women with giant fur muffs and feathered hats strolling in snow-covered Central Park. And pelicans and monkeys and bears just a tram ride away at the New York Zoological Park—I could hardly wait!

Of course, nothing was as I'd envisioned it. My geography of the city was all askew. And Greenwich Village, I had no idea. . . .

All that *noise.* So different from our quiet enclave in Chelsea. Automobiles and taxis always going too fast, always honking. A cacophony of voices—vendors calling out from pushcarts, hawking cheap necklaces and rings and scarves; children spilling out from tenements into the streets to play ball, chase rats, and yell epithets at each other and anyone who happened to be near. Greenwich Village was a carnival. We were, all of us, amused and delighted.

Still, it was disconcerting to discover that, as denizens of the neighborhood, we were *tourist attractions*. Double-decker tour buses regularly rolled through the quaint, diagonal streets—"Bohemian Excursions" they called them. Little boys stood at the end of Macdougal Alley, offering, for a quarter, to show passersby where Gertrude Vanderbilt Whitney had a studio. *Step right this way, ladies and gents, see where the rich lady woiks same as for a livin'!*

Macdougal Alley, our new address, was an artists' enclave, a little cul-de-sac just off Macdougal Street, between Eighth Street and Washington Square. Not long before, the alleyway had housed rows of horse stables, and a few were still in use—most days we could catch a whiff of horse manure or hear a faint whinnying. Often, we had to maneuver our way around horse droppings. And like the Village itself, the alley was not a quiet place. Wagons rolled in, groaning. Aproned loaders delivered blocks of marble or slabs of clay. Smocked and spattered artists stood outside their doors, chatting amiably—or not so amiably—about art or food or local politics. Children played on the cobblestoned lane: skip-rope or one o' cat or hopscotch. Dogs wandered in and out, usually managing to disturb a game of marbles or jacks. The children would leap up, whooping, and chase them away. Cats, ignoring the pandemonium, slept curled up on doorsteps, alongside potted plants.

Hidden in the back corner of the alley, behind Gertrude's studio at No. 19, was the Jumble Shop, a homey and colorful café. It was a popular gathering place for poets, artists, and musicians who'd sit into the wee hours talking, drinking, and eating. More or less in that order.

I fell in love with Macdougal Alley immediately. The children, the artists, the animals. It all felt quite like home to me.

margery

*T*here were only a few days before the opening for Pamela's exhibition. Francesco was wild with anticipation.

He kept calling Mr. Kennerley, the president of Anderson Galleries, asking questions, making changes. I heard him talking about publicity, people who must be invited to the reception, arrangement of the pictures, prices to be increased or decreased.

Alone, with me, he worried. Gertrude liked Pamela's art, of course, but did that mean Americans in general would feel the same? What if no one bought Pamela's work? What if they didn't even care for it?

I gave him all the expected reassurances. That Pamela could not fail. That her appeal was universal. At any rate, I told him, there was not a thing we could do about any of it.

By then I was glad Francesco was in control, I had no urge to interfere. Things had been quite calm between us for in the last few years. Still, there was an undercurrent, unacknowledged. We both felt it. Small things—perhaps he would stop midsentence, or I might give him a look I couldn't take back. There were voices altered, words ignored. We would pretend nothing had happened. But his old betrayal burned beneath the surface of our marriage like a peat fire. I feared it would take only a tiny spark to cause a conflagration.

With luck, I thought, it would not happen.

‡ ‡ ‡

Yes, well.

It did happen. Quite quickly.

When the moment came, somehow I steeled myself, turned away. But it went against all natural instinct, as if an ember had leapt from the fireplace, and I just let it sit on the rug, burn a hole right through.

pamela

Early on the morning of the opening, Daddy and I walked all the way uptown to the gallery at Park Avenue and 59th Street. He wanted to check on things one last time.

Anderson Galleries was huge, intimidating. My work—170 of my drawings and paintings—filled three vast, high-ceilinged rooms, hung on walls covered in great swaths of red velvet. The pictures were arranged more or less chronologically from newest to oldest. One room in the back was devoted entirely to the works of my earliest childhood.

Daddy was quiet. He kept rearranging his pocket handkerchief—I knew that meant that he was nervous. He must have been very worried that the crowds wouldn't appear, that no one would buy my pictures. I followed my father in nervous silence as he made the final rounds of the great halls.

As soon as the doors opened, rivers of people filled the gallery. Before long, it was difficult to move about. Many viewers had trouble getting close enough to see the pictures without leaning over someone's shoulder or standing on tiptoe. Mr. Kennerley said he'd never in his entire career seen a show mobbed that way. He'd never seen such sales, either. In the first week, more than a hundred pictures sold! The room reserved for my earliest works was almost stripped bare and had to be closed while new pictures were hung. Mr. Kennerley was especially pleased that so many of the purchasers were celebrities and members of New York society's elite—people with names like Frick and Vanderbilt and Hopkins.

The songwriter Jerome Kern could not decide which of my rabbit drawings he liked best, and so he bought three.

Americans, it seemed, liked my work very much indeed.

GIRL ARTIST AT 14
HAS EXHIBITON HERE

———

Anderson Galleries Show Work
of Child Who Took Italy and
England by Storm

———

PAINTINGS EAGERLY SOUGHT

The New York Sun
March 21, 1921

* * *

14-YEAR-OLD BRUSH WIZARD
AMAZES WORLD WITH GENIUS

———

Little Blonde Pamela Bianco, Here from England, Plays
with Home-Made Dolls and Creates Canvas Master-
pieces Between Times

New York Evening Telegram
March 27, 1921

* * *

CHILD'S PAINTINGS FIND READY MARKET

———

Society Leaders Take Many Pictures from the Exhibit of
Pamela Bianco, Aged 14

———

Purchasers include Mrs. J. H. Hopkins, Mrs. Harry Payne
Whitney, Mrs. Bayard Cutting, Mrs. W. K. Vanderbilt,
Miss Helen Frick. Jerome Kern, the songwriter, takes the
largest number of pictures.

The New York Times
March 30, 1921

margery

*T*he headlines in the newspapers were startling. Art critics gushed over our daughter, the *wunderkind*, the amazing child prodigy from across the sea. Stories about Pamela found their way into papers all across America, in towns I couldn't imagine, like Austin and Chattanooga and Indianapolis. Accolades poured nonstop from the heavens. Francesco ran around collecting them as rain in a bucket.

The pattern was now set. Francesco would manage Pamela's career. My job, as I saw it, was to counterbalance his wild ecstasies over her success, see that it didn't go to her head, ruin the girl. I'd steer her far away from the seduction of fame. In quite mundane, trivial ways. Teasing her if she did something silly or absentminded. *Our little miss genius has left her jumper in the alley again, has she?* Or, *I wonder if Rembrandt spent such a lot of time choosing which biscuit to have with his tea. . . .*

I'd remind her that she would be an artist forever, but perhaps not always a famous one. It was hard to tell what she thought. She always agreed with me. She seemed unaffected by it all.

But then the spark flew. Just one sentence.

One sentence from a review in the *Evening Telegram* incensed Francesco, ignited the old trouble.

We were having such a nice, quiet evening in our new home in Macdougal Alley. Francesco was reading the paper, and Pamela and I sat on the sofa opposite. Pamela was reading a book. I was tatting, finishing up a lace collar. The cozy silence was broken only by the clicking of shuttles and Francesco's contented *hmmms* as he approved what he read. Occasionally he'd call out to us, chortling, and read a bit of praise—"instinctively chooses the right medium" ... "colors of the most daring kind" ... "a marvel of modeling" ... "arresting good judgment and harmony. . . ."

Then, "Listen to this, Margery!" I looked up. I could see he was furious.

It was a mistake, I'm sure, it must have burst right out of him without a thought. For if he'd given it any thought at all, he never would have read those words out loud to me.

It is apparent to any one that Pamela is a genius. Naturally the question in all minds is what will be the result of this premature exploiting of her work?

Francesco ripped out the offending page, crumpling it into a tight ball.

"How dare that idiot talk about 'premature exploiting'? And *now*, for God's sake. She's not a child, she's fourteen! What do these people want? Do they think a girl with a talent as extraordinary as Pamela's should be hidden away until she's . . . what? Of marriageable age? On her deathbed?"

He ranted on and on.

"Pamela's old enough to think for herself now, she could decide not to exhibit if that's what she wanted, couldn't she? Nobody's making her do anything she doesn't want to do. That's right, isn't it, Pamela?"

Pamela look startled, blank, when he looked at her for assurance. She nodded her head dumbly. Then Francesco looked at me and in that instant realized his great mistake.

I was silent. I set down my lacework, behaved as if Francesco's outburst had never occurred at all. Spoke almost cheerfully.

"Francesco, Pamela and I are going out for a bit of a walk . . . we'll pick up a chicken for supper, I think."

By the time we'd put on our coats, Francesco was already bending over the Victrola. As the door shut behind us we could hear the opening notes of "Celeste Aida."

pamela

News of my great success at the Anderson Galleries traveled back across the Atlantic. Stories were printed in the London papers.

Diccon wrote to me.

I read about your American debut—I am terribly proud of my little friend who hikes in the rain and swims like a sand eel in the cold waters of Wales <u>and</u> draws and paints like Botticelli. . . .

I cried when I read his letter.

And I was back in the miner's cave in Wales, while the storm raged.

I felt him beside me, then, his arm around me, his hand hot on my skin.

I should be over there, not here. I should be with Diccon.

Well, he'd be here before long. In summer.

Summer. Summer. Summer.

It's all I could think about.

But I kept busy. Working, mainly—I was practically living in my studio. If I had free time, I'd head over to the Whitney Studio Club on West Fourth Street. Gertrude had started the club a few years earlier as a gathering place for artists. There was a billiard room and art library on the lower level. On the main floor, there were two galleries and a parlor where one could read or play cards or Parcheesi or just talk. The parlor was painted in brilliant colors, with floor-length curtains of deep sapphire, lined with chartreuse silk and tied with a scarlet cord. I thought it was rather like a gorgeous dress-up box.

Although I flew over to the club at every opportunity, I was mostly just an observer. I was shy, and the youngest member by far. The others regarded me as a child. At first, some of the artists teased me, bowing and brushing the floor with imaginary hats. *Hail to the little queen of the art world! Let me kiss your feet, I beg of you, that I may taste of your genius!* But they soon grew tired of that, and before long I was nothing special, just a girl with braids who sat in the corner with a book and might be listening in but who cared? Everyone seemed so jolly, so full of ideas, so interesting. There were hundreds of members, not just painters and sculptors, but also printmakers, illustrators, art students, and cartoonists—and even if I didn't join in, I felt like one of them.

There was a sculptress, Sara, who befriended me. She was nineteen; she said that before I arrived she'd felt like the baby in the group. To me she seemed the picture of sophistication as she darted airily about like a dragonfly in her slouchy gaucho pants, her flowing peasant blouses, and her ever-changing array of seductive little cloches that called attention to her fantastically green eyes. I felt the dullest housefly in comparison.

Still, it was all just a diversion. I was counting the days until Diccon would arrive.

At last, spring blossomed in the Village. Washington Square Park burst into beautiful blooms, all snowy-white magnolias and leafy elms and lindens a brilliant yellow-green. My fondness for our new neighborhood increased every time I took a walk. Even so, I couldn't wait to get out of the city, to be off on our seaside holiday at the New Jersey shore.

April. May. June. *Summer.*

Forever.

margery

*P*amela and I walked out into the night.
A strong March wind pummeled our backs, blowing my hair across my face. We turned up our coat collars and headed south, flinching from the beastly screech of the Sixth Avenue el train careening over West Third Street.

I remained silent as we walked. Pamela looked at me now and again with a sort of half smile that tried to be cheery. It was strange for me to be so quiet, and I knew it was upsetting her. But I wasn't ready to talk, wasn't sure what it was I wanted to say. I kept her arm linked in mine, held her close. I wanted to comfort her, but I didn't have the words, I needed just to keep walking, to get far away from the confines of our house. Away from Francesco.

We passed a young girl bending over in the shadows of an alcove, pulling a flask out of her shiny red boot. Farther south, mothers sat on the front stoops of tenements, drawing their shawls close, gossiping. A streetlight lit up a banquet of vegetables, a burst of rich color. Shiny red peppers, green-blue broccoli, orange-tipped squash blossoms. On Carmine Street a hurdy-gurdy man played his barrel organ music. A little red-capped monkey clapped his hands and held out a tin cup. Neighborhood children hopped and skipped and twirled. Pamela and I stopped, enchanted despite ourselves by this impromptu hurdy-gurdy ballet.

I began to feel I could breathe again.

I tried to collect my thoughts.

What will be the result of this premature exploiting. . . .

The reporter from the *Telegram* had hit a very tender nerve. The tenderest nerve. But it would not do to give in to the feelings his words aroused in me. I had made a pact with myself. Now I would walk through these feelings, exorcise them. I needed to be quick about it, not brood, as much for Pamela's sake as for my own. I knew how it must weigh on her, the tension between her parents. She'd be certain that it was all her fault, that she was to blame.

The silence became too much for her.

"Oh, Mam, you mustn't worry . . . you know . . . that's just Daddy. It doesn't make any difference, really it doesn't." *It's too late, anyway,* is what she meant. "I'm quite used to everything, you know, we can't change . . . I mean, I'll just keep on painting and drawing, it's not as if I can stop that. I suppose it's best if Daddy handles the rest. Like he always has. After all, he *is* my manager—and he always will be, I guess. . . ." She laughed nervously.

Did Pamela wish that things were different? Did she wish that her father had never brought her drawings to the gallery in Turin? Did she regret her fame, or did it make her happy? She never seemed affected by it, not that I could tell.

And what did *I* wish? It was all quite beyond me on that bitter March evening.

In the end, I saw it didn't matter. We couldn't address the real issue because we both knew there was no way to fix it.

Everyone knows you can't go back in time.

We crossed Sixth Avenue and wound our way through the warren of streets—Cornelia to Bleecker to Barrow. We stopped just outside the brightly lit window of Levy's butcher shop. A row of skinned rabbits hung by their feet, long and glowing pink. I tried not to look.

"Pamela." I held her away from me, my arms rigid, the way I always had when she was small and she'd done something wrong and I wanted her to know that what I was about to say was quite serious, indeed.

"Pamela . . . you know that this . . . this *craziness* won't last forever? I mean, you know that what's happening now is not the important thing . . . ? The important thing is that you are an *artist* no matter what newspapers ever may say, good or bad. . . ."

"I know, Mam . . . I know."

And . . . well, to this day I believe she did truly know. She had always understood, from the beginning. She'd known in Turin when I hadn't wanted her pictures in the exhibition. She had learned it all these years from bits of overheard conversation, seen it from my gestures and quick looks. Pamela would always draw and paint. She would never be anything but an artist. She would be quite content when there was no "craziness" at all.

"Daddy gets excited, but I don't."

I hesitated, looking at her carefully. She was all right, I thought. She's not worried about herself, she's only worried about me. And her father. She wants it to be fine again between us.

I gave her my best smile, the one that said, *Don't worry, everything's all right now.*

"Well . . . right, then. I'm glad, that's good."

I pushed open the shop door.

"Oh, Lord, I wish they wouldn't put those poor little rabbits in the window, don't you?"

pamela

*F*orever arrived at the end of June. Summer!

When I got off the train at Point Pleasant I looked around, almost expecting to see Diccon waiting there at the station. It was silly, but I couldn't help it.

Cecil and Teddy were already there, waiting for us at Old House with Agnes and her two-year-old son, Shane. Gene, however, was missing. The ever-elusive playwright was staying in the city to work. Cecil confided to us that she saw little of her son-in-law. She hadn't even met him until almost a year after the wedding. Cecil clearly had many reservations about the man her daughter had chosen. *He can be funny as hell, and charming, but only when he drinks and he drinks too damned much. And I'm not too sure I want to know how he treats her when no one's around. . . . I'll never hear a word from Agnes, though, she thinks the man walks on water.* Cecil would shake her head over Gene—what could she do?

I thought it must be terrible to have a daughter married to a man you didn't care for, who was drunk half the time. As I listened to Cecil prattling on I couldn't help thinking, *How happy Mam will be with Diccon for a son-in-law.* It would be such a natural thing. He was part of the family already.

Old House was set on a hill. It was a three-story farmhouse, airy, with large, sparsely furnished rooms. Nothing matched. Chairs didn't go with tables, bureaus didn't go with beds. *It's a summer place, a camp,* I can hear Cecil saying.

The strangest thing in the house was the hand. Whenever we referred to "the hand" we'd look about and speak in low, mysterious voices as if it were some dreadfully scary thing. From the inside of the fireplace in the living room, a very real-looking hand seemed to be reaching out, holding up the brick arch. Once white, it was now yellowed by smoke. It was, in fact, Cecil's hand—an artist friend had made a plaster cast and presented it to her. Unsure what to do with the appendage, Cecil had, on a whim, cemented it to the fireplace.

I remembered that hand. From long ago. How it had frightened me.

There were other things. Little bits of memory floated back.

The yellow wooden knobs on the kitchen cabinets, the creaking exactly halfway up the back stairs, the stuffed owl on top of the bookcase. And, on the third floor, my bedroom. It faced the front of the house, looking towards the sea. I remembered the slanted wall, the eaves.

I remembered the feeling of loneliness.

margery

*F*rancesco and I made our peace. Late that night, in bed, Francesco held me and murmured into the dark, "I am very sorry, Margery. Very, very sorry. I don't know what I was thinking . . . well, I was not thinking at all . . . you know how I am."

"I know how you are."

"It's all right then?" he said, after a while.

I was silent, but I didn't move away from him.

It wasn't much of a peace, really, but I would stick to it. I would never let the issue come between us again. Pamela, I understood, had been concerned only for me. She had always turned herself over to Francesco willingly.

No, in those days if Pamela looked distracted or concerned or wistful, I could be quite sure it had nothing to do with her father or her work or her future. Her mind was fixated on Diccon.

Quite a natural thing, I thought. What young girl does not dream of romance, *crave* romance?

I'd seen the pile of dime novels under her bed. *Verdict of the Heart, Dotty's Dilemma, Wife in Name Only.* And *The Dark Heart of Kitty LaRue*—I'll admit I thumbed through that one. What a nasty, calculating creature, stealing another woman's husband. But she paid for it, of course, she was sorry on her deathbed. As she should have been. . . .

What on earth did Pamela learn from these books? What ideas filled her head? She was—she still is—terribly gullible. Lord, I can still see the look on Pamela's face that time at Old House when Agnes started talking about how she met Gene.

Well, the fact is that Agnes had us both mesmerized. It was quite a tale.

At twenty-four, she'd published a few novelettes and some of her short stories had appeared in pulp magazines. She had ambitions, big dreams. She yearned to go to New York City, where every street corner held promise. In October of 1917, she left her family behind at Merryall and rode the milk train from the Housatonic Valley into New York. It was a noisy ride—she was accompanied the whole way by the clanking of the metal milk cans in the boxcar. As she gazed through the train window at the trees ablaze with red and yellow, she thought with some sadness of the country winter she would miss—the frozen fields, the icy woodpiles, the wind that could almost knock her flat as she came round the corner of the barn.

But her fit of nostalgia didn't last very long. Not with the shiny adventure of New York just ahead.

In the city, Agnes took a small room in Greenwich Village at the Brevoort. She called up an acquaintance, Christine Ell, who'd told her about a possible job—a factory job, but she could work short shifts and it would be steady money. Christine gave Agnes instructions to meet her at ten thirty at the Hell Hole, the back room of a bar called the Golden Swan, on the corner of Fourth Street and Sixth Avenue.

Agnes was uncomfortable as she waited alone in the dark, beery room strewn with beat-up wood tables. Christine was late.

"I lit a cigarette. Then I noticed a man sitting across the room. He was dark and still, and he was staring at me. . . . I could feel a sadness in his look and . . . there was a hardness, too. I thought he was probably someone not to be messed with. Then Christine showed up, and the first thing she did was greet the man who'd been watching me. She brought him over and introduced him, said his name was Gene O'Neill and that he wrote plays.

"Then Gene's brother, Jamie, turned up. He was wearing a black-and-white checked suit and a bowler, and greeted everyone with a cheery 'What ho!' He was walking painfully slowly, and he sat down in the booth carefully like an old man. The Hell Hole wasn't the first bar he'd been in that day! He did most of the talking. Gene never said a word. Christine leaned over to me and whispered that *Gene's not drunk enough to really talk . . . you should hear him when he does. He hardly ever talks when he's sober.* Anyway, after an hour or so Jamie and Christine headed off to another bar."

Agnes leaned towards us dramatically, to make sure we were paying close attention.

"Gene walked me back to the Brevoort . . . never said a thing. When we got to the hotel door, I politely offered my hand to say good-bye, but Gene just stood there looking at me with those sad eyes. I felt horribly awkward just standing there, so I just said, 'Well, good night, then!' Then . . . very slowly and clearly . . . Gene said the first words he ever said to me.

'I want to spend every night of my life from now on with *you.* I mean this. *Every night of my life.*'"

Pamela was motionless. She just stared at Agnes. I thought perhaps she might never move again.

pamela

No, Old House was not new to me. Now the house emanated the same mixture of warmth and safety laced with sorrow that it had so many years before. I'd almost forgotten. I was so small, then.

It wasn't long after the dinner party with Pablo Picasso that Cecco and I knew something was wrong. Daddy was quiet a lot of the time. He just sat with a book on his lap, not reading. If we tried to talk to him, he'd pat our heads absentmindedly. We heard our parents whispering in a different way. We mostly couldn't catch the words, but once, as I quietly approached the kitchen, I heard Mam quite clearly. There was the scrape of a chair, and the sound of a china plate set on the porcelain sideboard. Then my mother's low voice.

"You're not well, Francesco . . . we must do *something*. And that is all I can think of to do."

There was only silence after that. I tiptoed away and found my brother upstairs.

"Daddy's sick," I told Cecco.

Mam was sad-eyed when she explained to us about Daddy. *Not to worry, darlings, he'll be shipshape soon, but I must stay here to care for him.* She told us that Cecco and I were going away to live with her sister, Cecil. She would accompany us on the voyage over. She said we'd love America; we'd love Aunt Cecil and Uncle Teddy and all the girls. Teddy painted landscapes, and I could draw with him. The Connecticut countryside and the New Jersey coast had lovely open places to explore.

What Mam said was true, but it's certainly not the landscape or even Cecil, whom I did grow to love, that I remember from that time. It's loneliness, mainly. And how much I hated automobiles. The shiny Model T parked near the pier that would take me, unwilling, to a strange world. The jalopies that would roar up to Old House, waiting for sixteen-year-old Agnes to run out the door and hop in the back, off to have loads of fun with her friends. And this, most vivid of all: Mam driving off with Uncle Teddy to go back to New York, to get on the ship that would take her back to Daddy. I see her bright face haloed by the lemon scarf she's wrapped round her head. She turns and waves until she is out of sight. Cecco waves, too, yelling over and over, "Bye, Mam, see you soon! Bye, Mam, see you soon!" Cecco's house is made of brick, but mine is made of straw, collapsing in the slightest wind. I don't wave. Why should you wave when your heart has been ripped out?

For weeks I kept hearing motors, and dashed to my bedroom window hoping to see Mam rolling up the driveway, but of course she never did.

margery

Agnes talked of Gene a lot that summer.

She told us how miserable he'd been when they'd spent the winter at Old House a couple of years earlier, when he was working on *The Moon of the Caribbees*. The play was scheduled to open at the Provincetown Theatre in New York at the end of December, but they couldn't afford to live in the city in the months before the production, and going to Agnes's family home on the coast of New Jersey had seemed a good solution. Gene could take the train in to New York for rehearsals, and Agnes promised him that he would have his solitude for writing. *Absolutely no visitors,* he'd warned.

Gene had sworn off liquor, that was one good thing. He was determined to work. But that didn't make everything rosy for Agnes. Far from it. He was irritable, and she was nervous and angry. She'd done everything she could think of to make the house pleasing to Gene, to make it a quiet haven so that he could write in peace. She'd cleared the dining room when he decided that was where he wanted to work; she'd even had a carpenter build a special long table with two drawers so that he could more easily correct his manuscripts. She kept the coal stoves burning. She was a vigilant watchdog, turning away all visitors.

Still, Gene was impossibly churlish. Agnes said he found fault with everything.

"He complained about *everything*. . . . He'd say things like, *Who can concentrate with that god-damned windmill creaking all the time? Why do I have to wake up in the morning and find a cat on my bed? That is not a draft, Agnes, that is a fucking hurricane blowing through this house!* I tried to ignore him but then one day he found two bills from the hardware store in the mail and accused me of overspending. I told him I wasn't buying anything we didn't need and I'd had to get the windmill fixed.

"He said, 'Well, I can't for Christ's sake be worrying about the money on top of everything else. When are you going to start working?'

"Well, that did it . . . by then I was just red-hot mad and I went to my typewriter, jammed in some paper, and shoved back the carriage return over and over so that the bell kept ringing. Naturally, Gene wasn't going to hang around for my childish behavior, so off he went, just walked out the front door. When he came back, though, he was all sad-eyed, and he grabbed me and said *Promise me we'll never fight like that again. Promise me!* So of course I said *Never, darling! Never again!* But…"

Agnes laughed and threw up her hands. "Never say 'never'— right?" She was quiet for a while, staring out at the gray expanse of water.

"He even found fault with the ocean, for God's sake! He thought it was boring . . . everything was boring, boring, boring. He was like a caged lion, always running out to throw a tennis ball against the old barn over and over . . . didn't do any good, he'd be just as angry when he got back in the house. We just avoided each other. Then maybe he'd have a good day of work on his play, and he'd be jolly for a bit."

Pamela listened to it all, wide-eyed, and when we were alone she said to me, "I don't think I like that Gene very much."

We spent quite a lot of time with the O'Neills after that summer. Bermuda. Cape Cod. At some point I noticed that Pamela avoided Gene as much as possible. Francesco and I were ambivalent about him. We saw his moody side, saw he would be impossible to live with. Still, we didn't have to live with him. But Pamela would shut down whenever she was near him. It began, as I recall, after one of our holidays in Truro. She knew—or saw—or felt—something that we didn't. I asked her about it, but she just shrugged. *Well, I never did like him very much*, she said.

pamela

$\mathcal{F}$or years, Agnes O'Neill had hovered about in my consciousness like one of the colorful hot air balloons that dotted the
skies of Paris in the spring. And now the beautiful balloon had
landed, gracefully, in the kitchen at Old House.

Agnes. Exotic, unknowable, Agnes. The cousin who'd married a difficult playwright, who'd got Mam's Murano vase. I had
only vague memories of her from that time long ago when Cecco
and I'd spent a year with her family, when Daddy was sick. I mostly
remembered that she always seemed to be leaving the house to
go off with friends. After that, I'd seen her only in the few photographs that Cecil had sent to Mam. We always commented on how
much she resembled my mother. Though they were aunt and niece,
there were only twelve years between them, and they seemed more
like sisters.

Now that I could see them together, I knew the photographs
hadn't lied—they looked remarkably alike: shining, cropped dark
hair; a fine, long nose; and large eyes—though Agnes's were glittering, dark topazes, while Mam's were deep blue pools, infinite
and warm. They had similar proportions, and they moved with the
same elegance. Yet there was great difference. Agnes emanated a
kind of tension—a greyhound straining at the leash. Mam radiated
gentleness—a doe munching on a shrub.

Agnes sat with Mam and me at the kitchen table, talking of
Gene, her husband. It had started off such a romantic story. When
she told how she'd first met him, how he never said a word all night

until they'd walked back to her hotel and he told her he wanted to spend every night of his life with her—it seemed to me the most wonderful story I had ever heard. But then her tale took a sharp turn. She looked off into a corner of the room, took a deep breath, then confessed that she worried about Gene's drinking.

Just after they were engaged, she said, they'd stayed at the Garden Hotel, across from Madison Square Garden—a small, dingy place with a bar in the lobby.

"We were planning to leave in the morning for Provincetown, but when we woke Gene lay in bed grousing about the trip and the long wait we were sure to have at the station in Boston. Finally he got up and went into the bathroom. . . . He tried to shave, but his hand shook too badly to hold a razor, so he asked me go down to the bar and get him a milk shake with a shot of brandy. It was awfully creepy and dark. There were already a few men hunched over at the bar, and I felt sick when the bartender winked at me and said, 'Having a rough one, is he?' when he handed over the drink. It was horrible.

"I did think Gene seemed a little better after his milk shake. He shaved, then sat looking over some papers he'd spread over the coffee table. But I guess he couldn't concentrate, so he just sank back on the sofa. Then he told me to bring him an egg-nog—a couple of eggs in a double shot of brandy! He said that'd be breakfast, and he promised we'd get going after that. But we never did. Later he went out and got some Old Taylor and by afternoon . . . well," Agnes shrugged, "at least he made it to the bed before he passed out."

I didn't know what to think, really. *Milk shakes. Eggnogs. Dark hotel bars. Gene's hand shaking so much he can't hold a razor.*

That was no love story.

Yet despite her sordid tale, Agnes was acting as if all was fine, really. She didn't seem to have fallen out of love with Gene. But things weren't fine, you could see it in her eyes.

And it wasn't long before I saw it for myself, how bad things were.

I wondered, that day in Point Pleasant: Did all men and women—all marriages—have their ugliness? What about Mam and Daddy? Was there anything . . . could they . . . ? No, I decided. My father ordering my mother into a seedy bar to pick up an early-morning "milk shake"? It was impossible to conjure up the scene. Or anything of the sort.

I was beginning to doubt a lot of things, but of this I was sure.

margery

I don't know what Pamela saw or heard. But it's true the O'Neills were a strange match, Gene so silent and inward, and Agnes so open and expressive. And it was no secret that there was a volatility between them. Francesco and I caught glimpses of it often enough. I hate to think what Pamela may have witnessed. She is so vulnerable. Did Agnes tell her something? Agnes—and this is part of her charm—is not always . . . appropriate, shall I say.

Once, after Gene and Agnes went swimming with Francesco at Peaked Hill Bars, Agnes made a comment to me, something along the lines of I must be a happy woman. I deflected the conversation. I am my mother's daughter, I think of myself as a free spirit, an open-minded woman, happy to discuss just about anything. But I will not talk about the intimate side of my marriage. I simply don't see the point. Agnes, however, does not feel the same way. She's often talked about such things, about Gene, in the most intimate way possible, with no hesitation at all. Almost with glee, like the morning she sat in my kitchen, pushing her cigarette round and round the ashtray, nervously returning strands of sleek, dark hair behind her ear while she regaled me with her story about the night at Spithead, the stucco beach house they'd recently bought in Bermuda.

There was a lot of drinking that night—there always was that—and then the inevitable argument. Incensed, she couldn't remember about what, Agnes stomped out to the stone patio and flopped down on the chaise. At some point Gene walked out (he probably finished off a bottle of something first) and stared at her a while. Then he was on top of her, forcing her. Never said a word. Even put his hand over her mouth. *He was a beast. Christ.*

After she said that, she laughed a little laugh that was hard to interpret. But I don't think I misinterpreted that bit of pride in her voice as she told her tale.

We went to Spithead, once, and I can picture it all too clearly. The balmy night, the soft light emanating from the house, the glow of the pumpkin-yellow walls. The sound of waves gently lapping up against the breakwater—not that Agnes or Gene would have heard. Agnes, lying on the cushions patterned with cheerful azaleas, feeling, however mistakenly, that she has conquered Gene. Proud that she has him still. He cannot seem to stay away from her. And Gene, driven by raw lust.

Or, worse, sheer perversity.

Because by then he'd already made up his mind to leave her for Carlotta.

pamela

It was Agnes who showed me the barn full of family ghosts.

One sunny morning I was working in the kitchen. I'd arranged a teacup and a cutting of blue hydrangea on the red-checked table-cloth. Agnes had her elbows on the table, her delicate fingers wrapped around a large, cobalt-blue coffee cup. She watched me as I painted.

"You know, there's lots of stuff in the barn . . . old pottery and things . . . you might want to take a look, something might interest you."

And so after lunch the two of us made an expedition to the gray barn that sat behind Old House. Agnes showed me the cleared space on the east side where Gene had thrown his tennis ball against the barn wall for hours on end. As she wrestled with the padlock, she told me how she used to run around the barn with her sisters when she was a child, and how creepy she used to think it was, all full of dusty old things. But now she realized that there was a lot of family history stored there.

We climbed up the narrow, creaky stairs. At the top, we had to step over a crate of empty mason jars. The loft was dark. Cobwebs hung from the rafters, and a thick poison-ivy vine had climbed inside the east window, its tendrils growing every which way, attaching themselves to old luggage and shelves and anything in their way. It was hard to maneuver among the great collection of old shutters, furniture, kerosene stoves, washbasins, toys, and books. Agnes pointed out some heavy walnut furniture from our great-aunt Agnes's house in Philadelphia: wardrobes, a chest of drawers, a sofa, and a few Victorian chairs. Everything was covered with a thick dust. Agnes sighed.

"What's to become of all these things? No one wants them, but no one in our family ever gets rid of anything . . . we just keep collecting things. I suppose this junk will just sit here till long after you and I are gone. . . ."

‡ ‡ ‡

It's early morning. I wake to a soft breeze blowing fitfully over my face. I rise from my bed and stand for a long time by the window. Directly in my view is the old barn. I like the shape of it. A glance to the sky: clouds, lots of pale, unthreatening clouds. And this lovely sea air wafting about, invisible silken scarves. I make up my mind. *I'll paint outside today. The barn.*

I set up my easel on the lawn in back of the house, and place on it a small board, not much bigger than a piece of letter paper. I sit quietly a while, contemplating the shadows and lines and planes of the old barn. I know then what I will do. I open a few tubes of paint. I have to work fast, the tempera will dry very quickly. The scene grows in soft angles and primitive shapes. A gray barn. Rounded trees in deep green and bright lemongrass. A sky of lavender blue.

I bring the painting up to my bedroom and lean it gently against the mirror on the dressing table. I lie on my bed, studying it, thinking of what one could not see in the painting, of the pieces of family history collecting dust. The old leather prayer books, the discarded playthings, the Victorian bed of dark wood, the curved brocade sofa. I'd had so many homes in my life. I always seemed to be carrying my treasures and memories from place to place, my life in a knapsack. It was good to think that this barn, holding family secrets, would stay on this plot of land forever.

An image of my life flashes in my mind—a kaleidoscope.

Tapped here, then there, forever reassembling itself. I wonder if, one day, a pattern will hold.

I pick up the painting again, take it over to the faded yellow wingback chair opposite the window. I turn it over, steadying it on my legs, and write in pencil on the back: *The Old Barn. Point Pleasant, New Jersey. 1921.* I sign my name, the letters round, precise, perfect.

margery

Weeks went by, and I began to worry. We hadn't heard a word from Diccon. Pamela ran out every day to get the mail, came back disappointed.

I tried to prepare her for the possibility that he might not be able to make it. Unavoidable things happen, I said. Diccon's mother may have taken ill, or perhaps he'd had a job offer he couldn't refuse.

But Pamela was adamant.

"He *promised* he'd come see us in the summertime, didn't he?" she would say. "He'll be here, he won't forget."

Still, I worried.

pamela

$\mathcal{M}$iss Betts was not cooperating. It was a hot evening with only the occasional whisper of an ocean breeze to stir the heavy air, and I was crouched on the farmhouse porch trying to tie a magenta ribbon around the cat's neck. We'd had a jolly picnic earlier, a fortieth birthday celebration for Mam, and the ribbon was from the flowered hat box, Daddy's gift—a wonderful, drapey straw hat from Miss Emma's Dry Goods that my mother had been coveting.

I sensed something moving, and looked up.

Walking from the direction of the beach towards the house was a man carrying a large satchel. It looked as if it was a struggle for him to move forward at all. At first I wasn't sure, but then he put down his bag to lift his cap in a wave, and my heart lurched. I ran down the steps.

"Diccon! Oh, my God, Diccon, you're here!"

I stopped just short, unsure once again. This Diccon had a scraggly beard and bloodshot eyes and dirty clothes. He looked emaciated, older. He almost seemed an imposter. But then he grinned, and he was Diccon again.

"Don't stand there looking at me like that, Pamela . . . perhaps I should turn round and go back?"

"Oh, no, Diccon, it's just that when—"

Behind us the porch door banged, and Mam flew across the lawn. She didn't hesitate—she threw her arms around Diccon.

"Diccon! What a wonderful birthday surprise!"

She stepped back quickly. "Good God, Diccon, you need a *bath*!"

Diccon laughed. "As bad as all that, is it?"

Over supper, Diccon told us of the horrors he'd suffered at sea. He'd had trouble scraping up money for the voyage, finally opting to travel as a steerage passenger on an emigrant ship. Soon after he embarked he heard talk that the ship was "rotten," and only fit for cargo. He endured a public bathing with lye soap and paraffin, and a thorough search for lice. In the cabin he shared with three other men he couldn't sleep for the noise—the whole room vibrated with the endless pounding of the engines.

After twelve days crossing the Atlantic, the ship entered New York Harbor, where it sat idle for days in the stifling heat.

"It was like a coal furnace, with no place to hide. Coal dust poured over us, enough to choke us, and clouds of mosquitoes biting in a frenzy! It was Hell, and that is an understatement. I was comatose in that heat. . . . Don't know how I had the strength to leave the ship. I was happy to see that tugboat come up to bring us to Ellis Island, I can tell you . . . then guess what the captain yells to his mates? 'We got a great pile of shit this time, lads!'"

margery

I wonder now, was that when it began? That summer? Was that when Pamela's girlish crush became more . . . an obsession? A child, you cannot know. I was not looking hard enough, I did not properly judge the *depth* of her feeling.

Still, if there was anything to worry me about Diccon and Pamela that summer at the New Jersey shore, I do not remember it. My memory of that time is that it was both calm and glorious. Swims and beach walks and picnics and long, soft evenings and games of charades. And an industrious time for all of us. Diccon was writing a short story. Pamela was working for the first time in lithography, drawing trees on zinc tablets. Cecco was reading some important and very heavy book—Proust, I think it was—before returning for his last year of boarding school in England. Francesco was in the city most weekdays to run the bookshop he'd opened on West Eighth Street, just behind our home in Macdougal Alley.

It's not that I was blind. I could see how Pamela adored Diccon still. But she was just fourteen, and . . . well, at that time I suppose I could have missed things. I was a bit distracted that summer, self-absorbed. I had a secret or two of my own.

Of course my family knew I'd been writing a book for children. When Pamela and Cecco had asked what it was about and I told them it was about a toy rabbit who becomes real, they looked at each other, raising their eyebrows and grinning conspiratorially. *It's your Tubby!* they said in one voice. They'd always known that I was particularly fond of Tubby, the stuffed bunny I kept on my desk, the bunny with the loose seams and worn-off fur.

What I hadn't told anyone was that in April I'd had extraordinary news from Mr. Heinemann, my publisher. Without a word to me, he'd taken my manuscript to William Nicholson, told him that he was convinced it would be an instant classic. He asked the artist to please take a look, see what he thought. William, apparently, thought the same, and agreed to do the illustrations straightaway. It was almost more than I could comprehend.

And now Heinemann's had sent me the final proof of *The Velveteen Rabbit.*

I had told no one that the book was so close to being ready. Never before or since have I been so secretive. But I had my reasons for wanting to keep *The Velveteen Rabbit* to myself.

I wanted to hold on to that time with my father as long as I could.

The book—every character in it, every sentiment, every *everything*—was between Daddy and me. The bunny with ears of pink sateen who loses his shape and scarcely looks like a rabbit any more, except to the boy who loves him. The kind and wise old Skin Horse. The bracken and the raspberry canes and the fairy huts in the flower beds. The sadness. The joy. All of it.

Writing *The Velveteen Rabbit* was a gift from my father. It was a gift *to* my father. I would be happy to share my book with the world, but the essence of it would stay sealed in my heart forever.

pamela

I couldn't stand it. Diccon would be leaving Point Pleasant soon, and I just had to have him to myself for a while. I thought perhaps if we were alone, then . . . well, I didn't know, but something would happen. Perhaps he'd kiss me. Perhaps he'd look at me wistfully. *I know you're awfully young, Pamela, but in a few years, perhaps. . . .*

The silly dreams I had!

But how serious to me at the time. And so I plotted.

It was obvious that Diccon's interest in our family was intense, so one morning I mentioned the barn, the old family things in the loft.

"Let's explore, shall we?"

I led the way up the rickety steps.

The barn attic was mostly in shadow except for a great shaft of light breaking through the eastern window, active with powdery life. I showed Diccon the old hammock, the gray roping now brittle and broken. Ancient dolls and toys lay in haphazard heaps on their fragile bed—dolls missing limbs and eyes, their hair mostly fallen out from aged netting, dented tin cars and trucks, a mastless wooden sailboat.

Diccon marveled at the musty childhood relics of my grandparents, aunts, uncles, cousins.

"Shhh!" he said, and stood quite still. "Listen—the echoes of long-ago children."

I heard them, too.

I picked up a cloth doll, smoothing the worn checked dress as Diccon wandered across the room. He stood in front of a large bureau with a mirror in a scrolled frame of dark wood. He stared at his own thin face and smoldering eyes; he could see me behind him, watching. He turned abruptly and headed back towards me.

I froze. *It's going to happen; he's going to touch me.* As he moved swiftly towards me I could already feel his hand on my hair, my cheek, my neck. I gripped the doll, unable to move. *He's almost here. . . .* For a moment Diccon's figure was obscured as he stepped through the blinding shaft of light.

"Ah! Let's take a look at these!"

Diccon walked past me to a shelf against the wall where the old leather books were stacked. He rifled through them briefly.

"Oh, bad luck. I had thought perhaps one of your grannies had left an old Melville or a Hawthorne, but these are all to do with religion. Well, I've no use for any of these!"

My face grew hot. I tingled from head to foot. I couldn't move, yet I felt I might lose my balance. I thought I must look like a madwoman in my mortification, but Diccon didn't seem to notice a thing. He started to head back downstairs.

"Are you coming, Pamela?"

I lay the doll in the hammock. I walked to the stairwell, the blood still pulsing in my cheeks.

When Diccon left Point Pleasant and sailed home to London, he took with him a stack of sketches I'd made of him, and lots of other pictures.

I would have given him anything he asked for.

I was yearning for so much that I couldn't articulate. For Diccon, yes, but even more for . . . well, just for *everything*.

I began to work with an intensity I'd never felt before. Trees beckoned to me when the breezes stirred the leaves, and I had to draw them; I couldn't leave them alone. I did some pieces in pencil, tempera, ink, oil, gouache. But mostly I was working in an altogether new way.

In the city, Daddy had taken me to the printmaking studio of George Miller, who let me watch as he rolled the etched stones with ink and pulled trial prints. I was fascinated—it seemed such a *strong* way to make pictures. *You may sign it in the stone, or later if you like,* Mr. Miller said. *You would do a limited edition of course, and the stone would be destroyed.* I wandered around looking at prints while Daddy talked about the print runs and sales. *We'd want to do quite small editions, not more than thirty, perhaps—each would have a greater value.*

I couldn't wait to try it on my own, and boxed up sheets of grained zinc to bring to Point Pleasant. The tablets were light enough to hold on my lap. I liked the smoothness of the grease crayon in my fingers, the layering of lines on the thin yet substantial surface. I became obsessed with the technique. I did some still lifes, but over and over I returned to the trees—maples, sycamores, copper beeches, balsams. I wanted to transfer their strength, their texture to paper. I wanted to draw the beating heart of every tree. This new method felt to me the best way, and I worked with a sort of passion I hadn't known before. I felt a curious power as the crayon moved across the zinc.

Diccon wrote to me from Oxford. He said that his friends had made no attempt to hide their jealousy. *They were positively pea green with envy when they saw that my walls were covered with drawings by "that famous little Bianco girl"!*

Little! Did he really think I was just a little girl?

margery

*E*arlier, in the city, Pamela and Cecco had asked me if I would read my story to them, but I'd refused. "Not until I'm sure it's finished," I'd told them.

But now it *was* finished. I was ready to mail back the final proof, and so that night after dinner I made my announcement.

"Well, it's done. It's finished. I'm sending the final manuscript to London tomorrow."

Diccon spoke up immediately, "You will read it to us, Margery, before you wrap it up and put it in the post?"

"Of course, yes, I'd be delighted!"

And I was. Now that I was ready, truly ready, I did very much want to read *The Velveteen Rabbit*.

‡ ‡ ‡

Darkness draws round us. We are sitting around the dining room table at Old House. Francesco lights a few more candles.

My audience is old for a children's tale: Cecil and Teddy, Agnes, Diccon, Francesco, Cecco, and Pamela. Shane is asleep on the rug, curled up with his blanket.

I begin.

There was once a velveteen rabbit, and in the beginning
he was really splendid. He was fat and bunchy, as a

rabbit should be; his coat was spotted brown and white,
he had real thread whiskers, and his ears were lined
with pink sateen. On Christmas morning, when he sat
wedged in the top of the Boy's stocking, with a sprig of
holly between his paws, the effect was charming. There
were other things in the stocking, nuts and oranges and
a toy engine, and chocolate almonds and a clockwork
mouse, but the Rabbit was quite the best of all.

I lose myself in the story. Though I'd read my own words a
thousand times, rewritten them over and over, now they seem new
again. As if I, too, were meeting the Rabbit and the Skin Horse for
the first time.

"What is REAL?" asked the Rabbit one day, when they
were lying side by side near the nursery fender, before
Nana came to tidy the room. "Does it mean having
things that buzz inside you and a stick-out handle?"
"Real isn't how you are made," said the Skin
Horse. "It's a thing that happens to you. When a child
loves you for a long, long time, not just to play with, but
REALLY loves you, then you become Real."
"Does it hurt?" asked the Rabbit.
"Sometimes," said the Skin Horse, for he was
always truthful. "When you are Real you don't mind
being hurt."
"Does it happen all at once, like being wound up,"
he asked, "or bit by bit?"
"It doesn't happen all at once," said the Skin
Horse. "You become. It takes a long time. That's why it
doesn't happen often to people who break easily, or have
sharp edges, or who have to be carefully kept. Generally,
by the time you are Real, most of your hair has been
loved off, and your eyes drop out and you get loose
in the joints and very shabby. But these things don't

matter at all, because once you are Real you can't be
ugly, except to people who don't understand."
 "I suppose you are real?" said the Rabbit. And then
he wished he had not said it, for he thought the Skin
Horse might be sensitive. But the Skin Horse only smiled.

The little Rabbit yearns so, but he must be patient, he must
wait his turn. Still, he is a very lucky bunny, for the Boy loves
him truly.

Spring came, and they had long days in the garden, for
wherever the Boy went the Rabbit went too. He had
rides in the wheelbarrow, and picnics on the grass, and
lovely fairy huts built for him under the raspberry canes
behind the flower border. And once, when the Boy was
called away suddenly to go out to tea, the Rabbit was
left out on the lawn until long after dusk, and Nana
had to come and look for him with the candle because
the Boy couldn't go to sleep unless he was there. He was
wet through with the dew and quite earthy from diving
into the burrows the Boy had made for him in the
flower bed, and Nana grumbled as she rubbed him off
with a corner of her apron.
 "You must have your old Bunny!" she said. "Fancy
all that fuss for a toy!"
 The Boy sat up in bed and stretched out his hands.
 "Give me my Bunny!" he said. "You mustn't say
that. He isn't a toy. He's REAL!"
 When the little Rabbit heard that he was happy, for
he knew that what the Skin Horse had said was true at
last. The nursery magic had happened to him, and he was
a toy no longer. He was Real. The Boy himself had said it.
 That night he was almost too happy to sleep, and
so much love stirred in his little sawdust heart that it
almost burst. And into his boot-button eyes, that had

long ago lost their polish, there came a look of wisdom
and beauty, so that even Nana noticed it next morning
when she picked him up, and said, "I declare if that old
Bunny hasn't got quite a knowing expression!"

I feel an aching sadness when the doctor declares that the
Rabbit the Boy loves so very much is full of scarlet fever germs and
must be burned.
I really can hardly bear it.

And so the little Rabbit was put into a sack with the old
picture books and a lot of rubbish, and carried out to
the end of the garden behind the fowl-house. That was
a fine place to make a bonfire, only the gardener was
too busy just then to attend to it. He had the potatoes to
dig and the green peas to gather, but next morning he
promised to come quite early and burn the whole lot.
The sack had been left untied, and so by wriggling
a bit he was able to get his head through the opening
and look out. He was shivering a little, for he had always
been used to sleeping in a proper bed, and by this time
his coat had worn so thin and threadbare from hugging
that it was no longer any protection to him. Nearby he
could see the thicket of raspberry canes, growing tall
and close like a tropical jungle, in whose shadow he had
played with the Boy on bygone mornings. He thought of
those long sunlit hours in the garden—how happy they
were—and a great sadness came over him. He seemed
to see them all pass before him, each more beautiful
than the other, the fairy huts in the flower bed, the quiet
evenings in the wood when he lay in the bracken and the
little ants ran over his paws; the wonderful day when he
first knew that he was Real.
He thought of the Skin Horse, so wise and gentle,
and all that he had told him. Of what use was it to be

loved and lose one's beauty and become Real if it all
ended like this? And a tear, a real tear, trickled down
his little shabby velvet nose and fell to the ground.

Someone must rescue the poor Rabbit!

Luckily, I can.

Where the tear falls, a flower grows. It has slender leaves the color of emeralds, and in the center a blossom like a golden cup. The blossom opens, and out of it steps a fairy in a dress of pearl and dew drops. She kisses the Rabbit, and flies off with him to the woods.

"Run and play, little Rabbit!" she said.

But the little Rabbit sat quite still for a moment
and never moved. For when he saw all the wild rabbits
dancing around him he suddenly remembered about his
hind legs, and he didn't want them to see that he was
made all in one piece. He did not know that when the
Fairy kissed him that last time she had changed him
altogether. And he might have sat there a long time, too
shy to move, if just then something hadn't tickled his
nose, and before he thought what he was doing he lifted
his hind toe to scratch it.

And he found that he actually had hind legs!
Instead of dingy velveteen he had brown fur, soft and
shiny, his ears twitched by themselves, and his whiskers
were so long that they brushed the grass. He gave one
leap and the joy of using those hind legs was so great
that he went springing about the turf on them, jumping
sideways and whirling round as the others did, and he
grew so excited that when at last he did stop to look for
the Fairy she had gone.

He was a Real Rabbit at last, at home with the
other rabbits.

When I finish reading, everyone sits quietly. For a moment there is only silence and candlelight, and the faces round the table turned to me.

Then Diccon stands up and claps. "Brava, Margery!"

"Yes—brava, brava!" Everyone claps and cheers, and Cecil comes over and gives me a great hug. She compliments me in her rambly, muddly way.

"It's so absolutely *you*, Margery—children will adore you—I mean *it*, that is, the book . . . !" she says, and we all laugh.

pamela

*L*ike everyone else, Agnes adored Mam. In the city she'd often drop by Macdougal Alley, and they'd sit with their tea for ages, talking. In the kitchen, or out in the alleyway, depending on the weather. Most of the time it was just the two of them—I was usually in my studio—but I was at home with Mam when Agnes appeared on the day *The Velveteen Rabbit* arrived.

It was late fall, and glorious. Shadows fell cool across the pavement. I can still feel the air, newly crisp, smell its freshness.

Agnes was even more animated than usual. She had a big evening planned.

"Got some time to kill, d'you mind if I hang around here with you two? I'm meeting Gene at the Swan, then we're going to some fancy speakeasy on 44th with a swell menu or something. The sort of place Gene can't abide, but he got talked into it, I guess. We're meeting up with some actress and her husband—Gene's thinking of putting her in his new play, says he wants my opinion."

Agnes looked stunning. She sat all liquid and slinky in one of the new sleeveless flapper-style dresses that fell in a straight line to her calf, black chiffon with silver beading, and I could hardly take my eyes off her. She glittered like a chandelier in our homey kitchen. A princess among the scullery maids. Mam was wearing a long skirt and checked apron, and she was chopping onions and garlic. I was in my usual uniform of paint-splattered overalls, making a powdery mess of the Jell-O.

"Carlotta Monterey. What a name—d'you think she made it up for the stage? Isn't it a town or something, in Mexico? California, too, I think. Anyway, she must be persuasive."

Somewhere along the way we heard the mail drop through the door slot with a thud, but no one made a move to get it, not with Agnes entertaining us.

It was dark by the time she stood up to leave. She pulled a silk magenta cloche with a pleated band over her sleek dark hair, threw a wrap of rose-colored velvet rose round her shoulders, and kissed us good-bye.

We heard her voice from the hallway.

"A package for you, Margery. . . ." Agnes returned to bring it to my mother.

Mam looked at the return address. "Oh! Heinemann's. . . ."

She tore off the brown paper.

The Velveteen Rabbit.

There it was, at last.

Agnes stayed while we all admired the beautiful little book, all bound up and shiny and filled with William Nicholson's delightful pictures. Mam kept saying that she just couldn't quite believe it. There was much hugging and kissing and congratulating, and finally Agnes flew off, sparkling, into the night.

Sad, to think of her now, off to meet her nemesis, blissfully ignorant. I don't know if Agnes had a good time out on the town that night, but I do know that the memory of her first meeting with Carlotta Monterey must be seared into her heart forever.

When Agnes left, Mam and I retreated to the kitchen to admire *The Velveteen Rabbit* over and over, to exclaim over every drawing. We were anxious for Daddy to come home and share the excitement.

"Margery . . . Margery," Daddy murmured, as he turned the pages of the book with care. He had such a graceful way with books, such a reverence for them.

"*Straordinario . . . splendido—come sei*, Margery." He meant it. He looked at my mother with love born anew, as if she were a jeweled medieval book he'd just discovered buried in his store room.

Daddy put *The Velveteen Rabbit* down on the table ever so gently. He drew Mam to him. They swayed just a bit, drawing closer to each other, and it did not seem they would let each other go very soon.

I went to my studio.

I began to work on a lithograph of Washington Square. Tried not to think about what I felt.

Extraordinary, like you, Margery.

Agnes flying out into the night to meet her terrible beloved, Gene. Mam and Daddy, forgetting the world sometimes as long as they could touch each other.

I had no one. Whenever would I be really grown and find love and be truly Real? I was stuck fast. I had no hind legs, no way of moving at all. I couldn't run in the meadow with all the other rabbits.

I was jealous.

What was bright and real passed by outside my studio door, and I could not be part of it. I studied with envious eyes all the couples in the Village who walked together entwined and nonchalant and murmuring private things. I wondered what they did when they were alone.

But . . . how could I be jealous of my own *parents*? It didn't seem natural, it was a terrible thing.

margery

*A*ll this dissecting the past—what difference can it make? Pamela can do all the wondering she wants, she can think "if only" a thousand times, but we can't change a thing.

Still, I'm beginning to feel I was wrong this morning to push the whole thing aside. It might help Pamela get through this if she'd say whatever's on her mind. I'd do anything if I thought it could prevent another of her breakdowns. When she wakes, I'll ask her just what she meant, I'll let her talk all she likes.

For Pamela, it could be cathartic. But for me . . . well, it's the future I think about, that's what really troubles me. Pamela often says *I never do anything right.* It's not at all true, of course. When she's herself, she's quite wonderful. A good mother, a brilliant artist, an affectionate daughter. It's just that she loses her way. Her mind betrays her. She goes off, simply breaks apart. . . . Sometimes I get quite desperate, imagining what's in store. I can't help wondering, what if Francesco and I weren't around to pick up the pieces? What would become of Pamela then?

I've got to go check on her.
I'll just push the door open, make sure.

Strange, how she sleeps, her hands crossed over her chest. Her braids, uncoiled, spill down her sides. Watching her makes me feel uneasy. I can't put my finger on it, exactly. She seems locked inside herself.

A wax doll. As if she is . . . not alive.

Well, perhaps just one step in.

I know how absurd it is, behaving as one does with tiny children. You have to be certain they are breathing. You know of course that they are, but . . . well, you just can't walk away until you are sure.

There it is, the slight heave of her chest.

Is she dreaming? Beautiful dreams? Well, it's nice to think so.

How silly to stand here, watching Pamela sleep. A grown woman.

pamela

I heard Mam coming down the hall. I heard her opening the door ever so gently. She thought I was asleep, I'm sure of it. I'm good at that trick. Cecco and I used to have contests when we were little, to see whose eyelids fluttered quickest, giving them away. I always won. I have a knack for it, a secret method. I paint a picture inside my lids, an apple or a Madonna—anything at all. I think of nothing else, and the outside world simply does not exist.

I wish I could hold on to that, make everything disappear. But now that Diccon's returned, the toy train just goes round and round. Well, it won't stop now, I know it.

I wrote many letters to Diccon, I hate to think how many. I was so *determined*. Sometimes I would get a letter in return; more often he wrote to the whole family. He'd always say he would come to visit us just as soon as he could. He was terribly busy, though, writing stories and plays and poems. And he was strapped for money, just scraping by, running articles in the *Weekly Westminster Gazette* and writing book reviews. He couldn't be sure when he'd have a break.

What could I do? Nothing. I would just have to be patient. Diccon would come to New York just as soon as he could.

If ever I had known that almost four years would pass, that I'd be eighteen before I saw Diccon again . . . well, how could I have believed it? How could I have borne it?

Eighteen! A lifetime.

And when I think now . . . if I had known about Nancy. . . .

Well, I would not have been rational at all.

part four

‡‡‡

The Letter: January 11, 1977

428 Lafayette Street
New York City

....

Oh, Lord ... how long have I been pacing?
All this pacing, I know what it means.

I need a cigarette.

There. That's better.

I ought to clean this place up, air it out. It smells of cat and
stale smoke, I'm sure, not that I would notice.

Pamela watches Byzantine slowly eating his way through the
soft pellets. *Poor old Byzantine, he never gets outside.* The cat
lives on the sofa. Once it was a beautiful emerald green, but
now it's more like faded camouflage, mottled green and gray
and white, covered with a silky film of cat hairs. Pamela looks
around the place, and the usual litany of shoulds go around in
her head. *I should get the vacuum out. I should tend to the litter*
box. I should do something about all those dishes piled in the

sink. Soak them, at least. I don't want Lorenzo finding them, feeling he has to clean up after me.

The letter she is trying to avoid centers itself in her mind, plunks itself down like an unwanted guest.

Why did he write? What's to be gained?

I suppose I must open it. Lorenzo, she thinks. It must be about Lorenzo. Does he imagine that I will be the intermediary? What does he expect me to say? Oh, Lorenzo, you'll never guess who I heard from—your father! Isn't that nice, dear?

Well, I won't help. Why should I? If Robert had wanted to find his son he could have. At any time. It would have been no trouble at all. In all these years, we've never moved beyond a mile radius of Greenwich Village. All he had to do was to call long distance information. How many Lorenzo Schlicks are there in Manhattan?

Still, I can't help asking myself over and over, why?

All I can think is this: Robert must be dying. I try to picture the situation, try for just a minute to put myself in his place. He is ill. He putters around his house in the rainy woods of Oregon. Time is running out; he regrets the past; he wants his son to forgive him. He wants to make amends. Amends! I see what he's dreamed up, it runs like a bad play in my head. A frail and hoary old man, leaning on a cane, sees his son for the first time. The cane drops, and the men embrace. The son's bewildered wife and children stand in the background. The son, wet-cheeked, turns to his children. Come meet your grandfather. . . .

God. It makes me cringe. Still, I wouldn't be surprised if something like that is just what he's imagining. Robert always was dramatic.

Pamela studies the handwriting on the envelope. It is still vigorous, not the shaky script of an old man. No, the man is not dying.

She crosses the room to her writing desk, picks up the mother-of-pearl letter opener that her father brought with him from Italy. Such a pretty thing, it always gives her pleasure to hold it. Even now.

The knob on the spindly floor lamp has always been reluctant, but she finally gets it to turn. She settles herself in the chair, runs the silver blade through the top of the envelope.

‡‡‡

September 1, 1944

9 Livingston Place, Stuyvesant Square
New York City

(Midafternoon)

pamela

*T*he arrow flew silently, without mercy, across the ocean. It lodged in my chest.

A letter from Diccon, to tell us about a girl he'd met.

Nancy Stallibrass. Nancy was blonde and serene, he said. Something about the eyes of a fawn. He was quite fond of her, he said, and we'd adore her—she was a poet.

Adore her? I hated her.

It wasn't fair, it really wasn't fair. How could it be fair when I was stuck in New York and she was over there, with him?

Well, he'd only just met this Nancy person, it wouldn't last. If only Diccon and I could just be together again, it would all happen the way it was supposed to. He'd see that the child he remembered had disappeared. Our relationship would be quite different, now.

I scrutinized Diccon's letter. I decided to ignore it. It wasn't important. He never wrote that he was in love or anything like that. I shoved the idea out of my mind.

I buried myself in work, but it wasn't the same as it once had been. Daddy's business was slow, and he was bored, I suppose. He kept coming up with commissions for me that paid well. There was lots of extra work, illustrating and posters. It seemed important to him. But there was no time for painting what was inside of me. The dreams. What seemed most real.

Two more letters from Diccon arrived.

The first one made me laugh, at first. He mocked Nancy's mother, the very proper Philippa Stallibrass who thought Diccon an unworthy suitor for her daughter. He said that Philippa was aghast that Nancy had fallen in love with a writer, a man with no decent income. And to top it all off, he had the ridiculous idea of living in some hovel off in the wilds of Wales, it wasn't civilized, not natural at all. Philippa said that Nancy could never be induced to lead that sort of life.

But Diccon admitted that he wasn't entirely sure himself about what Nancy would make of the rough living conditions, and he'd come up with an idea—he thought it imperative that Nancy spend a week with him at Ysgol Fach, to be sure she could take the isolation. And Mrs. Stallibrass had agreed, provided that Diccon's mother went along as chaperone. *She is, naturally, convinced Nancy will run straight home in horror. . . .*

Diccon's reach was longer than I could have imagined. He picked up my heart like a teacup and hurled it against the wall.

Nancy was going to spend a week at Ysgol Fach. *My* Ysgol Fach! It could not be. I would not let that pale London girl have any of it—not the high grass and hollyhocks blowing in the wind, not the furred dunes, not the lazy sails, not the lacey shadows of apple trees down the hillside, not Diccon's hotcakes!

It wasn't right, it made no sense. Diccon—and Wales—were *mine.*

The second letter was brutal, too. But, in the end, it contained a gift.

Diccon was full of outrage. He wrote that he and Nancy wanted to become engaged, but that her parents, in their ridiculous and stupid way, had made him agree to a six-month separation. He thought it quite absurd, said that all it would prove was the obstinacy of their emotions. Philippa's idea was that they were not even to hear about each other. Diccon said that such an idea was something only a person as crass as herself could conceive.

He was furious, but he had seen no alternative but to agree.

I couldn't believe it. I had to read it many times to be sure.

Diccon was coming to New York.

pamela

On a dull March day in 1925 Mam and I stood at the dock waiting for Diccon to sail into New York Harbor. I was impatient for him to see me. I was *eighteen*, nothing like the child he had seen last. I was still short, but I had my new patent heels that I wore with everything no matter what, even my painting overalls. Just as Mam had promised, my baby fat had disappeared. And I had breasts—rather nice ones, I thought. I'd studied the breasts of lots and lots of nude models of all ages, some nothing more than little points, some large and heavy flopping down low, some—on the young women—sat on thin chests like little domes or circles of armor. Mine were more . . . Courbet-ish. When I'd seen Courbet's *Nude Woman with a Dog* I'd thought, *Hers look like mine.*

Over and over, I'd imagined Diccon's look of surprise. *Pamela, how beautiful you've become! A young woman now!*

How ridiculous, those flights of fancy. I feel my face getting red even now.

What actually happened is this: Diccon hardly greeted me at all. He looked flustered. He was uncharacteristically distant.

"Pamela! You . . . I almost didn't recognize you . . . but I suppose, yes . . . there you are!" And finally, reluctantly, he gave me a hug.

I suppose I'd given him a severe shock. I was hardly the little girl he remembered.

But he was here now, that was the important thing. Now I had plenty of time to show him how very, very different I was.

‡ ‡ ‡

Above Daddy's antiquarian bookstore on West Eighth Street was a tiny garret, with just enough room for a table and chair. Daddy offered it to Diccon to write in, to be alone. At first Diccon was immensely pleased, but he soon found he shared the space with an army of winged ants, a vast column of perpetual motion running from the baseboards up around the window casement. He realized that he simply couldn't work in the stifling, infested room.

Mam had her own writing room in our new place on Grove Street, so her old space in my studio was available. I told Diccon he could work there. He was hesitant; he said he thought he'd be a bother. I said he was being ridiculous, that he might as well have a light-filled space to work in, and, as far as I knew, there were no hordes of strange insects to worry him. And, *for heaven's sake,* there was more than enough space for the two of us.

Diccon and I never did bother each other in the slightest. That was one area in which we were always in perfect accord—we were equally intent in our work.

Diccon was writing a novel. It was concerned with child-hood, he said, but he was quite vague about it. *Oh, it's about some children in Jamaica who end up on a pirate ship. . . .*

I thought I saw many signs of Diccon's affection. I convinced myself I did. The lingering, impish smile he always gave me when I handed him his tea, his incessant interest in my art, his teasing sobriquets. *Pammikins, Pammy-pie, Little Miss Genius.* Often, he commented on my eyes, how they changed color, gray to blue to lavender.

"There—they've done it again—they're almost gray now. . . . Now look—I think I see a bit of violet—remarkable!" He embarrassed me yet made me feel pretty at the same time.

Diccon told many tales of Nancy Stallibrass and her parents. I couldn't help but be amused whenever he described his tribulations with the Stallibrass family, and laughed to the point of tears at his merciless imitations of the haughty Philippa. He talked of

Nancy's sensitivity, her poetry. But he never talked of love. I was sure that Diccon, now back in the heart of our family, was realizing how wrongheaded it was to think of a future as part of the Stallibrass family. They weren't his sort at all. It would be horrible. And it was no good having two *poets* marry.

But an artist and a writer, that would be quite different.

He does not love her, I told myself. *He cannot.*

I saw him posting letters to Nancy. One of them, surely, would tell her that they must break it off. That he realized he'd been in love with me all along. I almost began to feel sorry for Nancy.

Still, I wanted—desperately needed—proof of his love.

pamela

$\mathcal{F}$or the month of April, Daddy rented a rustic, rather shabby house in the Catskills. Diccon went along with us, and set himself up nearby in a small cabin. He buried himself away to write. We didn't see too much of him. I never found a moment to be alone with him at all. Why couldn't he make time to see us once in a while? It was horribly frustrating. Whenever he did show up, he always said he was sorry to be so absent. *But I'm writing furiously now . . . can't stop. . . .*

I knew all about the artistic temperament, the need for peace and quiet and all that, but I had to do *something*. Time was running out.

I walked over to his cabin one day. I knew he wanted to be alone, but . . . he couldn't write *all* the time, he just couldn't. Perhaps he'd like to go for a walk, or for a swim in the river.

"Diccon!" I called out as I approached the cabin, not wanting to startle him. I knocked on the door. "Diccon!" Pushing the door open a bit, I called his name again, more as a question. "Diccon . . . ?" The cabin was still, empty. *Fishing*, I thought, he must be fishing. I could find him by the river. I turned to leave, but then my eye fell on his writing desk. His fountain pen lay across a sheet of paper. Curiosity pulled me across the room. It was wrong, I knew. I shouldn't have been there at all. Perhaps I thought if I knew a bit more about his book, I could talk to him and . . . no, there was no justification for what I did. I was spying, there's no other word for it. I wanted to know Diccon's secrets. And what I found burned itself deep into my consciousness.

Diccon had not been working on his book. Before he capped his pen and pushed his chair back that morning, he'd just finished a letter. There was his signature on the final page. I read the last sentence.

Darling, darling, DARLING, I love you so I feel it will burst out of me suddenly like a thunderclap, & leave my body all cracked up on the grass.

If I read more I have no recollection. I may have read those words once or a hundred times, I don't know. I may have stood there one minute or one hour.

I walked outside in a trance. Diccon's words pounded round and round in my head. *I love you so. . . . Burst out of me like a thunderclap . . . Leave my body all cracked up on the grass.* Oh God, why did I have to read that letter? Did he love that Nancy so very much?

It was too painful to think of, it made me dizzy. Helpless, nonsensical thoughts crowded my brain, jamming up until I had no thought at all, just a sort of buzzing.

Then, a strange thing happened. A thought took hold, breaking through the logjam in my mind. Who, really, was this "darling" person? Well, perhaps it wasn't Nancy at all. Diccon hadn't said *Nancy, I love you so.* No, just "darling, darling, darling." Darling could be anyone, couldn't it? It could be *me.* Perhaps he was writing what he was too afraid, too shy, to say. I began to believe it could be true. After all, what he'd written was exactly the way I felt about him. He must have known that. The longer I considered it the more I believed it *had* to be me he was writing to, and if I never got the letter it would only mean he hadn't the courage to send it. Didn't we all put our deepest feelings down on paper, then later crumple up our thoughts and toss them away?

I was ecstatic. Diccon's words belonged to me. He felt his love for me like a thunderclap!

‡ ‡ ‡

I was sure I was right. And soon enough, I had proof. My spirits soared so . . . they could have lifted me over the tops of the tallest pines.

Diccon invited us all over for a campfire supper. In a huge cast iron skillet, he fried up sliced potatoes and some trout he'd caught in the stream behind his cabin. We drank bootleg whiskey in tin cups. Diccon was in a festive mood. He said he'd had a real breakthrough in his writing and felt like celebrating. He came and sat next to me, and the dank, woolly smell of his lumberman's shirt, laced with pipe smoke and charred fish, filled me with a familiar joy.

This was what I had dreamed of when I first learned he was coming back to America. I was close to Diccon again. He wouldn't stay away any longer, I thought. There was still time for everything to work out.

We all got rather rowdy. At one point Diccon, standing precariously on a rock, held out his cup and shouted out a toast.

"To the Biancos! No fairer, finer people on God's green earth! How I do love the lot of you!"

He sat down next to me again. He knocked his pipe against the log, then brought his face close to mine.

"'Tis true, Pamela, I love the lot of you!"

Of course I knew it was his way of telling me. He meant he loved *me*. I wanted to kiss him right then, his face was so close, but there was my family across the fire and all I could do was smile back at him. Happiness flooded all through me.

Diccon was mine. He'd meant that letter for me. I should never have doubted it.

pamela

*I*n May, when we returned to the city, Diccon stayed on in the mountains.

What was *wrong*? I couldn't understand why Diccon stayed in the country so long. The six months would soon be gone, he'd be going back to England. Was he really going back to Nancy? Would he leave without a word to me? I wrote him several letters, asking when he'd be coming back to the city, but he didn't reply.

I sank low, then.

Such a bleak time. It's hard, remembering it.

I stayed in my studio, sleeping late, rousing myself by noon to work into the small hours of the morning. When I was painting I was all right—it took all of me, brain and heart and hands, and I didn't think of Diccon then. I'd fall into bed exhausted, but when I woke I'd just lie there, staring at the wall, for hours.

Nothing is anything, I'd think. *What is wrong with me, why do I make a mess of everything? Why won't Diccon write? How could he love me, why should he? I'm nothing, nothing at all.*

Sometimes, late in the morning, Mam would come over.

"Goodness, Pamela—still in bed? You're missing a beautiful day!" She'd open the shutters, start some tea, say she'd just come over to let me know Daddy was off to Woodstock, or that she just thought she'd take a break from writing. But she was not just popping in for a visit, I realize that now. I didn't think of her feelings, how worried she must have been.

Why couldn't Diccon answer one of my letters? Why did he have to stay away so long? What was the use of his coming over from England if we never saw him?

I kept thinking of the one jolly evening we'd had, the campfire supper when he'd been his old warm and lovely self. I didn't understand anything. Hadn't he looked at me in that meaningful way, letting me know he loved me, *saying* he loved me? I was sure he had. I went over and over the events of that night, feeling Diccon's face so close, his eyes on me, his grin, his declaration of love, the way he'd repeated it especially for me.

I was terribly confused. Why did it have to be so hard, so mystifying? Why couldn't I have what everyone else had? All those couples in the Village, just outside my studio door, *they* were all quite happy. It seemed so simple—why couldn't Diccon and I be like them?

I wanted to stop thinking about it but I just couldn't.

In my studio I found a broken frame. I sat on the floor, and with my penknife I carefully cut off bits of wood until I had a little pile. I put the wooden shards in an envelope.

My letter was brief.

Dear Diccon,
I am enclosing for you a few pieces of firewood. You
may light your fire with them. I imagine that you are
having quite a nice time.
With love, Pamela

I posted the letter, returned to the studio, and picked up my knife. I cut at the frame, slowly, methodically, until there was nothing left of it but shavings.

pamela

*D*iccon never answered my letter. He ignored me entirely. When he finally did return to Greenwich Village it was only for the briefest moment—he'd booked passage back to London in two days' time. He did allow us to give him supper on his last night in the city. It didn't take him long to get around to the subject of Nancy. He was positively alight with joy.

"Well, I've done it—I've fulfilled my part of the bargain—and I've managed to write up a storm. Philippa has no grounds for complaint now . . . looks like I'll be a married man soon!"

I was silent while everyone around me chatted cheerfully, as if there were something to celebrate. Mam cast furtive glances at me. She must have been awfully worried by my silence; she must have been alarmed by my face of stone. She was powerless to stop me.

I pushed back my chair and stood up. Everyone looked at me in astonishment.

How I wish I could take back what happened next. . . .

I screamed at Diccon.

"I hope in future all your hotcakes burn and that all your children are acrobats!"

There was silence. Utter, terrible silence.

What had I done? What had I said?

I had no rational thought. I was an animal. I ran from the table.

The next day I stayed in bed. I lay there unmoving.

I could not move, for a sorrow heavy as a boulder was strapped to my back. Pressing on me, suffocating me.

Mam came over, sat by me. Asked if she could do anything at all. I knew that she wanted to unbuckle the straps, lift the burden from me, but it would not be lifted.

I shook my head. Slowly. Even that seemed an effort.

The heaviness was unrelenting, now clamping itself around me like a full body cast. I couldn't raise myself up.

Anyway, I didn't really see the point.

What good was anything? What good did it do to be grown up, to be pretty, to feel desire . . . if no one desired me? I was nothing to Diccon. I was nothing to anyone.

I'm smaller than the smallest ant. Someone should go just ahead and step on me. I'd feel better then.

I'm nothing, nothing at all.

‡ ‡ ‡

I won't think of Diccon. There is nothing to think about. You can't really think of what you don't have and if I try I might start pacing again and I couldn't bear that and I couldn't let Mam see me that way.

I'll think of the paintings. I can turn through them in my head like pages in a book. Each one crystallized. The chandelier. The pomegranate. The maze. Children like statues, frozen. I've painted them a million times.

All those ghosts. I'm afraid of the ghosts, but at the same time I want more than anything for the ghosts to return so that I can begin.

Why don't I just go ahead and paint, what is wrong with me?

How can I tell my mother about these things? Why do I talk and talk and say nothing?

margery

I wonder . . . *is* Pamela dreaming?

Well, no matter. Sleeping dreams are fine, you can pay attention to them or not. It's more the waking ones I worry about.

Everyone says dreams are wonderful things. *Hang on to your dreams*, people say. But that's not always good advice, not when the dreams you're clinging to are no more than a pretty bunch of balloons, with nothing at all inside.

I don't know why it is but sometimes you have to get quite far ahead before you can look back and see clearly how things were. Now I look back and there's Pamela, a young girl clutching a handful of ribbons, ribbons rising up to the sky, to a host of bright balloons. She runs everywhere with these balloons, and if one should slip away . . . well, she finds another somehow. She has to keep her dreams intact.

When I think how she must have collected dream upon dream, storing them up in her mind, sure that she would have Diccon in the end. . . . Well, it's no wonder she shattered so completely.

pamela

I mustn't bottle things up inside, I know it, Henry taught me
that, at the hospital. But that night I never thought of Henry. I
was simply too far gone.

*I'm smaller than the smallest ant. Someone should go just
ahead and step on me. I'd feel better then. I'm nothing, nothing at all.*

Was that what I was thinking when I ran out in the rain? I can't
remember. Probably. I remember feeling that way most of the time.

It was a hard rain. How it rattled on the skylight in my studio!
Insistent. Tapping out messages to me. It would not let up.

I ran out in the rain because my painting was wrong.

I ran out in the rain because of the money.

I ran out in the rain because of Daddy.

I ran out in the rain because of Diccon.

I ran out in the rain because I was eighteen and I was crazy.

I ran out in the rain because my painting was wrong.

Daddy had arranged for several shows that year—in Los
Angeles and Chicago, and at the Knoedler Gallery in New York.
They drew good crowds. Critics referred to me as an "established"
artist. Perhaps the reviews were less exuberant than they once had
been. Well, I was no longer something new and extraordinary. The
child prodigy had grown up.

My pictures sold reasonably well, I think. I never really kept
track. Whenever I got a check from a gallery I just signed it over
to Daddy. I could see he was not as happy, though, as he had been

in the early days. I suppose he wished for exactly what I didn't want—that I could be a child prodigy forever.

That day, he came into the studio, gave me a hug, said he was proud of me, did I know that?

I nodded. I even believed him.

He went over to the Victrola. He bent down to the stack of records, running his finger down until he found his favorite Puccini. *Madama Butterfly.*

I made tea, and we sat together on the sofa.

Un bel di. One beautiful day . . .

Poor Butterfly! She imagines her love returning to the harbor. She will wait for him on the hill, and he will appear, calling her the old names. *Little one. Dear wife. Orange blossom.* But he never comes. More than anything I wanted to be happy sitting there with Daddy, but the music and Butterfly's tragic story filled me with an ineffable sorrow. All I could think of was Diccon. Diccon, who couldn't even manage to leave the Catskills to see me. I tried to stop from thinking how it all might turn out.

I think there is no sadder tale than Butterfly's.

Daddy tried to get me to sing with him as we often did, but I just couldn't. When the first side of the record ended, Daddy didn't turn it over. He lifted the needle off the disc and set the arm down ever so gently, with the same great care he took when he turned the pages of his beloved, ancient books. He kissed my forehead and left. I didn't say a thing.

I think he'd wanted to talk about my work, give me some advice. I pictured him telling Mam he was going over to my studio, heard her say, *Why don't you just spend some time with her, forget her art for a while.* It was just a feeling I had.

I ran out in the rain because of the money.

My father was restless a lot in those days. He was always so full of ideas, I couldn't keep up with them all. He'd come banging through the studio door, and I'd wonder—what would be on his mind this time? A commission he'd found, or an exhibition he wanted me to see. *Come along, Pamela, just to get a few ideas, a new track, perhaps?* And off we would go.

He kept talking to me about what the public wanted, which were the most prestigious galleries, who was selling what. *I want to show you what Joseph Stella's doing these days, Pamela . . . the color. . . .* His talk made me uneasy. I knew he dreamed of big sales. I suppose it troubled me more than I knew at the time. I didn't want to talk of sales, I wanted only to paint as I wished. But . . . the money . . . I never could shake off the idea. And it didn't help that Gertrude had dropped by the previous week and mentioned, all nonchalant, that one day in the coming months, she wasn't sure when, there was a young artist from France coming over with his family and he'd need a place to stay, so we'd be wise to keep an eye out for apartments, to think about our next move.

Daddy and I never, ever talked of it, the money. But it was always there, trembling in the air between us, and when he left the room it hung over me, then dropped, catching me as a net.

I ran out in the rain because of Daddy.

It's true I would have done anything to feel again as I did that time after the exhibition in Turin, when the soldier came to the door with the box, the letter from d'Annunzio inside. Daddy, holding that letter as if he were Moses just handed the Ten Commandments. And when he put it down at last he beamed at me. Then he held his arms out to me, and it was just then, as my father lifted me high overhead, that I saw the brilliant icon. I painted it in my mind: a child stands surrounded by a myriad of golden rays—Mam and Daddy and Cecco, awash in the brilliant light, turn towards me; beyond my family are shimmering circles of admiring strangers—a great expanding halo.

I clung to this icon for years, carrying it with me everywhere, wearing it as a locket round my neck.

The icon was false. Gold shines forever, but I was not made of gold.

I ran out in the rain because of Diccon.

Diccon had deserted me.

But . . . I would not believe it.

Why would he never see what was right in front of him? Why was he so stubborn? I didn't understand one thing.

Diccon didn't love me. He loved Nancy.

Nancy! Why did she have to exist?

He was going back to England. *She* would have everything. I would have nothing. Nothing. Nothing. *Nothing.*

margery

That summer when Diccon came back to New York to spend his enforced six-month separation from Nancy, Pamela may have been eighteen, but she remained very much a child.

Still, by the time Diccon arrived, I was sure she understood. Diccon was *engaged*. There was no question. We had all discussed it. It suppose it was foolish of me, but I did think she had accepted that Diccon had found a girl he wanted to marry. She *seemed* to. She seemed quite fine to me. In fact, just before we left the Catskills, when we had that campfire dinner over at Diccon's, she was as jolly as I'd ever seen her.

Then Diccon came back to the city, and it was a horror. That dinner at our place. Pamela losing control, as if a great hand had given her a turn, and she went spinning like a top across the table, right over the edge. No one was quick enough to catch her. Screaming about hotcakes and acrobats! What on earth did she mean by that? She was not herself at all, she was a girl *possessed*.

It only went downhill after that. Blackness churned inside her for months, unrelenting. There was nothing I could do.

You could almost feel it yourself, the heaviness.

I watched over her, but nothing I did seemed to help. Then one day I got a call, and thought I saw a possible way out, a tiny light in all the darkness. Anne Carroll Moore, the children's librarian at the New York Public Library—a good friend of mine ever since *The Velveteen Rabbit* was published—called to say that her old friend Bertha Mahony, the proprietress of a children's bookstore in Boston, was having a series of artists' exhibitions . . . and, well, she said, it seemed natural to ask me if I thought Pamela would consider participating. Anne had no idea of Pamela's trouble. She couldn't have known that to me the idea seemed a gift from the gods. Something, anything, to get the girl going in the right direction.

pamela

I ran out in the rain because I was eighteen and I was crazy. It is a very dark time. Shadowy arms reach out, and I brush them away at first, but then they seize me, and I know they won't let go. I am not myself. The pain pulls me under.

For days, I can't seem to work. Instead, I pace around the studio. I'm in a muddle, I can't understand anything. I feel so terribly low. I feel not much of anything at all.

Late one afternoon, as night descends, I pace and pace. I don't turn on the lights.

The rain taps out messages. Tells me things. *Stop all this. Leave it. You are nothing, nothing at all. Just give it up. Leave it all.*

I listen to the voices. I have no choice. I cannot explain it.

A strange headiness overcomes me, almost a dizziness, like when I smoked my first cigarettes. The feeling expands in me, filling me, lifting me.

I think that I can *fly*.

With no thought in my mind I grab the money I'd stashed in the little kitchen drawer and run out into the night.

The wind hits when I turn onto Macdougal Street. Automobiles run through rivers at the side of the road, pushing curtains of water onto the sidewalk. The rain slams into me, my overalls are wet and heavy against my body. My braid flops like a dead fish down my back. The lights of the city are all in a blur.

Under a streetlamp I see the mass of color. I head straight for it. Flowers! I buy bunches and bunches of flowers.

I walk fast, careful to give other pedestrians a wide berth. I'm crazy with worry, terrified that my stick-out handle might knock into people, push them down. I have to be so careful! I am quick, jumping to the left or right.

The words in my head are all crackly. I don't think I say them aloud.

"What is REAL?" asked the Rabbit. "Does it mean having things that buzz inside you and a stick-out handle?"

"What is REAL?" asked the Rabbit. "Does it mean having things that buzz inside you and a stick-out handle?"

"What is REAL?" asked the Rabbit. "Does it mean having things that buzz inside you and a stick-out handle?"

I shove flowers at people who speed towards me. Some take them, some turn away from me and the flowers fall down to the wet pavement.

Fear seizes me. Fear of the darkness that chases me, that has nothing to do with night.

I walk eastward, faster and faster, until I have to stop. My eyes hurt. I put my hand up in front of my face to block out the network of lights flying across the Brooklyn Bridge, dropping into the river. To block out the steel cords like giant harp strings curving up to the sky, up and down again like a roller coaster. The dizziness returns.

I have to turn away.

I lie on my side, crouched, all taut. Mam rubs my head with a towel.

"Better now?" she says, quietly. It's almost a whisper. "Let's just get you out of these wet things."

She has trouble prying open my hands that press up in fists under my chin. She loosens my fingers, and I breathe in the cool and earthy smell of smashed stems.

I sleep fitfully for days, the dreams repeating themselves, all of rabbits and children and sunlit meadows and Diccon holding me, and they sound like good dreams, but they aren't.

"Real isn't how you are made," said the Skin Horse. "It's a thing

that happens to you. When a child loves you for a long, long time, not just to play with, but REALLY loves you, then you become Real."

"Real isn't how you are made," said the Skin Horse. "It's a thing that happens to you. When a child loves you for a long, long time, not just to play with, but REALLY loves you, then you become Real."

"Real isn't how you are made," said the Skin Horse. "It's a thing that happens to you. When a child loves you for a long, long time, not just to play with, but REALLY loves you, then you become Real."

I put my hands over my ears.

margery

$\mathcal{P}$amela had no interest in the children's bookstore. She was extremely reluctant, just as I'd expected. But in the end she gave in. It was only to please me, I knew that, but still I hoped it might pull her out of her trouble.

In January, we took the train to Boston.

It was a frigid Sunday morning. We battled icy winds and slippery sidewalks as we made our way to Boylston Street. Bertha welcomed us into her bookstore, pride lighting up her face. It was a very pleasing face, rounded and soft with that delicate flushing that is so attractive. She wore her warm brown hair piled loosely on top of her head, and her brown eyes almost closed when she smiled, like Alice's Cheshire Cat, but more cuddly, so that you immediately felt she was a friend. She looked to be just about my age.

Since it was Sunday and the store was officially closed, we had it all to ourselves. Bertha gave us a tour, and I saw that she had reason to be proud. It was a beautiful place. The bookshop had once been a private home, and it was naturally cozy and welcoming. There were wood-burning fireplaces to read by, and a winding staircase leading up to a long gallery on the second floor landing, a natural exhibition space. The drawings and paintings that Pamela had sent ahead were uncrated but still wrapped in brown paper. Bertha had arranged them in small piles.

Also upstairs was the children's reading room. A wall of windows reached from floor to ceiling, offering a bird's-eye view of the Public Garden and the lagoon where the Swan Boats would glide silently by come spring. On the other side of the room was Green-away House, a huge dollhouse. Bertha explained that Alice-Heidi, the official bookstore doll, lived there. The façade of the house was completely open so that children could easily reach in and rear-range furniture at will.

Pamela walked over and looked in all the rooms.

"But where is she?" she asked.

"Alice-Heidi? She's not there? Oh, she must be right . . . *there* she is, one of the children must have been reading to her." Bertha picked up the blonde-haired doll from a little wooden chair and set her down in front of the dollhouse.

We returned downstairs, and Bertha set out some coffee in a sitting area by one of the fireplaces. *The Velveteen Rabbit* sat on the little table in front of us, along with Anne Carroll Moore's new book, *Nicholas, A Manhattan Christmas Story*—the story of a little wooden Dutch boy visiting the city.

Pamela barely spoke. After a while, she excused herself and went upstairs to unwrap her artwork.

Bertha and I chatted about her business and about the latest crop of children's books, but after a bit she looked at me almost apologetically.

"Is Pamela all right, Margery? She seems rather . . . tired, perhaps?"

I was about to answer when I thought I heard Pamela's voice.

Startled, I asked, "Is there anyone else up there?"

"No, not a soul," Bertha said.

We went upstairs. Pamela was holding a drawing. And she was talking to it.

Aren't you a nice fairy, but why don't you . . . should you . . . hide behind that tree, if you can find that tree . . . run! Run! Run! Why it's right there, will you please move now . . . ? Why don't you hide behind that tree . . . ? Do you think there's a ghost . . . ? Are you afraid to see a ghost . . . just run . . . run!

I was too stunned to make a move at first. Through the huge windows dark winter clouds skittered across the sky. The light in the room flickered. Pamela all bright, then shadowed. Then bright again.

Pamela put the drawing down. She walked over to Green-away House. I watched, detached, as if I were watching a play, as she pulled out Alice-Heidi and set her gently down on the rug. She took a chair from the dollhouse and set it next to the doll. Then a desk, and a bathtub. She picked up Alice-Heidi again. *Oh I don't know, I don't know, I don't know. . . . She can wear the rose-colored dress. She can wear the rose-colored dress; tell her to wear the rose-colored dress. . . . Oh, is it lost? Have you lost it?*

I woke up from my stupor and went over to my daughter and put my arm around her and held her to me.

I looked at Bertha and the compassion in her eyes unnerved me.

"She really has been terribly overworked lately. . . . I'm very sorry, Bertha, but I must get her home right away, I'm afraid."

"Of course, Margery. Of course."

We managed to find a taxi. It was only once we were settled in the back that I noticed the tears running down Pamela's face. I pressed my handkerchief into her hand. I didn't ask her why she was crying, what was it all about, because I knew she couldn't have answered.

I was afraid that I knew, though. The tears of even a young girl can be the tears of an exhausted soul.

margery

$\mathcal{A}$t home in Grove Street—we'd had to move from Macdougal Alley to make room for the artist from France—Pamela moved trancelike around the rooms, picking up small objects—pencils, ashtrays, china curios, eyeglass cases, candles, silverware—and lining them up in neat rows. She had to make them perfectly straight. It was never quite perfect. She straightened the rows over and over.

She spent a week in bed. She refused to eat.

Sara called to invite her to dinner. I was surprised that Pamela agreed, and worried once she had left the apartment. She didn't seem right at all.

Late in the evening the phone rang. Pamela wasn't feeling well, Sara said. Francesco had to go and retrieve her.

She'd had too much wine, that was obvious. But that was hardly the problem. She kept us up all night, talking and weeping incessantly. Nine hours it went on. *Nine hours.* How is a thing like that possible?

She took to her bed again. She was delirious for days. Feverish. Talking gibberish. Francesco and I were frightened.

As soon as we could, when she was calmer, Francesco and I brought her to a physician. The doctor's words should not have surprised me, yet I felt each one as a jolt. *Nerves. Hysteria. Breakdown.* We all agreed—there seemed to be no choice—that Pamela should be admitted to Four Winds, a hospital in the New York countryside whose specialty was ministering to those of fragile mental health. The doctor said it was unlikely that she'd leave before the end of summer.

Four Winds, Pamela said. *It's a lovely name.*

margery

*I*t seemed such a long trip. We'd borrowed the Studebaker from Ira Gershwin, a regular customer at Francesco's store who'd become a great friend. Francesco was nervous—he had little experience driving in America. I tried to help, kept studying the Standard Oil map, but I was unused to navigating with maps, and we got lost. Under other circumstances, it would have been amusing, a great adventure. But tension permeated the automobile, swelling with every mile. I should have thought it would burst the top right off.

We rode mainly in silence. Francesco occasionally hummed softly. I kept flipping the map, folding and refolding it. I don't think Pamela said a word during the whole trip.

Eventually, we found Katonah, a pretty little village, and asked a policeman if he could direct us to Four Winds. He pointed ahead, said it was just down the road.

There was a long drive up a hill, and there it was. It looked more like a very nice hotel than a hospital. There was a lovely main house with a porte cochere with columns of stone.

It was dark inside. A highly polished wood floor. A large office. Paperwork to fill out. Then we all traipsed down the hall to Pamela's room. It wasn't a bad room. Two windows at the end looked over the high lawn behind the main building and to the woods beyond. The leaves were at their last bit of color. The room smelled of pine and ammonia and the mix of starch and faint perfume emanating from the nurse who never left our side.

We met Pamela's new doctor. Dr. Boardman. *Thank God,* I thought, *he seems a very caring man.* It was more his manner than anything, for he said very little, just that it would take time to sort things out, that Pamela would most likely not be home until summertime. But he would be sure to keep us apprised. We could call anytime we liked.

And then it was time to leave. Pamela was stoic. Or, more truthfully, she was like stone. We hugged her, smiling, assuring her that she'd be ever so much better and that we would write all the time and see her whenever we were allowed.

I was shaky as I walked to the car. Francesco fumbled a bit with starting the engine. We were both silent.

Eighteen, I kept thinking. *She's just an eighteen-year-old girl and how has she ended up here? How have we all ended up here?* I could not stop thinking that somehow I could have prevented this from happening.

I did not have a grip on my feelings. *We've abandoned her, it's like leaving your dog at a shelter. What have we done. . . ?*

The tension we'd felt on the drive up now turned to sadness, and I rolled the window down a bit to let some out. Hills and long driveways and stone walls and almost-bare trees rolled by as my throat tightened. The tears came.

I would have said, *I don't cry.* I never did cry. Not even on that gray afternoon when the carriage came for Daddy and I watched, dry-eyed, from my bedroom window. Or later, at the cemetery. I kept my eyes down, studied the laces on my boots when I heard that terrible sound, the thud, thud, thud. The dirt falling on my father.

But now I found I could not stop myself, and before I knew it I was sobbing. I just couldn't stop. Francesco had to pull over. He'd never seen me like that. He put his arms around me, held me tight. *It was the only thing to do, Margery.*

pamela

I was crazy.

Running out in the rain all night, talking to pictures, ranting at poor Sara and her friends, talking for nine hours.

What could they do but send me away?

There were no patterns on the walls at Four Winds, no pretty paper to occupy me. Just the mark on the ceiling—a stain like a sepia-ink drawing spread out from the far corner. It looked like a sailboat heeling in a strong wind.

I lay on my bed, imagined myself on the boat, sailing, sailing away to someplace I'd never been. Greenland. Tahiti. The coast of Africa.

I stood at the window, watched the seasons change.

Sometimes I'd venture out to the glassed-in porch, hold a magazine or book in my lap. I tried to read, to write letters, even to draw, but I could do none of those things.

One day I got a letter from Daddy.

My own dear Pamela,
I think of you so often and wish you were back home. I
know you will be back with us soon enough!
So many people ask about you, and the proposals
for your artwork sit here gathering dust. Mr. Sell at
Harper's has sent along an especially interesting idea
for you to do a poster for him. There is quite a lot
of money in that sort of work, if you should feel like

tackling it without any strain to yourself—it would be
an amusing job with quite a few greenbacks attached. I
am enclosing his letter so that you can ponder it.

I didn't read the letter from Mr. Sell. I folded it up along with Daddy's letter and put them both in the drawer of my bedside table.

I felt a pain at the back of my head that traveled down, clenching my neck and shoulders. I curled up on my bed. I squeezed my eyes shut and tried to forget the letter. I tried to name the regents of England in chronological order, then the Presidents of the United States. I didn't do a very good job. I looked out the window, and thought of nothing at all.

After a while I felt a little better. I was beginning to read some things, a few magazine articles. One day I found a new issue of *Harper's* on one of the wicker tables on the porch and idly thumbed through the pages. I stopped at a story by D. H. Lawrence called "The Rocking Horse Winner." The title caught my attention. I thought of Blue, our old rocking horse in Paris. I settled back on the sofa and read.

But soon I was sitting forward, all stiff. The story was horrid. I wanted to throw the magazine down, but I just couldn't. I felt ill.

And so the house came to be haunted by the unspoken
phrase: There must be more money! There must be
more money! The children could hear it all the time
though nobody said it aloud.

I gripped the magazine, powerless to stop. I read, horrified, as the boy on the rocking horse rode to his death. I sat there rigid and blind and deaf. My mind went black.

What happened next I don't remember. I suppose a nurse—perhaps it took two of them—brought me to my room.

I spent days and days in bed. I don't know how many. I wept. Terrible, improbable images plagued me. Huge rocking horses threatened to crush me, red-and-black-checked lumber shirts flew through the air, stacks of money soaked in puddles of paint. The sheets tormented me; I thought they were made of paper or canvas, and I clawed at them, tearing them into strips, tearing the strips into squares.

When I wasn't hallucinating, I just stared at the ceiling, paralyzed by a ceaseless drone of painful thoughts.

All the same thought, really: *I am nothing.* It was a wretched chorus. *I am a failure. What good am I to anyone at all? I can't do it all; I can't do anything. I've never been anything, not really. I've let everyone down. I hate the way I am.*

Dr. Boardman was in charge of my case. He told me to call him Henry. I wasn't very helpful to him, not for a long time. He asked many, many questions.

Tell me why you're here, Pamela. What happened on the porch, can you try to remember? Your mother—are you close to your mother? How about your father, can you tell me a bit about him? Let's talk about your childhood for a moment, shall we? What is it like being a celebrity, how do you feel about that? What can you remember that made you happiest? Saddest? Is there someone you feel has hurt you in some way?

There were long stretches of silence between Henry's questions; he always waited patiently for me to answer. It must have been very trying for him. I would look into his eyes and then beyond. It wasn't that I hadn't listened, I knew what he was asking me. Speech was simply too difficult for me. So I was silent. Or worse, out of the blue I'd go off on a rant on the bloody ridiculousness of Prohibition, or the life of Buddha, or some other crazy thing.

Over time I developed a fondness for Henry, with his avuncular manner, his silver hair decorating his head like crimped tinsel, and his habit of removing his glasses to clean them, then looking straight at me as if he could see me better. *But it wasn't true, was it?* I'd think. *Why did he wear glasses at all, then?* While he talked to me I'd study his eyes, eyes that seemed vulnerable, unhappy that their owner had exposed them so abruptly. But they were warm eyes, almost black, and they pulled me in.

I found my voice again, and began to answer Henry's questions. He asked me about my friends, what sort of friends I had. I explained that I'd never been to school so I didn't have friends in the ordinary way. I told him about the group of artists over at the Whitney Studio Club on West Fourth Street.

Henry asked me about my family.

I talked easily about Cecco and how close we had always been and how I missed him beyond bearing when he went away to boarding school, and how now, in America, I felt I was losing him a little. He was so busy with his friends at Columbia. How when he came to the Village he'd go off fencing with Daddy or just help him out at the bookshop, and how I wished I could be with them, then. I talked easily about Mam and how she loved Cecco and me and always managed to make things so cheery, how she helped us collect silver paper from chocolates to wallpaper the dollhouse, how she forgave me when I ruined my Easter hat, how she taught us to make boats and swans and tea kettles out of paper.

I began to tell Henry most anything I felt like.

I talked about Diccon and Wales and that I'd planned to marry him since I was thirteen, how he seemed to belong to me. How I never knew how to behave around him, how his behavior mystified me. How he got engaged to Nancy and went back to England.

I didn't talk much about Daddy, but one day I showed Henry the letter I'd stuck in the drawer.

How did I feel about that, Henry wanted to know. Did I feel my father was pressuring me? I avoided his eyes. I felt stupid. I wanted Henry to know, but I knew I would never talk about it. *Oh, no*, I said. *That's just the way he is.* I didn't want to discuss Daddy, though Henry always told me that everything was completely confidential, no one but the two of us would know about our conversations; he only asked me questions to try to help me. I couldn't have answered Henry truthfully anyway, because I never formed the words even to myself.

Henry tried mightily, in his gentle way, to get me to talk about Daddy. Eventually, though, he had to change the subject. Or he seemed to. He asked if I thought I was ready to paint, if I wanted to. Yes, I thought. Yes, I *wanted* to. A painting of a dancer. She invaded my thoughts during the day and my dreams at night. A dancer who feels lost, stuck, as if in a maze. Who, every time she thinks she's discovered an exit, collapses at the brink. The exit is a bottomless abyss. She moves woodenly. The colors are as dark and layered as nature at night.

Do you think you'd like to paint, Pamela? Do you feel ready? Henry's questions hung in the air.

"I want to." I looked past him to the window. "I can't, though. I don't know why . . . I just can't."

Henry nodded. He was quiet for a while. Then he leaned towards me and spoke with a quiet urgency. He talked about how there were many different ways to be strong, how there were times to do things and times not to do things, how I could say *no* if I wished to. It would help, not hurt, he assured me. *I promise you, Pamela, the world will not end.*

It was such a short letter, but it cost me dearly. I reworked each sentence over and over.

> *Dear Daddy,*
> *I can't draw very well at present. I have made an*
> *attempt once or twice but without success. I'll try and*
> *do my best under the circumstances. You may send me*
> *pen and inks, but I really cannot work well here, and it*
> *will be quite a while before I am home again.*

I sent him much love. Even so, I almost didn't post the letter for fear it would upset my father, for fear I would disappoint him.

pamela

*H*enry seemed quite interested to know about the different sorts of men I'd known, what I thought of them. I really didn't have too much to say, beyond Diccon. I mentioned Gene in passing, didn't say much. Of course the more I clammed up on a subject, the more Henry would return to it, ever so patiently. *I noticed you went quiet the other day when Gene's name was mentioned. . . . Is there something you'd like to tell me about him?* I'd shake my head or say, *Oh, no, nothing in particular.* But eventually we'd get round to it.

And so, in the end, I told Henry about what happened that night in Truro.

Peaked Hill Bars, Agnes and Gene's beach home in Truro, was a former Coast Guard barracks. A surprise gift from Gene's father. It was charming in its rickety way, but it felt terribly precarious. The beach had eroded perilously close, and the ocean lapped at the deck even on calm days. Agnes said Gene dearly loved the old, amphibious beach house. He found it a haven for his writing. The roar of the sea, waves knocking against the underside of the house—these cut him off from domestic sounds and gave him peace.

I didn't work well in Truro. I wasn't comfortable there, and drew more out of habit than inspiration. I did some angry-looking charcoals of dunes with sea oats bending in the wind, and a few line drawings of Shane. One sketch I liked: Agnes on the beach in her bathing suit, arms wrapped around long legs tucked up to her chin.

My feelings about Peaked Hill Bars were quite mixed. In some ways it felt more alive than Old House in Point Pleasant—the wind blew all wild, the beach was just out the front door, sea grass and cattails danced on the high dunes, and doors were always slamming shut as Shane ran in and out. But the very closeness of the ocean was disturbing. On fine days it was all right. But at night, or on stormy days when great waves battered the fragile structure, I was fearful. I couldn't help feeling that Peaked Hill Bars would simply be washed out to sea, carrying me helpless aboard.

I asked to sleep in the smallest room in the back. It was similar to my room under the eaves at Old House, with a reassuring landlocked view of sandy road, shrubs, tall grasses, and beach plums. There I felt protected from the dark rages of the sea. But I was not protected, it turned out, from the dark rages of Agnes's marriage.

One night Agnes and Gene walked into town. There was a party.

I was awakened by the sound of voices.

I knelt by the low window under the eaves. At first I saw only the high moon and the silvery light polishing the grasses in the stillness. Then two people appeared on the sandy path: Gene was walking unsteadily ahead of Agnes and occasionally turned back to yell something at her. Agnes appeared to be sobbing. I saw Gene gesturing. I could only catch a few of his words, ". . . here now. Are you happy? . . . that stupid ass of yours inside."

Agnes stood still. I flinched, feeling Gene's violence as he suddenly lunged at Agnes and yanked her by the arm. Agnes staggered forward as he pulled at her.

"Fucking *bitch!*"

Gene slapped Agnes hard across the face. Horrified, I watched as Agnes slowly slumped to the ground and sat silently. The sobbing had stopped. Gene stood over her.

"Jesus Christ, Agnes. You fucking drive me fucking crazy."

‡ ‡ ‡

The next day Gene and Agnes came downstairs as Mrs. Clark, Shane's nurse, was putting out the afternoon tea. I'd just come in from a swim; Shane sat at the kitchen table eating gingersnaps. Gene ruffled his son's dark-gold hair.

"Good?"

Shane looked up at his father shyly and nodded. Gene and Agnes exchanged a smile.

Gene turned to me.

"A swim – excellent idea! How is it today?"

I couldn't look at him. I mumbled into my teacup, "It's all right."

Gene laughed loudly.

"Moody, like the rest of us," he said.

"Did you ever mention this to anyone? Your mother?" Henry asked.

"No," I said, "I never did."

I had wanted to. I didn't want to keep it to myself, but when I thought about it, I knew I couldn't tell anyone. If I told Mam, she would, naturally, tell Daddy. And I knew what Daddy would do. He would be furious, and he would confront Gene. *What kind of man hits his wife?* And I was very sure that Agnes wouldn't want me to tell. She would be exposed, then. I didn't know much about these things, but I understood somehow how important it was to Agnes that everything looked to be all rosy with her and Gene. If I told what I saw, it would be hell for her, it would cause problems in the family, and she would never forgive me.

pamela

*H*enry helped me with so many things. He even helped me with my letter-writing.

In the middle of February, I sat at my desk in my hospital room, pen and paper set out. It was snowing again. White sky, white land, white trees. The firs were heavy, their lowest branches collapsing sorrowfully to the ground under their weight of snow.

It was the third straight day of snow. And the third day I'd tried to write a letter to Diccon. Each time I wrote, the lines slanted down severely from left to right. I'd write a while then look at the page, surprised by the hill of lines. It wasn't right. *Why were the words coming out that way?*

There was a brisk knock on the door and the now familiar "Hal-ooo Miss Bianco!" in Henry's jovial bass voice.

Oh good, maybe he can help with this letter-writing business.

And he did, just like that. He took one look at my writing and said, *I'll be right back.* When he came back he had a notepad in his hand.

"This ought to set you straight!" he said. It was a pad of squared paper.

I had no trouble after that.

After Henry left, I picked up my pen with renewed energy.

Dear Diccon,
At last I am well enough to write to you. I couldn't write
any sooner because my handwriting went slopewise

down the page, untidily like a steep hill and you would
have wanted to hitch it up straight on a crane with
hooks. This will be the first real letter I have written for
two months. I can keep my lines straight now because
Henry taught me to by means of squared paper. I've had
a most exciting time. It started by my getting measles
towards the end of November then about a month
ago I had only been up for a few days and I went to
have supper with my friend Sara and I hadn't eaten
any food for two days and I would burst into tears if
the telephone rang—to make a long story short they
gave me two glasses of port for supper and I guess you
know how wine affects me—but I didn't want anyone
to know I was drunk so I walked very rapidly round
and round all the chairs as though nothing were the
matter just silently weeping and giggling—then I told
Sara I wanted to wash the dishes for her, so I shut
myself in the kitchen, and drank some more wine, and
then really I don't remember what happened except
that I was shrieking and yelling and I was put to bed,
and I lost an entire week, just blank, and then I talked
cuckoo talk incessantly for days, and threw glasses of
water at people, and there were lumber shirts, and boxes
of powder floating around the room and I shrieked
because I couldn't catch them—and one day I talked for
nine hours without stopping. And now I go on writing
in the same way and can't stop, but don't read it if it
bores you. I tore up three pillowcases and two sheets. I
tore a pillowcase into one inch squares one night and
explained to the nurse that I was making book jackets!
And when Henry asked me what my symptoms were I
insisted on telling him the life history of Buddha from
beginning to end. I am quite sane now though you may
not think so—and only go funny for a few minutes every
two or three days. Now I have no interest in life and I'm

about sick of everything most of the time—but thank goodness I did get ill—I've felt so nervous and demented for years, and always wished I'd go crazy and get rid of everything. The trouble Henry says is that I've always kept things to myself, everything—and that is bad—it's the worst thing to do, never do it—if anything worries you talk it right out with someone, anybody it doesn't matter who, just talking about it puts it right somehow. That's what I shall do in future, only I would much rather there wasn't any future. There were millions and millions of things I could have talked to you about last summer, but I preferred to forget everything annoying and talk nonsense and joke. O bother, I believe I'm beginning to blither again, I must put a stop to it and write more sensibly if I can. Thank you ever and ever so much for the poem you sent me, and the beads. The beads are so beautiful and they made me awfully happy, and as soon as I'm well I can wear them. They are about the loveliest beads I ever saw, like little moons, and they are satiny when you hold them to the light. I am so glad to hear you have set the date and send you my very best wishes. I hear that your fiancée is very beautiful and I should love to meet her. Why don't you come to America for your honeymoon? Do please write me a letter someday soon and tell me all about it. I like to get letters but nobody much writes to me. This is a stupid letter. I'm now quite sure that I'm not absolutely sane yet, but as soon as I can I shall write to you again—to counteract the dullness of what I've written so far. Really, this is a funny world. And do you know that the last few years of my life don't worry me anymore, but continually my mind goes back to my early childhood in Italy, and I worry amazingly over all sorts of little things that happened then, and cry and fret about them. It is probably inconceivable to you that I should be so

*demented. Really I must stop now. I never wrote so fast
in half an hour before, and I think I'm slightly delirious.
But I think I will have this letter mailed nevertheless
as madness is nothing to be ashamed of. Only please
destroy this letter—there is enough blither in it to have
me sent to an asylum for life should anybody else read it.*

*It is now five days since I wrote this letter, and the reason
I did not mail it is that I wished to wait a day or two so
I might reread it. Now that I've reread it, I realize that
it's just as demented as I imagined it to be, because I've
written one sentence after another in quick succession
just as they came into my head, but Henry insists that
always I must say straight out what I want to.*

    *I have been dressed for four days. And I wear the
beautiful milky beads and nobody has seen anything like
them before and they all admire them. Today I went out
for the very first time in a taxi to see a nerve specialist.
It seemed like a dream all the time—nothing was real. I
think I'm going to be sent to a rest home (NOT a lunatic
asylum) for a few weeks, and after that I must be quiet
and hardly see anyone, and next summer perhaps I shall
be allowed to go to dances—but I don't care because I
don't feel like doing much anyway. Well that's all now
as this piece of paper is quite crammed with words.
And I wish you every sort of happiness, but I don't hope
your hotcakes may burn and your children be acrobats!
Though it would be nice to have one of them an acrobat
to amuse you after a day's work.*
Well do write—

I felt much better after sending that letter. I'd been so casual
about Nancy, as if it were nothing at all. It was just a letter. I'd
always written him letters; it was the natural thing to do. I felt I'd
set things right.

pamela

*I*n June, I began to paint again. Just the one painting, the dancer. She would haunt me forever if I didn't put her on canvas. I'd painted her over and over in my mind, working and reworking the brushstrokes endlessly. It took me weeks to finish the picture.

The colors in the painting are mostly dark—blues and grays and greens. A woman wearing a blue bell-sleeved dress stands on a stage. Her dress looks heavy, like satiny metal; the skirt twirls open, revealing layers of petticoats that rise in circular patterns like the cross-section of a fruit. Her dress conveys motion, but her body is frozen awkwardly. Her expression is somber. She is looking inward, unaware of an audience. She has no partner, she is alone. She is more wooden doll than woman. Behind her, the backdrop is a landscape, a hill flanked by two gray blockish buildings, like old barns. A leaden sky threatens rain. A tree like no real tree rises behind the dancer—it's more a tall vine rising into leaves that wreath a giant cluster of blue grapes. The dancer has one foot on the back edge of the stage and one foot just off, as if there were no painted wall behind her. She is about to step off into the abyss.

Days after I finished the painting, I penciled the title on the back of the canvas: *The Sad Dancer*.

I was ready to go home.

margery

*I*t was torture. I kept seeing Pamela when we left, looking small and lost and empty as we left her there in the dark room with its strange smells.

You'll be home soon, darling. We love you. Don't worry.

How could it seem like the end of the world at eighteen? Could we lay it all at the feet of Diccon? Was it just—just!—a broken heart? As simple and as terrible as that?

Well. Enough.

I must take my own advice, think of the here and now. . . .

I've not been honest.

I say I don't know why these things happened, I don't understand what caused Pamela's illness. But I do.

Pamela's melancholia—her breakdown—was not about Diccon. Not altogether.

It's true that she was willfully blind, that she would not let herself believe that Diccon's engagement with Nancy was real, and perhaps that pushed her over the edge.

But the truth is, Pamela would have shattered anyway.

What I mean to say is this: Pamela's illness had to do—*has* to do—with Francesco. There is such a closeness between Pamela and her father. They are alike in so many ways. They are alike in the blood.

Francesco's illness is quieter, though I imagine it's no less painful. His melancholia is more like a slow deflation, as if the life is being sucked out of him. He walks around the house with glazed eyes, sits with a book in his lap but never turns a page. He shuts out the world, travels to a place I cannot imagine. It is wretched to see. Still, there was never a question of sending him off to the hospital.

With Francesco, I can manage. Patience, watchfulness—and time—seem to do the trick in the end.

Francesco's bouts simmer like a low-grade fever. But it's not the same with Pamela. Pamela's attack like the plague.

There's nothing I can do to fix the hurt inside her. It scares me. I don't know what to do.

Well, here we are now, and I suppose . . .

There's nothing for it but to make the best of it, is there?

Who knows? Today could be the beginning of a bad time. But then again, it may be nothing at all. You simply do not know.

pamela

oves me not, loves me not, loves me not. Loves me not, not, not. . . .

The old hurts are like boomerangs. I can hurl them away all I want but they always come back.

Diccon crushes me like a tiny bug under his boot.

I lie on the floor of my studio, as miserable as the dwarf I have to draw though it's killing me. It's an excellent commission, I should be happy. Macmillan's hired me to do pen-and-ink drawings for Oscar Wilde's short story, *The Birthday of the Infanta*. But I hate the work. I can't escape the wretchedness of the story. Every line I draw makes me feel as naive, as tormented, as the little wood dwarf.

There'd only been one letter from Diccon since I came home from Four Winds. The letter was to all of us. He said he was sorry he hadn't spent more time with us while he was in New York. His book about the children and the pirates was coming along well. And he was glad to report that Philippa Stallibrass had capitulated in the end, even insisting on a large wedding at Holy Trinity Church and a formal reception at the Rembrandt Hotel. The wedding would be in February. He hoped for snow.

After that we didn't hear from him, but no one was surprised. After all, he was a very busy man.

Early the next year, a letter came, addressed just to me. The envelope was fat. The postmark was Harlech. Harlech! Oh *God*, I thought. I didn't want to open it. I didn't want to read about his wedding, his glorious honeymoon, how happy they were in Wales.

I sat on my bed a long time, staring at the envelope. *Well, nothing can be too shocking, Pamela, you know the worst,* I told myself. I tore open the flap.

It took a while to sink in.

Diccon was miserable. As desperate as he'd ever been in his life, he said. He would have written sooner but truly, he could not. He could not even pick up a pen. In February he had fled London for Wales, plunged into his own cycle of despair. He'd not eaten or slept properly. Writing was out of the question. He hadn't written a word for ages. He hated to admit the reason. He'd been such a coward and a cad. *He had not been able to go through with the wedding.*

He wasn't entirely sure why, even now. He said he cringed to think of his abominable behavior. He'd been a monster, inexplicably ignoring Nancy in the weeks before the wedding, hiding out in his flat, not answering her letters. He had been paralyzed. Panicked. He had no excuse for his behavior. Nancy's last letter had been brief. Coldly, in stark terms, she had broken it off. He was not to think of contacting her or seeing her again.

Diccon was not married.

I knew I shouldn't be happy about what had happened, but how could I help it?

I wrote back, cautiously. Just some words of consolation, some breezy family news. After that, we wrote each other often. I told him about the paintings I was doing, about the illustrations and all the commission work that was piling up. Diccon wrote to me about his novel; he was no longer secretive or vague. He wrote in great detail about the progress he was making.

I wrote faithfully, but I never asked him when he might come to see me, I never begged him to come to New York. It was bound to happen, and now, more than ever, I had faith that once we were together again we would never part. Surely it was inevitable . . . even preordained?

I was surer even than I'd been at thirteen that Diccon belonged to me, and could belong to no one else. We'd marry, quickly—why wait? It was all so simple now.

In the beginning of July 1928, we went to stay with Cecil and Teddy at Merryall. By midsummer Diccon wrote that he was brooding again. He wasn't altogether happy with his book; he'd reached a standstill. He wasn't doing any real work, he said. *Mainly I sit with the typewriter in front of me and watch the tedious comings and goings of the stupid bloody hollow-eyed pigeons on the window ledge. I've got myself in a hole — I've got to get away again.*

He was thinking of coming to New York to finish his book. Perhaps the Connecticut countryside and the company of the Biancos could cheer him up. Did I think it sounded like a good idea?

I wrote to say I'd be at the pier to meet him.

This was it, I thought.

This time it *would* be different. Diccon wouldn't behave as he had the last time; he wouldn't make himself scarce.

I had waited for Diccon so many times. But this would be the last time. My anticipation was all hot and fierce and embroidered with fantasy. I couldn't stop myself—my mind reeled with imagined scenes. Perhaps a long walk in the piney woods and hillsides of Connecticut. Wildflowers—wood lilies and jewelweed and wild indigo—would decorate our way. I'd pause to examine a bloom too pretty to pass by, and as I turned to show it to Diccon, he would step towards me and without a word kiss my eyes, my neck, my mouth. He would murmur his love, the love he had held back for so long. Or—perhaps a rainy night. After dinner and several glasses of wine he would simply take my hand. *Come, Pamela, let's not stay indoors with all this lovely rain.* We'd run outside laughing, and he would lead me into the little copse at the meadow's edge and kiss me hard, not giving me a choice. . . .

pamela

Sunshine warmed the city as I hailed a taxi on Broadway. How light I felt! Everything seemed to contribute to it: the sun glinting off the twin globes of the gas lamps, the warm leather of the cab seat, the pretty way the pleats of my dress flared when I crossed my legs.

I have not lost him after all.

This time, when Diccon came off the ship, the scene was as if scripted for a Hollywood film. It was almost silly. I saw him scan the crowd; when he spied me, he grinned—he looked absolutely thrilled to see me. He threw his arms around me. He said I looked beautiful. *Beautiful!* All the pain of the last few years melted then, dissolving into the heat of the city, vanishing into the happy pulsing of my blood.

It would be a glorious end of summer.

Our days at Merryall were tranquil and lovely, and as easy as the old days. Diccon's novel sped along—he said he had hopes that he might finish it while he was in America. And I was taking a little holiday from illustrating. Teddy had carved out space for me in his studio, and I was painting still lifes: three wild roses in a glass bowl; an apple, a pear, and a silver knife on a blue dish; a few wildflowers tossed on the tin kitchen table.

Diccon would drop by once in a while to watch me paint. He slipped in one day as I worked on the stems of some meadowsweet.

"It's wonderful to see you working again," he said.

"Working again?" I didn't understand. "But I've always been working!"

"Painting, I mean. Not those damned illustrations."

"But it's . . . Daddy says that . . ."

"Daddy! Pamela, *you* are the artist, not your father."

I didn't understand why he sounded so hostile. Surely he knew why I was spending so much time doing illustration work. I'd explained in my letters about all the contracts.

The old unease returned.

I was frustrated. Despite the string of fine and peaceful days in the country, all my efforts to be alone with Diccon seemed to fail. Every time I thought there was to be an excursion with just the two of us, Cecco or Cecil or *someone* would decide to go along. I'd suggest berry-picking or picnicking or swimming, but Diccon would cheerfully demur. *I've too much work to do!* Or *Tomorrow, perhaps!*

He made time for horses, though. Our neighbors, the Cassidys, had a horse farm. Cecil and Teddy had known Jane Cassidy since she was a child. She was a favorite of theirs—ours, too—with her high spirits, her irreverent wit, and her curly strawberry-blonde hair tied back with whatever she could find lying about—a shoelace, or the string off a feedbag. She was married to someone named Marion, but I never saw him. He always seemed to be off somewhere on business. Iowa. Or St. Louis.

When Jane found out that Diccon loved to ride, she told him he could borrow one of her horses any time he liked. Sometimes I'd look up from my painting to see Diccon cantering off into the woods.

I would have loved to go with him, but I didn't know the first thing about riding horses.

On a hot day in August, Diccon came to my studio, his forehead glistening with sweat. I'd say he looked wilted but his eyes were so fierce that really he looked like a madman. He declared he couldn't write a word. He was irritable and sullen, complaining of the heat.

I said, "Well, then, let's go to the lake!" And almost dropped my brush in amazement when he agreed. We packed a picnic and set off on the three-mile hike to Lake Waramaug.

By the time we reached the lake, we were famished. We spread out our blanket away from the families that were clustered on the beach. Our luncheon—deviled eggs, celery and bacon sandwiches, pickles, strawberries, lemon tarts—all quickly disappeared.

The lake glinted merrily, sequined by the sun. Children played in the water near the shore, diving under, their legs suddenly shooting above the surface, then bending and listing precariously. The littlest children sat at the edge of the lake, filling pails or splashing madly with their hands. Diccon began to speak of the children in his novel, why they behaved the way they did. He grew animated. He said that the children—despite their surreal and grotesque predicament as pirate captives, despite their feet being eaten by winged cockroaches and their hands permanently tarred and greased, and despite witnessing animal fighting and the pirates' prolonged attempts to cut off the gangrenous tail of a drunken monkey—despite all these things, the children remained innocent at core. They might seem like animals, but they were *innocent*. Diccon was sure of this.

He was silent a long while, his gaze fixed on the children swimming in the lake.

"I think I have it, Pammy—the title. I shall call the book *The Innocent Voyage*."

I nodded. "It's a good title, Diccon."

We sat there in silence a long while, lost in our reveries.

Eventually we decided to swim far out, to the middle of the lake. It was glorious to feel so alive, laughing and paddling about. The swim restored Diccon's spirits, and when we returned to the blanket, he told me how glad he was that we'd decided to make the journey. The lake and the breezes had cooled and refreshed me, but Diccon's words made me feel all warm inside.

‡ ‡ ‡

Late in the afternoon, I walked up the hill to the Lakeview Inn to find the ladies' bathing house. On my way back I stopped to look at Diccon in the distance, where he sat hunched over on the blanket. He looked like a little boy, with his thin back, his hair sticking out here and there, his neck all white and vulnerable. I was flooded with affection. The desire to hold him overwhelmed me.

I was foolish. I should have restrained myself.

Diccon didn't hear me approaching across the sand.

I reached the blanket and in one motion I fell to my knees behind him and wrapped my arms around his chest. My breasts and thighs, barely clothed in the thin damp cotton of my swimming suit, pressed against his back.

"It's *so* lovely here, isn't it, Diccon?"

I felt him jerk, then freeze within the circle of my arms.

Mortification, a sharp pain, shot through me in hot electric waves.

I released him.

I felt all empty. Collapsed. Not a real person at all. *Why do I make a mess of everything? What is wrong with me?*

I began to pack up the picnic things.

"Well, shall we go, then? We've a long walk back." My voice was dull.

On the hike back to Merryall, we talked of the most boring things. The weather. *Clouds are gathering . . . perhaps a storm tonight.* What might be for supper. *I think Cecil said she was making some sort of casserole.* Had we seen that hollowed out log on the way in? *Don't remember it; I think not.* It took all my effort just to put one foot ahead of the other. We were two soldiers marching home, stalwart and unified in our mission: remain friendly, cheerful.

And why not? Nothing had happened.

Nothing at all.

Words, I kept thinking. It was *words* I had trouble with. Henry had said I must always say what I felt. Why couldn't I just *talk* to

Diccon, ever? I burned inside, and I wanted to tell him how I burned. And I was so curious about everything. What was Diccon *thinking*? Did he think of me at all? What was he *feeling*? There was no way to tell.

I'd failed miserably in following Henry's instructions. In fact, I'd been getting quieter as the summer progressed. Now I was almost mute.

When we packed up to return to New York in September, Diccon said he thought he'd stay on in Connecticut a bit longer. Cecil and Teddy were heading to Pennsylvania; they said he could have the house to himself.

God, I thought. *Not again.*

I was angry. It was going to be just the same as when he'd stayed in the Catskills and never, ever came to New York. I knew it.

Diccon did not return to the city.

It took ages for me to catch on.

pamela

As soon as I got back to my studio, I began to paint again. I thought I'd surprise Diccon, do some "real" work, as he called it. My plan was to finish my illustration work during the day and paint at night. I got up even earlier, stayed even longer in the studio. It wasn't a wise plan, for I was trying to please both my father and Diccon, and it was all wrong. I was using my brain— my fevered brain—and my hands, but not my heart. I pushed and pushed, and in the end neither my illustrations nor my painting were any good.

I wrote Diccon from Macdougal Alley more than once, asking when did he think he'd be back in the city. Five weeks went by, and only one letter from Diccon. It made no mention of plans to return to the city.

My work did not go well. I got up at six and worked until dark making bloody drawings and half the time ripped them up as soon as I was done. I blamed Diccon for my frustration with my work. I fumed. *Why* didn't he write? *Why* didn't he come to the city?

And then I finally understood.

It was not a letter from Diccon that clarified the situation, but a conversation with Cecco.

I knew, of course, that Cecco looked up to Diccon, that they were great friends. But I hadn't thought they'd get together without telling me. We were all part of a family, weren't we? And so when Cecco came back from a weekend at Merryall and started to tell me about it, I said it would have been nice if he'd told me, I might have wished to go, too. Cecco just shrugged.

My thoughts were childish. Cecco was twenty-two that summer, a man. He had a job at the Museum of Natural History and a steady girlfriend. And he had decided to go up to Merryall for a weekend. Why should he consult with me? Oblivious to my precarious state of mind, he spoke casually of what he had witnessed in the country.

"Well, our Diccon appears to be quite busy."

"Writing, you mean?"

"There's that, of course, but what I meant was he seems to have attached himself to Jane Cassidy . . . it's the horses, I guess . . . they spend an awful lot of time riding."

"Riding . . . ?"

Cecco said that they rode together all the time, that they regularly went off on long moonlit rides.

I wrote again to Diccon. I shouldn't have, for I composed my letter after I'd downed a good deal of wine. I told him I'd spent all week drawing a dead queen picking fruit off a fig tree. I told him I hoped he was having a nice time with Jane riding in the moonlight while I had no moonlight at all, on account of the tall buildings. I told him I was generally suicidal.

I was furious with Diccon. I couldn't bother being angry with Jane. I liked Jane, she'd always been quite nice to me, and she was married, after all. I was sure it was all Diccon's idea to go riding, take up all of her time. But honestly, I couldn't see why he spent all that time galloping around the countryside when he was supposed to be so busy writing.

Diccon wrote back, ignoring everything I'd written. His letter was jubilant. He'd been in a black mood for weeks, he said, unable to write the ending to his novel. Then he'd gone out for a ride and somersaulted off his horse, landing flat on his back. The jolt was what was needed, he said, *for I rode back and straightway finished the story. All I required was a good shaking up. Which would go to prove that all books come from the liver.*

I suppose I knew even at that moment that Diccon had no interest in me. Not in the way I wanted. He was only interested in his book. And riding. I knew it, but dismissed all such thoughts.

I shut myself in my studio and played Italian operas all day and night. Mostly *La Traviata* over and over. I curled up on the old Oriental rug and listened, over and over and over, to the high sweet notes of Amelita Galli-Curci singing "Sempre Libera."

Sempre libera degg'io
Folleggiar di gioia in gioia
Vo' che scorra il viver mio
Pei sentieri del piacer
Nasca il giorno, o il giorno muoia
Sempre lieta ne' ritrovi
A diletti sempre nuovi
Dee volare il mio pensier.

I must always be free
To hurry from pleasure to pleasure
I want my life to pass
Along the path of delight.
At daybreak or at the end of the day,
Always happy, wherever I am,
My thoughts will ever fly
Towards new delights.

It was the only consolation I had.

margery

I've changed my mind.

I do think it would be good to let Pamela talk about whatever it is she wants to talk about, but I think I'll postpone it, after all. I'm afraid I'm not up to it.

I'll ask Francesco to talk to her. It all has to do with him, really, doesn't it? She has answered to him all her life, perhaps now he can answer to her.

They are so very close. How different it's been for Cecco and Pamela, their relationship with their father. With Cecco, it was always all so easy. Helping Franceso in the bookstore, fencing with him, discussing the papers he wrote when he was studying at Columbia. And Francesco liked to advise Cecco about his love life, not that Cecco paid any attention. But Pamela . . . it's not that Francesco doesn't love her beyond measure. But Pamela's talent—it's colored everything. She's grown up needing his approval in a way that Cecco never has. Not that he isn't happy to have Francesco's approval—or mine—it's just that he's never seemed, really, to need either of us terribly.

But Pamela, always trying to please her father . . .

How vividly I remember the time—she was only five and Cecco was six—when Francesco got it into his head that they must memorize "The Host of the Air." He does love his Yeats— even now, his battered old *Wind Among the Reeds* sits by his bedside. Still, it was a daunting task for a child, "The Host of the Air." Eleven verses!

Pamela took on the assignment as a sacred duty. I went to check on her before I went to bed one night, and she'd fallen asleep with the torch shining beneath the sheets, *Wind Among the Reeds* by her side. And just a few days later she announced that she could recite the poem. We gathered in the parlor, and there she stood, so small in one of those rather shapeless linen dresses I used to make for her, and she chanted, quite perfectly, all eleven verses. I can hear her child's voice now, speaking of the pain of love, not understanding a word of it.

Brava! Brava! Francesco called out, beaming and clapping.

Cecco had his turn weeks later. Even then, it took a good bit of cuing to get him through. It was clear he was miserable. Francesco just laughed.

At any rate, perhaps now Francesco can get Pamela through this, perhaps he can find a way to break down those barriers she puts up.

I'm not the one for that task.

pamela

I was miserable, but I was not the only one with a battered heart. Agnes was suffering, too. Gene wanted a divorce.

The reason was simple: he was in love with another woman. The beautiful stage actress, Carlotta Monterey. He and Carlotta had plans to leave for Europe soon. The quicker Agnes would agree to a divorce, Gene had told her, the better for everyone.

Unlike my agony, Agnes's troubles were exposed for the world to see. Gene's affair screamed out from the newsstands. *Eugene O'Neill Deserts Wife. O'Neill and Monterey—Parisian Tryst?* Every story seemed to be accompanied by the same picture, a softly lit portrait of Gene and Agnes in profile.

It was a very popular scandal.

Agnes did her damnedest to present a blasé face to the public. She gave an "authorized interview" to the *World*. She said—truthfully—that she had no idea where Miss Monterey was, but that Gene—and this part was not truthful—was touring with friends in France. When asked, she said no, certainly not, her failure to leave for Europe with him did not constitute what other celebrities have referred to as a "marital vacation."

To Mam and me, Agnes said she'd told Gene he could just go ahead and have his fling, for that was all it was, she was sure.

"Oh . . . he'll come back to me . . . he always does . . . all hang-dog as usual."

But she could not keep up the air of bravado forever. She sat at our kitchen table one morning, all crumpled, and I saw the invisible hand of Gene fly across her face.

She pushed a letter across the table.

I love someone else deeply. There is no possible doubt of this. And the someone loves me. Of that I am certain. You and I have often promised each other that if ever one came to the other and said they loved someone else that we would understand—that we would know that love is something which cannot be denied or argued with.

I was sorry for Agnes, who now seemed a caricature of herself, smoking cigarettes one after another, pushing them wearily round and round in the ashtray, heaving great sighs and shaking her head as if to fling the whole thing off. I was sorry, but I couldn't help thinking that leaving Agnes was the greatest gift Gene had ever given her. She could find a new man one day. Any man, practically, would be better than Gene. Of course, it was different for the children—by then Agnes and Gene had had another child, Oona, (*Oona—it's Irish for Agnes,* Gene had said proudly when she was born)—they couldn't simply find a new father, or a better father, one day. Eleven-year-old Shane was devastated by his father's desertion. He went all quiet.

Agnes and her children came to us for Christmas that year. Daddy gave Shane a Daisy BB gun. *Every boy needs one of these,* he said. *I'll take you to the park, we'll find a squirrel or two.* In the middle of the night we woke to sounds of repeated crashing and stumbled out into the living room.

Shane, tears rolling down his face, was shooting all the ornaments off the Christmas tree.

pamela

After Christmas, Diccon returned to the city. He dropped by only to let us know that he'd found a place to stay with "friends."

It was probably a good thing, not seeing very much of Diccon. I really was feeling overwhelmed, steeped in work. I still had a long way to go with *The Birthday of the Infanta*.

I was concentrating hard on the intricacies of a ruff adorning the neck of a young noble boy, when there was a knock at the studio door. Then Diccon's voice.

"Hello? Hello . . . Pamela?"

He stood next to me. I could tell he was uneasy. He looked quite fine in his charcoal overcoat, soft grey scarf, and rather beat-up fedora, but his manner was sheepish. His closeness, his pipe smell—it was too much. *I love him,* I thought. *I can't bear this.* I felt lightheaded. I tried to continue drawing, but I had to put the pen down. My hand was trembling. I knew that this was not to be a happy visit.

He was going away again, he told me. Jane Cassidy had invited him down to her winter home, Bellevue, in Virginia. Her husband was away on an extended trip to Des Moines—she thought Diccon would find it a quiet place to write. He could ride Sukey, his favorite horse.

How jolly.

"But you only just got here, Diccon. For God's sake, can't you stay in New York for at least a bit longer? It seems you're always trying to get away from me . . . it's true, isn't it?"

"Not at all, Pamela, it has nothing to do with you, really. . . ."

"Well, what has it to do with, then?"

"Just what it is . . . a chance to see a new part of the country, and, well, I've started on some poetry again . . . you know, I've found I do seem to work better in the country than in the city, I don't know why. Remember . . . in Wales . . . how I wrote . . . ?"

"I wish we could go back to Wales! We were happy there!"

"But Pamela, I don't see that this is about our happiness or lack of happiness. . . ."

"Oh, God, just go, Diccon. Just leave. I don't want to talk to you any more. I'm too busy, as you can see"—I waved at my drawings—"I've got to get these finished on time!"

The door shut with an accusatory thud. I turned to my drawing. Angrily, I wiped away quick tears, and kept working.

I hated the story of the Infanta.

Even if I hadn't been miserable about Diccon I would have hated it. It was a withering tale of a twelve-year-old Spanish princess, abominable in her mocking cruelty to the court dwarf who loves her. The young dwarf is plucked from a happy life in the woods solely for the Infanta's amusement, only to discover, by looking in a mirror for the first time, that he is ugly and deformed. He dies brokenhearted at the feet of the jeering princess.

> *. . . the Chamberlain looked grave, and he knelt beside the little dwarf, and put his hand upon his heart. And after a few moments he shrugged his shoulders, and rose up, and having made a low bow to the Infanta, he said:*
>
> *"Mi bella Princesa, your funny little dwarf will never dance again. It is a pity, for he is so ugly that he might have made the King smile."*
>
> *"But why will he not dance again?" asked the Infanta, laughing.*

*"Because his heart is broken," answered the
Chamberlain.*

*And the Infanta frowned, and her dainty rose-leaf
lips curled in pretty disdain.*

*"For the future let those who come to play with
me have no hearts," she cried, and she ran out into
the garden.*

For all her cruelty, though, the Infanta had the right idea. A
heart was a miserable thing. I could have done without my own.

pamela

I don't know exactly why Diccon wrote to me from Virginia.
Later, Jane would offer me her theory, that he was using a
twisted bit of logic, that he felt she was going to eat him alive and
he wanted me there to diffuse the situation. *He was all nonchalant,*
said he thought perhaps he'd write to you, see if you'd like to come
to Bellevue. He said you were fond of me and that you'd shown an
interest in learning to ride and perhaps I could give you a lesson or
two. I told him, "We don't need a chaperone, you know, Diccon."

But Diccon, stubborn as always, had gone ahead and invited
me down.

Of course, I should have refused. I should have known better
than to be pleased, but I told myself that it was his way of apologizing to me.

And so I wrote to say I'd take the train down. Said he must
teach me to ride a horse while I was there. Said I would bring down
the Infanta drawings, that I must work six hours a day because of
the contract. I sent him my love.

I'd never been to the South. I'd read about the old plantation
houses, but in my mind's eye they'd always turned into a sort of
English country house. Bellevue was nowhere near as grand, as
kingly, as the estate I'd envisioned, but it was entrancing nonethe-
less. The tree-lined drive was fairy-tale beautiful, with a spectacu-
lar branched archway overhead. It was ghostly now in winter, cast-

ing ragged shadows. The house itself was three stories of faded, pinkish brick, skirted by a huge veranda. Six columns supported a graceful second-floor porch. The home had been in her family for ages, Jane said. It had been a working tobacco plantation once, but they'd had to sell off hundreds of acres.

Inside, Bellevue looked as if not much had changed since Jane's grandparents—or perhaps great-grandparents—had lived there. The rugs in the parlor were rich but worn, the balding arms of the Queen Anne chairs were little more than a network of gray thread, and the wallpaper, mottled with amber stains, curled away from the wall. A statue of a boy blowing a bugle stood in the far corner. The little tableau on the mantelpiece was quite forlorn— two cracked Chinese vases set on trivets of carved black wood, a dented and tarnished silver candlestick, and a dusty beehive clock that always read ten past four.

Bellevue had seen better days, but it was a comfortable place.

Perhaps things will work out after all, I thought.

The very first morning, I asked Diccon to give me a riding lesson.

"Why don't you go out with Jane a few times?" he said, "When you've got the hang of it we'll all take a ride. I've really got to stay here and write."

Jane read my disappointment. She shook her head and made a "There's nothing to be done, so let's get on with it" sort of face.

In the barn, I stood by Lulu, a gentle old roan mare, while Jane went about saddling the horse. I breathed in smells of sweet straw and dusky animal, and pondered the array of leather and metal contraptions hanging on the wall, all a mystery to me.

"I may have to adjust the stirrup further, but let's give it a try." Jane came around to help me mount the horse. "Just put your left foot here, I'll help."

"Jane," I interrupted. "I really, really do wish to learn to ride. Truly—it's just that now . . . well, now we're alone I want to ask you a question, about Diccon. . . ."

"Which is?"

Nervously, I stroked Lulu's flank. I couldn't look at Jane.

"I feel I must know . . . it's difficult not knowing . . . are you and Diccon . . . ?"

"Lovers?" Jane looked amused. "One would think so, wouldn't one? But the answer, my dear, is no. If it makes you feel any better, you and I are in the same boat." She laughed. "And we're paddling about in circles!"

"Oh! Oh, well, then."

"Yes, well, then. So, now we can all be jolly good friends, don't you think? And I don't mind telling you, it's not as if I haven't *tried*—I tried rather hard, in fact, just before you got here."

I was aghast at Jane's directness, but thrilled, too, to be having this sort of conversation.

"You . . . you did? But what . . . ?"

"I don't know what goes on in the head of that man. But the other night, after dinner—we'd had plenty of wine!—we were sitting by the fire like an old married couple and, well, I guess I thought it was just about damned time, so I stood up, looked him in the eye, and said, 'Let's go to bed, Diccon.' And he just stared at me—you know that look, all dark and shooting disdain at you—it seemed to go on forever. It was awful, I can tell you that. Then I simply got mad and said, 'Oh, hell, Diccon. You really are *impossible*.' And he still didn't say anything for the longest time. I was feeling wretched, naturally, then you know what he said? He said, all slow and serious like he was lecturing me, 'I suppose, Jane, it's a notion I would have expected to come up with on my own.'"

She laughed, shaking her head.

"He was so incredibly serious . . . I just thought it was funny all of a sudden, and so I said to him, 'Well, Diccon, I *am* the hostess, you know!'"

"Oh, Jane!"

I laughed, too, but truly I was shocked. Jane was so bold. She wanted what I wanted and had simply asked for it . . . and she'd been *refused*. What would I have done in her place? But of course

I would never have asked. All this time I had worried that Diccon was having an affair with Jane. I believed Jane, though—it wasn't true. But I didn't understand.

"So, Pamela, you're here now—perhaps you can have a go. . . ."

God. The thought made me cringe. It was quite hopeless. I knew that now. But now another idea was forming in my mind, a very confusing idea.

"I did want . . . oh, never mind. But now I can't help wondering . . . does Diccon even . . . ?"

I couldn't say what I meant. But Jane could.

"Does he even *like* women, you mean? I've given it a good deal of thought, and I can't say, I really don't know, but I think perhaps he does, that he's all right, really. But he's so damned *English*—no offense, Pamela. I think he thinks American women are animals, pouncing on men as if they're prey. He prefers women who are . . . well, like our dear friend *Nancy*. He did manage to tell me that she never made a move towards him, and he said it in a very approving sort of way. It was all quite chaste, I'm sure, that whole business. . . ."

However the three of us managed to live under the same roof for even a minute I don't know. Over the next few days we gathered together the bits of kindling: silent tensions, moodiness, bursts of sarcasm. The pile grew. And then of course the inevitable happened. The match was lit one night and the fire raged, fueled by a great deal of bourbon and wine.

The next morning, pain crackled all through my head. I worried gloomily about what awful things I might have said. Plenty of awful things had been said, I knew that. I wished I could erase the misery, but the injuries of the night before returned to me, inexorably, in all their cruelty.

I tried to remember what had set if off. Had it been when I said to Diccon, "I've always thought you such a *good* person, Diccon, but you are just a hypocrite"? Or had that come later, after

Diccon had turned on Jane, scoffing at her "useless life." He had not been gentle. But then, none of us had been. . . .

"What do you do, Jane, I mean what is it you really do? You ride horses in the north and then you ride horses in the south, you open up and shut down houses, and that's about it as far as I can see. A woman with your intelligence . . ."

"Christ, Diccon, leave off. . . . I don't go around telling you what you should—"

But then he quickly turned on me.

"And you, Pamela, what's become of the artist you were? I'd really like to know that. Are you just going to go on diddling about, illustrating for magazines . . . forsaking your real self, your real talent?"

I trembled with hurt and fury. Didn't he *know*?

"You don't understand anything, not one thing . . . I . . . I have no choice . . . and anyway it's none of your business. . . ."

"But that's where you're wrong!" He glared at me. "You *do* have a choice! For God's sake I'd rather be starving in some rat-infested pisshole and write what I want than to do what you're—"

I couldn't let him finish. I didn't want to hear it.

"You want things to always be the same! You want me to be that little girl with the flaxen braids running around Wales, drawing apple trees, and now that . . ."

"Yes, I do. I wish you were that girl still." Diccon said it so spitefully. He stopped me cold. To my horror, he went on.

"You're not what I would have thought. . . . You've become a scheming woman, Pamela. I've seen it. . . . Why can't you be straight?"

"But . . . *you're* the one who's not straight, Diccon, avoiding me and my family. . . ."

"The problem is you refuse to grow up . . . it's a sickness, actually . . . you're attached to your mother with a bloody gold-plated umbilical cord! And your father, if he told you you ought to design nursery wallpaper, you'd go ahead and—"

He might as well have flung me across the room, cracking my head against the wall. Be done with it. I couldn't speak. Jane spoke for me.

"How *can* you, Diccon! You're cruel."

"I'm not cruel, I'm simply telling—"

"—And you're a pretentious lout! You care more about your precious writing than you do for any living person. You're a cold and insensitive man. Pamela's suffered too, too much, she really has. Why do you have to be so arrogant? You treat both of us as if we were helpless, as if we just couldn't possibly go on in life without your great *wisdom* to guide us. . . ."

Diccon's words had sapped all the life from me. I was exhausted. I wanted only to leave the room, to go to bed.

But Jane kept going.

"And you tease us all the time, Diccon. But I don't know why you bother. I mean, you'd never . . . you don't really even *want* to, do you? Was that what was so wonderful about your little Nancy— she let you preserve her just as she was, the little poet-virgin?"

Diccon stared at Jane, his blue eyes turned cold with disgust. With each beat of silence, the gulf between us—I knew his disgust was not reserved for Jane alone—stretched wider.

"Girls like Nancy," he spoke slowly, "and I used to put you in the same category, Pamela, despite evidence to the contrary . . . most often *do* wait. Most women do. Whores aside, that is."

Whores!

He despises me, I thought. I could not bear this final, brutal hurt. All the years of living with a bruised heart, of my insane *hoping,* suddenly compressed themselves into one ancient thought.

I couldn't stop myself. I screamed at him.

"You should've married me when I was fifteen! Everything would have been all right, then!"

Well, I'd said what I thought. I suppose Henry would have been proud of me.

‡ ‡ ‡

*What's become of the artist you were? You are a scheming woman.
. . . You've never grown up. . . . Your father . . . Your mother . . . Girls
like Nancy . . . Whores aside . . .*

All night I tossed under the assault of Diccon's words. His
attack had left little untouched, it was a massacre. But—had he
been justified? Had we instigated the battle? Had our attack been
equally devastating? Should I be full of self-righteous indignation,
or should I be full of remorse? I couldn't piece it together, and it
was too painful trying.

The next day we crept silently about the house. By nightfall,
Diccon was gone. He never said a word before he left.

I stayed on at Bellevue for another day. I was simply too
weary to leave. Jane and I sat on the veranda in great old rocking
chairs, wrapped in blankets, creaking back and forth. Half-heart-
edly, in little spurts between silences, we dissected the nature of
Diccon Hughes. *He really is too proud. I don't take it back—he does
care more about his writing than any living creature. Do you really
suppose he visits whores? Hah!*

Not that it did either of us any good. Our talk of Diccon was
idle, bloodless conversation. We had no heart for the topic.

It was the end for me. Slouched in my chair on the sagging
porch of a Virginia plantation, I understood that all was lost. And
what was lost was nothing, for it had never been. I had known that
for a long time, really.

Bellevue's fairy-tale drive beckoned, leading to emptiness.

pamela

I would not struggle anymore. Bellevue had changed things for good. I was utterly weary of walking around with little spears all through my heart. The sharp, bright shape of Diccon that I'd held within me for so long—all the fierce color of him—had caused only pain. Now I would reconfigure the world of Diccon.

With infinite care I painted over what I'd thought was love—the hurtful reds and blacks—with softer, muted colors. I took my collection of foolish, amorous reveries and rubbed them smooth, glazed them with a homey patina. I left intact the Diccon of my childhood, the eager young poet who tramped the hills, who sang Welsh songs, who made hotcakes on a battered old stove, who had once looked at me—and all my family—with love. I would hold on to that Diccon.

At bottom, I feared losing him altogether. I had to keep him as my friend, always. It was what he had wanted of me all along. What a fool I'd been to think it would ever be more than that.

pamela

*D*iccon never did come to see us in New York. My parents wondered aloud about his strange absence. I told them things had not gone well in Virginia, but they would never know the half of it. They didn't press me. Months passed.

In March 1929, *The Innocent Voyage* was published.

The first reviews were mixed. Critics seemed both repelled and fascinated by Diccon's shocking, unsentimental portrait of children—kidnapped children who never seem to miss their parents; children who quickly adapt to life on a pirate ship; children who do not mourn when their twelve-year-old brother dies a violent death; children capable even of murder.

Sales of the book started off slowly, but then several influential critics wrote glowing reviews and after that, things changed quickly. Suddenly Diccon was in constant circulation. We read about him in the newspaper—the readings, the luncheons, the cocktail parties. There were lots of interviews. By August, *The Innocent Voyage* was on the bestseller list.

Diccon was terribly busy now, sucked into his own orbit of fame. I wasn't surprised that I never saw him. But how strange, how painful, not to celebrate Diccon's triumph with him. He'd worked on the novel for years, and he'd shared so much of it with me. I knew he'd almost given up on it at times. And now it was as if the novelist I was reading about was a perfect stranger.

I held out no hope of seeing him. After all, what could we say to each other?

When I heard that Diccon's London publisher was going to print his book under a new title, *A High Wind in Jamaica*, in September, I was sure that Diccon would be leaving soon. He'd want to be home for the event. I hated to think that his last memory of me would be the wretched time at Bellevue. I wanted him to know, somehow, that I wouldn't pursue him as I had in the past. But I couldn't write to him for I had no idea where he was.

When Diccon sent me what was obviously a hastily written note, I knew that he, too, wanted to erase all the unpleasantness. He said he regretted the mess we made at Bellevue. Still he thought it would be best if we didn't meet. He'd booked a cabin on the *SS De Grasse* and would be sailing soon. He asked me to apologize to my parents for his rudeness in staying away. He said he'd write once he got things squared away.

I passed on Diccon's message to Mam and Daddy. They were perplexed by his behavior. Mam, typically, was quiet. She was hurt, but she would simply begin to think aloud: *I really can't understand why he couldn't at least call. . . .* And then she would drift off. Daddy, of course, was more vocal.

"Why in hell can't the wretched boy come see us? Does he think he's too famous? He's written a book, for Christ's sake, he's not the bloody pope!" Daddy ranted on. "Didn't he want to celebrate with us? Weren't we like family to him?"

When the two of us were alone, Mam tried to question me, gently, but I cut her off. She understood, though, that my infatuation had finally come to an end.

"Pamela, you have your whole bright future ahead of you."

That was all she said. I nodded.

It was ungodly hot as I walked, slowly, to the waterfront. The newsman on the radio that morning said temperatures had reached record highs in the city. Ninety-five degrees yesterday and the same expected today. Sweat soaked my hair and ran down my face.

I had no intention of seeing Diccon. But somehow I had to

see the SS *De Grasse* head out into the harbor, carrying him home. Away from me forever. I wanted to see it for myself.

I stood at the pier for an eternity. Finally, Diccon's ship slipped away, off into the gray horizon. I turned to go home.

The studio beckoned. There was a cover for *Harper's* due in two days, and several more commissions had piled up.

But I couldn't go back, not yet.

I wandered down the waterfront, past the looming dark tunnels of the pier, past open docks, past the longshoremen's taverns. At Christopher Street, I stood for a very long time by the riverside where leaden waves lapped at the seawall, hypnotizing me with the heavy *slap, slap, slap* of the water.

I am alone.

An era had come to an end. I knew that as surely as though I'd seen a great towering door swing shut across the harbor as the SS *De Grasse* vanished from sight.

margery

L ord, my head hurts. . . .
   But . . . there's one good thing about it. It's helped me make
up my mind.

I've decided that when Pamela wakes I'll send her home—
ever so gently—instead of asking her to stay for supper as I usually
do. I'll give her the roast I was going to cook tonight, and a few
potatoes. I'll tell her I think Lorenzo was very much looking forward to a nice home-cooked supper tonight with his mother.

I suppose I should look for some aspirin.

part five

‡‡‡

The Letter: January 11, 1977

428 Lafayette Street
New York City

....

January 8, 1977

My Dear Pamela,
I suppose you will cringe at that salutation, but that is still how I think of you, despite everything. You were a dear little thing, all that time ago. Do you still wear your hair all coiled around your ears? Are they silver coils now?

I am writing to you because I am coming to New York at the end of next week. A friend of mine, Edward Tawner, died quite recently. I hadn't seen him since I left the city, but we've corresponded over the years. He was a lonely fellow, I think, a quite minor but devoted poet, always writing me to celebrate when he got published in the odd poetry journal. Poetry was, obviously, our mutual topic of interest, and it seems he's left me his book collection. There's some wonderful stuff, first editions, Whitman and Pound and Sandburg (this one is signed!).

*I'm sorry to give you so little warning, but of
course I couldn't have foreseen this turn of events,
and Edward's brother Mason has let me know that
he is putting up the apartment for sale immediately
and would like to clear out his brother's things as
quickly as possible. Mason is seven years older than
Edward and in poor shape himself, so I agreed to
help him pack things up and ship the books to Oregon. After all, besides the brother, I appear to be the
main beneficiary.*

*My hope is that I can see you. I would like to talk
to you. Could we have a cup of coffee, at least? We can
talk about anything you like, but of course I am thinking of Lorenzo. Time, I'm afraid, is running out and it
would be nice to round things out, finally.*

*I have your telephone number and I'll call you
when I get into town.*

*I do hope you are well, Pamela. Please do say
you will see me.*

Yours,

Robert

Pamela sinks back into the chair. Reads the letter again.

She takes the measure of his words. Two long paragraphs
on this Edward person and his book collection. A brief paragraph mentioning Lorenzo. An aside, really.

She could almost laugh, it's so typical.

And this: *It would be nice to round things out.*

Round things out? Round things *out?* What does this
mean exactly—after forty-six years let's just fix things up,
shall we?

Well, it doesn't appear that he's dying, at any rate.

She could almost laugh.

Still, he is coming to New York, she can't alter that. The end of next week. She has to think. Today is . . . Tuesday. January 11. That means he will be here around the 20th or so. Or . . . no, he wrote this on the 8th. A Saturday. Perhaps he means he will be here at the end of *this* week. Why couldn't he have been specific? Just written a date?

Silly question. It's all pure Robert, this vagueness.

He never has liked to be pinned down.

‡‡‡

September 1, 1944

9 Livingston Place, Stuyvesant Square
New York City

(Late Afternoon)

margery

One more cup of tea. The Darjeeling this time. And another biscuit. A bit of strength before Pamela emerges.

She's bound to any minute now, I should think.

Perhaps she'll surprise me. Come out all rested, her old self. Cheerful.

What I wouldn't give. . . .

Well, fingers crossed. Pamela's perfectly capable of coming up with big surprises. Some quite a bit bigger than others, ones with large consequences. I'm thinking of Robert, of course.

Robert . . . that whole affair . . . now *that* was surprising all the way around. If I'd ever guessed what was really going on with Robert, I would have at least *tried* to make her see her foolishness. Not that I didn't understand the attraction. He was very appealing, with those moony eyes and lovely long, wavy hair. He had his own sort of style—I suppose he fancied he dressed himself as a poet should, and he may have missed the mark there, but the point was he did look good in his clothes. Natural—a true bohemian. You couldn't help but be attracted to him. And that naive charm of his. . . . No, Robert didn't worry me. Not at first, at least. It was the headlong way Pamela threw herself into the affair.

But it wasn't love with Robert. I don't know what it was, really. Francesco and I were glad at first that she'd found someone, a distraction, a man who brought her out of her shell. *Anyone*, we thought, to help her get beyond Diccon. And besides, the truth is when she met Robert she was sailing so high we couldn't have reached her if we'd tried.

In those days, Pamela had time for two things: painting and Robert. There was no time for us. She went all silent and mysterious. We never knew a thing. Not even the day Francesco stepped out of his bookshop to get his midmorning espresso at Café Reggio and caught sight of Pamela trotting down Eighth Street towards Sixth Avenue. In a white dress. Francesco was so astounded by the vision that he forgot his coffee and came straight to tell me.

"What was she doing running down the street dressed like that? Yes, I'm sure it was Pamela. For God's sake, Margery, I know my own daughter—and anyway, who could miss those braids around her ears!"

We came up with a few theories, none very satisfactory. Going to meet Robert for a romantic boat ride in Central Park? Perhaps she was modeling for a friend? Her clothing was certainly a mystery. I was sure that Pamela didn't own a white dress.

We could never have guessed the truth, that Francesco had just seen his daughter hurrying off to her wedding.

pamela

I see it now, the irony. Diccon leaving, everything disintegrating. It was the end of October 1929—barely two months after Diccon had stood on the deck of his ship watching the great financial institutions of lower Manhattan fade from sight. Everything slid downhill all at once. The stock market tumbled, then collapsed utterly. All of America was reeling. No one could understand what was happening. Poverty spread like the plague. Our own family fortunes, never grand, steadily diminished. We held on, but things were uncertain, shaky. Royalties from Mam's books trickled in; sales at Daddy's bookstore were almost nonexistent. Cecco took a job in the men's department at Saks Fifth Avenue. My illustrating commissions began to disappear.

On New Year's Eve, 1930, I turned twenty-four.

It was a somber birthday, despite Mam's efforts at cheer—the frosted angel cake with yellow roses, the presents wrapped in tin foil. Mam, Cecco, and I walked to Times Square to watch the ball drop. Daddy stayed at home.

The truth was it felt good to get away from him for a while, to join the anonymous crowd. Daddy was in trouble. He seemed to have shut down.

I thought of how much my father had changed since he'd had to close his bookshop. He no longer moved impatiently about the house. He sat still for hours, holding a book, staring across the room. Even the gramophone was silent. It was the money. It had to be the money. Everyone had lost so much in the Depression.

Eventually we were forced to leave our lovely home on Waverly Place. Still, we were lucky to have a roof over our heads.

Daddy was mostly silent. When he did talk it was scholarly gibberish, nothing to do with our life. More than once he called me over as he pulled out his most precious possession from his old steamer trunk. A Papal Bull. It was extremely old, extremely valuable. He would never sell it, though.

He spoke in a flat tone. He was expressionless, not his real self at all. He had simply faded altogether. He'd already lost most of the hair he'd been so proud of, and though he still dressed well, the details were overlooked—the folded handkerchief in his jacket pocket, the perfect shine on his shoes. My father, the man Diccon had once called a butterfly of a man, had folded his wings.

I looked at him as he sat hunched in his chair and felt a terrifying stab, a realization that so very much time had passed and so much of the good had gone.

"1511, Pamela. Pope Julius II inviting the Lateran Council. Look at this seal, the wheel pattern." Dutifully, I looked at the dull, half-dollar-sized circle dangling at the bottom of the ancient document. "People are ignorant, they ask if a Bull has a bull's head on the seals. Not one that I've seen." He ran his finger absentmindedly over the parchment. He droned on as if he were reading from a text.

"You know what the word 'Bull' comes from, Pamela."

Yes, I did. I had heard it all a hundred times. "*Bulla*—air bubble—such as rises in water during ebullition . . . also any small object of globular shape such as those gold or silver bosses that were worn for ornament on a string around the neck. The leaden seals appended to Papal Decrees were of just such a shape and, therefore, were called *bullae*. . . ."

He would look up to assure himself that I was still there. Daddy didn't care if I responded or not. And I did not respond, just stood by his chair. Patted his shoulder.

I was devastated by this phantom father. It was painful to see him, and I didn't like thinking about the reasons for his depression. There were the money problems, of course, but all I could think was, was it just as much . . . disappointment in me? Was I to blame for my father's illness?

It hurt too much to be around him, and I began to avoid him, hiding in my studio for days at a time. But I did little work. I paced and paced, uselessly going over and over the events of the last few years.

I'm to blame. I handle everything so badly!

Mam held steady, maneuvering her way around all the dark shadows of our home. She continued to write, books with happy endings. In 1929 she published *The Candlestick*, the story of an old wooden candlestick who'd been feeling rather useless and forgotten, then burned brightly one stormy night to lead a fisherman safely home. Now she was almost finished with *The House that Grew Smaller*, about a lonely, abandoned house who finds happiness shrinking first to playhouse size so that children will inhabit him. Then, abandoned again, he becomes even smaller, ending up a beautiful bird house, delighting all who pass by.

Now I see another truth, a sad truth, about that time. Mam continued to write her books not just because she was so steady in her nature, and not just because she had wonderful stories in her head and she knew they would give pleasure to so many children. Perhaps more than anything, she wrote to escape the madness that pressed in on her.

The noxious cloud of misery—Daddy's illness, the constant lack of money, my failure with Diccon—was suffocating. I was desperate to shake it off.

There was a glimmer of a hope to cling to, a possible way out. At the Whitney Club, everyone was talking about the Guggenheim Fellowship. *Why not?* I thought in a rare moment of optimism. I'd try for it—it would be the answer to everything.

I worked hard on my application. Gertrude agreed to write a recommendation. I had no confidence, though. And it turned out there was a great hurdle to overcome: I had never completed the process to become a citizen of the United States, and I couldn't get a passport until I did. I forced myself to do the necessary work, make the calls, fill out the paperwork. It would all be worth it, though.

If I could get the grant, I'd have the money to stay for months—maybe a year, even—and do whatever I wanted, paint whatever I wished. It would be just as in was in the old times.

If only I could go back to Italy . . . well, things would be all right then. It would be heaven.

When I got the congratulatory letter from the committee, the good news washed over me, a fresh and beautiful torrent. *God*, I thought, *it won't be long now, I can't believe it.*

Soon, I would be back in my beloved Italy!

Six weeks, I figured. I could manage to be ready in that amount of time.

margery

$\mathcal{P}$amela's wedding. Well, I wasn't there. I wouldn't know. Pamela said it was quite the scene.

But I'd rather not think of Robert right now. I'd just as soon forget him altogether, though that's impossible, of course—he is always here, hovering about somehow. We can never lose him. One simply cannot get around the fact that he is Lorenzo's father.

How infuriating it is. How is it that a person can trot into one's life for a brief second, then trot right off again and, when he is gone, everything is changed? So many people's lives that man affected, and off he goes whistling into the sunset. And not a thing we can do about it.

Poor Lorenzo. How he must wonder about his father. So many times I've thought perhaps we should track him down, try to get him together with his son. But I'd have to go behind Pamela's back. Whenever I've mentioned it to her, she would have none of it. Anyway, I'm sure she's right—if the man has made no effort to see his boy in all these years (and what kind of man is that?) then no good could come of forcing the issue. Surely it would make things worse.

Best to leave it alone.

At any rate, today of all days would not be the time to talk of Lorenzo's father. All I want is to be sure Pamela is all right, that's she not falling down one of those rabbit holes she stumbles into now and then. I'd just like to make sure she's herself, and send her on her way.

So any talk of Robert will have to wait. It could so easily set her off track. For ages after he left, Pamela was fragile. So *detached* from everything.

You would have thought that having a child would bring her to her senses, but she really could not care for Lorenzo, it did not come naturally to her. He was an easy, happy child, but he seemed to perplex his mother. She found it hard to know just what to feed him; she said it seemed to change all the time. Or I'd come home and there he'd be, asleep under the coffee table, Pamela reading or drawing in another room, and I'd realize she'd forgotten about naptime, about putting the baby in his crib. It was alarming.

All I could think to do was to get her and Lorenzo to Merryall. Out to the country, to ride it out. I have no idea, really, if being in the country had anything to do with it—it was such a long haul—but she did, finally, recover. She finished the drawings for *The Little Mermaid* before the deadline. At the end of November 1935, we returned to New York.

We weren't home long before a strange thing happened, something that hadn't happened in years. Pamela got a telephone call from a reporter. Someone from *The New Yorker.*

pamela

I did not leave for Italy in six weeks.
My American citizenship still was not finalized. I was very
anxious. How long would it take? Would I ever leave New York?
The more I tried to look on the positive side—*it will all work out
if only I can be patient*—the more morose I became. It was cold
in my studio. My artist's tools sat untouched. I even began to fear
the journey: the idea of crossing the ocean loomed up dark and
treacherous. I thought I simply couldn't handle it even if I ever did
get my passport. It wasn't going to work after all.

But . . . if I didn't go, I'd still be in New York with nothing
changed, and that was hell, wasn't it? Wherever I turned, whatever
I imagined, it was hell.

*I can't make things work. I always make a mess of things. Noth-
ing I do turns out right.*

Every day I wandered around the city, walking hundreds of
blocks, taking notice of nothing. I knew only that I was cold, I was
hungry, winter was hell. I felt a huge emptiness. I walked without
purpose. *Nothing seems anything,* I kept thinking. People brushed
by me. I heard the rattling rush of cars, the splattering of slush.

*Nothing seems anything. Nothing seems anything. Nothing
seems anything.*

The thought repeated itself endlessly, I couldn't close my ears
to it, couldn't stop it. An idea began to make its way through this
painful chorus. It would be simple. It would be the end of the pain.
I would focus on one thing. Taxis, I thought. *Taxis. I'll just walk*

out in front. . . . I would be free, then. It almost made me happy to think about it.

For several days I implemented my plan.

I would wait by the side of the street. Once it was a Brown and White. There were a few Checker Cabs, I think. I stepped off the curb when I was sure they were too close to stop. But they would dodge me. Brakes screeched, the taxis careened away.

Once or twice some kind person led me back to the sidewalk. "You all right, Miss?" The kind person would try to get me to talk. I couldn't talk.

It all meant nothing to me, except failure.

I had failed even in that.

pamela

I muddled through the days. The brightness of Italy faded.
Daddy rallied, though. He began to make the rounds of all
the best galleries, to find out what was selling. One day he waltzed
into my studio, confident and beaming. "Still lifes," he declared,
"that's what people want today!".

And so I worked on still lifes, and my heart grew heavier still.
The paintings in my studio did not please me. Something was terribly wrong.

I thought of how Daddy hovered around me sometimes,
trying not to tell me what to do, but then telling me anyway and
squeezing my shoulder and looking sheepish as if to say, *Oh, you
don't have to listen to me, of course, you must listen to yourself.* But
always I listened to him, I couldn't help it.

Everything overwhelmed me. I simply wasn't able to deal with
the most ordinary chores and obligations that faced me every day.
I couldn't seem to get out of bed until noon at least. My thoughts
were gloomy, and the familiar fog of despair thickened around me.

Still, there were the periods when I thought I was all right.
Then I worked and worked, though not in a good way. The large,
geometric canvasses of dreams and childhood and even fear rattled around in my mind, but I couldn't start on them yet. Not feeling the way I did.

I mixed cobalt violet, purple madder. The bright, rich paints
on my palette hurt my eyes. *White,* I thought, and mixed it in to
dull the hurt, working fast, driven—not by muses or by the welcome rush of brain and heart rushing to my fingertips, directing
the brush, but by the fear that if I stopped painting, the painful

thoughts would engulf me, drown me, as I lay in bed or tried to talk to people or to do anything in the ordinary way.

The colors didn't feel right, but I went ahead anyway and filled my brush with paint. *Are you angry about something, Pamela? Are you angry with someone?* Henry's voice whispered in my ear. I gripped the brush hard, as if I thought it would fly from my fingers. I painted in short, angry strokes. The studio filled with lots and lots of small, cramped paintings: flowers and fruits, fruits and flowers.

At Christmastime, I took to my bed. I remember Mam coming in, talking about Anne Carroll Moore—something about an anniversary at the library—and wouldn't I like to write her a note?

I couldn't think if I wanted to write a note or not.

From my room I could hear Lorenzo shouting a poem he'd just learned.

> *The camel in the gloaming*
> *No sheet for his bed*
> *The little lord Jesus*
> *Lay down at their head!*

I heard Mam's laughter.

"Isn't it 'candles' in the gloaming, Lorenzo?"

But Lorenzo was certain he had it right. "No! Camels with a hump!"

I wanted to be out there with them, but I couldn't. I couldn't move.

Perhaps I don't really remember those things. Mam probably told me later.

Daddy came in to my room, holding one of the still lifes I'd been working on. He said he hadn't realized there were so many—he thought he'd bring some of them round to a gallery or two. I said perhaps shouldn't we wait a bit. "Wait for what?" he asked, and I had no answer.

margery

The loud ringing startled me, and I hurried to the telephone table in the hall. A man identified himself as Eddie O'Toole, a reporter from *The New Yorker*. He asked to speak to Pamela. When I told her who it was, she shook her head and gestured with her hands to let me know she didn't want to talk. But I held out the receiver—she had to deal with life once in a while, I thought—and beckoned her over.

Pamela agreed to see the reporter, but immediately regretted it. Francesco, on the other hand, was elated. He still had hopes that the old days would return. Why, I can't imagine. Francesco's hold on reality often seems not so very much greater than Pamela's.

My own feeling was that I simply wanted her to get on with her life, and I thought perhaps talking about her work to someone outside of the family might jog her a bit, get her started again.

None of us knew what to think, really. Things had been so quiet for so long, we'd almost forgotten the days when the telephone never seemed to stop ringing, when there was always someone who wanted to find out what Pamela was up to.

Is that all that Mr. O'Toole wanted, to find out what she was up to?

pamela

*D*addy had luck with the still lifes. In February they were hung at Ferargil Gallery as part of a group show. I was meant to go to the opening, but I didn't feel well.

The show was reviewed in the *New York Times*. The article opened with a long and complimentary review of another artist, followed by a brief paragraph.

> *In another room at the Ferargil you will find flower and fruit paintings by Pamela Bianco, who some fifteen years back was a child prodigy in her earliest teens. These rather tight and hard and unyielding little canvases of hers are decorative, but they are not prodigious. Much that is unsatisfactory seems to lose vitality through a too facile rhythmic scheme or a too frequent use of mauve. They are clever, but that seems about all.*

"Bloody critics," my father said.

Some of the fruit-and-flower pieces were still in my studio, stacked on the floor against the wall. One by one I put them on the easel, covered them methodically with fat brushfulls of white paint. They stared back at me, hurting my eyes, mocking me. *We're all the same. Stilled life. Stilled heart. No good.*

I was quite ill. I went right back to bed. I stopped eating.

My mother and I talked.

We agreed that it would be best if I went back to Four Winds for a while.

pamela

*H*enry rescued me once again. The unbearable weight cracked and crumbled and fell away. I floated about, weightless. I breathed the spring air of the Village with joy.

I had forgotten that I could feel that way.

And so when I met Robert, he could never have guessed that I had just emerged from hell. It's not what he saw at all, he only saw me flying high. I had burst through all the clouds. I was ecstatic just to feel alive. To paint again.

I'd tacked the letter from the Guggenheim people on the wall next to the studio door. Soon I would be free—to draw and paint whatever I wanted, whenever I wanted. I could do anything at all. I was even optimistic about love, and daydreamed endlessly about falling in love with an Italian artist, or a baker, I didn't care. I'd live in Italy forever.

It would not be long now. I'd booked a berth for July.

Robert appeared at the end of April, an early spring flower. A daffodil, all stalky and new and hopeful.

It was late afternoon, unseasonably warm. The gentle rain that had been falling all day had stopped, and the sky hung low and soft, a blanket of dove-colored clouds. I was scrutinizing *Woman with Grapes*, trying to decide if it was absolutely finished. I dragged a lamp over to the easel and stepped back. Illuminated, the painting stood as a beacon in the middle of the room. Under a dense arbor, the nude figure glowed all alabaster as she reached up to pluck some fruit. The grapes glinted in the foreground, splashed by sun, begging the viewer to touch them. I couldn't help but be enchanted, seduced by my own work. I stood a long time, pondering. Perhaps a bit more shading there, under the leaves. . . . But I was happy. It was a good painting.

I heard laughter outside, and went to crank open the window. The sun was just beginning to break through the clouds. In the alleyway, neighbors were setting out chairs, lanterns, plates of food, and jugs of wine. I thought I'd join them. I was hungry, and it was a good time for a break. But then bits of the conversation reached my ears— Garbo and *Anna Christie*—and suddenly I didn't want to go outside at all. Everyone was talking about the new movie. How amazing it was. Greta Garbo had her first talking part, and she was electrifying the world. Garbo talks! Garbo *talks!*

I wasn't interested in taking part in that discussion. I was quite familiar with Gene's old play, *Anna Christie*. And everyone knew that my cousin Agnes had married Eugene O'Neill—I didn't want to go out there and talk about him, or his damned great success, or anything else to do with him. I despised him. The outside chatter wafted in, and I saw Agnes's pale face as she pushed that awful letter across the kitchen table. I saw Agnes in the shadowy dawn at Peaked Hill Bars, falling to the ground like a doll in the sea grass.

I certainly had many reasons to dislike Gene. Still, all this talk of the movie made me remember the time, years earlier, when my opinion of him softened somewhat. It was just days before *Anna Christie* was to open on Broadway. I happened to run into him—it was only a few minutes or so, but I saw a bit more of what made up the man, then. I thought that maybe he was all right.

On a dark, chill afternoon, threatening winter, I was walking down Broadway, heading home from the horse's veterinarian Mam had charmed into looking at our pets when they were sick. He didn't usually tend to small animals, he'd said, but who could look Mam in the eye and say no? I'd taken our white rat, wheezing, oozy-eyed Narcissus III—or perhaps he was Narcissus IV, I'm not sure which. The doctor had given me a small bottle of camphor oil and said it might make breathing easier.

It wasn't the best day to be out—a fine mist that hadn't quite decided to be rain was dampening the city. I was just a few blocks south of the Vanderbilt Theatre, daydreaming about the series of Greenwich Village roofs I was working on. At the corner ahead I noticed a man leaning against the lamppost, smoking. A very thin man, the kind that look all bony even in a padded wool blazer like this man was wearing. His hat was pulled low against the weather, but he kept looking up at the hotel. There was a clock on the roof, and I wondered if he was meeting someone. When I was almost upon him, he turned towards me, and I realized who it was.

"Gene!" I called out, reflexively, and instantly regretted it.

The eyes that turned upon me were as cold and menacing as a mobster's gun. But almost worse was that beyond the hostility there was such a pleading look. *Don't come near me*, it said. No one could feel comfortable with those dark eyes upon you, eyes overflowing with pain and anger and disdain. When Gene looked at me all I could think was: *How does Agnes live with him?*

But Gene's hostility, unmistakable as it was, melted away when he recognized me.

"Oh, it's you, it's all right then. Come here, I'll show you something."

When I got close, he took me by the shoulders and turned me so that I was facing the building he'd been staring at. The Cadillac Hotel, it said on the marquee. At first I thought maybe it was the hotel Agnes had told us about once, where Gene had stayed drunk for days. I was afraid he was going to tell me his version of the story. But this didn't look like the kind of place Agnes had described, it looked quite respectable.

"Up there . . . third floor . . . left side . . ."

I looked but saw nothing but a row of double windows. What did he want me to see?

"Right there—you see? I was born up there."

"You were?" I said stupidly.

"Yes, I was. It was the Barrett House back then. Damned nice apartment, my father always said. My mother hated it; she wanted a real house, out in the country, but of course my old man had to be near the theatre." He pulled a pack of Camels from his jacket. His hand trembled a bit as he took out a cigarette. He started to put it in his mouth, then looked at me. "Care for one?"

I nodded. "Thanks . . . yes."

Gene laughed, and then his eyes were black diamonds. "Thought you might—you're all cut from the same cloth, you Boulton and Bianco women!"

I juggled Narcissus, all wrapped up in a moth-eaten scarf, holding him close to my chest with my left arm so that I could hold the cigarette Gene was lighting for me. He never said a word about Narcissus, he acted like it was an everyday occurrence to have a smoke with a fifteen-year-old girl who was holding a white rat.

"Your father, he was . . ." I started to say, but Gene had just looked at his watch and he cut me off. *He was the Count of Monte Cristo, wasn't he?* I'd been about to ask, though I knew the answer— Agnes had told me of Mr. O'Neill's fame in that role, and how he could never escape it.

"Good Christ, I'm hours late, Hopkins'll never forgive me." He hesitated briefly, then kissed me quickly on the forehead. "Glad you stopped by my corner, Pamela," he said, and walked away towards the theater.

I stayed there, enjoying my cigarette. The smoke rose, delicate blue wisps spiraling into the mist. I took Gene's place, leaning against the lamppost, looking up at the Cadillac Hotel, and thought of what Agnes had told us about how Gene fought with his father all the time, how he blamed himself for his mother's illness—and how it was soon after his birth that she had begun to drug herself. I pictured a sad and ghostly woman moving past the third floor window, a baby crying.

I walked home thinking about Gene, about his unhappy childhood with an angry father and a mother quite removed from reality. I liked Gene a little better that day, felt a bit more kindly toward him.

It wouldn't last, though. After the divorce . . . deserting his children the way he did. . . . Well, I never did forgive him then.

I didn't want to talk about *Anna Christie*, but I did want to get out of the studio and into the sun, get something to eat. And so I dawdled about, cleaning my brushes and neatening things up, then returned to the window to eavesdrop. Mr. Hoffman, who owned the music store near the Brevoort, was telling one of his long-winded jokes. The coast was clear. I stepped outside.

"Pamela! Over here!"

There was a small group of people off to the left that I hadn't been able to see from my studio window. The sculptor Gaston Lachaise and his wife, Isabel, had set up camp just down from No. 17, Gertrude's studio. Isabel had tossed some brightly colored Indian fabric over a low iron table and set out a feast: a colorful array of crudités, wedges of white cheese, loaves of round bread, and bowls of olives and nuts. There were two young men with the Lachaises. I didn't recognize either of them.

"Help yourself!" said Isabel, gesturing to the food, her round face all jolly as I approached. She held out a glass of wine.

"Lovely. Thank you. How can I say no? And I was just absolutely starving, I must say." The gaiety in my voice took me by surprise.

"This is Frederick Schlick, Pamela, and his brother Robert. Fred's got a play about to go on across the street—no doubt you've heard. *The Joy of the Serpents?*"

"Oh, yes. Fantastic."

I had, in fact, heard about the play. It was impossible not to know everything that was happening in the Village.

Robert was the younger brother. He was handsome, in a very boyish way. There was an open, naive look about him. At first glance he seemed from another century, another world—he wore a Russian cassock shirt, and his wavy dark hair, unfashionably long and parted in the middle, seemed awfully daring. But his speech belied his exotic look. He looked up at me with frank surprise and admiration.

"You're Pamela Bianco? Gosh . . . it's . . . it's just such an honor to meet you."

I laughed. It had been a long while since I'd heard anything like that.

I stayed for a second glass of wine, and then one more. It was so nice there in the warm spring air. And Robert seemed so fascinated by me, I couldn't help but feel flattered. When Frederick excused himself, saying he still had some tinkering to do with his play, Robert looked at me.

"C'mon," he said to me in what I would come to know was his characteristically impulsive way. "Let's go—I'll show you Harlem!"

Surprising myself utterly—who was this carefree girl?—I agreed without hesitation. We caught the express train on Fourteenth Street. We sat side by side on the rattan seats, the fan whirring overhead, the train vibrating and shrieking as we sped north. We talked and talked. I remember that I fretted over my painter's overalls. Robert said they were absolutely perfect. He said he liked the way I wore my hair in braids wound around my ears.

"It's pretty, Pamela, and so . . . unusual. Shows that you're not just one of the pack, cutting your hair in a bob like every other girl in the world."

He looked at me expectantly as he talked. I thought of Diccon's eyes, sometimes marble cold, sometimes flaming with passion, and how so often they had made me tremble with unease. Robert's brown eyes were as innocent and curious as a toddler's. They made me relax, made me unselfconscious. He seemed so eager to know about me.

He told me of growing up in Oregon. A beautiful place, he said, but so rainy and dull. He'd longed to follow his brother to the excitement and glamour of New York.

I told him of growing up in Italy and how I was going back there soon.

"I shall eat lots of risotto and *tortelli di zucca,* and wash it down with lots and lots of wine. And chocolate . . . only in Turin can you find the most delicious, the very best chocolate. I'll bring you back some of my favorite from Cioccolato Stratta."

"You will?"

"Well, I shall try! If you're still here."

"Oh, I plan to be here forever."

pamela

"*R*obert was in love with New York.

He was only twenty-one, just out of college, when he'd left Oregon. Frederick had written such colorful letters describing his life in the city. The bars—Chumley's or The Golden Swan—where one might run into E. E. Cummings or even Eugene O'Neill. The impromptu parties in Macdougal Alley. The fabulous subway system. *Shazaam!* Frederick wrote, "And there you are on 92nd Street!"

Robert called himself a poet. He told me that in Oregon he used to write long, mournful poems full of futility and snow. But now, in New York, his poetry had changed. He found the city more exciting and magical even than he had dreamed. At the Metropolitan Museum or the New York Public Library he ran up the steps two at a time. He prowled around the Upper East Side, imagining himself lord of the Morgan mansion or the Frick mansion. He did sound very much the poet when he told me of how he felt that New York was like a changing vista of gardens. Greenwich Village was ragged and weedy, a wandering meadow of wildflowers. The Upper East Side was a clipped and ordered world of topiary, blocked hedges, and perfect rosebushes. But Harlem—Harlem was tropical, a regal display of rare orchids and birds of paradise.

Robert was having a love affair with all of the city, but his deepest affection was for Harlem. Everyone was so free in Harlem! He loved the laughter, music, poetry, and dark, smoky clubs. He loved all the people: the women who sang and wrote and painted, women with large personalities who loved other women; the men who sang and wrote and painted, men who wore ginger-lily perfume and loved other men. Robert carried around a notebook and wrote paeans to this new world.

Such cosmopolitan hymn
Was meant to be the mission of mankind,
That all around appears in Harlem here
Unfettered and unhampered, and becomes
The liberal justice of the body-soul
Shrouded in colors of close beauteousness.

I tried not to think of Diccon when I read Robert's poetry. I knew what his opinion of this young American poet would be.

Robert had discovered that the center of intellectual life in Harlem was a narrow walk-up at 2114 Fifth Avenue, Gumby's Book Studio and home to Mr. L. S. Alexander Gumby. All the poets and novelists and artists seemed to meet there.

Gumby was a natural-born collector of information. He'd been keeping scrapbooks since he was a young boy. "Mr. Scrapbook," people called him. He was always happy to show off his trove of artifacts—slave records, autographs from Frederick Douglass and Booker T. Washington, letters from Paul Robeson and Josephine Baker. He had thousands of pages, all organized by theme: "Prominent Negroes," "Ethiopia," "Football," "Radio," "Negro Business." He had exhibited his collection all over the East Coast.

At home, during unofficial times, Gumby dressed in bright kimonos, rising late to sit by his fireside table with its starched white tablecloth and silver coffee service. On the street he wore a formal suit, pale-yellow gloves, and a diamond stickpin. He carried a brass-topped walking stick.

It was at Gumby's that Robert met Bruce Nugent, a flamboyant artist and writer. It's also where he met Roy de Coverley. Roy was a poet, too, newly arrived from the West Indies. When I met him I thought he was rather beautiful—silken and willowy. Roy took to Robert, the eager boy who came from a land he could not imagine, a gray land of forests and fog and cold. Robert, short of money and living like a vagabond, moved into Roy's apartment.

All that spring, Robert and I ricocheted back and forth between the Village and Harlem. In the Village, we went to different speakeasies all the time. Chumley's or The Grotto or the Fronton Club. But in Harlem we almost always went to The Sugar Cane Club on Fifth Avenue, just three blocks up from Gumby's place. Roy would often join us. We'd stand outside the Sugar Cane while the invisible man in the booth decided if he'd let us in. Finally, the heavy, creaking chain would lift, the door would open, and in we'd go. When the chain dropped behind us in a great crash I always imagined that we had just missed being guillotined.

It was black in the entryway, and we felt our way down a dark and narrow stairwell to the basement, a crowded, underground heaven smelling of smoke and booze and exotic perfumes. Revolving lights played over the room, casting slowly changing hues, blue to red and back to blue again. Wood tables were pushed haphazardly against the walls to make room for the three-piece band that played in the corner. There was always a crush of dancers on the floor—men in striped silk shirts and tan, square-toed shoes; women in jewel-colored, low-cut dresses. We all shuffled and kicked and threw our arms skyward while the band played jazz tunes like "Black Bottom Stomp." The colors round the room flared up and fell like silent fireworks.

Sometimes, when the band played the opening notes of a slow song, a woman would step out from the crowd and stand in front of the musicians. She was short and fleshy, and she'd stuffed herself into a tuxedo. Her lips were deep-ruby red. She would sing "Nobody Knows You When You're Down and Out," and if you closed your eyes, you'd swear it was Bessie Smith herself.

Oh lord without a doubt
Nobody wants you

Nobody needs you
Nobody wants you
When you're down and out

Her voice, the words, filled me with a sort of sweet melancholy. Robert and I danced to the song—or, to be more accurate, we moved languidly across the floor—and I was dizzy with bathtub gin and Robert's heat, and the reds and blues blurred down to a slow purple haze.

There was a solace in those Harlem nights. For so long with Diccon, I had felt uncomfortable. Fearful. I had tried too hard. With Robert, it was easy. I never had to think; it was all a lark. I wondered if perhaps I'd never been myself at all until I met him.

Robert and I flew together across the heavens. That's how it seemed to me.

We made love one warm night, just as spring was turning to summer. Giddy with weed and gin and a night of carousing, we returned to my studio in the early-morning hours. I put my beloved *La Traviata* "Sempre Libera"—on the gramophone and danced without inhibition around the room.

Happily I turn to the new delights
That make my spirit soar.

I never could remember how it happened, exactly, but there we were, wrapped around each other on the Oriental rug. It seemed quite natural, really, just as in all things with Robert. I do remember that, afterwards, he played with my hair, mumbling about Ophelia. I remember that he left before dawn.

‡ ‡ ‡

Tonight, if we talk, what of this can I tell Lorenzo?

I could tell him his father was such an *interesting* man, that he was quite fun to be around. That he was very good-looking, and had a lot of friends. *Just like you, Lorenzo.*

I could tell Lorenzo that I am sure he inherited only the very best parts of his father.

margery

It was raining the day Eddie O'Toole came to interview Pamela. He was quite young, not a day over twenty-five, and looked closer to eighteen once he'd taken off his dripping homburg and exposed his boyish, freckled face. His red hair, all disheveled, endeared him to me straight off. Of course by the time he arrived at our place in Stuyvesant Square, the only reminder of Francesco's former glory was a reddish-gray ring round his head. But it had sprouted anew on the head of little Lorenzo, who darted round the parlor like a dancing flame as Eddie talked with Pamela. The boy's antics didn't seem to faze the reporter at all. Well, he was an O'Toole. He probably had lots of brothers and sisters.

Francesco and I sat with Pamela during the interview. We had to be careful. Pamela can be terribly reserved. Silent, in fact. And she can be quite gullible. She has no sense of self-protection, no idea of self-promotion. She would answer questions plainly, simply tell the truth. She has no idea of dodging issues, glossing things over. It drives Francesco crazy.

But in this case, I thought it went well. Eddie was patient and deferential. Pamela warmed up to him almost immediately, becoming quite talkative. She showed him the illustrations for *The Little Mermaid* she'd done in Connecticut. And she opened up about some ideas she had for future work, told him she wanted to write an ABC book for Lorenzo, then perhaps more illustrated books would follow. She even told him about the large canvasses in her head—"Larger paintings than I have ever done before!"

she said in a burst of passion. It was just then that Francesco took Lorenzo's hand and led him from the room, asking if he'd like a bit of hot chocolate.

I thought he was just trying to get the child out of the way, give the reporter some peace. For once I hadn't read him correctly. My antenna for these things is usually quite sensitive—I'm always on guard, ready to deflect this, patch up that. Sometimes I think that my biggest role in this world is the go-between. *Margery Bianco, Perpetual Conciliator.*

Part of the reason I didn't quite catch on was that as Pamela was talking to Eddie, I had opened a folder I held in my lap, a folder she'd put together of some of her old pictures. I was distracted by the top one. A line drawing she'd done in Turin, the day after her first exhibition opened—a portrait of me, sitting at my desk, wrapping up that beautiful Murano vase. A wedding gift for Agnes. What the picture doesn't show is the letter that's hidden under the wrapping paper. A letter from my sister Cecil, announcing that Agnes had run off and married a man named Eugene O'Neill, a playwright. No one had met the mysterious groom yet. It had all been quite secretive. Agnes had written to her parents, as if it were something rather miraculous, that her new husband had written several well-received plays. But Cecil was skeptical. She said that Agnes had never before shown any interest in the theatre, and she feared her daughter had tangled herself up with a ne'er-do-well scribbler. She was afraid that Gene would be more than happy to have Agnes support him with the income she made from selling her popular pulp stories.

I was thinking to myself . . . if only *that* had been his greatest sin. . . .

And so I missed the look of displeasure that must have crossed Francesco's face as he left the room.

When Eddie had finished his interview with Pamela, I accompanied him to the front door. It was already quite dark outside. I switched on the hall light. In the tiny entry, the tulip lamp lit up Pamela's little painting of a cherub haloed in gilt. It transformed the dreary hole into a merry, welcoming spot. Eddie stood for bit, admiring the painting.

"Do *you* think she'll exhibit again?" he asked. It took me by surprise.

"Oh, yes, I expect so," I said, too quickly. I'm afraid my doubts showed through. He held out his hand and thanked me profusely for the tea, for our hospitality. As he left the rain blew in, but I stood there a while and watched him walk down to the corner. The rain fell on him, a spray of yellow diamonds in the glow of the lamplight. He turned north on Second Avenue and disappeared from sight. What was *his* mother like? I wondered. What sort of life did he have, what sort of future? What would he write about Pamela? I even wondered, did he like the rain?

That night, after Pamela had gone to bed, Francesco and I retreated to the kitchen. He didn't wait long to let me know that Pamela's exuberant declarations about her future plans had irked him terribly. As I poured Vermouth into our favorite little green glasses from Italy, I ventured, "It went rather well with our young Mr. O'Toole, don't you think? Pamela was certainly—"

"She was certainly foolhardy, is what she was." And that was when he told me he'd had to leave the room so that Pamela wouldn't see his irritation. I told him I was quite grateful for that.

"An ABC book for God's sake! *That* is the future she envisions? And some vague thing about large pictures. . . ." He was talking too loudly; I was very afraid that Pamela would hear. I gestured to him, nodding in the general direction of the bedrooms, and we began to whisper conspiratorially.

"How will it look to people when they read that the girl who astonished the world now wants to draw an ABC book for her son, and oh, by the way, when she gets ready, after she's properly prepared, after she's *learned to draw* . . . don't look at me like that,

Margery, those were her words . . . and after she's *learned to draw*, well then perhaps she'll paint some really big canvasses."

I told him that Eddie hardly seemed the sort to write a negative piece, he seemed particularly empathetic to me. I pointed out that Pamela had been at her most charming, that her confessions showed her lack of guile, and that I thought she had shown a great deal of optimism regarding her future work. But Francesco was not to be moved, and we were both aware that I felt there was some truth in what he said.

At any rate, we both thought that was the end of that. That Eddie's visit was the end of the affair. We had only to wait to see what *The New Yorker* printed. We hardly expected a second call.

pamela

*I*t was a very erratic love affair. Sometimes Robert would disappear for days and days—but I didn't mind that. I now knew
what I'd been desperate to know, and the knowledge made me
feel all light and beaming. Prideful. Whenever I passed a young
woman on the street I'd think, *Do you know? I do!*

I was ridiculously happy, grateful for this strange gift Robert
had given me, but I was not in love. Beneath everything, I felt it,
the falseness.

Our lovemaking was infrequent. There were no truly tender
moments; there was no lingering. Robert seemed awfully childish,
somehow. We never talked about anything important, like what
we really thought about love or art or family or any of the problems of the world. He was quixotic, chasing after anything that
sparkled, dropping it when it lost its luster. He liked trotting me
around, liked telling people who I was. I knew all this, but I did not
like to admit it to myself. I wanted to hold on to the brightness—
the lightness—as long as I could. To Robert, I was a grand sparkler,
and I basked in his idea of me. It was good, a relief, to be happy in
this new and frothy sort of way.

I did not obsess over Robert, I just let things go on as they
were. After all, I had Italy. Italy was my true obsession. God—to
be on my *own*, free to paint whatever I wished, whenever I wished!
To find an Italian lover with soulful eyes. A man who wanted to be
with me always. He would come to my studio, and we would make
passionate love. He would stand in the morning light, admiring my

paintings. Then he would turn to me. *Straordinario . . . splendido—come sei, Pamela.* No, I was not in love with Robert.

So what happened next makes no sense, I realize.

Of course I should have stopped it, but it seemed to have a life of its own. Robert formed an idea he couldn't let go. He kept talking about *marrying* me. Well, more about a *wedding.* He said, "Wouldn't it be grand?" We'd have a ceremony in Harlem. He said he'd talked it all over with Gumby, who was eager to host it at his salon. They'd stayed up late one night, planning the whole thing, the music, the decorations. They decided Bruce Nugent ("Brother Bruce" they called him) would be the best man. They made up a guest list. It would be the social event of Harlem that season.

It wasn't real, I told myself. He didn't mean any of it. I never thought it was real. *Marry* Robert? It was crazy. He wasn't the "right" one, I knew that. And really, we'd only just met.

Anyway, he never actually proposed, he just started talking, talking. I never objected to his plans, I just laughed a lot, and kept telling him he was crazy.

"I've found the dress!" Robert said to me one day, dragging me away all the way down to Broome Street and, in his usual exuberant fashion—just for the thrill of it—farther south to Chinatown crammed with red and yellow and green buildings hung with banners and glittering with gilt. And the horrible stench!—a sort of awful stew of raw sewage, roasting meat, bitter herbs, raw fish, and incense.

We made our way back up to Little Italy, to Mulberry Street, overrun with hundreds of pushcart vendors. The dress was in a tailor's shop. Robert had seen it in the window when he'd gone to see about taking in a pair of trousers. When he asked about the dress, the tailor had shrugged and said it was just for decoration, that he'd be happy to sell it. It was a fancy Italian peasant dress, white, with a low square neck and fitted bodice and layers of lace over white cotton. The neckline was embroidered with gold and emerald thread. The dress was nothing like the ivory silks and pearls I saw every

Sunday in the *New York Times* wedding portraits. But Robert had a knack for that sort of thing—it turned out to be just the right dress for me. I went into a cramped little closet to try it on and when I emerged the tailor beamed. *"Bella! Sarà una bella sposa!* You will be a beautiful bride!"

Robert looked quite pleased with himself. "I *knew* it. It's absolutely the perfect dress for you!"

I shrugged and smiled sheepishly.

I let myself be propelled forward, bit by bit. This little ceremony that Robert had concocted hardly counted as a real wedding, did it? It was as if we were acting out a fairy tale, or a silly play. I was just playing the role he'd handed me. Robert would tire of it soon, I thought, go on to the next thing.

But he kept insisting, and I kept going along. I ignored the rational—horrified—voice inside that was lecturing to me all along. I simply turned myself over, as I had from the beginning, to the make-believe joy that Robert Schlick had brought into my life.

I told no one about the upcoming event. Not even Mam and Daddy. I don't know if they would have made me see how foolish I was being. Cecco had married his longtime love, Barbara, the year before. They had gone about it in all the right ways—a long courtship, a year's engagement (Cecco had saved up, bought a small but perfect diamond), and a beautiful wedding at St. Bartholomew's. There was no question that they were a well-matched pair, little question that it would be a good marriage. And here I was, running around in secret, planning to marry a man I barely knew. But I was sure of two things: that when it was a *fait accompli* Mam would accept it graciously, and Daddy would be happy not to have to pay for a wedding. Besides, Robert said he wasn't telling his parents, either, not till later.

On June 21, 1930, about thirty people assembled in Gumby's parlor. A crowd stood outside. Word had spread fast that something *big* was happening at Gumby's. It was warm, and windows were open.

All the people in the street were making a racket. Brother Bruce stuck his head out and yelled, "Y'all shut up till you hear de ladies start singing de saints marching in song. Den you kin do what you lak. You got dat?" Then he turned to us, pulled down the corners of his vest, and spoke as if he were a professor in a lecture hall. "I believe, my friends, that the crowd is tamed. You may proceed."

The altar was a podium Gumby had borrowed from the neighborhood elementary school and decorated with a garland of white carnations. To the left of the altar stood the chorus: six ladies dressed in jewel-colored silk dresses, feathered hats, and high-heeled shoes. To the right was Gumby's prized piano. Robert's friend Teo Hernandez played his own jazzy version of Wagner for my entrance, followed by a slow and quiet "Rock of Ages." The chorus hummed while Gumby raised his baritone voice, and said a few things about Robert and me that I don't remember. Robert slid the little gold filigree ring we'd found at a pawnshop on my finger. Gumby theatrically pronounced us man and wife. Teo began to pound on the piano, and the chorus sang joyously:

> *We are trav'ling in the footsteps*
> *Of those who've gone before,*
> *And we'll all be reunited*
> *On a new and sunlit shore.*
> *Oh, when the saints go marching in,*
> *Oh, when the saints go marching in,*
> *Lord, how I want to be in that number,*
> *When the saints go marching in.*

The people inside and out on the street clapped and sang and danced. Bruce, in his yellow silk shirt and white linen jacket, worked the crowds as if he were the host, kissing everyone on both cheeks while holding out his cigarette in a long ivory holder set with green and red enamel.

My wedding.

The social event of the season.

pamela

A few days later, Robert and I told Mam and Dad.
I held out my left hand, feigning bright assurance. "Guess what?" To which Mam exclaimed, "Oh, you're engaged!"

But when they learned the truth they took it quite well, just as I had thought they would. I was twenty-four, after all, a year older than Mam had been when she'd married Daddy. And theirs had been a whirlwind courtship, too. Mam hugged Robert—she seemed to be genuinely fond of him. I can't say the same for my father. In a misguided bout of enthusiasm, I'd shown him some of Robert's poetry.

The pattern that we'd established before our marriage remained unchanged. Robert would show up sporadically, and we'd go off to a party, or to Gumby's, or perhaps to a play. Sometimes we tagged along with Frederick and his friends at the Golden Swan.

We never discussed our living arrangements; it seemed unnecessary, I suppose. There was only a little time left before I was to leave for Italy.

It was obvious, anyway, that I couldn't have Robert sharing my studio in Macdougal Alley. And I could hardly join Robert in the apartment he still shared with Roy.

To be truthful, my focus was not on Robert. At times I just forgot about him, forgot that I had a husband at all. *Husband,* I would think. *What a strange-sounding word.*

I was rather single-minded.

Italy.

I folded blouses and skirts with care, slipped stockings into my sky-blue satin case with navy frog fasteners, wrapped glass perfume bottles in cotton rags. As I packed, my eye kept traveling to my left hand, now adorned with the delicate gold ring. Such a pretty little ring.

When finally the day to set sail arrived, Robert came with me to the dock. We were in high spirits. We embraced quickly and laughed. I waved happily from the deck. Robert waved back with the enthusiasm of a crazed man.

The terrible, strange burden of marriage was lifted from us both.

Robert, the wedding—it all did seem a dream as I crossed the sea. *What had I done?* We had no money, we had no plans. Still, I found it strangely easy to push these worries aside. For as long as I could make it last, Italy would be my world. Surely Robert and I would work out things when we settled down together in New York. There was plenty of time.

In Turin, I rented an apartment not far from our old place. I was overjoyed to see that all the places were just as I'd remembered: the house on the Via Cassini, the chestnut-lined streets, the vast and exquisite Valentino Park, the Po River, the churches and museums, the wide piazzas.

Months later I moved on to Florence, where I returned again and again to the Pitti Palace, home to the Medici grand dukes. Starstruck, I stood looking at the portraits and busts of the great Lorenzo Medici, the supreme patron of the arts. The force of the man was everywhere.

And everywhere, the Madonnas! *Madonna of the Sea, Madonna of the Chair, Madonna of the Steps, the Castle Madonna, Madonna of the Grotto.* Soon, I thought, I would paint Madonnas, too.

After Florence, Rome. After Rome, Venice. I fell in love with each city in turn. Mostly, though, I was in love with my freedom. I could do anything. Go anywhere. I could do nothing. Go nowhere. No one knew!

Never had I known such freedom.

‡ ‡ ‡

When I arrived back in Turin, I had a letter from Mam. She wrote that Peaked Hill Bars was no more. The house had been unsafe to live in for a long time, collapsing little by little. And so it should have been no real surprise to learn that finally, one day, a storm came and the ocean rose up, sweeping Gene's beloved beach house into the roiling waters. The news gave me a jolt, but I would not miss the place.

Then Robert wrote from Copenhagen, where he'd gone with Roy. They were collaborating on a book of Roy's poetry. The title was: *The Poems of Roy de Coverley, Together with a Lyric by the Editor.* The editor being Robert. I thought it was not a very good title. Robert's letter was mostly about Roy's book and all the wonderful people they'd met in Copenhagen, but he also had sad news from Harlem. The Depression had claimed Gumby among its victims. He'd been forced to close his studio, sell off many of his rare books, and store all his scrapbooks in a friend's cellar. Worst of all was the emotional toll—now Gumby was spending his days in the mental ward at Riverside Hospital in the Bronx.

In a postscript, Robert wrote that he was coming to visit me.

Robert . . . in Italy? I had mixed feelings about that. I didn't like to think of losing my solitude. I was engrossed in a painting, the one I would later always refer to as "my Guggenheim Madonna," and the work consumed me entirely. Almost since setting foot in Italy, I'd wanted to do a new sort of Madonna, but no setting satisfied me. Woods? Rocks? A church? All too dull, too static. Nothing made me happy. The answer arrived one morning in a package of laundry wrapped in brown paper. When I unloosed the string, the smell of starch hit me hard—instantly I was back in San Remo. I smelled the fresh ocean breezes and the starched laundry blowing on the line. And all at once I had a vision of the open sea and a young woman standing by the water, draped in a scarlet robe. A child stood at her side; he was no small babe, but a young boy, and in his hands he held a golden ship. *Madonna of the Sailors.* Yes, that was it. I was sure.

My Madonna claimed me. Now I was close to finishing it—I had only to fill in the background, paint the golden fabric that draped, wavelike, around mother and child, and my painting would be done.

Robert and I hadn't seen each other in fourteen months. When he arrived, it was early October and Turin, predictably, was shrouded in fog. It rained. I'd dreamed of picnics by the river, or hikes in the country, but that sort of thing was impossible.

Anyway, it seemed that all Robert wanted to do was eat and drink. Mostly drink. We traipsed around the city until the early-morning hours. He'd acquired a more sophisticated air, he'd somehow lost the naive boy from Oregon and become citified, a world traveler, throwing in Danish and French phrases whenever he could. He never got out of bed until noon at the earliest. Sometimes he didn't shave. His hair had grown even longer, and he had a rakish look with his cossack shirts during the day and now poets' shirts at night, and his gleaming, buckled boots and his flashing grin. He was terribly attractive. I clung to his arm as we roamed over the city. I saw how women looked at him. I saw how everyone looked at him.

Robert talked and talked, but it was all about Copenhagen, and about how well Roy was doing, how the Danish people seemed to look upon him as a god. We never spoke about our own life, about what we might do when we got back to New York. He asked little about what I had been doing or what I was thinking about. He did admire my Madonna. He said the colors were gorgeous.

I'd look at him in the morning, splayed across the sheets, and wonder so many things. *Who are you? Do you love me? Do I love you? Are you glad we got married? What will we do when we get back to New York?* But I never really asked him those things, I wasn't brave enough. Besides, I told myself that maybe love didn't matter right now, that love was what would happen when we finally got around to living together. But it was all foolishness, and among these thoughts the truth intruded, startling me. The words might as well have been shouted through a megaphone. There was no escaping them as I stared at the naked man on my bed.

Here lies another disaster.

Robert was gone before the week was out. He said there was a book festival in Copenhagen he had to attend.

I knew then I'd been fooling myself, that none of it was Real at all.

And I was what I'd always been, a rabbit with no fur, no hind legs, nothing more than a sewed-up sack of sawdust. I couldn't move properly. It wasn't fair, it wasn't fair at all.

At the end of December, I booked passage home.

I hadn't planned on returning to New York so soon. I had hoped to stay in Italy until spring, but I knew now it couldn't happen.

I'd been to see a doctor.

I wrote to Robert; it seemed that he ought to know.

I wrote to Mam and Daddy that I was coming home, but I didn't say anything about the baby. I thought that everything would get sorted out once I was in New York.

margery

Oh, lord. What was true then is still true today. Francesco has never wanted to let go.

When Eddie O'Toole came calling, Francesco thought that things would change, that people would sit up and take notice. I told him that Eddie had asked me if I thought Pamela would have another exhibition, and he looked at me as if to say, *What an odd question, of course she will, you're not doubting that are you?* He was quite emphatic, he told me Pamela would have another exhibition soon. It would be brilliant, he was sure of it.

A few days after Eddie's visit, the second call came. Another reporter from *The New Yorker*, somebody named Kinkead. He said he just had a few more follow-up questions to ask. Could he drop by for a few minutes?

Francesco took it as a good sign. They must be really interested. It would be a big story. I wondered what more there was to ask. Eddie O'Toole had been quite thorough, I thought.

Mr. Kinkead was nothing like young Eddie O'Toole. He was exceedingly self-assured. Late thirties, perhaps, with the physique of a boxer. His face was soft and ruddy—a grown-up Campbell Soup boy—but his eyes were sharp and black. I suppose he was what you would call a "seasoned" reporter, all no-nonsense and questions one after another, rat-a-tat-tat. He made us all uncomfortable. He kept asking Pamela questions about money all the time. How much did she make on this exhibit or that exhibit? He asked about her social life—was she part of the wild party scene that Greenwich

Village was so famous for? He wasn't rude, exactly, it's just that he managed to ask rude questions in a polite sort of way.

Worst of all, he kept asking Pamela how she felt about no longer being famous. Well, it didn't make any difference at all, she said. *I didn't paint to be famous. It was all the same to me.* But Mr. Kinkead didn't seem to believe her. He kept pressing. *But do you feel you're living up to your promise, to what all those people like Augustus John and John Galsworthy said about you?* It was rather amazing, how his face could look rather kindly with words like that coming out of his mouth.

Francesco and I tried to step in. We tried to explain that Pamela was born to be an artist, that nothing could take that away. But he simply wouldn't drop the subject.

We were very relieved to see him go.

When we heard nothing from *The New Yorker* for months, Francesco called the magazine. The story was on hold, they said. There were many considerations of space when putting together a magazine. If he wished, they would call him when they had more information.

There never was a call.

The New Yorker Memos
Winter 1935–1936

Outside, Stuyvesant Square Park was gray and indistinct in a blur of rain. A young woman of small stature and calm features entered the room with a lively little boy of three and a half who had a shock of red hair and an ingratiating kid's grin.

Back in New York after three years of silence, she is hoping to take up her painting again as soon as she can do some illustrating and "get on her feet again." She and her husband have separated, and he has gone back to his people in the West. She does not talk about that, but it is quite apparent from the strength underlying her features and her quietly smiling admission that there have been many problems to meet, that the last few years have not been easy to pass off lightly.

"I will never give up painting," she said. "At first I hope to get some illustrating to do until I can get back on my feet again. Then I want to paint from life—portraits, landscapes, nudes, everything until I am absolutely sure that I know how to draw everything as it is found in life. Then when I am sure I know how to draw, I want to paint things I imagine myself, things that I don't have to look at in life but will be right. . . . I want to do much larger paintings than I have ever done before."

From an interview with reporter Eddie O'Toole
December 1935

———

Mr. Ross:

This Where-Are-They-Now report on Pamela Bianco, the child wonder painter, is an excellent example of muffed and incomplete facts. If I rewrote it, people would say, 'Well, just where is she now, and for God's sake where has she been?'. . . In short, the story of Pamela Bianco's great drop from world fame to motherhood in New York is not at all told herein. What has happened to her and her great promise since 1921, when she hit this town like a comet? That is the only story we want.

Memo from James Thurber, chief rewrite man, to editor Harold Ross
December 1935

———

She knew most of the artists down in Greenwich Village, she said, but in response to a blunt or specific question most of the time Miss Bianco could only raise her eyebrows, or look puzzled. She didn't live a very gay life, she said.

From an interview with reporter Eugene Kinkead
January 1936
(The story was killed in the spring of 1936.)

pamela

*T*he crossing was rough, and I was wretched. I had been feeling nauseous even before I'd stepped on board. I hardly ate, and mostly stayed in my cabin. I must have looked a forlorn, starved ghost when I got off the ship—Mam's alarm as she looked at me was palpable. She clasped me to her.

"Oh Pamela, you're awfully pale! Let's get you straight home."

Mam and Daddy were, naturally, concerned. They wanted to know about Robert, what our plans were. I told them Robert would be back in New York soon. I said we hadn't quite worked out where we would live, that the baby had come as quite a surprise to both of us.

Take your time, Pamela. There's a roof over your head as long as you need it.

I'm afraid I took that quite for granted.

Robert returned at the end of the year, in time for my twenty-fifth birthday. After an overnight visit, he took off for Harlem.

A few weeks later Daddy saw the notice in the *Tribune*. On Friday, January 8, 1932, the author Richard Hughes had married Frances Bazley at her family's estate in Gloucestershire. I felt Mam watching me carefully. But she had no cause for concern, at least not in that direction. If my expression was grim it had nothing to do with Diccon. I had too much to worry me at home.

Robert was unreliable, to say the least, but now his absence—and his utter silence—stunned me. Surely we could talk a *little*, there was so much we had to talk about! I tried to think of the baby, but it was hard to concentrate. I couldn't picture anything.

In June, Lorenzo—named after Lorenzo de Medici, the great patron of the arts—was born. A healthy, red-haired baby.

Robert came to the hospital, bearing flowers, on the day his son was born, and a few weeks later he came to see us at Grove Street. I can still see him standing there, his brown eyes all earnest and panicked at the same time. He kissed me and grinned. Mam and Daddy left the three of us in the living room and retreated to the kitchen, where they busied themselves making tea. They spent longer than necessary, thinking to give us privacy.

Robert and I didn't say anything for a while. We both gazed at the baby sleeping on my lap.

"Would you like to hold him?" I asked. Robert seemed startled, but he nodded. I handed over the warm little bundle. Robert stared at Lorenzo. I thought he looked as though he might cry.

"I . . . I'm afraid I'm not too good at this, Pamela. I'm very sorry." I could see that he wanted to say more. He looked at me in a pleading sort of way, as if I could help him along. I didn't want to help him along. I was silent.

My parents needn't have bothered to stay so long in the kitchen. By the time they emerged with the tea, Robert was gone.

I was quite calm.

"He just needs more time. He's not used to all this," I said, without looking up from the baby.

There was silence as Mam put the tray on the table.

"No one's used to all this, I'm afraid," Daddy muttered.

pamela

Robert never came back.

He sent me a letter. When I read that letter, I took to my bed. I couldn't help it.

I was weighed down again. I knew the signs. I didn't try to fight it.

I couldn't care properly for Lorenzo. Mam cared for him.

I read Robert's letter over and over and over. I should have just ripped it up, but I kept torturing myself. I imagined the scene in Harlem so many times, I saw it so clearly, that I believed it to be true. . . .

Roy stands behind Robert in their now-empty apartment, his arms crossed over a purple silk robe embroidered with dragonflies. In exasperation, he puts paper and pen in front of his friend, my husband.

"What you have to do, Robert, is tell her the truth. For God's sake, you can't just leave without a word. Now *write*. I'm not moving until you've finished."

Robert fingers the paper.

"You're right, of course. But what do I say? I can't think."

"*Jesus*, Robert . . . just say what's true . . . it doesn't have to be long. Say she's beautiful, the baby's beautiful, but you just cannot be a husband and father. You wish you could be. You're sorry."

When he finishes, Robert hands the letter over to Roy.

"Okay? D'you think it will do?"

Roy reads the letter quickly. He lets out a great sigh, rubs a long finger over his silken forehead, and hands the letter back to Robert.

"Oh, it will do all right."

I worked unhurriedly. I was meticulous.

I pressed out the letter with the palms of my hands, then folded it in half. I ran my thumb along the seam twice, then opened up the rectangle again. I made neat triangles by bending the top corners of the paper toward the middle, again running over the seams with my fingers. *Triangles, fold the flaps inward. Open with the thumbs. Fold flat. Another set of triangles, another square. Fold up the flaps.* Just as Mam had taught me when I was a small girl. Then the final opening with thumbs. A boat appeared. A boat with a nice flat beam and angled bow and stern. It was perfect.

I picked up my umbrella.

"Mam, I'm going out for a little walk . . . not for long, I promise . . . could you just pick up Lorenzo if he wakes?"

I'd waited for a rainy day. I didn't want it to float for long.

I headed west on Barrow Street and walked the few blocks to the Hudson River. At the end of the dock two beat-up skiffs rocked against each other in the current.

There was a breeze from the north. I was relieved: I didn't want the tiny boat to drift back to shore. I turned my face into the wind; a fine pelting of rain made me blink. Squinting, I saw a large boat heading downriver. A ferry. As it got close I could see it was the *de Witt Clinton.*

I walked to the end of the dock and stood a while, listening to the pinging sound, the symphony of water drops on the stretched silk of the umbrella.

I took the paper boat from my raincoat pocket and pulled the little filigree ring off my finger. I wedged the ring into a fold. I held the boat parallel to the water before I dropped it, but still it fell over as it hit the waves.

The boat drifted southward on its side, toward the ocean, in a fast-moving tide.

Water soon weighed the vessel down, and the cargo—a few words in blue ink and a bit of gold—was lost forever.

My dearest Pamela,
You know that I have loved you very much. You have
always been very beautiful to me. The baby is beautiful,
too. But I have realized that I can never be a husband
and father. I would be no good at all.
Roy and I are leaving tomorrow for Oregon. We can't
afford this apartment any longer.
I will think of you always—
Your Robert

margery

I do wish Francesco would get home. It could make all the difference in the world if he's here when Pamela wakes. She tends to put on a brighter face if he's around. With me, she feels she can fall apart.

Francesco can get quite lost in his work, though, forget all about the time. It's been such blessing for him to have that little studio uptown, a quiet place to work in. A bit of space to himself, room to store all the old bookbinding tools from Italy. He's been so excited about this book. A small volume, he said. Poems.

I'm glad I thought of sending Pamela home with the roast. It will be best all way round. Better to be alone with Francesco tonight. And God knows I have no inclination to cook. Not with this pain that seems to have its own schedule, crashing through my head like a freight train, then leaving only to come back with a vengeance. Just the thought of cooking is excruciating—the noise of the knife across the cutting board, the banging of pans.

When Francesco gets here, I'll ask him to make vegetable soup. There are plenty of vegetables left in the bin. It's his specialty; he won't mind a bit.

I'd better write out the recipe for Pamela. She can get muddled when it comes to cooking. Oh . . . and the bay leaf, the spices . . .

she may not have those. I'll wrap them in a bit of cheesecloth for her, put everything in the blue wicker basket.

Do I hear . . . ?
  Yes . . . footsteps . . .
  Pamela's awake.

margery

*T*hank God. Just the miracle I'd prayed for. . . . She'd lost that dreadful look. She almost seemed—it's too much, really—but she almost seemed *cheerful*.

"You look awfully serious, Mam," she said. "A penny for your thoughts!"

I'm sure I saw it, a bit of a twinkle in her eye.

Well. Perhaps, after all, she just needed a nap. Lord, all that worry for nothing! And she positively brightened when I gave her the cut of beef and the potatoes. Sometimes it's just thinking what to cook that's the hardest part.

Pamela *seems* to be herself again.

There's reason to hope, after all.

How lovely . . . a breeze. . . .

And there, shadows moving. Clouds.

Perhaps we'll get a storm after all, clear the air. How nice to think it will be cooler tomorrow. A glorious thought.

Is that . . . thunder?

God, my head. . . .

It's cracking in two.

....

September 1, 1944
(Early Evening)

Francesco Bianco is walking down Fifth Avenue. In two blocks he'll turn east—he likes to take 28th Street so that he can stop by St. Stephen's. The Brumidi paintings. The *Crucifixion* that towers over the altar never fails to move him. He is not a religious man, but he loves the paintings in this church, all the saints and angels. And he is proud that the artist, Constantino Brumidi, is a fellow Italian.

Just as he nears the church, he feels the rain, and quickly, deftly, he tucks the handmade book under his coat. He presses it to his heart with his right hand, and pulls down his fedora with his left.

It's a beautiful book, the most beautiful he has made. He has told Margery it's a special edition he's doing for a local poet. He hasn't told her the whole truth, though—that the local poet is himself, that he's dedicated this book to Margery.

He's played out the scene in his head many times. He'll tell her, *The poetry may be no good, Margery, but at least the illustrations are superb.* The book is strewn with Pamela's exquisite woodcuts of flowers. And of course Margery will be astounded, will look at him with those eyes that never fail to reach deep inside him. Tonight they'll go all soft, fill with happiness. And love, even still.

She will tell him how beautiful the book is, and he will bask in her light. He is savoring the anticipation, as if he were a small child carrying a clay animal or a tin angel he's made at school, anxious to show his mother, to hear her words of praise. He can barely wait to get to Stuyvesant Square.

He is home.

He pushes open the door, calls out, *Margery?* And it is this that he will keep going over later, it is this that will keep him up at night, how he *knew*. How the silence was somehow different. How heavy it all was.

He heads to the kitchen.

Margery!

For the second time in forty years of marriage, Francesco collapses to his knees before his wife.

pamela

I

September 1, 1944: Evening

*T*hank God Mam wrote out the instructions so I couldn't go wrong. Something usually does go wrong—I forget to grease the pan, or I set the oven for the wrong temperature. There aren't any carrots, but that doesn't matter. Lorenzo isn't fond of carrots, anyway.

Dinner's in the oven. I can't believe it.

I almost laugh as an image comes to me, one I see in the magazines all the time: a pretty woman wearing a cheerful apron, stirring something wonderful atop her new General Electric stove, smiling as if she were having just the *best* time ever.

I've been wondering now, about Robert, about whether to talk to Lorenzo about his father or not. I'm beginning to think that perhaps it isn't a good idea, after all. I thought, *What could be the harm*, but now I realize that Lorenzo would be sure to ask, *But why did it end? Why did he leave?* And I would have no answers.

And, well—I'm afraid it might only make things worse for Lorenzo, make him miss him having a father all over again. He's had more than enough of that.

Someday I'll talk to him about Robert. But not tonight. Tonight we'll just enjoy our lovely roast beef.

What . . . oh—the telephone! The loud, shrill sounds startles me, I'm so lost in my thoughts. But as I scurry out to the hallway I'm lighthearted—I'm sure it's Mam, it usually is, and I'm anxious to let her know that the roast has survived my ministrations and is safely in the oven.

It's Daddy's voice at the other end of the line. I know it is, of course, but it doesn't really sound like my father, it sounds like a hollow man.

"Pamela . . . your mother. . . ." There is silence.

"My mother what? Is she all right?"

"She fell, I don't know. . . ."

He says that Mam's at St. Vincent's.

I drop the telephone into its cradle, run over to the hospital.

They can't tell us what is wrong, exactly, not yet. A stroke, perhaps.

My mother lies in the hospital bed, lifeless. Pale and small as a faraway, wispy cloud. Her eyes are closed. The fragile lids lie all limp over her eyes like pie dough rolled too thin. I have a crazy thought, that Mam is a doll, and I can simply prop her up and her eyes will fly open. But she isn't a doll. She isn't my mother, either. She is a terrible thing.

I hold her hand, talk to her about Lorenzo, the roast, the weather. I tell her that soon we'll have her home. But Mam doesn't respond, she doesn't even squeeze my hand.

Seeing my mother like this makes me nauseous, dizzy. I'm afraid I might vomit. I don't know how to deal with this sort of thing, a blow like this, as though someone had kicked me in the stomach but I can't yell out in pain. This hospital room with my mother all ghostly is incomprehensible to me. And a fear beyond any I'd ever known paralyzes my brain. I am terrified that Mam will never open her eyes again.

Daddy's face is rigid, and I know he fears it, too. He paces and paces, goes over to Mam's bed, puts his hand on her cheek, or on her brow, then walks away.

pamela

II

September 2, 1944

I call Cecco. He takes the train up from Washington.

Now we are all in Mam's hospital room, Cecco and Lorenzo and Daddy and I. The room is quiet, the light dim. There's a window, but the roll shade is drawn more than halfway down and no one thinks to open it.

We come and go, the nurses won't allow us to be there all the time. But Mam never seems to notice whether we are there or not. She doesn't even respond to the sound of Cecco's voice. We had thought she would, somehow.

Nothing changes. Mam just lies there.

Her eyes remain shut. *It can't be true,* I keep saying to myself, *Mam's eyes must open, they must. Please just one more time.*

But I am so afraid that they never will and what could be worse than that, whatever could be worse than never again seeing how my mother loves me.

margery

III

September 3, 1944

Cecco . . . is that Cecco's voice?

No . . . no, that is a man's voice. Cecco is a little boy.

There he is, I see him through the window, in the backyard. What a perfect day to be outside playing—all that lovely sunshine!

He's with Pamela, they've made a little castle, a heap of stones, and now they're digging a moat, jabbing at the dirt with rocks and sticks. I'll just bring them some soup spoons. . . .

pamela

IV

September 4, 1944

*M*am's eyes do not open. Three days after she enters the hospital, she is gone. A cerebral hemorrhage, the doctor tells us.

Cerebral hemorrhage.

I imagine the beautiful circuitry of my mother's brain, all blue and green and yellow loops, red blood flowing without a hitch. But then I see them—the insidious black tendrils of my illness, of Daddy's illness, winding their way through that humming place, choking off a bit here, a bit there. . . .

May 1945

Francesco descends the dark stairwell at the subway station on Christopher Street. It is eight months after Margery's death.

He is disoriented, unused to the place, and he puts his nickel into the turnstile with the hesitancy of a tourist. On another day he might have admired the blue-and-amber mosaics on the walls, but this is not another day. He has left his hat at home. He moves to the far left, stands close to the platform, looks northward for lights.

The conductor of the train sees something ahead. Something all conductors dread. *Jesus!* he calls out, and shoves the brake switch as far and as fast as he can.

pamela

Spring and Summer, 1945

I have to call Cecco, he has to know.

It was a dizzy spell, I tell him.

Cecco takes the train north once again, this time to sit by Daddy's bedside. Francesco will surely recover, the doctors say, but he is not a young man, and with the all the fractures and the broken collarbone it's bound to take a while.

Daddy gets better, a bit. But he isn't the same. Francesco, the charmer, the most social of all of us, can bear to see no one. He barely seems to tolerate his own children. When he's well enough to travel, Cecco brings him back to Washington, hoping that there, with a change of scenery, with no memories of Margery in every corner, he'll get his strength back.

Cecco calls me often. Daddy seems to make an effort at first, venturing out to the living room, chatting with Cecco and Barbara, and his grandchildren. But then something happens, lethargy sets in. He will not leave his bed.

"It's as if he's turned his face to the wall," Cecco tells me.

Daddy fades rapidly. He rarely speaks. He refuses to eat. Cecco says he thinks that Daddy has made up his mind. That I should prepare myself.

I am calm when Cecco calls to tell me the news. I have been waiting for this call. The official cause of death is bronchial pneumonia, but Cecco and I agree that bronchial pneumonia had little to do with it, that Daddy died of grief.

We are just saying good-bye when Cecco remembers something.

"Oh—Pamela, he left a book for you, his old Yeats. I'll send it to you straightaway. And there's a letter."

And there's a letter.

I've worried so that I could not be with my father when he died. I've imagined how it would have been. I would have held his hand, and told him how I'd always loved him. But what would he say to me? I could never imagine that part.

The package arrives from Cecco. I tear off the brown paper. And there it is, Daddy's old clothbound book of poems, the green faded almost to yellow in places. So lovingly worn. I see it in my father's hands.

The envelope is small, a single page inside. The handwriting is shaky, nothing like the beautiful, bold script that I remember.

Cara Pamela,
Be not afraid of greatness.
That is what I wish to tell you, though
Shakespeare said it first.
That is the simple part, something I hope you
already know. Now, here is what keeps coming to me, as
I lie here day after day.
I see you clearly, Pamela, such a bright little girl,
in your linen dress and sturdy brown shoes. You stand
in the parlor in Chelsea, reciting "The Host of the Air."
All of it perfectly! I was a stern taskmaster, wasn't I?
I hope not too stern. I always thought we understood
each other, you and I?

Yes, Daddy, we did.

At the end of the letter, Daddy wrote, *I send you my love, dearest girl.*

I hold the letter to my breast, press it to my heart.

‡ ‡ ‡

My parents are dead.

How can I believe it, that they are truly gone? That I'll never hear their voices again?

Yet . . . I hear them all the time.

Now you are famous . . . now all Italians are happy to claim you as one of their children!

Pamela . . . you know that this . . . this craziness won't last forever?

People are ignorant, they ask if a Bull has a bull's head on the seals. Not one that I've seen.

Listen to this dress, Pamela! 'French blue silk crepe blooming with a copper and gold floral design, a tracery of metal lace. . . .' Gorgeous, don't you think?

Bloody critics . . .

Sometimes I walk to Stuyvesant Square, stand in front of my parents' old apartment. I see Mam at her writing table, Daddy engrossed in a book. They know I'm there, though, and they look up at me. Their eyes are full of concern.

I am in a bad way, as it all sinks in. I dream of putting stones in my pockets, slipping down into the gray waters of the Hudson. *The peace.* How I long for peace! But inevitably, when I let my thoughts drift in that direction they always run aground.

Lorenzo.

Lorenzo, though he will never know it, saves my life. He gives me the gift of his existence, the only reason I can find to stay with the world. I will not allow myself to find solace in the cold river water, I will not. Lorenzo can afford to lose no more. The boy has never seen his father. Now, his only grandparents are gone. I will not take his mother away from him.

part six

‡‡‡

*And [the Fairy] held the little Rabbit close in her arms
and flew with him into the wood.*

*It was light now, for the moon had risen. All the
forest was beautiful, and the fronds of the bracken
shone like frosted silver. In the open glade between the
tree trunks the wild rabbits danced with their shadows
on the velvet grass, but when they saw the Fairy they
all stopped dancing and stood round in a ring to stare
at her.*

*"I've brought you a new playfellow," the Fairy
said. "You must be very kind to him and teach him all
he needs to know in Rabbit-land, for he is going to live
with you for ever and ever!"*

*And she kissed the little Rabbit again and put him
down on the grass.*

"Run and play, little Rabbit!" she said.

*But the little Rabbit sat quite still for a moment
and never moved. For when he saw all the wild rabbits
dancing around him he suddenly remembered about his
hind legs, and he didn't want them to see that he was
made all in one piece. He did not know that when the
Fairy kissed him that last time she had changed him
altogether.*

From *The Velveteen Rabbit*
by Margery Williams Bianco

pamela

I

I am working again!

Not painting, I've pushed that behind me. For a long while I kept telling myself that I ought to. I thought . . . *should I try? Is it what I ought to do? And if not painting, well, what do I want to do?*

Now, I know. I suppose I've always known.

The books. Illustrated children's books. *Beginning with A.*

The thoughts—the ideas for books—come to me almost all at once, beckoning me.

Such a sweet realization, a relief. As if I'd been walking along on a dark day and up ahead there is a sudden sweep of light on the ground—I look up to see a blue hole in the clouds. The sky opening like an invitation. It is more than that. A gift.

I understand, now, that I no longer have to please . . . well, anyone at all.

At first, the thought seems a terrible betrayal.

Then, a source of wonder.

Whatever I choose to do, I won't be letting anyone down.

I can only disappoint myself.

I fly straight sunward, through the blue portal.
And on the other side, I am not what I have been.

‡ ‡ ‡

The ABC book for children is really all worked out, it has been for a long time. Twenty-six children—and twenty-six poems—have been living in my head for years. Alexander, Barbara, Catherine. I'll do pen-and-ink drawings of each girl and boy, set them in frames of lace and diamonds and rosettes and ribbons.

I publish *Beginning with A* in 1947. After that, my books for children come one after another. One every year.

I have no thought of trying to be the writer that my mother was. It would be impossible, anyway. My voice is not my mother's voice. I do not have her wise heart. What I do have, what I want to capture, are memories of the childhood that she made so bright all those years ago. In my books there are many different mothers, but they're all Mam.

It's Mam who fixes the party dress in *Playtime in Cherry Street* when her daughter has ripped off the lace collar and sleeves to make a Valentine for a friend. It's Mam who prepares the tea party for her children in *Joy and the Christmas Angel*—grapes packed in sawdust, cheese in silver paper, angel cake iced with ribbons and rosebuds. And it's Mam in *The Doll in the Window,* who helps the little girl out of her predicament when she *means* to buy presents for her siblings but really wants to spend her Christmas money on a doll for herself.

My mother is with me every day as I write and draw, just as if she were still sitting at her little writing desk in the corner of the studio in Macdougal Alley.

In the winter of 1948, I find a new place to live. Colonnade Row, on Lafayette Street, near Astor Place. Lorenzo and I are thrilled.

Such an elegant old building, all decked out in marble and Corinthian pillars. We think it's quite grand.

We have the top-floor apartment, and above that, a rooftop studio with a large, slanting skylight. The studio is lovely, the perfect place to work on my drawings and books. For the first time in years we have space to move around—although for the most part, it's just me. Lorenzo is rarely home these days. He's almost twenty now, and busy with photography and the National Guard and all his friends.

My easel sits in the basement, gathering dust. Thoughts of putting my dreams onto canvas have all but disappeared.

II

*I*t's just a random thought, really. A whim. The sort of thing you don't usually follow up on. It's October 16, 1954, and a notice in the paper catches my eye. A young Spanish artist is showing his work in an uptown gallery, and the opening is tonight. *Why not?* I think. A good excuse for a nice, long walk.

The evening is clear and sharp. I stand still for a moment, breathing in the cool autumn air, a jumble of fresh-fallen leaves and rainstorms and first frost that makes me think of Merryall. I've dressed perfectly for this chilly weather. The new soft boots that lace on the side, and my favorite skirt—wool and angora, flounced at the hem and cozy as a blanket. A breeze riffles through my hair, now chin length. The short cut makes me feel light all over.

On East 73rd Street, I walk into the Mason and Dyer Gallery filled with a rare, inexplicable happiness.

I take a quick glance around. No surprise here—it's the usual mix of fashionable and artsy. A clump of guests stand by a table laden with cheese and fruit and sparkling champagne glasses. *Perhaps one before I leave*, I think. I know it's shyness, really, the reason I don't head over to the table. But I have, in fact, come to see the art.

I stand in front of a large, roughly painted canvas—giant nudes with pitchforks and blue orbs, the outline of a cityscape in the far background. I scrutinize the painting. Despite its lack of grace, its jarring contrasts, Gaugin jumps into my mind, and I think: What if Gaugin had never left Paris, what if he had never traveled to Tahiti? What if he worked all those years in the city, penniless, growing angrier, wishing he could leave, never seeing a way? Perhaps he might have painted something like this. I like the painting . . . well, I like the idea of it, but it's too crude, undeveloped. *Well,* I am thinking, *if I happen to speak to the artist during the evening I could reference Gaugin. . . .*

"Care for a glass of champagne? I seem to have two of them. . . . "

A male voice, just behind my right shoulder.

It takes a moment to shake off my Gaugin reveries.

I turn to see a slim, gray-haired man in a charcoal jacket holding out a golden flute.

Yes, I *do* care for a glass of champagne, thank you very much.

"Georg Hartmann," he says, raising his glass to mine.

Definitely not the young Spanish artist, I think, relieved.

And then, there is this thought: *I like this man.* The soft jacket. The beautiful timbre of his voice, the slight accent. The kindness and elegance in his demeanor. And the eyebrows. Who would have thought that eyebrows could be such an attraction? When Georg laughs, the inner tips move up towards the center of his forehead, and he looks as open and innocently happy as a child.

He walks me home. He is an artist, he says. He paints some; mostly he does etchings. He knew who I was when he came over with the champagne—apparently someone at the show had pointed me out. He was something of a prodigy himself, he says. *Won the top prize in Munich about a hundred years ago. . . . I was sixteen.* I give him my most brilliant smile.

Georg is sixty-two. He has curious, black eyes. He listens well. When we reach Lafayette Street, I touch his arm as we say good night. *Moleskin.* As surprising and inviting as Georg himself. I feel its velvety softness, and the strength of his arm beneath, long after he's gone.

As I putter around the apartment, too excited—too *happy*—to go to bed, a strange thought astonishes me. I know that I am going to marry this Georg Hartmann. I am quite sure of it. I can't say that it's just the same as it had been with Agnes and Gene, when Gene had walked Agnes home and said, *I want to spend every night of my life from now on with you. . . . I mean this. Every night of my life.* I can't quite say that. But I'd been comfortable with him from the moment he'd offered me the sparkling golden flute, and somehow I know that it's not a feeling that will disappear.

We marry within the year. I am a bride at forty-eight.

‡ ‡ ‡

I'm astounded by my luck.

Doing nothing much of anything, we are happy together. We sit for hours, wrapped together in a huge old afghan, reading. I read Elizabethan historical novels one after another; Georg reads any book on World War I air battles that he can find.

He rents the studio next to mine. If we want to visit each other we've only to climb out of our skylights and scuttle over the rooftop, high above the colonnades, like great dark pigeons.

Now, at long last, I have nothing left to wish for. I am envious of no one. Together, we are part of all that's bright and real, one among the couples in the Village who walk together entwined and nonchalant and murmuring private things.

I can talk to Georg about anything. Perhaps it is all the years of living alone, of having thoughts pent up inside, but I find myself chattering all the time, telling him everything that comes to mind. I tell him all my secrets, and he tells me his. Somewhere along the way, I mention my old obsession, the series of large canvasses.

"Oh, but that part of me is finished, it was all so long ago," I tell him.

Georg, however, sees otherwise. He says he can tell my passion is burning still. He will not let it go.

"You must paint again, Pamela. Give it a try, it will be like a rebirth. I'm sure your work will be better than it's ever been! Besides, I want to see these new paintings, don't keep them in your head. . . ."

Full of misgivings, I rescue my easel from the cellar. It's rusty in the joints, all covered with cobwebs. I dust it, wax it. Set it up in the studio. Stare at it. It has been so many years since I've held a paintbrush in my hand.

I clean the studio, reorganize it, find any reason not to begin.

At last, one day as snow falls softly on the skylight, I start work on the first canvas. Once the door to my old dreams opens, the pictures spill out. A collection stuffed for years in a far corner of my mind. They are all still there. I've held on to everything. The patterns. The settings. The children. The ghosts. I lie awake at night, remembering. The turmoil, all frozen in geometric scenes.

Details. Mam's beaded purses. The prismed chandelier in the hallway in London. The flocked pomegranate wallpaper from my room in Turin. The French carpet in Gertrude's grand parlor at the Ritz. I remember how I felt when the world was such a dizzying place. Mazes, and other designs of entrapment, burn in my mind. The beautiful childhood that I couldn't control. I will paint it all.

Soon I'm working on several canvasses at once. I paint all day, and into the night, just as I did when I was a young girl in Macdougal Alley.

The work is complicated, and progress is slow. I am painting in excruciating detail—hundreds of tiny brushstrokes for a sleeve, a square of garden, a column. It takes me three or four years to finish some of the pieces. Stacks of sketches for future paintings fill the makeshift shelves under the studio eaves.

My dreams acquire names.

The Chandelier. An ornate painting, a crowd of patterns. Vertical. Horizontal. They surround a girl rising from the bottom of the canvas, pinned against the patterns by a dress of jewels, stiff as an altar. She is so tall that if she turned and walked, her head would hit the giant chandelier streaming endless crystal pendants.

In *The Appointment*, the bust of a girl sits atop a column on the left side of the picture; the bust of a boy on the right. Below them a ruler-straight path of blue-green is bordered by a sunken garden maze of violent green, an endless vista running off the painting—the depths seem unfathomable. A tiny girl in a white dress and red sash is in the path, holding out a silver hoop. If she stepped off the path, she would step into an abyss.

And *Pomegranate*. An ecstasy of geometry, image upon image. The shattered Christmas ornaments that Shane's blown off the tree. A kaleidoscope—bits of broken glass reordered, stacked in layers, delicate and precise.

Dream after dream. All the ghosts.

I work patiently, with the infinite care of a restorer. Everything is in place.

By the winter of 1961 I know that I have more than enough paintings for an exhibition. But . . . *could* I have a show? Do I even really want to?

The truth is: I am afraid.

The New York art world is now a mystery to me. My last exhibition was twenty-five years ago! If I have a show now, how will I be judged? I tell myself over and over that it doesn't matter. But fear quickly tramples all the joy I've felt as I worked on the paintings.

I've been painting in a cocoon. I'm crazy to think of an exhibition—it's far too risky. What if critics—if the public—find these new works wanting? What toll might it take? I try to convince myself not to worry about such things. I've painted just what I wanted to paint. I have not painted for an audience.

Still, I am paralyzed. I stop working. I hide in my studio, arranging and rearranging the paintings. Fretting about everything.

I remember my father's letter. *Be not afraid of greatness.*

But I am afraid. I'm afraid of just about everything.

I think of the time, so long ago, when Daddy had worried

about the critics. And my mother had worried about me. The time Mam and I stood outside the butcher shop, its window displaying the awful row of pink, skinned rabbits.

What's happening now is not the important thing . . . the important thing is simply that you are an artist no matter what the papers may say, good or bad.

I know my mother was right, that she's always been right. Still, I can't seem to make a move.

It's Georg, of course, who gets things going. He understands my fear.

One evening when I don't come downstairs at my usual time, Georg comes into my studio and finds me standing by the huge skylight, staring out at the darkening sky. Gently, he lays his hands on my shoulders.

"Call David tomorrow, love. He's one man, not the whole outside world. See what he says."

David Herbert is a gallery owner I've known for a long time. I respect him. He will tell me the truth.

‡ ‡ ‡

We climb the four stories up to the studio.

Sunlight moves around the room, lighting up this painting, then that, then flickers out as great clouds travel slowly across the skylight.

David shakes his head slowly.

"They are magnificent, Pamela."

Joy—and relief—hit me like a blow to the back of the knees, and I'm afraid I might stumble. I feel weak and pathetic. Never in my life have I so thirsted for praise.

"Oh, yes," David goes on. "We shall have a show. My only regret is that I can't bring this changing light into my gallery— what a drama!"

A few days later David shows my paintings to Robert Rosenblum, a professor at Princeton who's just published a book about cubism. The book's been very well received. Rosenblum says he's intrigued by my work, says it's refreshing to see art that seems to pay absolutely no attention to current trends. And he agrees to write the introduction for the catalog.

> *Fantastic geometries . . . disquieting magic . . . the explicit imagery of hallucination . . . where the simplicities of one-point perspective unexpectedly oblige us to tumble into a rabbit hole. Very rarely, an artist emerges whose work seems blissfully ignorant of the twentieth century. Pamela Bianco's painting startles and refreshes for just this reason.*

III

*I*n May 1961, my exhibition opens at the David Herbert Gallery. The opening party is a blur. I am blind with nervousness. Despite all my lectures to myself, despite my deepest convictions, I teeter on the brink of panic. I haven't a shred of confidence. I make David and Georg promise to stand by me the whole evening, to prop me up if necessary.

Afterwards, they assure me the affair went well, but I remember little.

My worries come to nothing. The critics are wildly enthusiastic.

They compare me to Balthus, to Magritte!

Just as when I was a young girl, leading lights of the art world come to see my paintings. And I sell a great deal, more than half the paintings in the show. David is ecstatic. He is thrilled, too, by the roster of purchasers: Joseph Hirshhorn, Edward G. Robinson, the Museum of Modern Art, the Chase Manhattan Bank, Gloria Vanderbilt, Zero Mostel.

The sales of my paintings bring in the first decent bit of money that Georg and I have seen for a long, long time. There have not been many luxuries over the years. But now we intend to celebrate.

We go to Balducci's and buy whatever strikes our fancy. Perfect Bosc pears and a package of coffee from France. Pâté de campagne with cornichons. Butterflied lamb and chutney and spaetzle. Italian cheeses and risotto. Petits fours—two chocolate and two white—and Harlequin biscuits. A bottle of *Veuve Clicquot*.

We toast our good fortune.

1965

IV

*G*eorg is dead.
I still cannot comprehend it. Such a sudden thing.

I found him that day, his head resting on his drawing board. I thought he'd fallen asleep.

I tried, for a very long time, to waken him.

I didn't handle his death well. The blackness returned.

I was in a hospital for quite a long time, in the city.

Even now I'm not sure I've recovered, not all the way.

I don't tend to things well.

It's difficult. The bills pile up.

Now my eye settles, as it does so often, on the little picture across the room. Georg's etching. I never tire of looking at it. It's a portrait of me, but there's so much of Georg in it. I can hear him telling me that he's caught me exactly, if he does say so himself, that he's captured that wary look I have—and a certain smugness. *Smugness!* I'd say, *I don't believe it for a minute.* And we would laugh.

Things were bright all round, then.

Georg is dead.

part seven

‡‡‡

‡‡‡

January 1977

428 Lafayette Street
New York City

pamela

Friday, January 14

I

*T*here's no use reading the letter again. It's etched in my brain by now.

> *Could we have a cup of coffee, at least? We can talk*
> *about anything you like, but of course, I am thinking of*
> *Lorenzo. Time, I'm afraid, is running out and it would*
> *be nice to round things out, finally.*
>> *I have your telephone number, and I'll call you*
> *when I get into town.*

I have to make up my mind, decide what to say to Robert when he calls.

Damn him. He's got no business writing after all this time. Such a stupid letter, putting Lorenzo in as an afterthought. An aside.

But the phone is going to ring any day now, any minute, and I will have to say something.

The letter sits on the table, a constant bother, niggling at me like a spider you've discovered in the corner of the room and you can't quite decide whether to smash it and flush it down the toilet, or just let it be. Hope it will go away. But it won't, of course. It's still there *somewhere*, isn't it?

What on earth should I do? Should I see him, hear what he has to say? Or tell him no, it's too late. I can't think. It's so unfair to do this now. Despite the ridiculous letter, the talk of his friend's book collection, this can only be about Lorenzo.

But . . . forty-six years—it's simply too late! If Robert had wanted to find his son he could have. At any time. It would have been no trouble at all. In all these years, we've never moved beyond a mile radius of Greenwich Village. All he had to do was to call long-distance information. How many Lorenzo Schlicks are there in Manhattan?

It's too late!

This last-minute business is so typical. He's thinking only of himself, his needs. People never change, do they? Most likely I wouldn't recognize him if he walked by me on the street, but one thing's clear—he's just as selfish and impulsive as he was all those years ago. And just as careless, thinking he can get away with anything.

At any rate, I suppose I have him to thank for this: he brought my mother back to me today. If it hadn't been for Robert, I wouldn't have had that little accident, and I never would have given Mam's book a thought at all.

This morning, the spilled tea, it all began with that. I was rattled—I've been so jumpy and distracted ever since I got Robert's letter. I poured my breakfast tea and carried the cup and saucer to my office—just a corner of the parlor, really, with my writing desk and the tall bookcase. I had a vague idea that perhaps I'd open the bills I'd been avoiding, but really my mind was still on Robert, turning over and over what I might say if he called and would I talk to him at all. I reached over to set the cup on top of the bookcase. It was an automatic gesture, I didn't really look. The teacup tipped over and the hot liquid raced right towards Mam's rabbit.

I was in a panic. I swiped at the tea with the sleeve of my blouse. If Tubby got wet, I knew, it would be the end of him. Such a fragile and insubstantial creature, and so *old*—almost a hundred years! A soaking would turn him to nothing more than a little heap of mush. A dreadful thought.

Don't look at me that way, Tubby.

Mam's rabbit gazes in my direction, his eyes all starry-blind. Even so there is a sadness in his look. He sits on the bookshelf . . . well, no, he can no longer "sit" at all, he just occupies space in a lumpy sort of way. When my mother was a little girl, Tubby was quite a fine, soft thing to hold, all puffed up in rich brown plush, but now you have to look very hard to find any of his old self—the faded bits of fur hidden among the folds of worn cotton. Mam said his eyes were once black and snappy, polished bright as Daddy's boots. Now they're broken buttons, mother-of-pearl, cross-stitched with white thread. That's my handiwork. A poor job, I'm afraid. No wonder he can't seem to focus.

I managed to rescue Tubby, but the bookshelves were a mess, all that tea dripping down, and as I cleaned I pulled out the row of my mother's books. *A Street of Little Shops, Poor Cecco, The Candlestick.* Then her first book for children, *The Velveteen Rabbit.* How long had it been since I'd read that book? Thirty years? More? Once, though, I had it almost memorized, and the words of her story burned in my brain. All that wisdom parceled out with love and humor and simplicity.

Not that any of it did me any good. I didn't understand a thing.

I took the book over to the chair, held it unopened in my lap. In the pool of light, the glassine cover shone like a glaze of water. I ran my hand over William's simple drawing of the bunny who knows nothing of the world, all alert and eager and innocent.

I read *The Velveteen Rabbit* ever so slowly.

In my mind I was back at Old House, and I could hear the warm, clear tones of my mother's voice as she read her story to us the very first time. It's impossible to read the book without hearing her—the story *is* my mother's voice.

My reading was really more remembering, though, because every paragraph, every drawing, made me stop and think of how, long ago, I yearned just to understand, to be part of the world of men and women together. But I was not one of them, I was pieced together differently, and I never could run with the other rabbits in the meadow.

> *"What is REAL?" asked the Rabbit. "Does it mean*
> *having things that buzz inside you and a stick-out*
> *handle?"*

I'd no idea what she meant when she wrote about being Real.
My mother's wisdom was wasted on me.
Now her words prick me with shame.

> *"Does it hurt?" asked the Rabbit.*
> *"Sometimes," said the Skin Horse, for he was*
> *always truthful. "When you are Real, you don't mind*
> *being hurt."*
> *"Does it happen all at once, like being wound up,"*
> *he asked, "or bit by bit?"*
> *"It doesn't happen all at once," said the Skin*
> *Horse. "You become. It takes a long time. That's why it*
> *doesn't happen often to people who break easily, or have*
> *sharp edges, or who have to be carefully kept. . . ."*

I shattered so easily . . . my edges were like glass.
I am so sorry, Mam, I'd like to tell her now.

If Mam really were here, I know what she would say about this letter of Robert's. She would be thinking of Lorenzo, she would suggest, ever so gently, that I should do this for my son. And perhaps even for myself.

Forgiving Robert might release a burden of your own, Pamela.
My mother knew all about forgiveness. She was an expert.

II

*G*od—the telephone!

The loud ringing of the phone startles me so that I almost jump off the chair.

Robert? My God, could it really be Robert? So soon? I'm not ready. . . .

I walk over to the phone, so flustered that all I can think is this: *It can't be Robert, but if it is, well I can just hang up.*

The receiver is heavy. Cold. I don't want to put it to my ear. I hold it away a bit as I answer.

"Hello?"

"Hi Mom, glad I caught you."

The relief is immense, but I've been so tense that I can hear that my voice sounds thin, constricted.

"Oh, Lorenzo, how *are* you darling?"

"Fine, Mom. Look, I was wondering if I could drop by? I wanted to chat with you about something if you have some time."

Something catches inside me. *He wants to chat about something. Well, ask him what it is. But no, it's probably nothing at all, don't be ridiculous.* I think these thoughts even as I answer him and they make me hold back.

"Oh, well. Lorenzo. Of course I'd love to talk to you, darling, it's just that I'm . . . just a bit under the weather today. Would tomorrow do just as well?

"Oh, okay, sure. That's fine, Mom. You didn't sound so hot when you answered the phone. When should I come over?"

"Come for tea, why don't you. Around four?"

Saturday January 15

I

I'm looking forward to seeing Lorenzo now. When I put down the phone yesterday I was all nerves, full of dread. I knew that it didn't really matter what was on Lorenzo's mind—the fact is that when I see him I will have to bring up this business about his father. I simply can't avoid it any longer. The man is coming to New York, and who knows what he might do, what he might say?

But now I've worked it all out. I feel almost calm. I've thought about Robert's letter until I can think no more. Last night, I made up my mind. Just tell Lorenzo the truth. *This letter from your father came out of the blue. Here it is. What do you think we should do?*

I'm still a bit nervous, I can't help it, but I'm pleased with this plan. I like the idea of including Lorenzo in this turn of events. I like the simplicity of it—no need to overexplain. No awkward apologizing, not at this point. God knows that now, when it all seems to be catching up with me, I regret that I've avoided talking of Robert over the years. But I never thought any good could come of it. Lorenzo knows that. And I know that he forgave me for this long ago. I'm sure of it. He's always been such a devoted son.

I feel almost happy.

And now, there's an errand to run. I'll go pick up some sort of treat for Lorenzo's visit.

The day is cold, overcast, a promise of snow in the steely sky. I dress carefully. The old winter silk chemise, dotted with holes along the seams, but it still keeps me warm. The heavy Irish sweater. Two pairs of socks. The no-nonsense boots I got years ago on sale at Saks—quilted black fabric outside, lined with fake gray fur.

At Balducci's I decide to splurge. Four éclairs instead of two. Might as well have plenty. Lorenzo might want two. I grow more light-hearted with every moment. The ruddy, middle-aged man behind the counter is so friendly! He ties a strawlike ribbon twice around the white box with great care. Gently, he nestles the small rectangular box into a nice bag, one with handles, and hands it to me with a smile.

"Always my favorite, those éclairs. Hope you enjoy them!"

Outside, the wind has picked up. I can feel the cold right through my coat. Maybe it was looking at all that lovely food in Balducci's, but I haven't gone far before I realize I'm not just cold but also very hungry. I remember that there's a diner I like on 12th Street. I'll get some coffee. Maybe a grilled cheese sandwich with tomato.

I head over to Fifth Avenue, walk north, and turn east onto 12th Street. There it is, the familiar faded blue awning. Jake's Luncheonette. As I get near, I have the impression that it is busy. Through the large front window ahead I can see a crowd of heads rising above the booths. I'm almost to the door when I stop.

I can't move. An icy fist clenches tight in my chest.

I've taken in the scene all at once. But I cannot make sense of it. . . .

It's the jacket sleeve, the man's arm flung across the back of the bench. His back is to me, but I know that jacket, the herringbone weave, and the red scarf tucked inside. I've seen them, just like that, a thousand times. *Lorenzo.*

But it isn't the sight of Lorenzo that's got me stuck there, as if the sidewalk had turned to quicksand. It's the man across the table. An old man, white hair in a ponytail.

Well, there can be no mistake about it. It's Robert all right.
Robert.

Lorenzo.

The sight of these two mesmerizes me. They are *laughing.*
And there is something . . . something about the way Lorenzo is
so relaxed, about the way they both gesture with their hands, lean
in toward each other. I can't see Lorenzo's face, but Robert's is animated. They do not look like two people who have just met, who
are tentative, trying to think of what to say next.

I want to leave, but I am riveted, watching the two men in
the booth as if they were playing a scene in a movie. Robert, with
the collar of his dark jacket up, just so. One of those opera scarves,
white with fringe.

How perfect.

At last I find the strength to move my limbs, turn around.

I walk up Fifth Avenue, my head swirling. *What, exactly, does
it mean? Has Robert been here other times, been with Lorenzo? Or—
have they been talking by phone for years? How long has this been
going on?*

I keep going back to it, how they looked so comfortable
together.

And then I remember my own thought, just the other day.
*All he had to do was to call long-distance information. How many
Lorenzo Schlicks can there be in Manhattan?*

I'd been scornful, then, thinking how easy it would have been
for Robert to find his son. But . . . why is it I never thought about
Lorenzo . . . that he might try?

I should have thought . . . why did I never think of it?

*All he had to do was call long-distance information. How many
Robert Schlicks can there be in Portland?*

Is that how it was? And if it was, how long have they . . .?

It's all I can think as I climb the stairs, holding the banister
with one hand for support, clutching the bag of éclairs in the other.
How long?

How foolish I have been.

II

*I*t is almost one o'clock when I get back to my apartment. For a long time, I just sit on the couch, coat and boots still on, the bag with the éclairs in my lap.

Absentmindedly I pet Byzantine. His purring is steady. Loud.

I think of Robert in his well-fitting jacket with the upturned collar. How *happy* he looked, there in the diner, talking to my son.

Forgiving Robert might release a burden of your own, Pamela.

My mother might as well be sitting here right next to me, speaking those words aloud.

There is no telling how long I stay on the couch.

Well, there it is.

I rise from the sofa, put away the coat, the boots. I set the box of éclairs on the kitchen counter. I find the drain cover and push aside the pile of dirty dishes to secure it in place. I run the hot water, squirt some dish soap into the sink. When the dishes have disappeared under a cloud of bubbles, I turn off the water. I sponge off the kitchen table, the painted blue relic that's stood in our family kitchens ever since I was a small child in Paris. I open the overhead cabinet, find my favorite ones. There never was a matched set, Mam always liked it that way.

So—three saucers, three cups. Roses, Willowware, Queen Elizabeth. I set them on the blue table.

Now there is only the note I must write. There's just time. It won't take long. There's not much to say.

I write "Lorenzo" on the envelope in large script. I dig around in the junk drawer, find the Scotch tape, and head downstairs.

III

I cross the lobby to the front door. I haven't put my coat back on. This will only take a minute.

Four strips of tape, each lined neatly around the edges of the envelope.

There. It's done.

Tomorrow the dishes will be clean, put away. I'll wash my hair. I'll put on my nice wool skirt. The one that's flounced at the hem. It's awfully old, but it's still in good shape.

Won't Lorenzo be surprised to see me dressed up for a change?

He'll know it's all right, then. He'll know right away.

Lorenzo darling—

Please forgive me, but I'm afraid I'm still just a bit under the weather today. Could you come over tomorrow instead? I promise not to postpone it any longer.

If you don't call me, I will expect to see you here at 4.

And please do bring your father with you.

Saturday January 15

Evening

*W*ell. Tomorrow, then.

I'm weary after all that's happened, but I don't want to lie down. I know I wouldn't sleep, I'd just go over and over everything, maybe start to worry about tomorrow, and I don't want to do that.

I'll go up to the studio, do some work on the portrait.

I push open the door of the studio and hear the scurrying of mice. *They'll be nesting among my rags. God, this place is a mess.* I've meant to clean it up for ages. But the task always seems overwhelming, it's never a good time.

It's awfully cold in here. I find the old shawl that I keep up here for the purpose, wrap it around my shoulders. From a dark corner I pull out a small chair, the one Mam used at her dressing table. Now there's a pattern of frayed holes in the old chintz, and the once-plump seat cushion has long been flattened into a thin disc.

I'll just take a look around. See what needs to be done.

But I don't want to look for the nests of mice. I don't really want to investigate anything too thoroughly up here.

I settle back, look up at the skylight. Evening has fallen, and the skylight is aglow.

All those lights in the city now. Not so many stars anymore.

Perhaps, if I sit here long enough, I'll see a star.

It's uncomfortable on the old chair, it's too low, really, but I'm too tired to move. I look at the unfinished painting on the easel, a portrait of two girls. It's barely begun—no faces, just the bodies blocked out. I can see so clearly how it will look in the end, the almost-twins with their black rectangles of dresses overlaid in ornate semicircles, neckpieces and wide ribbons covering their fronts like armor made of lace.

Somehow, though, I've lost interest in the portrait.

I take down the painting from the easel, replace it with a blank canvas.

I stare, I cannot take my eyes away, as the painting appears.

A dark stage. Somber blues and greens. The colors of night.

The Sad Dancer.

The frozen dancer blinks. She looks out, to somewhere beyond an audience, and bends down low, into a wooden curtsy. Slowly she rises, blinks again. Legs unsteady, feet dragging, she exits to the left. The stage is empty now.

The heavy curtain closes. Opens again.

A swath of gold light pours across the wooden floor.

The studio grows darker.

The painting glows.

It's Diccon I hear first. He's singing one of those old Welsh tunes he always loved.

Then I hear more voices, people laughing.

On the stage I see them all, all the familiar faces, lit up as if by candlelight.

Daddy is having a grand time, laughing with Diccon and Gabriele d'Annunzio. Gene glowers from the corner, pouring himself a glass of whiskey as Robert, standing a little too close, talks to him animatedly. Agnes leans over a little table, confiding something to Cecco and Georg. Mam sits in the center, her attention on the child in her lap—little Lorenzo, his red curls glowing copper in the candlelight.

The kaleidoscope in my mind settles into this golden scene.

In the morning, I'll begin a new painting.

A Madonna, I think. Mother and child, faces candlelit. Half-sun halos, disks of gold.

I don't know. I'll decide tomorrow.

I'll paint just as I feel. Just as I wish.

Pamela Bianco, 1922 (age 15)
Courtesy George Eastman Museum, © Nickolas Muray Photo Archives

Line drawing of Margery Williams Bianco
by Pamela Bianco, c. 1918

Agnes Boulton O'Neill
*Courtesy of Linda Lear Center for Special Collections and Archives,
Connecticut College, Louis Sheaffer-Eugene O'Neill Collection,
© Nickolas Muray Photo Archives*

Eugene O'Neill, c. 1919
Courtesy Eastman Museum, © Nickolas Muray Photo Archives

Peaked Hill Bars, Truro, Massachusetts. From left: Margery
Williams Bianco, Shane O'Neill, Eugene O'Neill, Edith and
Frank Shay (friends from Provincetown Playhouse), Agnes
O'Neill, Francesco Bianco, Margery Boulton (Agnes's sister)
Courtesy of Linda Lear Center for Special Collections and Archives,
Connecticut College, Louis Sheaffer-Eugene O'Neill Collection,
© Nickolas Muray Photo Archives

Richard Warren Hughes, known as "Diccon"
c. 1924
Photographer unknown*

***Madonna with Angels and Children* by Pamela Bianco, 1918 (age 11)**
—*author collection*

The Old Barn by Pamela Bianco, 1921 (age 14)
—*author collection*

Pomegranate by Pamela Bianco, 1957-59
*Digital Image © The Museum of Modern Art/Licensed by SCALA/Art
Resource, NY*

The Appointment
The Joseph H. Hirshhorn Bequest, 1981
Hirshhorn Museum and Sculpture Garden, Smithsonian Institution
Photography by Cathy Carver

I'm Zita, just a gipsy lass.
They found me on a mountain pass.
Day in, day out, I wandered there
With thorns and catkins in my hair;
They hunted for me day and night.
And rescued me with lanterns bright!

Illustration and verse from Beginning with A by Pamela Bianco (1947)
Reprinted by permission of Oxford University Press USA.

endnotes

Regarding the Authenticity of the Story

*D*iscovering and collecting the various pieces of the puzzle that eventually arranged themselves into *The Velveteen Daughter* was a wonderful obsession. It continues to amaze me that this story has not come to light before now. To my knowledge, no biography of Margery Williams Bianco has been published, and Pamela Bianco has been forgotten almost entirely.

A reader who finishes a fictional work based on a true story always thinks, *How much of that was real, I wonder?* I hope that the following will provide a sense of how much of *The Velveteen Daughter* is "real." As you will see, a great deal is.

The Bianco family. The story of Pamela and her family is historically accurate in terms of where they lived and when they lived there. Francesco was, in fact, an antiquarian book dealer and had stores in London and on West Eighth Street in New York. (The Gershwin brothers were known to frequent his shop.) He was an expert on Papal Bulls. He did, in fact, fall onto subway tracks soon after Margery died, which resulted in his death. The trajectory of Pamela's fame and her art career is documented in numerous newspaper accounts, in the *New Yorker* archives, in university collections, and in family letters. Margery did suffer the loss of her father and sister when she was a child. Cecco attended Columbia University, was a fencer, was stationed in Germany for a while, and eventually got a job in Washington.

The Diccon and Pamela relationship. This not-quite-love affair between Pamela and Diccon, which constitutes a good portion of the novel, hews closely to the truth as depicted. The trove of letters in the Richard Hughes archives at the Lilly Library at the University of Indiana (Bloomington) provided the basic tapestry upon which I could embroider events. Other facts were gleaned from Robert Graves's biography of Richard Hughes. The initial meeting in Wales is based on fact. Diccon was engaged to Nancy Stallibrass and the description of that relationship—Nancy's officious mother, the insistence on a six-month separation, and Diccon's cold feet just before the wedding—is all factual.

Pamela's depression/madness. Sadly, her episodes of depression were all too real, and took place as described. She was hospitalized more than once at Four Winds in Upstate New York. Pamela herself documents her breakdown at age eighteen in a letter to Diccon written from Four Winds. The disease caught up with her at the end of her life, and she was institutionalized at the time of her death in 1994.

Eugene and Agnes O'Neill. Agnes was Pamela's cousin, and the relationship between the O'Neills and the Biancos was, in essence, just as depicted in the novel. The Biancos often visited them at Peaked Hill Bars in Truro, Massachusetts, and at their home in Bermuda. Agnes's account of her courtship and early years of marriage are taken directly from her own memoir, *Part of a Long Story.* The O'Neills' volatile marriage has been well documented.

Gabriele d'Annunzio. The famous poet-warrior-lover did write a poem, reproduced in many newspapers, describing Pamela as a "new flower." He also gave her a wooden box and told her to keep all future correspondence from him in it.

Pablo Picasso. It is true that Picasso was a friend of the Biancos during their Paris years. However, the scene in the novel when he and Fernande (his real-life girlfriend) come to dinner is wholly imagined.

Anne Carroll Moore and Bertha Mahony. Moore, the legendary children's librarian at the New York Public Library was a close friend of Margery's. She was also a strong supporter of Mahony, who opened The Bookshop for Boys and Girls and founded *The Horn Book* magazine.

Robert Schlick. Pamela married Robert in Harlem in a ceremony at Alexander Gumby's salon almost exactly as described. A book dealer in California, who owns a copy of Schlick's exceedingly rare volume of poetry (*The Supplement Poems*, 1930), found two holograph accounts of the wedding tucked inside his edition, and he kindly shared copies with me. Soon after the birth of Lorenzo, Robert did run off to Oregon with Roy de Coverley, a minor actor-poet-journalist of the Harlem Renaissance. To the best of my knowledge, he was never heard from again.

Alexander Gumby was a well-known figure of the Harlem Renaissance. He had a book salon and regularly hosted parties for the literati. Perhaps his biggest contribution to American culture are his 161 scrapbooks chronicling the history of African Americans from the early nineteenth to the mid-twentieth century. An online exhibition was launched in September 2011 at the Columbia University Libraries' website.

Georg Hartmann. Pamela married Georg when she was forty-eight. Besides that, and the fact that he did etchings, I could find no other information on him.

Artwork. I invented the "apple tree at dawn" picture, the goat Pamela draws with Picasso, and the drawing purchased by d'Annunzio. All other paintings, drawings, and lithographs referenced are Pamela's actual work. She did paint the unsuccessful mauve fruit and flower paintings, although her white-washing of them is an invention. Her triumphant return to the art world in 1961 is fact.

Invented characters. The following characters are entirely fictional: Signora Campanaro; Sara, the green-eyed sculptress; and Dr. Henry Boardman at Four Winds. (Pamela does mention a "Henry" who helped her with her letter writing, but I do not know to whom she was referring.)

Invented places. The Mason and Dyer Gallery, where Pamela meets Georg for the first time, is fictional.

Letters. All letters between Diccon and Pamela are based on letters in the Richard Hughes collection in the Lilly Library at the University of Indiana (Bloomington). A letter found in the Butler Library at Columbia University from Francesco to Mr. Henry L. Bullen written on Christmas Day, 1928, provides the information on Papal Bulls, which Francesco relates to Pamela when he is ill. Robert's farewell letter to Pamela, which she turns into a paper boat, is fictional, as is the "deathbed" letter from Francesco to Pamela. The 1977 letter from Robert to Pamela is also fictional.

questions for discussion

1. What is the relationship between Pamela and Margery? Do you find it problematical? What about the relationship between Pamela and Francesco?

2. How does Pamela's illness manifest itself? When does it begin? Do you think it was inevitable (simply inherited), or do you think it had to do with circumstances in her life? What was the cause of her breakdown?

3. Do you agree with Margery's decision to allow Francesco take charge of their young prodigy daughter? Did she reconcile herself to her decision? What do you think you would have done?

4. What is your opinion about Agnes and Eugene O'Neill? What effect did the O'Neills and their relationship have on Pamela?

5. What role does the classic children's book *The Velveteen Rabbit* play in the novel? Do you see any correlations between the themes of that story and the events portrayed in *The Velveteen Daughter*?

6. What do you think of Francesco? What are his feelings about his daughter? His wife?

7. How do you interpret Pamela's feelings and actions with regard to Diccon? Is she willfully blind? How did their relationship develop, and how does it change?

8. What does Pamela reveal to Henry, her doctor at Four Winds? What is it that she cannot tell him? Why?

9. Why did Pamela marry Robert? What do you think of Robert? Do you think Pamela was right never to talk of Robert to Lorenzo?

10. What are Pamela's actions and feelings at the end of the novel? What do they say about her state of mind? Do you think she has changed since we first see her in the opening chapters as a young mother?

11. Many primary materials are quoted in this novel? Does this make the narrative more effective? Is it distracting?

12. How do you feel about the fictionalization of the lives of Pamela and Margery?

acknowledgments

Working with She Writes Press was both exciting and fascinating, and I will be forever grateful for the enthusiasm, the caring, and the professionalism of Brooke Warner, publisher, who somehow managed to run the business and still take time to actively participate in various decisions about this book along the way. I am also indebted to the gifted Julie Metz, who designed the extraordinary cover of this book, and to Lauren Wise, who dealt with an editing kerfuffle or two (or three) with calm and good humor.

I was extremely fortunate to work with Caitlin Hamilton Summie of Caitlin Hamilton Marketing whose thoughtful insights and tireless, stellar initiatives have more than a little to do with whatever success this novel finds.

Writing *The Velveteen Daughter* required years of research, which resulted in the use of many primary and secondary sources. While the research was riveting for me, I would have been helpless in the follow-up work without the assistance of Barrett Briske, who magically procured permissions for me with impressive efficiency.

Heartfelt thanks go to Nancy Schlick, who was married to Lorenzo (Larry) Schlick, and who took the time to meet with me on more than one occasion to talk about Pamela and Larry; also to David Wirshup, owner of Anacapa Books in Carmel, California, who provided copies of two unattributed hand-written descriptions of Pamela Bianco's wedding which were invaluable in creating the wedding scene with accuracy, and also a copy of a letter from Robert Schlick to Alexander Gumby, dated January 29, 1933, which relates Gumby's fate during the Depression.

Many readers helped me along the way. To these in particular I am grateful: Ellen Ruffin, Curator of the de Grummond Collection at the University of Southern Mississippi, and her assistant, Katie Windham, my very first readers who kindly let me know that my early chapters were not quite ready for prime time; Anna South of The Literary Consultancy in London, whose confidence in my writing lifted me up at a time when I was most discouraged; Barbara Esstmann, who threw both champagne and rotten tomatoes at various drafts (more tomatoes than champagne, I'm afraid); Leslie Pietrzyk and all my fellow students at the Writers Center in Bethesda; Ron Gutierrez, a reader I met online through a writing seminar, who was enthusiastic from the beginning, and who has unfailingly cheered me up many times over the years; the indomitable Kay Brinnier, who showed great interest in my work from the beginning; Christopher Rhodes, who did everything he could and who believed in this book; and all the wonderful people at Vermont Studio Center, where various versions of this novel took shape.

Also: My dear friend Lindsey Lang, who championed my work in all its stages; Mo Henderson, my hometown head cheerleader, along with all my other book club friends who supported me throughout this very long process; Carol Ridgway, who caught some embarrassing errors; and John McClure and Patrick Joyce, who took a bit of this journey with me.

And, of course, family: My sister, Lisa, and her husband, Stephen, who kindly read my novel in an early stage and gave it high marks despite its not being the sort of book either one would choose to read; my son, Jake, always my fan—thank you for the love and support, and for opening the door to your friend, Matt Martz, who gave me encouragement and a push in the right direction; and my husband, Toni, the steady rock amid my roiling waters—thank you for that, and for the incomparable Twr Dwr.

I save until last my profound gratitude to someone I have never met, whose name I do not know. But I would like whoever wrote the *Kirkus* review of my novel to know that his or her praise has made all the difference to me.

‡ ‡ ‡

Also, I am very indebted to the following individuals, universities, and museums that gave me permission to use material from their archives:

Quotations. The Hyman Kreitman Research Centre for the Tate Library and Archive in London, for use of Margery Bianco's letter to Jimmie Manson; David Wirshup, owner of Anacapa Books, Carmel, CA, for copies of material found inside his rare edition of Robert Schlick's *The Supplement Poems: Written during the Composition of The Imagination, A Poem in Four Books*: two unattributed holograph manuscripts from eyewitnesses describing the Harlem wedding of Pamela Bianco and Robert Schlick, and a letter from Robert Schlick to Alexander Gumby dated January 29, 1933; Lilly Library, Indian University at Bloomington, for access to and use of Richard Hughes's papers; The Literary Trustees of Walter de la Mare and the Society of Authors as their representative (London), executor of the estate of Walter de la Mare, for permission to use excerpts from de la Mare's poems *Autumn* and *To Some Most Happy Men*; Rosemary A. Thurber and The Barbara Hogenson Agency, for permission to use *The New Yorker* memo written by James Thurber to Harold Ross; Condé Nast Licensing for permission to use *The New Yorker* memos written by Eddie O'Toole and Eugene Kinkead; Hal Leonard LLC, for permission to reprint lyric from "Nobody Knows You When You're Down and Out", © Universal Music Corp., words and music by Jimmie Cox; and Jane Kaplowitz Rosenblum, for permission to use excerpt from Robert Rosenblum's catalogue essay for Pamela Bianco's 1961 exhibition at the David Herbert Galleries, New York City.

Photographs and illustrations. Cover photograph of Pamela in her studio © The Vassar College Archives and Special Collections Library, Louise Seaman Bechtel Papers, Folder 5.63; Cover detail from *The Velveteen Rabbit* cover drawing by William Nicholson

resources

Boulton, Agnes. *Part of a Long Story*, Doubleday 1958

Budny, Virginia. *New York's Left Bank, Art and Artists off Washington Square North 1900-1950*, published by the author, 2006.

Columbia University, Butler Library. The Alexander Gumby Collection.

Columbia University, Butler Library. Francesco Bianco Letters.

Friedman, B. H. *Gertrude Vanderbilt Whitney*, Doubleday, 1978.

Gelb, Arthur and Barbara. *O'Neill*, Harper and Bros., 1962.

Graves, Richard Perceval. *Richard Hughes*, Andre Deutsch, 1995.

Hyman Kreitman Research Centre for the Tate Library and Archive, London

Indiana University at Bloomington, The Lilly Library. The Hughes, R. Manuscript Collection.

Jullian, Philippe. *D'Annunzio*, Viking Press, 1972.

Kirkland, Winifred and Frances. *Girls Who Became Artists*, Harper and Bros., 1934.

Manson, J. B. "The Art of Pamela Bianco." *The International Studio Magazine*, July 1922.

Moore, Anne Carroll, and Miller, Bertha Mahony, eds. *Writing and Criticism, A Book for Margery Bianco*, The Horn Book, 1951.

New York Historical Society.

New York Public Library. Anne Carroll Moore Papers.

New York Public Library. *New York Times* Archives.

New York Public Library. *New Yorker* Archives.

New York Public Library. *The Greenwich Village Quill* Archives.

Norman, Charles. "To the Memory of Francesco Bianco." The Literary Review, Farleigh Dickinson University, Autumn 1957.

Rhodes, Anthony. *The Poet as Superman*, Mcdowell, Obolensky, 1959.

Rosenblum, Robert (author of *Cubism and Twentieth Century Art*, Thames and Hudson,1960). The catalog introduction for Pamela Bianco's solo exhibition at David Herbert Galleries, New York City, 1961.

Schaeffer, Louis. *O'Neill Volume I, Son and Playwright*, Cooper Square Press, 1968.

Schaeffer, Louis. *O'Neill Volume II, Son and Artist*, Cooper Square Press, 1973.

Seaman, Louise. "About the Biancos." The Horn Book, March 1926.

Smithsonian Institution. Joseph Hirshhorn Collection.

Summers, Leonie. "Pamela Bianco." England and Co. catalog essay from the Pamela Bianco Retrospective Exhibit 2003.

Thomas. D.C. *A Formidable Shadow, The O'Neill Connection,* Lulu Press, 2014.

Untermeyer, Louis. "The Drawings of Pamela Bianco." Century Magazine. 1922. Vol. 104, pp. 423-426.

Vassar College. Archives and Special Collections Library, Louise Seaman Bechtel Papers.

Whistler, Theresa, The Life of Walter de la Mare, Gerald Duckworth and Co. Ltd, 2003

books by
margery williams bianco

The Late Returning, 1902
The Price of Youth, 1904
The Bar, 1906
The Thing in the Woods, 1914
The Velveteen Rabbit, 1922
Poor Cecco, 1925
The Little Wooden Doll, 1925
The Apple Tree, 1926
The Skin Horse, 1927
The Adventures of Andy, 1927
All about Pets, 1929
The Candlestick, 1929
The House That Grew Smaller, 1931
The Street of Little Shops, 1932
The Hurdy-Gurdy Man, 1933
The Good Friends, 1934
More about Animals, 1934
Green Grows the Garden, 1936
Winterbound, 1936
Other People's Houses, 1939
Franzi and Gizi, 1941
Bright Morning, 1942
Penny and the White Horse, 1942
Forward, Commandos! 1944

books written and
illustrated by
pamela bianco

pamela bianco
solo exhibitions

1919: The Leicester Galleries, London
1920: The Leicester Galleries, London
1921: The Anderson Galleries, New York
1922: The Print Rooms, San Francisco
1923: Cannell and Chaffin Gallery, Los Angeles
1924: The Knoedler Gallery, New York
1924: The Art Institute of Chicago
1925: The Bookshop for Boys and Girls, Boston
1926–1927: Rehn Galleries, New York
1936–1937: Ferargil Galleries, New York
1961: David Herbert Gallery, New York
1964: International Gallery, Baltimore
1969: Graham Gallery, New York
1970: Santa Barbara Museum of Art
1974: Greenwich Library, Connecticut
2004: England & Co., London

about the author

*L*aurel Davis Huber grew up in Rhode Island and Oklahoma. She is a graduate of Smith College. She has worked as a corporate newsletter editor, communications director for a botanical garden, high school English teacher, and senior development officer for both New Canaan Country School and Amherst College. She has studied with the novelist and short-story writer Leslie Pietrzyk (the 2015 Drue Heinz Literature Prize winner for *This Angel on My Chest*) and has participated in several writing residencies at the Vermont Studio Center. She and her husband split their time between New Jersey and Maine.

Author photo by Danny Sanchez

SELECTED TITLES FROM SHE WRITES PRESS

She Writes Press is an independent publishing company founded to serve women writers everywhere. Visit us at www.shewritespress.com.

Hysterical: Anna Freud's Story by Rebecca Coffey. $18.95, 978-1-938314-42-1. An irreverent, fictionalized exploration of the seemingly contradictory life of Anna Freud—told from her point of view.

Little Woman in Blue: A Novel of May Alcott by Jeannine Atkins. $16.95, 978-1-63152-987-0. Based May Alcott's letters and diaries, as well as memoirs written by her neighbors, *Little Woman in Blue* puts May at the center of the story she might have told about sisterhood and rivalry in her extraordinary family.

Shelter Us by Laura Diamond. $16.95, 978-1-63152-970-2. Lawyer-turned-stay-at-home-mom Sarah Shaw is still struggling to find a steady happiness after the death of her infant daughter when she meets a young homeless mother and toddler she can't get out of her mind—and becomes determined to rescue them.

Stella Rose by Tammy Flanders Hetrick. $16.95, 978-1-63152-921-4. When her dying best friend asks her to take care of her sixteen-year-old daughter, Abby says yes—but as she grapples with raising a grieving teenager, she realizes she didn't know her best friend as well as she thought she did.

Beautiful Garbage by Jill DiDonato. $16.95, 978-1-938314-01-8. Talented but troubled young artist Jodi Plum leaves suburbia for the excitement of the city—and is soon swept up in the sexual politics and downtown art scene of 1980s New York

All the Light There Was by Nancy Kricorian. $16.95, 978-1-63152-905-4. A lyrical, finely wrought tale of loyalty, love, and the many faces of resistance, told from the perspective of an Armenian girl living in Paris during the Nazi occupation of the 1940s.